PRAISE FOR GEORGE FOY'S
THE MEMORY OF FIRE

"Foy's latest novel expands the gritty, high-tech, near-future setting of his *Contraband*. Foy sets this story of memory and love in a finely detailed setting."
—*Publishers Weekly*

"Hemingway meets magical realism . . . While much of the texture of this book is quite different from that of its predecessors, it has the same density and complexity of setting and intensity of feeling, and the same anger. Foy belongs with Gibson, McAuley, Spinrad, and Sterling on the short list of contemporary writers successfully working the territory pioneered by Bester, Brunner, and Pohl & Kornbluth."
—*Locus*

"Foy presents a near-future world in which the environment is degraded, governments are decentralized, and armies of homeless compete for survival like animals in the wild. . . . Foy's . . . detailed, moody rendering of a future San Francisco is winningly paranoid and disturbing."
—*Booklist*

SPECTRA BOOKS BY GEORGE FOY

Contraband
The Shift
The Memory of Fire

THE MEMORY OF
FIRE

A NOVEL

GEORGE FOY

BANTAM BOOKS
NEW YORK   TORONTO   LONDON   SYDNEY   AUCKLAND

This edition contains the complete text of the
original trade paperback edition.
NOT ONE WORD HAS BEEN OMITTED.

THE MEMORY OF FIRE
A Bantam Spectra Book

PUBLISHING HISTORY
Bantam Spectra trade paperback edition published February 2000
Bantam Spectra mass market edition / March 2001

SPECTRA and the portrayal of a boxed "s" are trademarks of
Bantam Books, a division of Random House, Inc.

ISBN 0-553-57886-3

Published simultaneously in the United States and Canada

Bantam Books are published by Bantam Books, a division of Random
House, Inc. Its trademark, consisting of the words "Bantam Books" and
the portrayal of a rooster, is Registered in U.S. Patent and Trademark
Office and in other countries. Marca Registrada. Bantam Books,
1540 Broadway, New York, New York 10036.

PRINTED IN THE UNITED STATES OF AMERICA

OPM   10 9 8 7 6 5 4 3 2 1

FOR EMILIE

ACKNOWLEDGMENTS

Thanks are due to Pat LoBrutto, Evelyn Cainto, Tom Dupree, Jonathan Matson, and Liz Orr, for believing in this book.

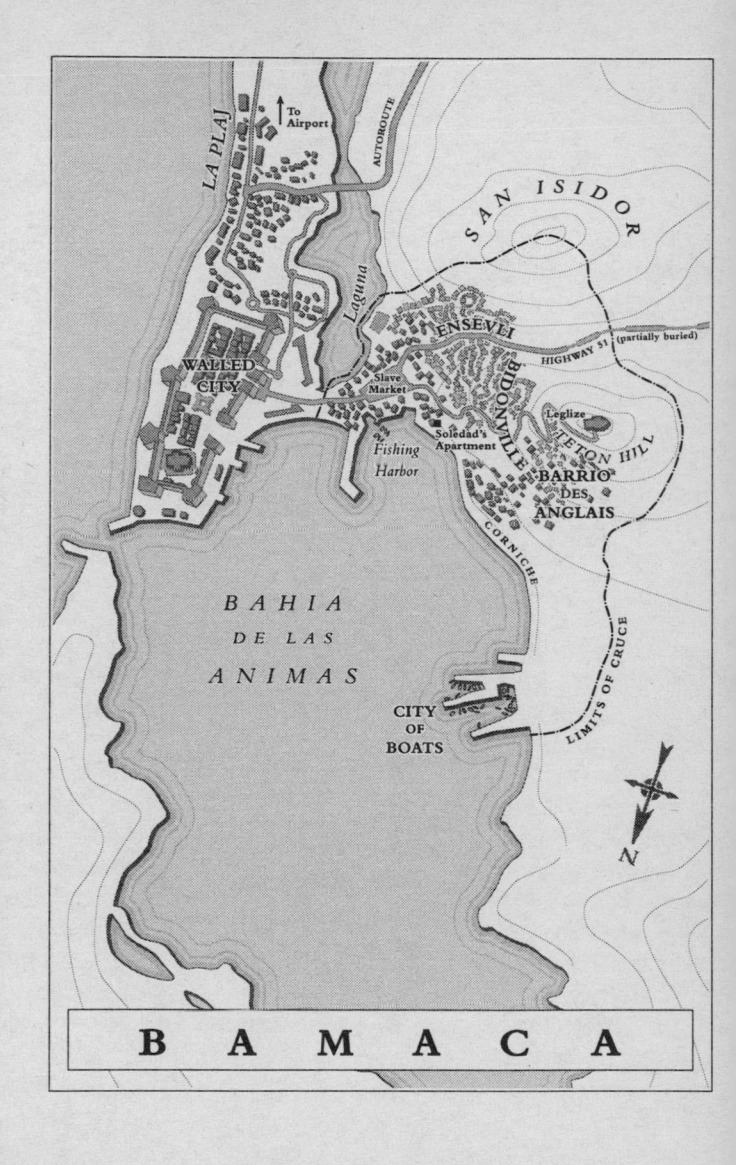

To Airport

LA PLAJ

AUTOROUTE

SAN ISIDOR

Laguna

ENSEVEI

BIDONVILLE

HIGHWAY 51 (partially buried)

WALLED CITY

Slave Market

Leglize

Soledad's Apartment

KETON HILL

Fishing Harbor

BARRIO DES ANGLAIS

CORNICHE

BAHIA

DE LAS

ANIMAS

LIMITS OF CRUCE

CITY OF BOATS

N

B A M A C A

THE MEMORY OF
FIRE

ONE

SHE LIES IN BED, watching the flames come for her.

She knows them by color, she has seen these fires so many times, seeking out the grave robbers, the emerald poachers, the gold smugglers, the Adornista guerrillas they are not affiliated with. Now the flames open like mouths in the direction of the garbage wall of Ensevli; it is one of two ways the army can come at the *cruce* from the land, if you rule out the volcano, as everybody does.

She stabs her heels into the mattress and bends her knees, sliding herself deeper under the sheets. She should crawl out of bed and get dressed but she has never seen the fires so close. In this she is like a town dweller who does not walk in jungle and knows only from the zoo that glow of pink at the corner of a panther's mouth or the splinter of coral when a cloud viper smells prey with its tongue. This morning, though, violence in all its colors has broken out of the *selva* without notice. Despite the panic rinsing the inner wall of her chest, she lists the explosions rising half the height of her window: scarlet with a flash of amaryllis, framed by oily black smoke streaked with platinum, of RDX explosive from the howitzers; silver, that even at a distance can visit your pupils with pain, from phosphorus shells.

Worst is the napalm, shifting curtains of jellied gasoline stuck horribly to the fractal rooflines; napalm like lava stolen from the volcano's crater, napalm so richly orange at its center it seems it must ignite even things it does not directly touch—which she believes, in any case, to be how it works. Over everything, lit by the fires that created it, the lighter ash of her *cruce* burning; rising in the dawn breeze till it mingles with the wisp of steam always curling like a lost thought from the summit of San Isidor.

Her head throbs. Her hands are clamped to her ears so hard the palms mash the cochleas as she tries to dampen the noise fire makes. The blast that comes after the red color is loudest, it literally shakes this crooked apartment the way a hound would shake a rabbit, pressing the very air from her chest. But all the other noises—the ripple-smack of napalm, the accelerating run and thunder from the jets, the fast tom-tom of helicopters—weave in and out of each other, crescendo, diminuendo, to create a flurry of sound-fists punching inside her to the place where music is made, and finally clinching cold around the flora there. It seems impossible that so much noise could cram itself through her narrow window in this tenement by the old fishing harbor, a full kilometer from Ensevli. On a normal day you can hear a thousand different noises come through those louvers: the middle-C clink of terra-cotta coffeepots, the rukkling of doves, cats mewing, the conspiratorial whisper of sea wind, the thud of fish boxes, the coughing of a smuggler's launch, the high-seventh of Cloodine calling her daughters; and always, even at dawn, the friction of *requinto* guitar, a voice moving into song, sad or teasing or angry, the rhythm of *bombo* drumming held back just the space of a laugh. Yet even those memories add up to zero compared to the chaos of sound now coming at her through the same window. And finally it is the contrast between her lazy mornings and what woke her today that causes her to scream, so loudly it tears ridges in her throat, hands crushing her ears harder to hold the scream in and the noise out but it doesn't work, the noise keeps coming, red-yellow-orange. She twists away from the window and falls to the floor, spraining her lower back.

The pain is hard and clean as a fisherman's knife and it slices through the shock that noise brought. She sits up, grabbing at her spine. The tiles of the floor are the hands of stone corpses on her buttocks. Dolores, she thinks, and part of her mind is amazed that it took her so long to think of anything but fire, and part of it finds that commonplace. She sprints toward the hallway, away from the window, slamming the door behind her.

The noise is still infernal here but it's half what it was in her bedroom. She stumbles through the dark to Dolores's room. This part of the apartment faces the ocean. Curtains dance as the humid and fish-smelling wind pushes through the window. She finds herself wanting to shriek at the breeze, curse it into silence for blindly, repetitively, doing what it always does, when fire is now so close. She actually tries to yell, only to find that her mouth is already open, and she has never stopped.

Anyway, the bed is empty, the blanket flat. The bottle of kohl Dolores paints her eyelids with stands open on the ledge. Behind the breakwater, the bay has gone the sultry indigo it turns just before sunrise, and the sun itself, invisible below the horizon, has touched its own match to the cumulus clouds coasting west on the Trades; but this fire is distant, as light as a girl's blush and, above all, silent.

A jet screams over the dovecote, banking jerkily, climbing more like a geometric expression than a flying thing. Its wings, too, turn rose as the sun's rays catch them. She swivels in the tremble of afterburners, fumbling for the phone. It is dead. It didn't work well at the best of times and now they must have cut the lines.

But it bothers her, for she cannot talk to Jorge, and one of the first people they will want is him. With a wash of warmth to her chest—from shame that it took so long to make the equation come out—she repeats it to herself: "They will want him *first*."

Back in her room, her eyes deliberately avoiding the window, she puts on earrings—unmatched balsa birds, a vulturine parrot, and an *agobequi*. She can't find a matching pair from her drawer but maybe this is not so important given the end of everything. She picks up her accordion case. The heavy instrument wrenches her twisted muscles and she gasps. It's an indication of the bad effect of too much noise on her that she is halfway to the front door before remembering that she is naked as a porpoise, except for the earrings; but already her mind was at Pytagoro's Cadillac, where Jorge was going last night, where he has tended to spend all his nights since they stopped spending nights together. She throws on the long peasant skirt she wears to perform, a loose blouse, she has no time for sandals or underwear. Some perverse nook of her psyche whispers, among all the noise, *You're doing it because he likes you without knickers,* while another segment of her brain replies, *Nonsense.*

The tenement feels empty. Maybe that is because noise still drowns out the details of sound that are the baseline of life in this place. In the dark stairwell the concussion of explosions has shaken dust from cracked walls and ceilings. Her bare toes sink into grit where it lies in drifts against the tiles.

Human voices on the second landing squeeze through gaps in the shellfire. The door to Cloodine's flat is ajar. Soledad pushes it open. Cloodine huddles in the archway of the next room, the correct position for earthquakes. Her daughters squeak under her sheltering and ever-pregnant stomach; the little boy shrieks in her arms. "Jako," Soledad yells at her, "Where's Jako?" Thinking, Cloodine's new boyfriend should be here to shelter her from this. In the sheen of a propane lamp the whites of Cloodine's eyes are like reflections of a new moon; she gestures at the coffeepot, mutely offering a *tinto*. The reflex of hospitality is all she can make work for her now. Soledad stares at them for another second or two, feeling under her panic a new distress boiling for the kids, so ridiculously small and soft. But in the end she owns nothing to help them with, no words to comfort them from the direction she is going. Anyway they all knew this would happen, sooner or later.

At least there is no shelling in the heart of this quasi-independent city-state they call the *cruce*. On the Corniche, the harbor road, people lurk in the purple light, staring upward at flashes of fire reflected from the buildings. A gang of emerald poachers carrying shotguns and machine-pistols moves disorderly but fast down the Corniche, toward Ensevli. A smuggler's boat revs huge gasoline engines at one of the piers while men and women chain-load crates into its cramped hold. Still bartering, she thinks in disgust, still running contraband while the *cruce* burns, although how they will get around the frigate now blocking passage across the harbor entrance she has no idea.

A Cadillac-bar owner is padlocking his shutters. Soledad starts to run, the accordion case knocking painfully at her thigh, because Pytagoro might be closing, might already have closed due to the attack, and then she will have no idea where Jorge went. He would never go back to des Anglais in the midst of this. As she rounds the base of the disused lighthouse she sees kerosene lamps shining like gentle quasars under the canopy of Pytagoro's, people moving darkly inside. A fisherman she has never met offers in courtly terms to take her offshore till this is over. Afterward, he says, they will go to Isla Cythera and screw in the shallows and make many babies. Half of her wants to split off from the rest and get in his rotten sloop, so badly would she love to leave behind this noise and the bitter smoke of devastation. The other half tells him to fuck off. The fisherman shakes his head, looks down the quay for another client.

Her breath is almost gone by the time she gets to the Cadillac. They have closed the glass doors that usually are shut only in the rainy season and when she pushes through them she understands why: the heavy glass muffles the explosions without and there is actually something to listen for inside, nothing more than the lyrics of people arguing and the rasp of *requintos* and a harp, it is so normal for Bamaca that she would never ordinarily notice; but this morning it pushes tears into her eyes and strains her esophagus at the thought of how much she loves this town.

A dozen people live in caves the cigarette smoke makes in the umber gloom of kerosene lamps. It is hard to distinguish who is Jorge and who is not; most are older men and they all smoke and many of them play dominoes, as Creoles tend to do in times of mourning. Several sport the same shaggy brindled sort of beard that Jorge wears. One wears Arab robes and turns away from her as she comes in. No one looks up when she calls. She stashes her accordion under the Cadillac itself—the two chopped-off halves of a Coupe De Ville, all gleaming and chromed, that such bars mount against the wall as a pulpit for casse-co jockeys—and walks among the tables to Pytagoro's corner. The men's eyes touch her as she moves. She is conscious of her thighs rubbing under the skirt, as if the men could know her nakedness in the heightening of senses associated with peril.

Pytagoro plays dominoes alone. He racks up the bones, spreads them expertly on the table, shuffles them again. He keeps his eyes on what he is doing as she comes near.

"Have you seen him, Pytagoro?"

"Qui?"

"For God's sake!"

He motions to a chair, a grandiose gesture that mocks as it invites. She does not sit.

"Play *Mericain* with me."

"I have to find Jorge, they—"

"Play with me, Soledad."

"Damn it, you know what they'll do to him!"

Pytagoro looks up. He holds his head sideways, like a curious rooster. He has large eyes with stained whites and a giant Adam's apple and all his various orbs pop as if pushed by some force bottled up within. His nose is hooked and fleshy; hairs an inch long curl from its nostrils. His lips are sculpted like the bank of a river in spate. A *basuko* pipe is stuck, flotsamlike, between.

The mathematical clicks of the bones resound clearly above the music, and the gunfire.

"Play," Pytagoro says. "The world has its period, *non*? And today the *cruce* is its *coño*." His laugh winds up, a bus changing gears underwater. He wipes a tear from his left eye. "If you win, I'll tell you where he is."

"Isalop!" she hisses. Bastard. His lips stretch. Then she does sit down, keeping her knees locked together, as if to contain the rage expanding quick as one of those RDX fires. It is useless to argue with Pytagoro at the best of times, and the contrariness that is the prime expression of his personality seems to have tripled now that the *cruce* is burning around them. She is about to argue anyway, it's all so ridiculous. Then she shrugs, thinking, *Mericain* will take only four minutes to play.

And Pytagoro, because of that very contrariness, will keep his most inane promises.

She selects seven of the ebony slabs from the pile. A light hand, she can tell immediately: a paired six, three deuces. Pytagoro slaps down a six-five, she follows with a five-two. They play fast, as is the custom, cracking the tiles like rimshots on the zinc. Lamplight rolls shadows across their hands. To her surprise Pytagoro is dry of bones for her last two deuces and she wins the first game. Two, then five men stroll over to watch. During a lull in the shellfire a heavy machine gun opens up, its explosions more regular, deliberate; and the *requinto* player shifts to follow the rhythm the M-60 makes, a 4/2 rhythm, somehow she and the bar owner slip into the same meter, slapping the bones *bom, bom-bom-bom,* and she knows the rhythm even before she consciously recognizes the tune, *boom bu-boom, bom-bom, boom, boom (boom),* it's the exact beat of *"Si mou estoma fue un chien"*:

> *If my stomach was a dog,*
> *I would walk it through the halls*
> *where you had been*
> *to catch your scent.*
> *If the world was a knife*
> *I would cut the sky*
> *and draw no blood, no,*
> *nor morning either;*
> *ah, but of these girls*
> *who wander through*

their tunnels in the rain,
tell me
how many of them
cradle my heart
the way a tree grows around
a bullet?

And it's as if the verses are claws that rip at her because they are Jorge's words; just as the notes are hers, notes that spilled out of the Fourneaux-Dallapé accordion now locked up and mute under the dark Cadillac juke. She misses a crucial set and loses the second game. Trying to regain control over her thoughts, she bums a butt from Pytagoro's pack, her fingers trembling slightly as she lights it, using fire from a votive Yemanja-Marie in the corner; but the jag of tobacco does not help. The bar owner is one slab down on her from the outset of the third game, and he plays two blanks in a row and wins the match.

She gets to her feet, still trembling. "So?" she rasps. Pytagoro looks up at her for the second time this morning, and says nothing. She remembers how much he loved even the news of disaster; she can tell from the salience of his eyes how much more he adores the real thing. *"Isalop,"* she hisses at him again. She walks under the juke and carefully lifts the accordion. The M-60 is silent now, and the rhythm of other weapons seems to have altered in undefinable but crucial ways, as if they had switched from her 6/8 merengue to an earlier dance where music had not yet been refined from the lusts and wounds that fueled it. The players have dwindled into improv, letting a scrape of harp keep the beat. "Play with us, Soledad?" the *requinto* player calls softly, jerking his head vaguely upward, "play *against* this," but she shakes her head, surprising herself. Before today she always agreed to play—it was the path of least resistance for her, and today you would think it that much more tempting—but she goes to the door. "He went to Legliz," the Arab calls as she goes, and she spins, cracking the glass with her thick instrument case.

She knows this man. In earlier, happier times he was in love with her, and followed her around this enclave like a lost duckling. He closes his eyes as if to disavow the information he just imparted.

Pytagoro, in the corner, is laughing so hard now the tears make snail paths down his cheeks.

"He went to the convent, *non*? *Que tragédie*." And Pytagoro is shouting against renewed rocketfire now, sobbing openly, he is so thrilled with himself, "in the autumn of your life, in the agony of this *cruce,* to seek refuge with the sisters of craziness. *Non?*"

Once outside she stares up at the heights. From this angle Ensevli and the eastern portion of the *cruce* are hidden by the Cadillac as well as by the row of bars, brothels and godowns it is set within. Teton Hill, with Bidonville rigged about its base and Barrio des Anglais higher up the northern flank, is clearly visible. At the top, looming like a guilty conscience, the barbicans and crenellations of Legliz girdle the yellow limestone walls of the convent and finally the white marbled towers of the church of Santa Karen.

The clock of the fishermen's chapel reads 5:53. From this perspective the sun is just licking the horizon, but at the altitude of the convent it has become day. The embrasures and bailey glow red as arterial blood and even the cold ash gullies of the volcano seem to retain warmth in the fresh illumination.

She walks faster, pushing through the air-shocks of shellfire, across the Slave Market—and she was wrong about no shells hitting the *cruce*'s center. Because Lo Pano is gone. The crazy tower that once bore countless Udine boards, marquee signs and ticker-tracks, all wired together and hung anyhow to mark the twenty-four-hour barters that were sign and center of the *cruce*'s life, has been blown into a tangle of steel and wiring and charred wood scattered like an abandoned children's game over five hundred square meters. She has to tread carefully to avoid stepping on strange chunks of motherboard and glass. A wedge of Udine still displays

earlier exchanges: TOSHIBA-TRANSCOM PARALLEL DRIVER,
270 BARTER-CHIPS; MANIOC, 12 C/SAC; GM 12-V STARTERS,
22 CAYMANS-PIÈCE. But nothing is left of the Flash Shack
where they kept the terminals and sat-relays that talked to
cruces in Brazil and even North America.

Now the only activity is like hers—hurried, avoiding,
furtive. A boy picks through smashed circuitry among the
splintered struts. Men grunt carts toward shelter, or hustle
gaggled families away from the sound of artillery. It is hard to
drag the Fourneaux-Dallapé on the level bricks of the market,
harder still to walk uphill on the cobbles of the convent road.
The muscles of her lower back seize up slightly every time
she takes a step. Her bare feet bruise on the unyielding stones.
Sweat stings her eyes. She has a weird, airy thought that
maybe she got all of this wrong. After all, she made a big mistake once about Jorge's aptitude for fidelity, so maybe she's
wasting her time worrying about his ability to save his own
life. She recognizes this as a notion that might make sense on
a normal day but does not necessarily apply when fire is all
around them. And it begs the question of what she would do
if she did not have to look for him.

After the road splits off for des Anglais its uphill spur becomes a dirt track where the Bidonville people pried up
stones to build walls for their shacks. Children coast toward
the harbor on homemade go-carts. Families wheel mopeds
piled with pots, chickens, bags of food. Donkey carts and mototaxis creak under cargoes of bootleg *pinga,* spindles of pirated software, counterfeit Kogi stelae, all the industries of
Bidonville. She dodges and pushes against a flow of people
moving downhill. The noise is much stronger up here, though
this part of Bidonville is probably only a little closer to
Ensevli than her apartment was; it's just that, with altitude,
there is less to break the sound.

Far more smoke is visible now, it climbs overhead in the
light wind and then folds back toward the fishing harbor in
backdraft from the perkling crater. Ash falls in gray flurries.
She can smell the smoke's sour breath, feel grit rasp the back

of her mouth. A condor flies overhead, or something like; it has the shape, the cruel bill, the spread-feathered wings, but it is too big and its angles too precise and anyway condors don't have tiny propellers at their tail and slits in their resin fuselage out of which blare overamplified, discordant voices. She drops the case and slaps her hands against her ears again until the condor passes.

As she takes her hands from her ears and drops her eyes toward the next corner she notices a woman standing still in a glassless window to her right. She has hair like polished coal, tied rigorously back; a crimson shawl, a worried expression, big hands ever ready to catch a child should she stumble. And Indio cheekbones, gray eyes hammocked on wrinkles, and the overpainted mouth that sang Soledad lullabies from the jungle. A squat woman in a cheap sharecropper skirt. Her mouth frames the single word: *"Reviens."*

Soledad closes her eyes tightly. *"Lombuage,"* she tells herself firmly—an illusion. Maria Gisela has been dead almost three years now. When she opens her eyes again the apparition is gone. She pushes it from her mind, thinking only, It's normal that tensions pulling so hard in such different directions in her brain should leave areas of slack where dreams might wander in. She starts walking again, slower. Her legs drag backward toward gravity, it's as if they avoid taking a path other than that of headlong flight. She forces herself uphill anyway, stopping for breath at first every minute, then every thirty seconds, shifting the accordion from shoulder to shoulder but resuming her climb every time till she has reached the last stretch of path at the top of Teton.

It was the song that made her do this, she decides. The song in the Cadillac. Not only because it reminded her of Jorge but because it connected through him to his daughter. And that, in turn, like an electrical current flowing into everything it touched, lit up the memory of the two kids nestled soft as ducklings under Cloodine's skirts, and also what she once felt for Jorge; and all of it has fused like shorted wiring inside her.

Because if Dolores has not already run for safety on a fishing sloop then she will be with her father. Or at least Jorge will know where she is, and then Soledad can drive them both toward safety, away from the heights. And now it is anger, rather than an inability to think of anything else worth doing, that drives her upward again; fury because he has no business coming up here, rage because she should not be reacting this way, squandering the precious division between them here where the explosions are louder, much louder, and from a different direction.

She stops abruptly.

This curve in the track is still hemmed in by shacks, but now she stands almost under the deep bastion of the convent.

Her wrenched muscles burn like a red-hot pipe buried in her lumbar region. Despite her caution she must have cut her foot in the Slave Market because her left footprint is accented by damp brown stains. Sweat drips down her earrings onto her collarbone; it runs between her breasts; it has soaked her pubic hair and drips down her inner thighs. Left hand at left ear again to muffle the renewed volume, right hand grasping the strap of the accordion case, she limps to the corner, to the earthen square before the convent's main gate, where she can see better.

The heights of Teton are too steep here to build more than one layer of shacks on a given level. You can look through gaps in the huts above the rows of similar huts tumbling like dice to the des Anglais district, and farther, past the Slave Market and the fishing harbor to the Walled City, and the dark facades of the Customs building where the General Staff and their F2 advisers must be watching through binoculars, directing over radio and computer links the artillery strike on the *cruce*. But what she stares at is the two brigades almost next to her: *guaqueros,* grave robbers, she knows some of them from the Cadillac they frequent. Some are digging a short trench with gold diggers' picks while others set up green tubes, three-inch mortars out of crates still marked CORPO DE EXERCITO XVII/BOA VISTA; pointing them north toward the coast road, where a column of smoke rises in front of armored personnel carriers lined up like matte green beetles at the approach to the *cruce,* coming from the opposite direction from Ensevli—a flanking action that bypasses the City of Boats but will squeeze the rest of the *cruce* like a vise.

Beside the *guaqueros* a tall man with a white beard, a Ping-Pong paddle in one hand, waggles his arms ritually. "No, no, no," he scolds, "*left* engine, *left* engine!" A policeman's hat is perched on his head but there are no flics in the *cruce,* anyway he wears the light blue smock of a Legliz patient. His directing of air traffic seems to work, in the sense of making things happen; where he was pointing, a red mushroom grows fast in the heart of des Anglais. It carries on its mottled skin bits of stone, mirror, tile, a car door. The mushroom becomes the size of a small house, then bursts, turning to smoke and sound and a gust of air that physically pushes Soledad back a pace, fanning her hair behind as if she stood in the first swipe of a hurricane.

Debris patter. One of the *guaqueros* yells at her. She cannot make out his words through the numbness of her ears. His intent, though, is transparent enough. He is waving at her, then at the convent postern, linking the two in time and space so she will get the hell into shelter before the hostile artilleryman tracks closer—or perhaps it is his own weapons he wishes to protect her from. For the other *guaqueros,* startled by the explosion, have triggered a mortar aimed at too acute an angle. Its projectile arcs almost directly above them and lands closer to the *guaquero* positions than the earlier shell.

Another backdraft happens. Overhead, a "condor" swoops from behind the convent tower, sunlight flashing in the lens of its betacam. A *whup-whup-whup* of engine noise rises from behind the clerestory. She picks up the Fourneaux-Dallapé, holding it like a puppy in her arms, and runs across the earth of the square under the swordlike shadow of a giant green chopper gliding around the northern slope of Teton, the *whup-whup* suddenly louder than fire or jets—and finally under the ocher walls of the convent bastion rising fifteen meters

overhead, into the black pool, the cool, the humid night behind the postern.

The walls of Santa Karen were built of mortar mixed with
bulls' blood to withstand the agitprop and sappers' charges of
pirates. They are five meters thick. The rare windows are only
a few centimeters across so cannonballs cannot get in. The
entrance tunnel runs left and right. She turns left toward the
main body of the church. Within five paces the roar of chopper and the crashing of shells are wrapped in stone, isolated
from her ears. After fifty paces they are gone.

The convent smells of incense and ether and herbs like
verveine and *sauge* that the nuns use in their ministrations.
The light splashing from the gate fades behind her. The corri-
dors are of brown stone and whitewash, but with no power
for lightbulbs the colors soon are folded into charcoal and
then black—until the process is reversed, here by a stone
lamp set in a niche, or there, by an open door. A deep-
sea glow illuminates portions of the rooms behind these
doors. As she passes she sees robed nuns tending stacks of
ancient murmuring televisions. The huge sets are lined up
before rows of blue-smocked men and women. She can tell
when she nears one of these rooms, not only by the glow but
by the simple rhythm scratching out of the deadness of stone.
The nuns all carry instruments, usually marimbas or tom-
toms, on which they cheerfully bat the different timings of
their therapy.

One sister stands apart from her patients at the third
therapy room. Soledad slips inside to ask if she has seen Jorge
or any other *crucistas*. The nun puts a finger to her lips, then
goes back to scratching at the surface of a rasp, matching her
rhythm to that of a highly charged dénouement in a Mexican
soap opera. Soledad stares at the nun, attracted despite herself
by the woman's absorption in a different discipline. She wonders for a second if she herself might not belong in this cool
blue silence, in the comforting glow of irrelevant drama, she
with her visions of the dead and beats of wrong music claw-
ing at her from the barrels of recoilless rifles; but almost

immediately she turns and limps onward, grimacing from the pain in her back and in her cut foot. The accordion feels three times heavier than when she first picked it up. Her body lusts to ditch it, but she has an uneasy feeling that she is on a one-way trek and there will be no time to come back. And she cannot lose the Fourneaux-Dallapé, not when so much else is tentative or on its way out. Now, apart from Dolores and, God help her, even Jorge, the accordion is all she has left for a reference point.

She finds a flight of stairs, going down. The stairs are lit only by a votive pietà nailed in a niche. The wounds of the Christ are melodramatic and bloody. From the level below, women's voices arrange themselves in straight melodic lines out of the dampness and dark. Soledad recognizes the tune they are singing: it's a *telenovela* theme arranged in Gregorian form. The chant swells as she passes Byzantine archways to her right. Tapers have been placed behind the indigo stained glass lining this hidden chapel where nuns and patients together sing "Pain in the Afternoon." Beyond the chapel lies a row of cells, some lit by tapers, but all empty of human sound.

The clear voices fade behind her.

The ground under her feet moves. It lowers a few centimeters, then rises back to trip her up.

Immediately afterward comes a bubble of pressure, muffled by the ten thousand tons of stone the convent is built of. Someone screams briefly a long way away. The plain chant has stopped. Dust powders Soledad where she lies across the accordion case. She picks herself up, and once more hoists the Fourneaux-Dallapé. It takes all the strength she is capable of. Her heart is banging loudly; somehow the now-total darkness amplifies it like a *bombo*-skin. The blue reflection of chapel behind her is gone. She starts to run, ignoring the hurt in her foot, scraping the texture of wall with her left hand for guidance. The corridor twists left, or maybe joins another hallway. She tastes something raw, familiar in the back of her throat. Faint light grains out of the black oblivion, allowing her to make out another downward flight of stairs. She needs to go up but she descends anyway, under the low arches of the tunnel, because reflected against the floor at the stairs' base is a much stronger light and a white and growing noise that does not belong at all in this cool, shadowed place. The light wavers, flickers, as if beckoning her.

Her lungs twist. Still coughing, she rounds a corner deep in drifted dust and there it is, what she flees, what she seeks: fire. Fire the color of blood and lions—thus RDX from the four-inch recoilless maybe, or from air–ground rockets. Fire raging in a hundred dancers of light and color with their five thousand servants of smoke. And the noise is now total and clear, it is helicopter and mortars yes of course, it is the music fire makes, sure, the laughing cracking cold saraband of flame, but it is more also. Behind it the patterns of howitzers, the patterns of jets and attack choppers have locked in fully, she understands them now and it is *cuto,* the 6/8 rhythm of *"Si mou estoma,"* the rhythm of Jorge's song. But the beat is unvaried where it should be loose, and broken in false places; so that now it is no longer Jorge's but *his* song, the man of the incomplete seventh, the Yanqui with no face. And she understands the fullness of their plans, in attacking the very rhythm of the *cruce.* And she knows beyond the shadow of a doubt that there is no escape. For Dolores will be found, and Jorge will be found, and when they catch Soledad they will—

She drops the accordion, puts her hands to her ears, and turns away. The Fourneaux-Dallapé is immediately forgotten. She knows nothing but retreat, back up the steps. The stones lift under her, higher than before. Fire is in front of her now as well as behind her and she is trapped like Jorge, *too long*! Without the slightest warning in sound or sight or feel she is blown backward—she is flying like the birds of her earrings, touching neither floor nor walls nor ceiling of this buried passageway. And the beat of *cuto,* twisted and perverted, rises and then is sucked into the infinite and terrible Esperanto of explosion. And flame comes at her face, warm and impossible to resist, its hot hands reaching for her skin.

She screams, raising the pitch and volume of her voice to match the voice of chaos but of course she is unable to. Her voice and her body are lost as blast, noise, and heat intersect the parabola of her flight, and there is nothing left now but the defeat of prayer. Even the small jade fact of her enduring love for Jorge's daughter has fallen in the lifting; all she knows is the complete surrender in her. For most of Soledad's life she has fought against noise and bad music and now at the end they will triumph. Yet even this knowledge is not so great as the pathetic and humiliating wish that she be free of the fire that is now about to touch her.

TWO

SHE WAS STILL SCREAMING when she woke up.

Even when she stopped—because everything else had stopped: the first hot lick of flame, the noise of explosions spiking beyond the ability of ears to absorb or brain to analyze, the searchlight ache of fire seen too close, all vanished from her senses in a flicker—even when she had stopped screaming she could hear her scream continue, using silence as sounding board, like the last sustained cello note, pianissimo, fermata, at the end of Britten's *Third Quintet,* an allusion (she remembered with fine irrelevance) to the famous "dying away" in Mann's *Doktor Faustus.*

Where there had been fire, it was now dark. Where there had been noise, only the echo of her own voice remained. As her consciousness caught up to the available input it figured out that truly nothing else existed—no recognizable sound, no background noise even, nothing around her.

No Dolores, above all. No Jorge. She could feel her body, in a trick she had gotten used to over the last three weeks, mimicking that absence: long fissures running from throat to pelvis, open to reveal a matching void inside her, where the people she loved used to live. She knew that, were there light to see, her skin would be as brown and smooth as before; the cracks lived in her mind, in her mind's picture of itself. But there was nothing imagined about the nausea following from all of this, rising so fast inside her gorge she barely had time to lean over the side of the bed before puking, violently, on the rayon wall-to-wall.

She sat up, wiping her mouth on the back of one wrist. It

was not entirely dark in this room. The noctiluc strip on the ceiling extruded an opal smear. The greenish glow to the left was the workstation, hooked up to the motel's network. Its screensaver showed two women undressing each other. When they got to panties level the screen would dissolve to two men, or a man and a woman, fully clothed, ready to start the cycle again. The noctiluc reflected on a glossy velvet painting of the Golden Gate Bridge over her bed, as well as on the cellophane everything was wrapped in here: the toilet seat, the virtual-reality mask, the portion of bed she had pulled her sheets from in the course of dreaming.

So quiet, without fire. She was certain now—though of course she had no evidence to support this theory—that it was the very depth of silence that had woken her. Already she was familiar with the background of sounds that usually populated this motel: the moans, real or feigned, of by-the-hour clients; the rumble of Magicffingers beds, jerking and subsiding in synch with whatever 3-D fantasy her neighbors had rented on the workstation; the overamped Shifta-shinjuku ballads from the twenty-four-hour jagger disco in the basement; the loudspeaker from Love Handles, the "Sex Shoppe" next door.

All gone. The blue burn of neon from the Love Handles sign reflected on a wooden fire escape across the alley. Eddy Street, to the left, was invisible and silent, though it too was always auditorially fat with exhausts, the blandishments of touts, the whoop of sirens sniffing out the inevitable fallout from noise in this part of the Tenderloin.

A whiff of breeze, heavy with humidity, tickled her forehead. It reminded her of her apartment on the morning of the attack. The memory was like a blow. She slid over the mattress toward the workstation, punched ENTER, and then OPTIONS. The women were replaced by the words

WELCOME TO THE NIRVANA MOTEL
YOUR VIRTUAL BASE FOR EXPLORING THE PLEASURES OF
OF THE BAY AREA

followed by a menu tree: ROOM SERVICE (food, cocktails, marital aids); FACE-SUCKER RENTAL; VIRTIX LIBRARY; MAGICFFIN-GERS®; WEBSEARCH; E-MAIL.

She pushed the cursor to WEBSEARCH and clicked. The screen shivered, and stayed the same.

She clicked again, then slid to other options. Each time the screen shivered once more, as if it did not like what was going on, either, but could do nothing about it.

The 'saver came back on. It was the men this time. They were fully dressed. Expressions of blond and manic delight racked their pretty faces.

She put on the same cheetah tights, loose blouse, and plastic sandals she had been wearing since she crossed the Tapon de Darien. She moved to the door and, unlocking it carefully, opened it just enough to see.

The corridor outside was mushy with dead air. She moved down the hall, padding quietly on the stained runner. From the top of the stairs she could safely observe the lobby. The doors leading into Eddy Street were propped open.

The chair the night porter used was empty. The front-desk workstation displayed the same screensaver as the one in her room. She knew the desk terminal had a long delay before the 'saver came on. Of course the clerk abandoned his post sometimes, to go to the toilet, to score a can of Zero Cola from the machine out back. But Soledad had spent a lot of time in the lobby over the last thirty hours, trying unsuccessfully, via questions scrawled on notepads, to pump information out of the clerk, and she had never seen the screensaver pop up.

And where was the clerk anyway, while the front door was wedged open like that?

(fire licking her stretched fingers)

Her heart banged away. Sweat prickled her forehead. She took a long breath. There was no fire here; the flames were all in her head. Probably nothing more was going on than a police raid down the block, or a jis' bust; something to pull the night porter from his furtive patching into the rooms' VR, or tempt the jaggers blinking from their music-jisi cocktail, or room residents from their strictly metered pleasure.

She shook her head, the decision—almost instinctual, after three weeks of living hunted like a *selva* panther—already made. She strode back to her room, locking the door behind her. Her bag was ready. When the sum total of your possessions was a fresh box of tampons, a half-empty pack of cigarettes, a lighter, a pair of mismatched balsa earrings carved to resemble jungle birds, and thirty-four Cayman cashchips, your bags were always ready. She slung the strap over her shoulder, moved toward the window. And stopped, staring at the monitor.

On the screen, the love couples had gone.

It was not their absence that brought her to a halt. She was used to things being merely absent. What stopped her was the image, vivid even on this antique Compaq.

Women and children running in blurred colors down a broad stretch of cracked tarmac toward her, people lost and sick, you could tell from the way they tried different directions then stopped, confused.

Music played very softly from the cheap Dolby arranged to complement the VR, but it was bad music, like a Virtix drama track played backward: minor chords, busted rhythms. "Uncaring" was the word that came to her, *uncompassionate* tunes. A man in close-up, eyes rimmed with panic. His face faded as smoke pumped thickly between him and whatever captured his image. He turned, picked up a wayward child, and ran to the left, but he could not work his legs well enough to wade through the smoke. In fact it was not smoke but the air around him becoming gray like fog, thickening, turning black, turning solid—the people struggling as their arms and legs, their toes and lungs, were set in something like hardening concrete, like a fly in amber, *como une mouche prise dans l'ambre.*

Soledad's hand gripped her throat. Between slams of diastole the words echoed in her head, the words of Jorge's poem, one of his last:

*The men, the children, slower and slower they turn . . .
and the air around them thickens. . . .*

She stepped onto the workstation's top, out of sight of the
monitor, but the tampered music snickered from the Dolby
and even as she opened the window and twisted on the sill
until she was hanging from her hands the words whispered in
her head:

*And even their lightest hopes like flies trapped in amber
are caught as the air turns to cement.*

And she dropped.

It was not much of a fall, perhaps a meter and a half. She
landed too close to the motel wall, bounced off the breeze-
block, and fell backward on the tar surface, the breath knocked
out of her.

The cool air abraded her throat. Flat on her ass, gasping
for oxygen, she looked around quickly. Beyond the paling,
the wedge of Eddy Street visible from this alley was empty
except for the bruised blue of the sex shop neon blipping on,
off, and on again.

She wasn't really thinking. It just *felt* early to try the
street, as if the part of her psyche rubbed raw and bloody
when the *cruce* was destroyed could not face something as
big as this unnatural silence of San Francisco. She got to her
feet, tripping on a poorly balanced grate that clanked in the
obvious quiet. Readjusted her bag and climbed all the way up
the fire escape of the next building, stepping on the outside
edges of the steps so they would not squeak. The institutional
bulk of the Federal Building occupied the horizon in front of
her. The Nirvana Motel reached into the sodium orange of
light pollution on the alley's other side. The roof of the building she stood on was full of odd black shapes she supposed
must be air-conditioning and heat pipes. The roof was fenced
with razor wire, the fire-escape gate illegally padlocked, to
protect the sex shop she supposed. She started to retrace her
steps, then paused beside a casement window two floors from
the ground.

The room inside was dark, except for the "standby" indicator of a personal computer and a strange curve of moving, colored light, in size and dimension like a wedge of melon, against the invisible floor.

It was a "half-sucker"—a three-dimensional virtual-reality mask. She had a Virtix model in her room in the motel, though she possessed no UCC card to unlock it. And she had used one in Bidonville, at a pirate-software workshop she visited once with Jorge. You put the 'sucker on and played a program, and then it was as if you had stepped into a different world, with all the depth and dimensions and colors of the real.

In America, she had noticed, people used them for everything: to go to virtual banks, to talk to their parents, to order groceries.

Someone clearly had dropped this one in the place she or he was sitting when whatever brought silence to Eddy Street intruded on viewing time.

The thing with this half-sucker was, one side of its screen was rimmed with a long slice of blue, blue that blinked in a way that seemed viscerally familiar. She turned her head slightly so that, across the alley, the wall of the Nirvana moved into her direct line of sight.

The reflection of the sex emporium sign flashed, went dark, flashed, went dark. And every time it flashed, so did the blue in the half-sucker. And every time it went off, the half-sucker's blue did the same.

But the half-sucker itself was in shadow and shielded from the neon's glare, and there were no other windows or mirrors in the room to account for stray reflections.

The window was cracked open—another sign of dysfunction in this high-crime neighborhood. Soledad yanked it halfway up, wincing as the nerves in her back complained. She scissored over the edge, dropped to the floor.

Gently, with hands that did not tremble, she picked up the headpiece and eased it on like huge glasses so that the screen dropped over her eyes.

And a roadway appeared, empty of cars, before her. It could be any street, in San Francisco at least, with its twist of slope, its line of wooden buildings, a sequence of pushwalls, or interactive ads, quiet now that no one was passing to interact with. A series of street lamps, various signs:

SLOPPY SECONDS NIGHTCLUB
LIVE! NUDE! SEX ACTS!
HOLLY THE HOOKER—SAFE AND SANITARY—HOT
AND HAPTIC

and, perhaps a hundred meters down the thoroughfare, a huge cerulean neon sign with letters three meters high spelling out

LOVE HANDLES
★ SEX ★
FOR THE HEFTY
★ SHOPPE ★
BIG VR LOVELIES
TOSHIBA SUITS

—flashing to the same beat inside the face-sucker as the wash of blue outside the window of this diaper-smelling bedroom.

A logo in the corner read: FLASHNEWS LIVE.

She needed no confirmation but it was there anyway, behind Love Handles, showing clear in the 3-D image: a five-story motel with its own orange sign, unblinking but half broken, so you could read only VANA . . . TEL of the full name of the motel she had taken refuge in.

She glanced downward. The scene automatically shifted to match.

Trucks blocked the width of Eddy Street in the foreground of the VR envirocam. Black, square armored cars. Trucks with wire grilles over their windows and darkened police lights on their roofs. Huge bulbous vehicles with twin turrets mounting both recognizable machine guns and the thick snouts of weapons she had never seen before. Buses with arrays of satellite dishes and the greenish blur of computer displays shining through smoked windows.

A handful of figures stood in the shadows between the trucks. They carried bulletproof armor and rifles lumpy with secondary launchers. Their helmets had half-suckers built in and they stood with heads cocked in a way that indicated they were listening to something other than the odd quiet of this night around them.

In the dizzying spread of 3-D across Soledad's own glasses, the men looked so close and so real, it felt as if she could reach out and pinch their Kevlar accoutrements.

Nothing moved, apart from the men, and the flash of sign.

"Adornistas," the announcer was saying sotto voce over Soledad's Dolby. "Another source mentioned possible links with the Putamadres street gang, or even a Ludd-Kaczynski cell. One thing's for sure, Ornette—I mean, take a look at the muscle on Eddy Street tonight—there's no way this suspect is an *ordinary* terrorist, like the federal spokesman said."

She swallowed, still gazing at the display in front of her. The street looked very beautiful, the pastels of porno neon and the drifts of signs all narrowing with perspective down the line of curb. It would be so nice to walk down that sidewalk as an ordinary citizen, unnoticed, unsought, without men or their instruments of fire looking for her. The impulse to cry squeezed at her chest, but in the three weeks since the burning of Bamaca she had not cried once, nor uttered any other sound for that matter, except—and even this was only a suspicion on her part—in the dreams that haunted her sleep.

The need for sobs subsided. She pulled the 'sucker off, got to her feet, and climbed back onto the fire escape. She knew what to do now. Walk down the stairs, crouch on the mossy cement of the alley, fit her fingers to holes in the grate she had tripped over earlier. The grate was cast iron but despite the old ache it brought out in her back she could lift one corner of

it. Once the end was wedged over the opening's rim she slid it
most of the way off the hole it covered.

Looking down at the inkiness of the hole, at the glimmer
indicating water at its center, she remembered how she knew
what course of action to follow here. It came from talking
about gringo movies with Jorge, even the dated ones that
made it, three years after first release, to the theaters in the
Walled City. For in the thrillers, when escape was blocked
and all hope was finally lost, the hero almost always pried up
a manhole cover and made his way out through the sewers.
Jorge said Doctor Fernsehen had written a sidebar on this
syndrome in one of his books. She hoped the police had not
read Fernsehen, or if they had, that they had not yet drafted
guidelines based on his writings. She swung her legs into the
hole, found the rungs, and climbed down till the opening was
at neck level. Then she braced her shoulders and yanked at
the grate till it dropped back into place.

The tunnel at the bottom of this hole contained water only
a few centimeters deep. It smelled, predictably, of diluted shit
and mold and garbage. It was also, of course, black dark.
From her sack she fished her pack of Galaxys and, resisting the urge to light a cigarette, removed by feel the lighter
tucked inside. The lighter's flame sprang high and steady
when she flicked the flint wheel. She flinched, and thrust it to
arm's length from her face.

Two farther circles—concrete, iron flanged, rust stained,
thick with algae, a meter and a half in diameter—sprang into
the yellow circle her lighter made. A brown trickle of thick
water at the bottom of their arc ran parallel to Eddy Street
into further darkness in both directions.

She chose the path toward the soldiers. It was a lesson
from her life in Bamaca, to confront problems rather than flee
them. It pleased her—despite the memories of sadness silted
up in her stomach, despite the panic higher up—that bits of
her vanished self could surface, like a sober driver, to take the
wheel now and then in emergencies.

So she slogged down the left tunnel. Bent almost double,

moving crabwise, flicking the lighter occasionally as she progressed. The slish of her footsteps fluttered down the tunnel and bounced and returned in humid stereo. Something scurried behind her, and was still.

Twenty meters or so farther on she stopped. A thick metal grate divided this tube from whatever lay beyond. It was set immovably in concrete. She stared at it, her thumb scorched from the lighter's trigger, trying to breathe normally.

Then she reversed her tracks and crossed back under the manhole she had come down and crabbed on, down the opposite tunnel, under the Nirvana, toward the eastern part of the Tenderloin presumably. Forty meters, a hundred meters. She had lost track of distance by the time she reached another grate, barring this end of the sewer also from the main conduits.

Like a fly trapped in amber, Soledad thought.

She released the lighter's toggle, dropped onto her haunches, and bowed her head. For some reason, panic was not the prime force in her now she had run out of options again. Panic had triggered her sober driver, but even that driver was out of tricks. Beyond the grate, or grates—for there were two here, one leading straight ahead and one right—she heard water, a small river by the sound of it, rushing in the many-chambered darkness. In the water's sound she made out high notes, major As like Dolores's voice, like her laugh which always had resembled a sequence of marimba touches. That was the beauty of water: all its scales. In the middle registers, the murmur of trade, *cruce* commerce that she used to hear twenty-four hours a day from the Slave Market, commerce that had as much to do with arguing and meeting and explaining your vision of soursop husbandry or Hawkleyite economics or how best to fry *butifarras* as it did with how many barter-chips you wanted for a barrowful of reject Guyanese underwear.

And in the deep registers, Jorge's voice, ranting as he sometimes did to the point where it made her blush with embarrassment for him. She was not sure if she really had heard him say this, but it was something he would say: "These sewers are vital in Yanqui films, because the tunnel is their Thanatos, with all the Viennese connotations—but, as Fernsehen says, this is the symbol they have chosen in video for their culture, their entertainment society, what they call the Flash—a tunnel of perception leading to openings, rooms that promise to be full of light and riches and release from the ills pulling you down, but that (so you see as you enter) are fully as dark and crammed with ennui as the tunnel you just left; only after the next chute, at the end, is another glimmer of light. If you're lucky, it will take only twenty years before you understand these rooms are all the same room. Yeh, these tunnels are all the same tunnel, and you were trapped before you started to escape."

The whispered "Jorge" started inside her somewhere but as always never rose higher than her throat. The voices faded briefly into the sound of water. When they returned they were different, farther off, and lacking the fluidity of Lanc-Patua dialect. Men instructing each other over radios. She could not tell, in this chamber of echoes, which tunnel the voices came from, but she had to assume they had come down the same tunnel she crouched in, the one leading back to the motel.

In the dark, her now-total powerlessness became a fact as solid as the darkness here was complete. She knew it was in her mind but the thing was, the inside of her mind was black and the inside of this tunnel was black and no border distinguished one from the other. Thus the powerlessness took substance, building form she could almost see out of the vibrations of what she could not, mass intangible, sound inaudible. And so when it shifted and became that black hole of her nightmares, the place so terrible that the weight of its horror sucked everything of grace and hope faster and faster toward the shape with no feature, the person without trait, the man *behind* the men coming for her down the tunnel—she had no borders left to hide behind.

All that was left then was what had been forcing her

onward; all she had was the physical, reflexive terror of
something she could not remember, perpetrated by an enemy
she could not recall except by what she had named him—the
faceless gringo.

And coupled with that terror, a habit of survival, the momentum of days during which she and the *contrabandistas*
who helped her had somehow eluded the gringo and all the
various uniforms in which he dressed his power. Survival
in that time had become a habit, like travel; in many ways
travel and survival had turned into the same thing, metaphors
for each other's engine, for knowing when you got up each
morning that you would have to be somewhere else by sunset.

One found shelter, one looked behind. One was most wary
when changing modes of transport.

Whatever the background, the drive left over from three
weeks of running was sufficient to raise her in revolt one last
time. So she scrambled to her feet, the useless protests beating as usual against the locked door of her throat. She grasped
the two grates, each with one hand, and shook violently. They
were made of iron bars six centimeters in diameter, buried
deeply in concrete: immovable. Yet one of them, the right-
hand one, swung out easily, banging her in the forehead and
causing her, in its treacherous absence of solidity, to slip and
fall backward in the muck, dropping the lighter.

It took a long time to find the lighter. Her hands were
trembling so hard they required almost as long a time to clear
the lighter's jet so flame could come out. Then gas hissed and
flame exploded, bright and expansive. She gasped as usual,
and had to squinch her eyes to look.

What she saw was faint bead marks at the top of each bar
of the open grate where the iron had been cut by a torch and
then filed so the cuts would not show easily. A rusted wire,
once hooked to a nail inside the tunnel beyond, had broken
when she yanked at the grate. The grate itself now swung
wide to reveal a few meters of cement pipe leading into yet
another version of the dark.

An illegal tunnel, then. Without investing another second

of thought in the mechanics of it, she picked up her bag, crawled over the lip, and wired the grate shut behind her. This passage was tighter than the previous one, but it was dryer, and she could manage a more squeezed version of the crab-walk she had adopted early on. The sound of river faded, was rivaled and finally replaced by the *slish-brush-slish* of her lo-comotion. One hand rasping the cement side, just as she had done so long ago in Santa Karen. Feeling for when the tunnel might end. She kept expecting it to stop but the walls con-tinued, slick and without pause or grate. The rhythm of her movement eliciting songs that shared that meter.

"Chanson de Los Altos."

"Of What Use Is a Root."

The rhythm built cramps in her muscles until she had to stop, kneel, and straighten her back along the axis of tunnel to relieve the pain. She began to measure time by the halts her lower back imposed. Two stops later and the tunnel sloped downward slightly. After the fifth stop it turned right. Water gushed from a smaller conduit to the side, further soaking her clothes. When she flicked her lighter to examine the conduit she found a sign over the pipe. FLOOD BUILDING SD-41. It sounded ominous.

Then light brought scale to her tubular environment. A curved glare, similar in shape and, at this distance, size to the glow she had seen within the curve of face-sucker; a flicker of light bent by the shape of her tunnel into an arc.

Voices faint as memories of infancy grew out of the glow. A smell of roasting meat and wood smoke frayed a way through nervous preoccupation to touch her fear, and boost it by association with the remembered smoke that rose and min-gled with the volcano's steam.

She stayed in the position she was in when she first saw it, curled against the wall like a piece of stale bread. But her sober driver was still on duty—or maybe it was that, with no other options left, the single remaining course of action was not so hard to take.

Very slowly and carefully, she crawled on toward the light.

At three meters, even one meter from the opening, the voices were still faint. The smoke, though, was strong in her nostrils. It squeezed in thin streamers through the grateless hole and stung her cringing eyes. She crawled to within a finger's width of the opening and, a centimeter at a time— locking her lungs tight so her breath would make no sound— eased her right eye past the rim.

It was a catchment basin. The ceiling was high, and a series of tunnels pierced the chamber walls at different levels. Tall cement bulkheads sectioned the chamber into different, smaller compartments. Every cement surface was covered with sheaves of wet, black algae. From where she squatted she could see through a sequence of giant metal sluice gates, all cranked open, that connected the different chambers. A column of pale orange light fell from the ceiling of the chamber closest to her, and smoke wove in and out of this column from a rusted barbecue grill set in the sludge of the chamber's floor.

Soledad pulled back, a fly's whisker at a time. She desperately needed to breathe but could not bring herself to release her lungs.

A man had stood next to the grill, prodding a piece of meat with a wire. Soledad found herself checking back over her memory of what she had seen, because it seemed so unlikely; yet every detail of him had been strong and uncompromising.

He wore a suit cut in the monkey-jacket fashion popular a few years ago, once elegant, but now stained and ripped. Long trousers torn into shorts. Dress shoes and a silk tie, all battered. Hair shiny with oil, and fashionably ponytailed. An obsolescent notebook computer hung from a rope tied around his waist.

The man had been in three-quarter profile, pricking the meat with one hand like a fencer, talking into a cellphone held in the other. But his profile was wrong. The light had

been poor, but it was not bad lighting at work here; his face
was distorted, scars running so thickly down his cheeks that
they collapsed his nose to one side and almost shut the socket
where his left eye should have been.

She covered her mouth to muffle the hiss of air finally
sucking in.

She had seen more in that quick glance.

In the chamber beyond had been a group of men dressed
like the first, every one of them talking into cellphones by
the light of a dozen torches wavering greasy flame against
the seeping concrete bulkheads of the catchment basin. And
every one of them held up a pink slip of paper toward a series
of posters tacked on the farthest wall.

They had been calling out. Locked as she was in the visuals, she had not made out what they were saying. From the
shelter of her tunnel, though, she found she could now distinguish words.

"A sign," one man called.

"A sign is nigh," another responded.

"Hoffa!" from a third.

"I swear euros in (undecipherable)," the first voice said.

"You can't cash his credits," another chimed in. "They're
bogus."

"Boooogus credits," someone moaned.

"Forty harddollars," another voice ventured, "in Zero Cola
cans?"

"Gotta pay off the *Lord*," from a voice very close by.

"Credits to Hoffa . . . for our meltdown."

Soledad leaned forward, slower than before. The grill man
stood in the same position, still talking into his cellphone. It
was he who had talked of payoff. The group beyond had
shifted, so she could make out details of the posters. She recognized the images, and felt surprise and even a wry pride
that she could know anything in a country so different.

One poster showed a face, burned but less scarred than
these men. He was wrinkled with age and his arms were out-

stretched in a rain of UCC cards. She recognized him from articles in the *Diario*: it was Hoffa, the American millennialist preacher.

Another was a painting: a woman, naked, with jet black hair and lambent skin against a black background, a thin ribbon sectioning the smooth skin of her neck.

Manet's *Olympia*.

The tunnel trembled gently around her, then was still. The grill-master rolled the meat on his barbecue. The meat was a small animal, somewhat bigger and longer than a chicken. The torchlight emphasized the characteristic twisting of the men's facial tissues that was a symptom of Kundura River swine flu. Soledad was vaguely astonished to find victims in this city, in this country. The Kundura had killed 18 million people throughout the world in the space of seven months, but mostly in poor regions like the slums of Mexico City or parts of the *selva* where the vaccine had been, for one reason or another, unavailable.

The grill-master adjusted his half-sucker. The movement drew Soledad's eyes upward, and she saw the reflection, bunched in the screen's convex curve, of his collapsed septum, the concentric rings of scar tissue—and too late, behind the reflection, his single open eye, staring directly at her.

He dropped his cellphone and in one swift movement turned and lunged at the tunnel opening. She pulled back, convulsively, breath exploding in a loud "foo!" as he grabbed her blouse. But she was in the wrong position, squatting with her weight still forward. Also he was strong and, while she struggled as hard as she could within the confines of the tunnel, he popped her out of the opening as easily as a bottle opener removing a cork. Then he twisted her, ripping her shirt, putting his scabbed legs out of range of the kicks she aimed. With one forearm barred across her neck, he threw her against the slimed wall of the catchment chamber.

"Easy," he grunted. "I'm not gonna hurt you."

Soledad shook her head violently. In the absence of

speech, it was the only way she could protest: *No don't hurt me, no don't hold me, no, let me go.*

The man did not slacken his grip. He flipped out the half-sucker's mouthpiece.

"Click up, team," he yelled into the mouthpiece. "Hoffa done brought us a tasty li'l guest."

Soledad let go of the straps of her bag, which was caught between her back and the wall. She brought her fist up in a roundhouse swing at his face, dislodging the VR mask. He caught her arm and bent it behind her till it hurt. Beyond her assailant's head came a noise of shuffling and muttering as the other men clambered through the nearest sluice-cage into the tiny chamber where the barbecue smoked. Their torches, wildly throwing shadows around the random angles of this utilitarian pit, emphasized in fire colors their ravaged features, twisted noses, cyclopean squints. The light fell on Soledad's face as well, on her left arm, splayed melodramatically against the cold wetness of the wall behind her. And she felt her astonishment at the weirdness of all this give way to old, habitual panic—because despite all the desperate effort she had put into avoiding this, she was going to be hurt and probably raped here, *now,* rather than in the myriad other times and places possible so far.

Yet before panic had fully moved back into its old digs in her mind, two then four of the Kundura men drew back hurriedly. They pulled at each other's lapels, shouting into their phones:

"There it *is!*"

"There it is—"

"The *sign!*"

"Larissa?"

"Larissa."

And, reverently:

"Hoffa save us!"

Now her assailant let fall his forearm. He, too, pulled back, doubtfully at first, then more quickly as his perspective altered with distance. And there they all stood, in a hunched and solemn ring, eleven men with maybe fourteen open eyes between them staring fixedly at a woman splayed against a wall so thick with algae that blackish green dripped over the thin white berm of her forearm. Amid the shuffling of the crowd, another poster was for the first time revealed behind them, a Plexiglas movie gel printed for display on an old-fashioned billboard. It showed a slim woman with short black curls, one arm over her left breast, which otherwise would have been visible through the tear in her long and elegant blouse; wide eyes of almost stratospheric blue; a mouth with a classic *V* shape that for half its length on either side disappeared like a river canyon into the fold of her cheeks; the other arm pulled backward by the dark greenish mass of what was supposed to be an Arcturan beast, whose paws melted over her arm rather like the slime dripping over Soledad's.

Larissa Love.

Between the face and its strong cheekbones and the similar disposition of props, the resemblance between Soledad and this heroine of American *telenovelas* was uncanny.

Even the men who looked from side to side as if in doubt ended up focused on her again, their tongues wet with the sibilants of the soap star's name.

"Larissa."

And, from a tall one in a full face-sucker:

"What do you want from us? We have Cayman cash-chips—"

"Dachshund steaks, too."

"UCC cards," volunteered a short man.

("Bogus," someone whispered, and was hissed fiercely by his fellows.)

"Access codes." The tall man's face-sucker nodded to itself.

"Yes," another added. "We were all partners at Derivatives Projections. We have their *encryption,* Lara."

"They changed the passwords realtime." It was the tall man talking now. They shushed him also, but he shook his face-sucker impatiently. "We had secret sites on the Wildnets," he continued, "memory futures, Flash-speed projections." The 'sucker's screen bounced torchlight in her eyes. "And we *knew*—we had it from a source at Glaxo-LaRoche—the flu shots would be more lethal than the Kundura. Oh, Lara, we can offer you electronic manna, if that is all you want."

"What *is* it you want, Larissa?"

The men stared at her.

Soledad licked her lips. It was a reflex only. She knew, even as she opened her mouth, that nothing would come out. And of course it didn't matter because these men were toying with her, they so clearly lived beyond the touch of both law and woman there was no reason they should let her go without taking something of value. Still, the momentum of flight was around, with all its rules, especially the one about if there was no choice left then you chose what was left open to you. And if it was a game they were playing, it was up to her to make the next move.

So, pulling her arm from the scum of the wall, she lifted it all atremble in the direction smoke went, her index finger wavering but still pointed distinctly at the color of street lamp that shone through the crude chimney of the barbecue room.

Everyone but the full-sucker man looked where she was pointing.

"She wants sky," somebody told his cellphone, quietly.

"Sky."

"It's a sign."

They looked at the full-sucker man, who continued staring at Soledad. Her figure was a tiny spider in the reflection of his screen.

"We don't dis signs," full-sucker whispered, "not any-more."

The men took a pace or two back.

"Sky," one of them repeated, almost in wonder.

Then, raggedly but together, the men shuffled toward the nearest sluice gate, each motioning at Soledad to follow.

————

THEY WALKED FOR A long time through tunnels of different sizes. Some had walkways to one side, a few were narrower than the drainage tunnel under the Nirvana Motel. One was hip-deep in chilly but fairly clean water. After a while Soledad lost what little hold she'd had on the evolution of time. The destruction of time pulled the curtains off her fear and morphed the stage-set world of torchlight into a sort of brain-cabaret where all the associations of this bizarre procession—the file of dark monsters, the womblike slosh of the sewers, the blending of escape, death, hell, ritual sacrifice, and possible rebirth—were allowed to play out with little reference to cogent script.

At one point she was certain she saw Dolores's face in perfect facsimile, white and determined in the scatter of torchlight on the swollen sewer they marched beside.

She had no clear idea of where or when or how far along they were when the column stopped. Someone hauled open, with great screeching of rust, a hatch in the tunnel's side. The opening where the hatch-cover had been was neither dark nor light but blue-gray; it was a color such as Soledad felt she had not seen for years, with enough silver to highlight the dust and torch smoke suspended in it. Two of the men stooped through, while the rest shrank back in the walkway-tunnel, so far that one of them fell backward in the stream of sewage with a loud splash, to the hoarse acclaim of his companions.

When she clambered through the hatch she found herself in a high chamber full of pumps and gnarled equipment, also illuminated in gray. An opening for a three-meter fan let in even stronger and more silvery colors. The full-sucker man unlocked a door and pulled it wide open. Now silver completely filled the rectangle and splashed among the dust-caked valves and gauges, forcing Soledad's eyes to shut against the glare.

"You have morning, Larissa," the full-sucker man said, with a curiously formal gesture, half bow, half introduction.

Soledad stared at him.

He gestured again.

"Thank Hoffa, you have morning."

Slowly, disbelievingly, Soledad stepped into the dawn.

THREE

THE UTERUS THROUGH WHICH Soledad was reborn into the predawn of a San Francisco day was a tall cubistic sump of concrete that served to drain the landscaped environment of a tall shopping mall.

The mall was full of spiral escalators, "drama courts," and cantilevered balconies designed as a post–Information Age statement ten years before by the ubiquitous architect Vanny Kemp. Its sump doubled as access ramp for a maintenance tunnel serving the Bay Area Rapid Transit subway, which probably accounted for the trembling Soledad had felt earlier.

She made her way up the ramp unobserved except by a handful of people, mostly black or Mexican (she heard the *chingados* peppering their muttered phrases)—all dressed as unhip as she, or worse even. They huddled under sheets of polyethylene or cardboard against a switchblade rain and gunmetal mist that were in part responsible for the mercury color of the incipient sunrise.

At the ramp's top she moved away from the mall, deliberate and slow, keeping an eye on a security detail idling in golf carts near the main entrance. A "tilt" commuter plane passed low overhead, heading for the commuter port at Hunters Point. She ducked instinctively and found shelter beside a sculpture of fake glass that changed from azure to rose as soon as she came close and stayed that way until she left.

A police chopper thudded its way between low towers behind the mall and disappeared. Electric buses full of cubicle-serfs hummed down an avenue bordering the landscaping. On the wall of an aluminum-faced building down the street,

cartoon figures even she could recognize—Bugs Bunny, Betty
Boop, Planet Blast—flickered, deep with 3-D, on screens
twenty meters in height.

She shivered. The air tasted harsh, like barbed wire in
breathable form. The rain resoaked her blouse. She was so
full of exhaustion it felt as if earth's gravity had multiplied by
a factor of six and she was having trouble keeping her knees
locked against it. The jump from the Nirvana window had
definitely resprained her back; it hurt worse than it had for
many days. She walked along the street and came to a shelter
of a type she had noticed earlier on the streets of this city; a
place with transparent walls and roof and even seats. It contained noctiluc strips, UCC-card readers, and jacks to the
Flash for those needing more speed and security than a wireless link could provide. There was a turnstile arrangement,
also with a UCC reader, but someone—probably one of two
black kids stretched out sleeping with heads cradled on car-
polo bags inside—had fried its mechanism with a disposable
mazer, the prongs of which were still bonded to the magnetic
strip.

The shelter was otherwise empty. She sat on the floor with
her back to a Lucite bench and dragged her fingers through
her hair. She was too tired to think about what had happened
last night. She had left her bag in the catchment basin, but she
would sooner walk into a burning house than return to the
loco domain of the Kundura survivors, assuming she could
even find her way back. In that bag however had lain her only
resource—the three extremely hot, highly valuable "triage"
programs she had picked up after a looter dropped them in
Bidonville. She had been getting ready to flog them in the
jaggers' disco under the Nirvana when the police changed her
plans.

Without the programs she was broke, and broke, she was
at the mercy of every flic or Migra agent who took an interest
in her. Almost worse, she was now unable to buy info on
how to find the *cruce* that she had been told was still alive

somewhere in San Francisco; alive and serving as sanctuary for refugees from foreign Hawkleyite enclaves like the one she had fled.

She had never imagined it would be hard to find the Yanqui *cruce* once she got to this city, but even the *coyotes* she crossed the border with had never heard of it.

Her hair was matted with sewer filth. She was not going to improve it with her fingers. She was not going to think about how the flics had found out she was at the Nirvana, or why they had seemingly mobilized a battalion of commandos to arrest her; or how close she had come to getting caught.

Just thinking about thinking about it made her chest feel like it was being pumped full of concrete, like that image on her motel workstation. With her chest turning to rock like that, little room was left for the travel-survival drive that had powered her, independent of feeling or even much thought, until now.

She wanted so much to sleep, and to wait as she slept for the capture she had fought so hard to avoid ever since the *cruce* burned. It made no sense after all to stay in this exhausting conscious world when Dolores and Jorge—when all the loose, inefficient, warm, complicated relationships of her *cruce,* all the rhythms and savory flavors and fishy sea breezes—had been eaten alive by fire.

Yet the tension she needed to keep going had also tainted her exhaustion so that she often found it impossible to go to sleep, even though unconsciousness was the only way to break that exhaustion.

One advantage of these tropisms of travel and flight was, never mind their survival value, they usually (though not last night) prevented dreaming.

Another was, they gave her something to do when she was conscious.

So she examined, through the Lucite, this awakening city, noting in the tiny margin of mind still unseared by flame and chase how prettily the odd-shaped towers—they had been built in the form of cylinders, pyramids, or rectangles, with chunks removed at random intervals, naively ostentatious—gleamed against the haze that absorbed the increasing power of morning. One whole wall of an office block had been painted with a mural by Joachim Boaz; she knew his dark colors, his inward-twisting monsters, from prints Jorge collected.

Wishing she had a cigarette, but her pack of Galaxys was gone with the bag.

When she lowered her gaze, she caught sight of a small palm tree, and the simple vision of that spiky interloper amid all this phallic cement and steel brought her mind straight back to Bamaca—only instead of fear, now it was longing that filled her abdomen, a longing as warm and liquid as the Bahia de las Animas, a wish: that she could go home now, this second, even though the *cruce* was gone and largely burned out, even though they had found Jorge's body in three pieces and buried them in the mass grave in the *pepinador;* though Dolores was vanished also and F2 had flooded Antioquia Province with posters of Soledad, looking, come to think of it, just like the poster of Larissa Love that the Kundurans—

The turnstile banged.

A pair of flics walked in. The two black boys sat up instantly. Then, slowly, they got to their feet, hands not touching their car-polo bags. The cops had their FNs trained on the boys' stomachs.

After the first scan of the shelter they ignored Soledad. This meant the regular flics were not on the lookout for Soledad specifically, which made perfect sense to her. She was used to how F2 worked, familiar with the Hawkleyite explanation: the secret police never told the regular police what was going on, because of the danger of security leaks they said, but mostly because one security org would never cede a millimeter of territory to another, and information was always the most important form of territory.

The flics concentrated on getting the gangbangers to lie down while they relayed the scan via vidcams to headquarters.

They did not object as Soledad walked calmly out of the Flash shelter, crossed the street, and disappeared in the buzz of traffic.

———————

DESPITE HER EXHAUSTION SHE kept moving for the balance of the day.

At first this was still a function of her habitual fear. If you kept moving you were harder to track. Also, while walking, she was less cold and shivered only half as hard. She followed the busy streets, the gridlocked avenues, avoiding places like parks where migrants might congregate and draw the attention of the flics. She found a piece of cloth and tied it like a scarf around her hair so she would look less like herself and, incidentally, less like that soap opera actress. She crossed an endless Chinese area that reminded her of scenes of Shanghai that Jorge once described; more proximately, those narrow, vendor-crammed streets brought back, with the usual heartwince, memories of similar alleys in Bidonville. Past newer office towers, thick with Vanny Kemp's vegetation-draped balconies—some of them even clothed, the wayKemp suggested one dress such buildings, in folds of colored nylon, a "skin of life" battened and draped to move with the wind. Up a steep lane lined with cafés and bookstores and young women in glasses and sandals being ogled by bald, bearded men, who of course also brought Jorge to mind.

And, after a while, she realized there was a specific rationale to being on the move like this in San Francisco for someone as hunted as she.

Because these Californians never stopped moving, either. On the skyways closed to trucks and other dirty traffic the Suits trotted down sidewalks or jogged the faster escalators, heads down, stampeding at high speed to unknown destinations. At the same time, on the half-suckers or digital vests many of them wore, they talked and watched videos and e-mailed diagrams to the people they were about to see, or to those they had just left, or both; glancing automatically at the pushwalls they passed, with the interactive screens that either picked up on a jambook's transponder or decoded the shape, speed, and fashions of the closest passerby and flashed an appropriate message.

LEAVE THE RATRACE—VACATION IN MICROCOM
THEMEWORLDS RESERVE HERE

WHY LEAVE ATTRACTION TO CHANCE?
WHEN YOU USE EARGARD™ ANTI-ODOR SCENT,
OUR GENETICALLY ENGINEERED PHEROMONES DO THE
WORK FOR YOU!

FOR A PREVUE OF THE WILDEST VR RIDE OF YOUR LIFE
PLUG IN YOUR JAMBOOK
—★—
HERE

The pushwalls, she decided, sped this city up more. They shouted and played loud tunes at you—well, not at her, the algorithms were good enough to figure out from the rips in her blouse and the smudges on her cheeks that she was not a likely prospect—but at people who looked like they had equity. They sprayed samples of perfume or smells of Tibetan deep fry or Nic-less tobacco smoke at people wearing the right brand names. To men in suits they touted their ability to predict the next Infocrash. You could stop, press your UCC-card strip to their shifting facade and make reservations at a restaurant, for a Clam Fetish concert, or a themeworld vacation park. Eco-commuters in rock-climbing shoes used them. Gangbangers zipping on illegal power Rollerblades in and out of traffic would brake, slap on their UCC card, and call a girlfriend, just for the pleasure (via a workstation vidcam) of seeing her in black garters and automatic censoring patterns four meters high on Grant Street. Even the homeless—of whom, since the last Infocrash, there were crowds—watched the pushwalls that never spoke to them. And these lost humans moved quicker also to keep rhythm with the pace of limited-life commodities being displayed on the surrounding streets.

The teedees, of course—the victims of teledysfunction—clustered around the screens until they were moved along by the nightprods of the flics. Along with the clang of cable cars, the buzz of messenger drones overhead, the thumping beat of Neodisko, the hiss of tires on tarmac, that cheerful buzz and whistle of the Flash seemed to Soledad the drumbeat that kept the rapid-fire pace of these Frisco streets in synch and moving.

TOWARD DUSK, COMING BACK from the harbor where she had walked in a trance of hunger and fatigue all afternoon, she found herself in a neighborhood walled with caricatures of Tiki palisades, "medieval" moats, and other fanciful entrances. Giant signs tethered to dirigibles half obscured by the thickening mist announced various theme parks—all of them, it seemed, ending in exclamation marks:

JULES VERNE
UNDERSEA RESIDENCE
LIVE WITH KILLER SHARKS!

VISIT THE LAND OF
FLUFFY THE MEGADESTROYER
AND HIS ROBOT VIXENS
BE A BUZZROCKET FOR THREE HOURS!

1908!
EARTHQUAKE!
(WHICH WAY OUT? YOU DECIDE!)

On pushwalls outside or through the portals she caught glimpses of people in elaborate roller coasters being bounced, turned upside down, dropped and picked up at freeway speeds. Most of the rides were virtual, sound and sights communicated in gory 3-D via full face-sucker gear and even bodysuits. A few were total-environment parks, old-fashioned stage-sets rigged like pushwalls to perform on demand. In "HolocaustWorld"—billed as "A Tasteful, Thought-provoking, Emotional Experience through the Greatest Tragedy of the Last Century"—people stepped aboard cattle cars for a ride to an ersatz "Auschwitz" where blond, blue-eyed Californian surfer boys dressed in SS uniforms smilingly handed out soap, bottles of Apollonaris water, and towels ("Yours to Keep as a Souvenir!"), pointing the way to the showers.

The earthquake in particular cut through her great hunger to smack Soledad with a casual backhand of fear. In this park, full-sized buildings toppled to dust and others were consumed by lavish fires, the heat of which she could feel even this side of the palisade; until the lights went out and, like magic or slo-mo in reverse, the buildings rose up again in the gloom the crowds had left behind.

She walked along the palisades, discreetly checking Dumpsters at the service gates to theme park food courts. GENUINE 1849 CHUCKWAGON FARE! SAMPLE LAB-GROWN GREAT WHITE! FEAST ON *PAIN IN THE AFTERNOON*'S HEALTHGRILL DELICACIES! the signs read. But these areas were clearly prime targets for other homeless. Every crate and plastic bag had already been picked as clean as its equivalent in the Bamaca *pepinador*. After rifling eight trash bins she had found only one useful item, behind the snack bar for Dirty Harry World ("Are You Feeling Lucky Today?"). It was a small kitchen knife with half its wooden handle broken off, which she wrapped in newsprint and stashed in the waist of her tights.

The other side of this street consisted mostly of the back of haptic sex parlors and Vietnamese *chō* restaurants. The smell of spiced beef-noodle soup was so strong and savory that, in triggering the gastric reflex, it actually hurt. She was clambering up a bin half hidden by a junction box of fiber-optic, tangles of thick wires snaking into a haptic arcade, when a voice called out low and strong: "Hey, sister!"

She looked around, a hand creeping to her waist and the steel shank of the *cuto*.

A tall mestiza stood hipshot under a pushpanel beside the arcade doorway. One hand held a ridiculously outmoded handbag with a UCC card cable attached. The other clutched both a cellphone and a Nic-less cigarette. Her eyes in the red glow of the pushscreen were pink and steady. She wore a street version of the Italian "split-screen" fashion; the left side of her face was heavily made-up, and the corresponding side of her body clothed to match in a long dress. The right face, by contrast, was not painted, and that half of her body was skimpily clad in miniskirt, tank top, and Lucite-heeled boot.

Soledad slid down from the bin. She stood half shielded by its metal corner so she had room to run if necessary. The woman came closer, looked her up and down, and threw out her hip once more.

"Wanna make three hundred bucks in four hours?"

Soledad stared. Three hundred dollars was almost six hundred Caymans—two weeks' wages in the *cruce,* and a decent day's pay even here.

The woman clicked her tongue, misinterpreting her silence.

"Girl, it's *legal. Seguro.* Safe as chatrooms. You never touch the john, not once. More important, he don't touch you."

With three hundred dollars she could hold out for a while. She could buy a change of clothes and info about the San Francisco *cruce*—if it even existed which, in the smoky depths of her hunger, she was beginning to doubt. Most of all, she could buy a meal and maybe a place to sleep, and time to figure out what in the name of Exu she was going to do next, among the bleak landscape of new circumstances arising out of this day.

Soledad leaned forward and tugged at the UCC-card cable,

shaking her head. The tall woman squinted, looking at Soledad's lips.

"You can't talk."

Soledad shook her head again. The woman chuckled.

"Girl, that don't matter—they don't want you to *talk*. And you don't have to worry about credit, either. It's all cashchips, this business."

She turned, beckoning with the cellphone.

"Come on in, I'll clear it with Ali Khan."

———

ALI KHAN WAS A thin Pakistani *habikusha,* a man with one side of his face burned in the short Kashmiri nuke war. He wore jeans and a T-shirt that read SOMEBODY IN MIAMI LOVES ME. He wore green Industrial Islam beads and did not believe the tall woman when she said Soledad was mute. He didn't go for the deal, anyway—complained and yelled behind a particleboard door while the tall woman, whose name, it seemed, was Sha'Oprah, yelled and complained at twice the volume because somebody called Backus was not where he said he'd be and she *knew* what he was doing and she was going to find him and cut his balls off, tonight; and if Ali Khan didn't let her she'd leave anyway, and take the other girls with her.

Ali Khan didn't stand a chance. When they came out of the office he slouched sullenly in one corner, watching a bank of twenty video screens of which eight were lit. The working screens showed small cubicles containing a single pushpanel and an orthochair. In each of them a naked man, sheathed in a transparent, blue-tinged johnny, rubbed a plastic 3-D pushpanel, or swiped a cashchip through a reader to pay for another round.

Sha'Oprah took Soledad by the hand and led her into a cubicle. Three walls of the cube were faced with bare particleboard, and the fourth with the same type of pushpanel Soledad had seen in Ali Khan's video screens. The tall woman took a transparent johnny from a medical cabinet.

Close up, Soledad saw it was made of rubberized polyethylene, with tubes of no-copy blue leading from a wall connection to a hole in the suit's back to patches of the same material located at strategic points in the suit, most thickly around the crotch and buttocks. When Soledad had stripped and suited up—it was surprisingly easy, especially with Sha'Oprah's help, since the suit split in half then refastened with strong Velcro—Sha'Oprah pointed at a bank of lights and switches to one side of the pushpanel.

"When that green light goes on, you're in business. He'll tell you, over the speaker, what he wants you to touch, as if you can't figger that out anyway. When the light goes off you stop, or when you hear a bell—that's the kum alarm; it's hooked up to something in his suit that senses liquid, means it's time to get the suit washed. Your suit don't have that problem, sugar." She chuckled.

"Now these are the important ones." She touched a rheostat. "Intensity level. You control his by how hard you touch the panel, but what *you* feel depends one hundred percent on this switch only. Danger zone"—she turned the rheostat so it pointed to an arc of red all the way to the right—"that's for S and M; you never, never go near that 'less you're bent that way. I keep it at zero except"—the ballroom face winked—"for the cute ones.

"And this is the alarm button, case he won't pay. Or if you get a freak."

She turned toward the door, and hesitated.

"I should tell you, there's a few more freaks around than usual. They brought in a pack of special ops advance boys for that big trade conference, and they been hitting some of the haptics pretty hard. There's one—" She shook her head, and opened the door.

"Anyways, they can't get into your booth. Just hit that button if things smell bad. Use this"—she pulled a bottle out of the cabinet—"for inspiration." She chuckled, one last time. "You have fun now, sugar."

The door clicked shut behind her.

ODDLY ENOUGH, FOR A while anyway, Soledad did have
a kind of fun. The first two "johns" were tourists, traveling together. She could hear them talking to Ali Khan in the reception area, hiding their nervousness with jive about a brothel in
Minneapolis, so young they were almost boys. The first was
half drunk. He talked very slowly in a flat-voweled accent.
Seeing Soledad standing stark naked in the plastic panel before him braked his speech down to the point where he was
almost as mute as Soledad. He touched her; he touched his
panel, and what he did was reflected in the panel before her.
The suit gently squeezed her breasts and smoothed her stomach in response to electronic messages from the panel he
touched. Smiling vapidly at his own audacity.

She touched him as she thought he wanted, and within
less than a minute the alarm went off and the screen in front
of him went blank. Soledad was left feeling disappointed. It
had gone so fast she had felt not a hint of pleasure—no time
even to trigger the priest-seeded guilt at her own aptitude for
promiscuity—a guilt that she knew lay somewhere in the
darker part of her, deeper even than the layers of sadness un-
derpinning her fatigue.

At the same time, she was slightly awed by the power that
her body, even through the medium of a touchscreen, had had
over this fledgling man.

The second one was better-looking. Soledad, fortified by
a couple of gulps from the bottle, which bore a label reading NIGHT TRAIN and contained apple wine, turned the intensity meter to two, then three. This one also had had more
experience and he had time to find the small fin of pleasure
between her legs and she felt, she observed herself feeling the
pressure exerted through the medium of the tiny hydropumps
in her suit; she had even time to feel the first warmth there
and the beginning wetness that came with it before his alarm
sounded.

More Night Train. The exhaustion was coming back, now

the novelty had worn off. She smiled at herself, at the thought that in less than an hour she already had started to develop a *putain*'s anesthesia to the touch of men.

The third was a Suit in his early fifties. The clothes he hung up had the Neodisko look she'd seen downtown—wide collars and silk shirts disguising bulletproof Kevlar. He had no beard. His eyes were slightly made up, and his hair was what they called "lit," thickly woven with tiny fiber-optic tubes plugged into a power pack at the collar, so that in the dark it appeared braided with purple-blue light. He was a talker; he relaxed in the cubicle's orthopedic chair, asked her her name, and how she liked "it." She turned her back when requested to do so. But then, with no further warning, he started to yell, calling for Ali Khan, saying he wanted a "screamer," he wasn't going to pay a hundred and twenty bucks for some haptic cunt who wasn't even a screamer. And Ali Khan was agreeing with him, saying the Suit could have his pick of the rest of the girls while he fired this one's ass right now. Then a third voice chimed in.

"I *like* 'em silent," the third voice said quietly.

"Hundred and twenty bucks, with-talk or no-talk."

"Who wants to hear what the cunt has to say anyhow?"

"Sure," agreed Ali Khan, who obviously had no position that could not be turned by money.

This john's voice was fairly high and, above all, assured. He undressed with his back to the screen. He was squat and heavily muscled, with graying crew-cut hair. The fluffer strapped his johnny shut, smiling fixedly, and disappeared. He turned to the screen: very small dark eyes, a narrow chin, big shoulders with tattoos, large nipples, and no penis—it took Soledad a full five seconds to absorb the info that this was, in fact, a woman.

"You don't look Guatemalan," she said, moving toward the screen. "Unless you're from the coast."

Soledad felt a hard pressure on her left nipple, a pinch that even at intensity level three made her gasp. She grasped the rheostat and turned it down to zero.

"Toca-me," the woman said in a good Central American accent. "Touch me here."

Soledad hesitated. Then she pressed the woman's breast on the screen. A green tattoo surrounding the nipple read BORN TO KILL.

"Harder," the woman said. "Go on, I'm not made of candy, do it harder. They used to do it hard," she added in a half whisper, "in Honduras. We weren't supposed to be in Honduras but they did it hard anyway. Touch me here"—she turned and spread the lobes of her buttocks, and then pointed at her crotch—"and here.

"We did sensitivity training," the woman continued in a conversational tone, "at John Wayne High. We never tortured anybody, no matter what those fat-ass senators said. What did they know anyway? We did it in Manila; we weren't s'posed to be there either. *Harder!*"

Soledad found she was sweating. It was hot in the cubicle, but that was not the reason. There was a wrong feel to this, a "smell" Sha'Oprah might have said, like being in a car coming down the Teton road and suddenly feeling the brake pedal go soft. She thought about pressing the alarm button, but Ali Khan would certainly fire her if she called for help before something happened and then she would never get the money. She pushed with the palm of her hand at the spiky facsimile of crotch mounded plastic in the screen. It felt odd to her—she had never touched another woman's pubis before, only her own, so this felt like it was her own *chatte* except, unaccountably, it was on another body.

"We tied down the *Frente* boys. We didn't hurt them at first. We fucked their girls in front of them. The Honduran girls give blow jobs hard. I want you," she said, "to give me a blow job."

Soledad pulled her hand from the screen. She did not know what a "blow job" was. The woman in the screen lay back on the orthochair and spread her legs, and the screen tilted with her.

"Coga-me," she whispered. "Like I'll *cogar* those bitches

in Oakland Navy Yard. Hawkleyite bitches. You watch the
newsscreens," she added. *"Fuerte! Aora!"*

Soledad kept staring at the panel. She knew how to *cogar*
because Jorge had done it to her. She would have to use her
tongue like a finger. She would have to overcome her revulsion, not so much at doing this to a woman, but at doing it to
this woman who claimed she raped other women in the jungle. And then, past the five-second delay of her disgust and
fatigue, what the woman had just said registered in Soledad's
brain, dispersing her vague plans for cunnilingus like dande-
lion chaff in the wind.

But the woman in the screen, the woman with the Born to
Kill tattoo, wasn't waiting. She rocked off the orthochair onto
the balls of her feet, staring at the screen image of Soledad
standing with one hand almost defensively on her breast, staring back.

"Cunt," the woman hissed. Her chest heaved. Her voice
was low and vicious. She jumped, forward and up, almost
three feet in the air, and kicked to one side, her legs disappearing beyond the scope of the cubicle's envirocam.

In Soledad's cubicle, the wall beside the haptic panel split
cleanly. One of the woman's shoulders appeared in the split,
wrapped like a joint of veal in the johnny, cracking the wall's
right side under the instrument board. Her hands gripped the
board and pulled it and a hedge of fiber-optic wiring backward into her own cubicle.

The speed and violence of the assault had frozen Soledad.
The mundane act of pulling out the board snapped her from
her trance. No way to hit the alarm button, it was gone with
the instruments, so she hopped backward toward the door and
was immediately spun around by the rope of blue tubes mooring the tail end of her haptic suit to the 3-D panels. She lost
her balance and fell heavily on her back and outthrust elbows;
half winded, fighting for breath. In the pushpanel she saw the
squat woman peer at the controls, Soledad's controls, twist
something decisively with two fingers, then drop the board
and move toward her own mounded screen.

Soledad rolled to a sitting position and fumbled with both hands for the suit's Velcro straps behind her. The woman's hands touched the lower right half of the pushpanel in her cubicle, and closed.

The pain that hit Soledad's groin was as sharp and intense as anything fire had ever done to her. She arched up, fell back again. Through the speakers she heard the squat woman making noise, a sort of contented gurgling. Soledad twisted, leftward this time, away from the door, finding her blouse and tights rolled against the two-by-four molding where she'd left them, and the cold *cuto* in the middle.

The S&M setting she was thinking but what her mind really said was *make that pain stop now immediately* and there was no time for the niceties of Velcro, no time for anything but the blade she pulled free of clothes and newspaper into the neon to slash down at the hydraulic umbilical cords transmitting pain to her from the woman's panel.

When she saw the knife, the squat woman stopped gurgling. *"Puta,"* she said happily. The tendons of her left hand curved like snakes.

What air was left in Soledad's lungs simply vanished; the pain was that great. She stared downward, where the powerful micropumps in her suit had shot their pistons clean through elastic epidermis and into the muscle of her inner right thigh, about three centimeters from her crotch. The blue of johnny went purple down to her left knee as blood seeped between plastic and skin.

"Figure I'm about a quarter inch from your femoral artery," the woman whispered. "Drop the shiv."

Soledad closed her eyes, opened her fingers. The *cuto* made a clink against the cement floor. Something else clicked in the speakers.

Abruptly, the pistons withdrew, out of her flesh and into their nylon sheaths. The pain immediately lessened. Soledad's breath came in noisy gasps. She opened her eyes and stared at the panel, at the black muzzle growing from the right side of the screen; behind the muzzle, the taut brown fist and miniskirt half of Sha'Oprah. The squat woman went still as a cliff as the pistol poked rudely into her left ear.

"Hands where I can see 'em."

The squat woman's hands rose slowly to her neck.

Sha'Oprah picked up the control board, using the whole stretch of her body, never allowing her eyes or the gun to leave the squat woman's face.

"Freak," she said, pushed the pistol hard enough to shove the squat woman sideways a step, and glanced at Soledad. "Coulda hurt you bad. Clean yourself up," she added, "get outta here. Backus wasn't where I thought, I'm goin' back to work."

Soledad stared at her. She was doing too much staring in this place, she thought dully. But the pain was so much less now, and in the luxury of that absence she couldn't be bothered to think of a more rational way to cope.

"Go on." Sha'Oprah jerked her chin leftward. "Ali's got a first aid kit. I'll take care of this."

Soledad shook her head. Her hands had pressed between her thighs, reflexively, to hold blood in, to keep other things out. She pulled them free. Her fingers were warm and reddish-brown. Sha'Oprah hissed softly. Soledad picked up a broken piece of particleboard and, using her blood as ink, quickly daubed a rough dollar sign on its surface, then held it where Sha'Oprah could see.

"Dag," Sha'Oprah said. "You only worked here an *hour*."

Soledad kept staring at her. Sha'Oprah shifted her weight from miniskirt to dinner dress and back. Finally she shrugged the handbag off her bare shoulder, and tossed it out of sight of the panel envirocams.

"There's a fifty-buck chip in the zipper pocket," she said. "Take it or leave it."

Fifty dollars would not be enough for a motel room.

On the other hand, with the info the squat woman had, all unknowingly, given her, maybe Soledad would not require a motel room tonight.

She ripped off the johnny. The screens in the reception

area showed four men touching landscapes of resilient plastic, plus the still-life-with-gun. Ali Khan held a shotgun on Soledad as she limped around searching for the first aid box. The box contained gauze, with which Soledad wiped most of the blood away, and a couple of yellowed bandages that she used to cover the neat double punctures the turbopump pistons had punched just south of her pubic hair. The pain had become more of an ache, like the one in her back; active but bearable.

Soledad found Sha'Oprah's bag, opened the zipper, removed the chip. She slid on her own clothes. They were damp, smelling vaguely of sewer, but as different from the johnny as a home-cooked meal was from industrially packaged *junque* food.

"*Acha,*" Ali Khan commented. "I knew you were trouble, slut; soon as you come here I knew."

Suddenly, for no reason, Soledad felt like laughing. Instead, she reached into her cubicle, grabbed the bottle of Night Train, and swigged off a quarter of the applejack. Ali Khan shrugged, and shifted the shotgun so it pointed at Soledad's crotch.

She tucked the *cuto* in her waistband and walked carefully up the stairs into the fog.

———

An hour and fifteen minutes later the memory of Ali Khan, Sha'Oprah, and the haptic parlor had been assigned to the sweet pink-colored sections of the brain where nostalgia was nourished by the tensions of what was happening in the here and now.

At first Soledad had been pretty pleased with herself. She had bought a bowl of soup from a *chō*. Then she found a bodega that sold real tobacco and bought a pack of smuggled Peruvian Camels. Fueled by the broth, refreshed by the cigarette, she limped to a BART station she had seen on the way to the Embarcadero themeworlds. On the pushmap by the ticket booth she discovered that Oakland, as she suspected, was not far from San Francisco; in fact it lay directly across the bay defining the city peninsula to the west, only one stop away at its closest point from the station she stood in.

She ran her finger across the 3-D capes and islands on the Oakland shoreline. The names of streets and landmarks were brought out as if through magic by the heat of her hand.

Just south of a highway leading to a bridge over the bay, and on the northwest or mainland side of a channel between Oakland and an island called Alameda, she had found, in tiny print, the words U.S. NAVY SUPPLY STATION. This she figured was the "navy base" the squat woman was talking about.

The thought of the squat woman made Soledad shiver. She had slid the cashchip through a machine, punched the OAKLAND button, and received a ticket in return. The train was very warm and clean. Despite the ache in her thigh, she almost fell asleep in the five minutes it took to cross the bay.

That had been the high point. She got off in a new concrete plaza poured in the same style of offset and vine-covered balconies that was popular in San Francisco. The vines were dead or dying and the plaza, washed the color of piss by sodium lamps, was almost empty of people. When she warmed out the naval base on the ticket booth map the station guard had stared at her crotch for a second or two, so that Soledad knew the bandages were not holding in the blood. He shrugged, and pointed to a quiet street leading into a row of new developments, designed on the same lines as the plaza, where the various brick cubes of living quarters overlapped each other in a series of balconies, terraces, and roofs.

She had walked, it seemed, for kilometers, more and more bemused, smoking and staring through the few windows in the development left uncurtained. And in every single window she had seen, more or less, the same tableau: a squat box in a site of ceremony and, around it, in various postures but always connected to the box by phone cords, the people who lived in that apartment. In each window their features were obscured by full- or half-suckers. In each window they moved, slowly or fast, in response to the dynamics of whatever drama was coming at them in fully interactive 3-D across the B-Net cable.

Once, in two separate apartments, she had seen two families jerking simultaneously in response to some presumably violent scene, and had known, from the similarity of their rhythms, that they were watching the same drama.

Although she assumed the curtained windows marked scenes of more traditional domestic activity, what amazed Soledad was this: not a single one of the windows she could see through held anything other than the sight of people dancing to 3-D stories sent across the Flash.

It should not have surprised her. She had always heard that Americans spent the vast majority of their time, when they were not sleeping or working, on the Flash. Jorge once said that the only political issue that mattered anymore in the U.S. was how much it cost to gain access to the broadband Nets.

The development came to an abrupt halt at a metal barrier a half kilometer on.

At that point the residential buildings gave way to a street of garages, burned cars, and gutted houses where no one lived.

Now, twenty minutes later, she was lost. Worse, she was getting scared. The soup and the Night Train had worn off and her weariness was back triple strength and her inner thigh was throbbing, not as badly as when the injury was inflicted but bad enough. The burned houses gave way to empty lots between disused factories of brick and corrugated iron. This was very different from what she had ever heard about America. Even Jorge—who, though he did not despise gringos like some of the *crucistas,* had very unkind things to say about their big corporations—had never mentioned areas such as this. The fog was so thick now that it was like an enormous gray animal that moved over the tops of factories and then lifted for a few seconds as if to scout where it was going.

The street she had been following ended at the gates of a power plant. The road to the right was full of weeds and she turned left. Most of the street lamps here were broken, and the only light for long sections came from cans full of garbage burning in empty lots, turning the fog around them red. Men and women, all of them Negroes, stood around the fires like black ghosts, like the souls of the unshriven around the infernal pits Father Jean-Carlos used to preach about.

A group of men detached themselves once from a fire and followed her. She ran, ignoring the thigh pain, through a sequence of alleys and hid behind rotting railroad coaches until they were gone.

Another time, a convoy of cars raced down the street she was on. They were all ancient cars she recognized from the *cruce*, where nobody had credits to buy new ones: Chevy Impalas and Novas, Oldsmobile Custom Cruisers, Dodge Darts. But where in the *cruce* every car and truck was painted and repainted with orchids, suns, rainbows in the hot colors of the tropics, here each car was black or a variation of black. Queer objects were bolted to the hoods and roofs: cow skulls, metal jaws, a jukebox, an electric organ, entire computers, panels of blinking green lights. The windows were black and the mufflers loud. They roared at her like dark dragons down the shattered tarmac, forced her to leap to the sidewalk, leaving her shaking, and coughing from the thick exhaust.

A ship's horn sounded low and loud to her left. Soledad slowly followed the wall of a boarded-up welding shop and turned left. Where there were ships, she reasoned, there was probably navy. So far, except for a sign saying U.S. NAVY CONVOYS STOP HERE, and another that read CHINESE NATIONAL MARITIME AGENCY, she had seen no evidence of navy or ships or harbor. This roadway was more gone to weed than the earlier road. On either side rose the sheer gray concrete walls of

ancient warehouses. Their windows were boarded and broken. Giant cisterns perched on I-beam gridwork over their
roofs. One of them, for a reason either too obvious or too obscure to worry about, had been crudely painted to resemble a
toilet. Two rats ambled casually from an abandoned container
next to a series of shuttered loading docks. They watched
Soledad with minimal interest before going about their own
dun deals.

The roadway ended at a cliff almost as high as the warehouses, made entirely of scrap metal. A black crane loomed
over the scrap, gawky as a Bahia heron. The foghorn sounded
again, behind the cliff. A vague hint of music floated briefly
to her ears as the fog shifted, then vanished. The pain from
her wound, mingled with the exponentially swelling exhaustion, prevented her from lifting her feet all the way. Her shuffle made lisps of sound between the walls.

She could not see if the roadway ended at the scrap-metal
cliff or if it turned right and left along its length. She failed,
also, to notice a worn plywood sign, with half its letters
chipped away, that read:

U.S. NA
NO TRE AS I

A rumble of engine.

At first she was unsure of its provenance because the concrete took sound and bounced it in different directions. As
she approached the scrap cliff she became aware that it was
made of junked cars—she discerned headlights, crushed cabs,
wheels. For a second she had the uneasy feeling that the cars,
twisted and rusty as they were, had decided to start up in
the midnight hour and fill this street one last time with their
rusty symphony of holed manifolds and loose tappets and
"La Cucuracha" horns.

But the engine noise was louder now, and behind her. She
turned. Her hand flew to her knife and then, slowly, dropped.

A huge squat thing sat at the entrance to the alley she had

just entered. In the first instance, that was how she compre-
hended it: as a thing, not animal, not human. It was rounded,
gleaming, black as a swamp beetle, bigger than twin elephants, about three meters high and four across. A swollen,
rounded hump sat on top of the main carapace, and that hump
was ugly with feelers and antennas and eyes on stalks and
even a rudimentary snout, long and open and dark.

The top hump moved slightly. The antennas and mouth all
shifted, and the eyes blinked and changed as they shifted to
match, keeping her in the target area.

And then it was her perception that shifted, and she saw it
for what it was: an armored car, only far rounder and bigger
and more silent than any she had ever encountered, and running on strange bulbous tires like black balls and—

And it came at her. The engine rumbled up a register, and
it began to move. She was so shocked that for a crucial instant she could only stare.

In that second, the tension between what she had lost and
the effort it took to flee got the better of her.

She would stay right here, she thought numbly. She would
stand and let them get her. She was out of strength and out of
luck and low on blood and sick of running. And it felt good,
no it felt wonderful at last to give up this struggle that she had
always known in her gut was doomed. It felt *right* to accept,
even welcome, the brief pain and subsequent oblivion that
had swallowed the *cruce,* and in so doing reject this hard,
misty, cold country that demanded ever-increasing energy to
do what her heart said was not worth doing in the first place.

She took a step toward the thing, hands loosening as her
arms came down, a classic gesture of rendition.

The armored car's eyes focused on Soledad. Tiny red
beads, and wide gridded green eyes like those of a fly under
magnification.

It accelerated; now it was running at fifteen kilometers per
hour.

A tongue of fire licked from its snout. It roared, as if suddenly enraged beyond endurance, a blast of cacophony like

crashing trucks and screams and the hiss of snakes all amplified a thousandfold and hideously distorted.

Then flame burst at her in an orange fireball, and light screamed from a half dozen apertures, blinding her—and something deeper than her emotions, deeper even than her gut, took over. In a flash as quick as that flame she understood what was happening: that her body was what powered her, and had been powering her over the last three weeks—not noble dreams of revenge, not stubborn refusal to submit to Jorge's killers, not even some half-elegant habit of transit but the low hardwired urge of muscle fiber and nerve juice to flee the pain and death they were programmed at all costs to avoid.

Realizing it made no difference. Grief forgotten, acceptance vaporized by the sight of flame, she turned and ran, heedless now of pain, without thought without sound, she could not scream or breathe; she had nothing left to give to the world but this final rout, the tatters of herself, an expression of flight.

The snout on the secondary turret adjusted, steadied, briefly shook. Fog wavered in the trajectory between the armored car and Soledad. Her sprinting figure was lifted by the shock wave, drenched by the soporific gas sent down its path. For a split instant she was conscious of lying on the roadway, gazing at the giant crane above her head. Only it was not a crane, or rather it was meant to resemble the living as opposed to the mechanical kind, a form of heron—for someone had bolted a giant yellow beak on the cab, and red and yellow "feathers" on its head.

Then nausea rose over her, like a fog coming from inside her body. The gas engulfed her. She coughed twice, and blacked out.

The vehicle slowed, came to a halt a few yards from the unconscious woman. The roar of loudspeaker was cut off abruptly. Its engine idled. The fireball also dwindled, with the hiss of pressured avgas, till only a lick of flame showed at the flamethrower's mouth.

For almost thirty seconds the periscopes and infrared eyes of the armored car gazed at Soledad's form, and everything was still in the dead-end alley.

Far overhead, the crane-bird began to move. Its cab twisted on silent bearings. The words TOO-WEET!, sprayed in phosphorescent paint, became visible on its front. At the same time, its jib lowered and extended over the alley. A giant counterslung claw used for picking up scrap dropped silently from sheaves of cables until it hung suspended in night five feet over the armored car's secondary turret.

A hatch opened in the turret.

The claw dropped and covered the turret completely.

The claw's cables tautened and the claw was dragged shut, shrieking over the slick black metal to the point where its tungsten-tipped teeth found the joint between turret and chassis, and caught.

A helmet appeared in the hatch. The engine of the armored car raced. It reversed, explosively and too late, for the cables were winding in and with no apparent effort the claw lifted the car, swinging and still revving, into the fog-heavy air.

As the crane's motors hummed, its giant arm also lifted. The armored car, twisting, still changing gears, rose floor by floor to roof level and then above the level of the warehouses on either side, above even the tops of the giant cisterns. When the claw and its cargo were ten feet higher than the nearest cistern—the one painted to resemble a toilet—the jib swung so that its pulley was positioned exactly over the cistern's open top.

A smaller pulley spun. The claw whinged. Then, as its teeth pulled clear, it opened.

The armored car fell into the cistern. There was a liquid sound, almost like flushing, and a sheet of water spattered like rain squalls into the alley below. Shouts rose tiny as the tankmen scrambled out of the hatch and found themselves swimming in eight feet of moldy rainwater.

A figure climbed slowly down the ladder of the crane and

limped into one of the warehouses. A thicker bank of fog covered the Alameda peninsula at that point, and when the figure reappeared from around one corner of the warehouse, an observer might have been forgiven for supposing it had morphed into a different form of life altogether.

It wore wide goggles and steel-toed boots. A stripped-down jambook computer was looped over one shoulder. Under a utility belt laden with tools and baling wire, it was dressed entirely in elegant black clothes of a cut and quality that had gone out of style a third of the way through the twentieth century. It rode a vehicle that looked like a cross between a Norton motorcycle and a fiberglass brown recluse spider. A long iridescent scarf snapped in its slipstream as the figure rumbled its machine across the alley and stopped next to Soledad's prone body. It dismounted, picked her up, and stuffed her carefully into the spider's black mantle.

Then the figure climbed back aboard. With a burst of engine, it accelerated down the alley, toward the cliff of junk cars. Perhaps it was a trick of the fog, but from the perspective of the alley it seemed to veer neither left nor right, but disappear without a pause into a mangle of crushed Buicks at the cliff's center.

The note of its engine hung for a beat or two in the damp air and then it, too, faded and was gone.

FOUR

SOMETHING IS WRONG WITH the Fourneaux-Dallapé. The lower A-sharp (or B-flat) is not working. This makes sense, because her thumb has always been heavy in that register; but on the same accursed day the upper D splits, coming out rushed and breathy on that note while it also gives vent to a quavering, reedy F, or sometimes F-sharp. She bought the instrument from Schaumberg Fils, the oldest and most respected musical firm in the capital, but they are notoriously expensive and anyway she does not want to go to the capital, for other reasons.

She asks around the Conservatory, focusing on the organ department but also seeking information from other reed-instrument teachers. In the Walled City, it transpires, only two people work on organs or reeds and neither will touch an accordion. Finally at lunch one day a string player of all things, a man by the name of de Weick, first viola for the Cathedral Symphony Orchestra and a gifted musician but one whom many in the Conservatory suspect both of Adornista tendencies and smoking too much coca paste, tells her of a man in the *cruce,* outside the Slave Gate, who specializes in automata. De Weick brought him in when nobody else could figure out a mysterious wheeze in the cathedral organ's Barker-slide, and he solved the puzzle in three hours.

There are two problems. One is that the violist has no address or phone number for the man, and Bamaca phone directories cover only the Walled City. The other, of course, is that he is in the *cruce,* which everyone knows to be lawless territory, a place even the police won't patrol anymore; a haven for emerald poachers, guerrilla sympathizers, anarchists, tomb robbers, and other untrustworthy riffraff, and not the sort of area a young woman should walk around in alone.

After four days of trying to play around the problem she makes up her mind to take the Fourneaux-Dallapé to the capital, though she suspects, no, she *knows*, down where her emotional deep currents wash and make direction, she will end up trying to contact Miguel, even if he expressly forbade her to look him up in the city—though she might, in her frustration and eventual despair, finally stoop to camping out in the café down the street from his apartment in the hope and terror of catching a glimpse of Dona Serena, his wife and the mother of his three-year-old son and (not coincidentally) the daughter of Sandoval, the deputy minister of trade and close friend of General Ochoa Campos, commander of the Sierra Division of the federal army.

On the day she makes that decision she has to attend a faculty meeting of the piano department. This is technically her group; she trained in piano until getting seduced, at roughly the same time, by a boy in the *campo* and the music of *Vallenatos* and all the slutty-complex play of accordion within those ballads. The chancellor allowed her to teach accordion at the Bamaca Conservatory on condition that she be affiliated with Piano and teach two undergraduate courses in keyboard technique.

The chancellor's hire, of course, was taken as a combination of massive threat and deliberate insult by Moreno, the chairman of Piano. At the faculty meeting, curiously, Moreno does not direct his usual unsubtle barbs at her. The principal issue appears to be the allocation of locker space during the rainy season, an issue she cares nothing about. She had to cancel a tutorial with one of her more talented pupils, a young Kogi from the hills who tends to fall asleep in lectures because he works as a road laborer to pay for tuition. Now, watching her colleagues argue more and more heatedly—Moreno wiping sweat off his bald dome with a lace kerchief,

Klein alternately popping pimples and stabbing fingers at everyone because he has more locker space than Parisot and believes he is entitled to it—she decides, with no possibility of changing her mind, that she will take the Fourneaux-Dallapé to the *cruce* this evening, after her last class.

She sets out around five. The municipal bus runs to the Slave Gate only and she must register at the police checkpoint there. A sleek black tank with skirts instead of wheels keeps its weapons trained on the gate. The flics look at her papers and stare at her but say nothing as she humps the instrument out of the shadow of the walls into the broad-splashed sunlight of the *cruce*.

And no one pays attention to her. That is the first thing she notices. The Walled City is full of gloomy underwater alleys where everyone looks at you from the side, but here no one seems to give a shit.

The second detail that snags her attention is the music, because music seems to live here almost, it swells in different volumes from all directions: mambo from transistors, a lone harpist singing "Luna de Habana," a raunchy Afro-Peruana ensemble perched on an open truck, the cries of vendors who tend to sing their wares in full scales, G to upper G, E to upper E. Somewhere an accordion and a guitar together draw out "Puta Rosa," oldest and most lyrical *Vallenato* of the central coast. Along with the music she becomes aware of colors; that's exactly how she is aware of them, *with* the melodies, as if colors were the visual expression of the notes that clash or meet but in any event swell and flap around her. For in contrast to the dark stone and black shadows of the Walled City, everything in and between the different cardinal points from which music comes here throbs with the enthusiastic frequencies of light. The houses around the Slave Market are daubed in bright yellow and russet, the cobbles are worn down to coral, the stalls spill with bright dyes, spices, parrots and shiny auto parts, bright Indian clothing and ripening fruit, all pressed between the translucent aquamarine of the fishing harbor and the phtalic greens of jungle tumbling down the lower slopes of San Isidor and the royal blue of sky broken into different parts by the volcano's steam and the billowed castles of creamy cloud finally making landfall after their long drift from Africa.

She ambles on awhile, forgetting the load on her shoulder, bemused by the number and volume of people after being confined for so long to the half-deserted streets of the Walled City. Though there is no shortage of shady-looking characters, a good third of the crowd consists of families tangled in the invisible trajectories of semicontrolled children. Despite what Miguel always told her about this place, despite the two brawls she witnesses in the course of her short walk, she feels no threat from any quarter.

The parrots in particular fascinate her. There are many more kinds for sale than she sees even in Ruedo, in the upper limits of the *selva*. One, a small macaw with a particularly smoky indigo hue to his wingfeathers and a bright canary breast, holds her gaze so long she trips over one of the guy ropes to a *butifarras* stall, knocking a stick of grilled fish balls to the ground, incurring the vendor's wrath. She buys the kabab to mollify him and expends that goodwill asking if he knows the automaton maker. But he shakes his head, pointing toward the market's center and a rickety tower covered with antennas, satellite dishes, spotlights, lasers, and literally dozens of electronic signboards. There are also newszippers, massive railway notices, advertising panels, and all the corresponding lights and wiring. The tower even has a makeshift shack for an office, wedged halfway up its spindly, twenty-meter legs. It seems likely to her a stronger than average wind would knock it down and all its hundreds of randomly strung guywires with it. "Ask there," the *butifarra* vendor growls. "Ask at Lo Pano." As she approaches the tower she sees that its various boards constantly shift announcements, like the "departures" panel at a busy train station, though no railroad would offer retail prices for happy-bananas from a *cruce* in Ghana, or the going rate for locally made Quichey tomb figurines, or "guaranteed" jisi-yomo works for jagger consumption.

The only access to the tower office is up a rickety ladder she doubts she could negotiate with the Fourneaux-Dallapé. Luckily the office seems to have spilled downstairs to a half dozen battered desks where men and women wearing the black cellphone belts of *crucistas* type at scuffed laptops or yap into walkie-talkies and phones that all seem to be buzzing at once. It's hard for anyone talking softly as she does to get somebody's attention but finally a young woman stranded between calls notices her, and looks up in a thick and unbelievably battered ledger the name Soledad spells out over the market din.

The address turns out to be a *pilotis* house, a massive wooden structure raised on pilings against the rainy season floods, behind stone countinghouses near the fishing harbor. The automaton maker, whose name is Haddad, is in his mid-thirties, very pale and thin. He answers the door and simultaneously shows out a client, who mumbles something and turns his face from Soledad as he slips away down the street.

Haddad talks fast, dresses in loose Arab clothes, walks with a limp. He has hurt his arm—at any rate he wears a bandage near the elbow which he picks at then smooths back nervously. He asks questions, moves to the next subject without waiting for an answer. Thick blinds block the dwindling sunlight and lamps provide the only real illumination inside the *pilotis*. The house is orderly and almost completely filled with workbenches and hundreds of shelves sagging under the details of machines.

Haddad puts the Fourneaux-Dallapé on a bench and hooks sensors to both treble and chord parts as well as to the bellows mechanism. He straps a virtual-reality mask to his head, pulls out screwdrivers of varying sizes, and begins taking the machine apart.

Soledad watches him nervously. His fingers are long and work with speed and surpassing dexterity. Thus, gradually, her nervousness over entrusting the precious instrument to a total stranger living in some kind of Kropotkinite free-port and referred by a *basuko* addict to boot, dwindles, to be re-placed by a different kind of discomfort; for Haddad's fingers seem to work entirely by feel, delicately opening and probing the accordion's innards while his eyes, under the half-sucker, remain fixed mostly on Soledad's. And after a short while she begins to get the feeling that, at the same time his fingers pry open the bellows plate and undo the thumbscrews that keep the reed ligature tight, what he sees in his optic nerves is those hands taking off her dress, and her panties, opening her to the blank gaze of his desire.

She clears her throat, turns her own gaze to his shelves: memory boards; a bank of coupler-tilts for a church organ; a loose assemblage that includes an ancient laptop and battery pack, three electric motors taped in a roll, clear plastic tubes ending in a leather sheath, all belted together in a canvas harness. Also, a complicated clockwork mechanism that appar-ently exists only to lift billiard balls up a conveyor belt to the top of an endlessly complex system of chutes, slides, and trapdoors, at the bottom of which the balls knock over and then right again a row of men dressed in the ornate robes of the National Literary Academy.

Her face, she knows, is the color of mango, and it is not so much because of his gaze as because of the response it elicits in her. She feels no attraction for this strange, pale technician; that is an absolute fact. Yet she can feel the tingling in her nipples that she recognizes as the first breath of correspond-ing lust, not for Haddad in particular, no, but for anyone, for touch, for companionship and by extension (and by absence) for the contact Miguel fails to offer her, by virtue of his living somewhere else, being married to someone else, and working for someone so powerful that he must run their affair, his and Soledad's, like an espionage operation of the highest

sensitivity in order to keep his enemies unaware of the wee-
est hint of impropriety.

She gets to her feet, intending to walk out of Haddad's
sight, but now his gaze has lowered and he is talking to the
instrument, as if he'd shifted his desire from the owner to
the machine itself. "You lovely, lovely thing," he whispers, holding up one of the gold-alloy reeds that make the
Fourneaux-Dallapé so sweet in tone and so expensive to fix.
"This is the F, obviously, and it is cracked, luckily I have contacts with the gold smugglers, we can get a new one made for
only a little more than brass. The A reed is intact, I think, but
there the armature is rotted, and I will have to cut away your
mahogany, yes, and sister in a new piece."

He talks the way his hands work, deliberate, caressing,
soothing. And the fact that he can redirect his lust so easily,
like engaging a sprocket in one of the hundreds of machines
with no earthly purpose lining his walls, entirely subtracts
from Haddad the feeling of threat. All that is left is the first
lick of desire still tingling a little under her brassiere.

She lights a Galaxy, walks to the window, pushing aside a
stack of computer manuals so she can open the blinds and see
out. The oil lamps in a hovel across the street light small
rooms against the blue dark dropping like a falcon's caul
from the volcano, now that the sun has disappeared behind it;
evening has arrived. The tall tower of the southwest bastion
of the Walled City rises dark against the disorderly skyline of
palms and Bidonville dwellings. "I am going to a party later,"
Haddad calls from behind her, "in Barrio des Anglais, it's being thrown by a poet and a musician also. You can come if
you want."

But the excitement she felt earlier has her thinking now of
Miguel, or rather probing the void of his absence the way
Haddad examined the emptiness of the Fourneaux-Dallapé—
fingering deep, where echoes are made to swell the tones music will produce. Perhaps it is the change in perspective—she
has not left the Walled City or the Conservatory or her routine

with or without Miguel for so long that even going to the *cruce,* to the Slave Market, feels like the kind of adventure that can make you reassess your whole life. Whatever the reason, the fact that for a whole year and a half she has geared the turbocharged V-8 of her love to a man who visits her twice a month (three times during elections) suddenly seems far stranger than this pale machine fixer, this surrounding enclave of tomb robbers.

For the space of a drumroll it is her life that suddenly seems bizarre, the Walled City that appears perilous and odd with its tight routines and shawled *dueñas,* its bankers in polished cars, its priests patrolling the Cathedral close in pairs, its shutters up every night at eight as if pirates still raged at the gates instead of the predictable and profitable cruise-ship Yanquis vomited forth to spend their dollar-credits on folk art manufactured in the sweatshops behind the airport. She tries to think of him, Miguel. What she always recalls clearly are his kindnesses toward her, when they are together: the gifts of spice and video spindles, the small and unexpected caresses in places she likes—the back of the neck, the upper stomach. She misses also the sharpness of his mind. In contrast to the shoptalk of the Conservatory faculty, she can spar with Miguel the way an adept of the épée practices with another fencer of similar skill, rejoicing in the skid and speed of steel.

When she tries to visualize him though—his narrow Castilian face, his dark hair that will not line up the way he wants, his too-thin legs—all she sees is an approximation, like a shadow of her memory of him. And she realizes she never sees Miguel accurately and whole, only one small detail at a time; and perhaps this is the way she processes and understands him.

Thus, for the second time in two days her usual reluctance to do anything different is threatened, then engulfed by a despair—that what she refuses to leave will end up drowning her.

Now Haddad is writing up a slip. "The accordion will be

ready in two weeks," he says. "I can have it delivered for an extra charge." She takes the slip, thanks him. Haddad's eyes are distant behind the clear portion of the sucker-screen; he has written her off. Her heart beats harder, and she winces in annoyance.

"That party," she begins, drawing a breath and then coughing quietly on saliva. "I was thinking—were you really inviting me?"

He shrugs, but his eyes have slid back to her face—curious, cautious, still interested. It's as if she can hear him thinking, *This one does not behave like other women, but underneath, surely, her needs are the same.* She is content to keep things simple, to put up with his clichés, if what it gains in the end might for a while anesthctizc the feeling of despair that just filled her to capacity.

"You want to go?" Haddad's voice brcaks, like a boy's, and he grunts to cover it.

"Sure," she agrees, simply.

———

SOLEDAD HAS SECOND THOUGHTS almost at once. She knows, vaguely, where Barrio des Anglais is—it's the neighborhood where rich merchants built houses, after the pirate menace faded, halfway up the slopes of Teton and thus protected from both the volcano's occasional spews and the neap tides that periodically washed the waterfront, and also in a perfect position to catch the prevailing sea breeze. It was not the fault of the merchants that they could not foresee the troubles that would come with independence, or the collapse of the sugar market, or the influx of rural poor that became a flood of poverty and makeshift architecture rising around des Anglais all the way to the convent. Now Haddad takes her through some of the thickest densities of these slums, this Bidonville—places of great intricacy, guyed with coir ropes, jury-rigged of waste wood and cardboard and bits of old cars. Rats trace the edges of streets in quick gray movement. The smell of open latrines, of the cuisine of indigence—manioc, breadfruit, trash fish—is everywhere. So is activity that in the Walled City would be shut down at once by F2—gold bartering, emerald sorting, copying of CDs and info spindles. The wisdom in the Walled City is, these people would cut your stomach open, without a second thought, to steal your shoes.

And yet, while these people are obviously poor, they all seem too busy to pay attention to her. Even the ones not working are hauling water or tending kids, and those who don't do that play guitars, mostly *bandolos* and *requintos,* on balconies, in bars, or on alley corners. A distant explosion shakes the ground, and no one even looks up. After a while she loses her second wind of anxiety and observes with interest, even amusement, the life filling these steep alleys the way blood inhabits an artery.

Haddad is her other source of worry, for before leaving he took the harness apparatus off its shelf and looped it over one shoulder and she finally put two and two together—the bandage in his arm, the 3-D goggles, the tubes, the pumps—it is a jag mechanism, a way of meshing the intake of various genetically engineered psychotropics with the evolution of a particular story told through the VR deck. But he does not put on the goggles as they walk and she ends up losing her concerns over this also; it is a foretaste of how she will let down her defenses on other fronts before the evening is over.

The apartment they are going to, the poet's apartment, is on the very interface of des Anglais and Bidonville, on the highest floor of a creaking merchant's house, built over a balcony and linked to the top two floors of a stack-dwelling raised on the eroded slope beside it. She hears music and the massed chatter of people before she spots, high up, the ocher glow of oil lamps and the black shapes of guests moving and dancing in that light. Electric bulbs are strung over the Doric columns of a rooftop grape arbor. Two metal VW bodies that form the roof of the adjacent stack-dwelling are lit as if ready to tow this whole architectonic nightmare into the violet night. Faded blue sea horses are painted on the lintel of the old mansion. She and Haddad climb the broken steps like swimming upstream into a river of smoke and liquor and food smells and talk, and are absorbed into the party the way new nutrients are sucked into the food chain of the South Atlantic.

Someone hands her a glass full of liquor. Someone else asks if she's seen "Victor." A very drunk girl with blue-black makeup and luminous green eyes asks her for a cigarette. The liquor is *pinga,* laced with juice of *guanabana,* or soursop. The two liquids, one golden, one cream, swirl into each other like candy cane in her glass.

Tafia. It tastes delicious. The walls are of yellow and blue stucco. She makes her way carefully through the crowd, watching the different views that the half moon delivers like platters of freshly opened shellfish through large louvered windows: San Isidor, Bidonville, the Walled City, the bay and the ocean behind. Watching the birds, for there are birds everywhere in this apartment, parrots mostly but also a miniature macaw with smoky indigo wingfeathers and a yellow chest, identical to the one she saw in the market. A cage full of black-billed *agobequis* is suspended from the grape arbor on the balcony, and they preen and squeak mightily, excited by the modified salsa a combo plays in one corner.

Couples lazily swing on hammocks strung between columns and wall. Vines full of golden flowers give off a scent of treacle. The walls are lined with shelves, most stuffed with books, though some also bear various collections: miniature sailing ships in bottles, antique tools, jade frogs, stirrups, Quinchamali flasks. Scarred wagon wheels, ships' figureheads in the shape of mermaids, angels, fierce Indio warriors—all bleached white as bone cement—occupy the corners.

In a side room, a much-pounded Mason & Hamlin baby grand bears a freight of blue lupines. Arriving guests arrange new flowers on an outdated Zenith television set, daubed with Umbanda-Cargo symbols, that stands on a plinth in the principal room. A voice grows out of the crowd, a man's voice saying, "You have as much chance of success, yeh, if you oppose the little conveniences on which people build their justification as you have of forcing the mountain to take back its mud slides." It is fitting that her first perception of Jorge comes through his words and his voice. He has a moderately deep, slightly rough voice, like a piece of old mangrove that has been sanded and varnished but still retains in a certain unevenness of texture a record of its growth and travels. She turns, looking for the speaker. He is instantly recognizable to her—a tall, handsome figure with a precise angle to his neck. Hector Ruiz de Castro, she thinks; he is a famous singer of *Cumbia*. Her mouth hangs in astonishment that Ruiz, who owns a mansion in the Walled City and a finca in Saint Jean and a new Lexus, should be here at this party in this outlaw *cruce*—and then Ruiz speaks, saying nothing much in a register half an octave higher than the textured voice from before.

Ruiz shifts leftward, and the man beside him laughs. It was not Ruiz but the second man who talked about the mountain taking back its mud. She leans forward, intrigued—she has finished her *tafia* and already her inhibitions are starting to slip and hang off her like clothes three sizes too large. He catches her movement. Their eyes meet. And what she is aware of then is green, dozens of different greens melted together in the intensity of the man's gaze, or maybe she provides the intensity that makes them melt in that first instant. She is aware of the rest of him: the stocky peasant body, so different from Miguel's; the strong hands, the slight stoop; also the strong Basque nose, graying hair flung untidily back, eyelids and cheekbones that make shelter of shade. But it's the green that will always color her first impression of Jorge, and thus, forever, her memory of him.

She turns away, of course. She has not drunk enough to stare. Finds Haddad standing at the balcony next to her, gazing at her, the virtual-reality goggles slipped all the way over his eyes, swaying slightly to a scarcely audible beat creeping from his earphones. She lifts one of the earpieces, asks, "Who's that?" pointing discreetly at the green-eyed man. Haddad's lips lift in a slight snarl, a comment is being made here, she is not sure why, but he answers, "Jorge Echeverria, the poet I told you about" and then turns away, toward the sea, where the lights of the Walled City and the anchor lights of yachts and the propane lamps of the conger fishermen make a whole constellation in the inky darkness that matches in its own way the splash of stars overhead.

She drinks another *tafia* and starts talking to the *agobequis,* even humming to them a little, the drinks are that strong. She knows she is staying in the rough vicinity of her host because she was intrigued by him, by that brief swipe of phrase, the "Yeh, if you oppose the little conveniences . . ." that seemed to find chinks in the crowd's noise to land in her vernal eardrums. Though he and Ruiz are surrounded by a crowd of people who obviously feel the same way, through cracks between shoulders and necks he looks in her direction occasionally and their eyes meet again, encounters of green and blue. Which makes her happy, excited even. Just to flirt with someone, anyone, would make her happy at this point, she realizes. Add to that the feeling of escape, of mild danger that comes from visiting for the first time this forbidden city— factor in the *tafia*—and you go a long way toward explaining this high. She refills her glass, grinning for no reason, and catches a glimpse of herself in a gold-scrolled mirror beside the bar. Her cheeks are dark with rum. Her hair streams like black electricity from her shoulders, her eyes seem to her like aqua searchlights, almost mad in their intensity. The *V* of her mouth, in grinning, has partly unwound the long ends of her lips, which normally hide in a diagonal fold of skin on either side.

The music pauses. In the gap of sound a woman's voice takes precedence, and people fall silent as they pay attention to the dominant input, for she is talking loudly, almost shouting.

"—for all of you," she is saying, "I have thrown the shells again and again."

"How can you be so sure, Mother?" a woman asks. "Do the shells even tell you the Lotto numbers?"

Laughter splashes. Soledad, making her way back to the room where the macaw is, notices a well-known economist from the university passed out shirtless in one of the hammocks. She maneuvers nearer the laughter. Haddad follows her as he has followed her all evening, without fuss, four or six people behind.

"Evil will surround us like atoms of light," the voice continues.

Soledad sees a woman swaying between a man who wears the black kerchief of a tomb robber and the teenage girl with thick blue and black makeup. The woman is dumpy and black-skinned with hair tied in a white cloth. She wears dozens of medallions that show in relief the half-Catholic, half-African saints of Umbanda, and the token offerings of Cargo.

A *mounchey;* a priestess of the folk religion most people in Bamaca practice or at least pay attention to because it is so thickly layered in the stones and other peoples here.

This *mounchey* wears no shoes and her hair is long and neatly braided. Her eyes are rolled up in her head, she splays her arms and fingers horizontally. "They are many colors, these spirits of the night, as many colors as light makes, but you will know them as you know your own sons and daughters. *Aaah!*" she screams, and falls backward. The arms of a half dozen people catch her and let her down easily to the floor, still yelling.

"Legliz, the fishing harbor, are full of their pig snouts! The sea will make fire, the land will piss water—"

"And the volcano will shit *pinga* and everyone will be happy," someone adds. That takes the tension out, and seems to shut up the *mounchey* also, for she promptly falls asleep on someone's sandals. Soledad turns, meaning to locate Haddad and get a sense at least of how to leave this place, and finds Jorge Echeverria beside her. He nods, half bows; his manners are Spanish and cautious. "She is a good *mounchey,*" he says, "I have learned a lot of things from her, though I do not believe them, but in the *associations* they made with what I was thinking, they proved useful."

She nods, wondering, Does he always talk so pretentiously? At the same time she likes the fact that, pretentious or no, he seems immediately to look for meanings beyond the obvious.

"What is it?" she asks him, pointing at the indigo-feathered bird.

"A blue-winged macaw," he replies. "*Putain,* I have no idea what his real name is. I only buy birds because they are pretty and they sing like children."

They talk a while longer about nothing much—the taste of *tafia,* whether it's better to mix the *pinga* with soursop or mango (they both prefer soursop), and whether the moon is made prettier or less subtle by the haze from the volcano. They agree on that as well. She has wondered before about the role of such early and inconsequential agreements in building an illusion of compatibility on higher levels; does it forge some association with pheromonal attraction, with illusion, with the idea of association itself? She tells him, vaguely, about the Conservatory. He says "But you should work here, not in that larval orgocracy." It is not her first exposure to Hawkleyite jargon. He wears a loose linen shirt, and pants of the same material. No shoes, a small Cargo amulet on a string around his neck. His fingernails are dirty.

Then Ruiz calls him away and silence falls again. She climbs the companionway leading from the merchant's house to the stack-dwelling. People are leaning out of the VW windows above her to find the reason for this silence. Ruiz plinks notes from a Spanish guitar and Jorge starts to recite. And at first she thinks Holy Mother, the pretension never stops, though she knows her reaction is partly due to jealousy, because she would be so utterly unable to stand up like that in front of strangers and perform her own work.

Anyway the faces around clearly don't agree with her. They are serious, as if Echeverria were reaffirming something so important to them that the styles and egos surrounding it do not matter anymore.

And then she starts to listen, without professional prejudice for a change. And in her own chest and head she finds the words are also affirming something worth saying, something important in a different way. Though what it says to her could not be the same as what it says to these *crucistas;* her take on it is personal and has to do with Dvořák's piano concertos which provided a lifeline in another time when she was also being drowned by her own lack of courage, and laziness, and inability to move.

> *When I tell you I have nothing left*
> *I don't mean just "nothing."*
> *I mean, when I hunt for bones on the beach*
> *there are no bones, not one, only red waves*
> *from Africa, rolling the days*
> *I gave you like stones.*
> *I mean, when I eat a* guanabana
> *expecting that taste of raspberries and moon*
> *I only taste vinegar and the smoke of a village*
> *where the army has never been,*
> *again.*

Applause at the end—solid, not sycophantic. No one bothers to mix *tafias* anymore, they are passing around bottles of straight *pinga.* The band starts up once more. It is almost immediately eclipsed by a chorus of shouts as two *guaqueros* square off on the balcony's northern edge. The string of fiesta lights glints on the blades they hold, in practiced fashion, out and loose and parallel to the floor at a perfect angle for finding the space between two ribs, left hands wrapped in the painted silk kerchiefs the tomb robbers affect in their time off.

An old man with one eye grins. He clicks dominoes from hand to hand as he lovingly observes potential mayhem. The overly made-up girl clings drunkenly to one of the men, trying to kiss him. She is impeding the fight, and he shoves her away angrily.

Then Jorge steps into the circle of *duella*. He takes the girl by one elbow and the look he gives her as he does it is so deep in grief and helplessness that Soledad turns away, feeling emptied, and walks off to search for Haddad, who it turns out is right there, the usual six people behind, staring fixedly at her while the 3-D video plays in his goggles and the music thumps in his headphones and the jisi yomo and *basuko* and synthetic adrenaline spike alternately through three tiny pumps into his wrist IV, in patterns fed back between the music and the jag program running silently in his jambook computer.

———

SHE LETS HADDAD LEAD her back to the fishing harbor. He wants her to come to his *pilotis* but she refuses, gently. Normally she might be harsh with him, to make sure he gets the message loud and clear, but he holds the Fourneaux-Dallapé hostage and she does not want to piss him off over something so stupid. Even so, he is angry—he disconnected the intravenous hookup earlier, when they left the party. Now he doffs the VR goggles as well and stares at her. They are in the lee of an all-night seafood dealer. The fishermen gaze at them curiously as they trundle half Hondas full of the ugliest fish Soledad has ever seen, and dump them into boxes on the fishmongers' scales. The smell is thick with sea salt and fish intestines and diesel oil, the flavor of harbor.

"You're falling for Echeverria," he mutters, and repeats the accusation louder.

"I'm not falling for anyone, that's what I'm trying to tell you," she snaps back, "anyway he obviously has his hands full with that drunken girl."

"Hah!" Haddad laughs, and turns away, catching a sob in his gullet; it's the jisi yomo, she thinks, it brings the emotions out. "He has his hands full all right," Haddad continues, "but that's his daughter."

Then he walks away down an alley, leaving Soledad to

stare after him; to stare at the acetylene lamps of the fish shop; at the sign that reads, around the corner of the alley, over the shop's sign, APARTMENT TO RENT 4TH FLOOR 50 CAYMANS MONTHLY. At the ugliness of the fish, their black leathery skin gleaming with sea ooze, their huge yellow teeth, their bulbous eyes stuck out on stalks twenty centimeters long, as if the fish itself could not bear to stay too close to those sticky globes; mouths half the length of their body and stretched like the grin of hell's most sadistic goblins.

"Merde," she exclaims, looking only at the fish now. Yet what she is really commenting on is not their surpassing ugliness but the power of the excitement that came surging back inside her at Haddad's words. Because of the way the excitement faded when she thought the dark-haired girl was his paramour, she can measure exactly how much of that emotion stemmed from the first spark of infatuation, and how much was created by the dangerous anarchy of what she has just done by slicing herself away from the advice of Miguel and her father and all the harrumphing residents of the Walled City who would have her never go farther than the La Plaj casinos, or her father's *estancia* near the mountains. Nor is it the Walled City that is the culprit—she understands this also, despite, or maybe thanks to, the burn of *pinga* in her brain. The real culprit is a superstructure to the self-knowledge she'd had before, a knowledge *about* self-knowledge.

Because she can sit back as she did earlier and soberly analyze that fucking propensity she has for procrastination, for habit, for letting what has already happened by itself determine what has not yet come to pass—*and still, despite that understanding, and in the midst of thinking about it, allow it to continue;* like standing in the middle of the capital highway watching the express Onibus bear down on you, all the while knowing you are too torpid to move your limbs, aware that the driver's eroded brake pads will never stop the bus in time.

And the pressure of self-directed rage this thought produces, and the remnants of the heady delight she felt at the party, and (it must be said) the *pinga,* propel her away from the fish shop to the waterfront proper where she paces perilously near the edge of the wharves, smoking one cigarette after another, eliciting calls of caution and invitation from the fishermen and smugglers until fatigue and the beginnings of an *aguardiente* headache cause her to head for the Slave Market, toward the gates of the Walled City and the command post of the federal police—brightly lit, as if to call her back home like a mother would, as lost and confused and abandoned as she feels this night.

————

SHE DREADED RETURNING TO her apartment, after the thrill of leaving the Walled City, after the colors of parrots and music and forbidden areas; but when she wakes up the following day her apartment does not seem so bad—dark and cool and safe inside its fat seventeenth-century walls; sheltering and protective of the person who lived inside. Her own baby grand is piled high with music manuscripts. The pictures on her dresser serially recount the stages of life that made her who she is: the hut by the tungstite workings, her dog Pablito on the finca's lawn, her mother grinning too widely as she tried to get away from the camera's lens. Miguel in evening dress, caught by a newspaper photographer at the opening of a play she was not permitted to attend. The phone rings when she is in the shower and she lets the answering machine pick up, though there is only one person it could be. When she checks it—drying herself lazily as the tape runs—she hears Miguel's voice, intimate in timbre, separated by distance and the poor quality of both tape and telephone cables.

"Sandoval wants me for the committee on airport security next week, so I can't make it. I got him to promise me the week after, and I have a reservation at the Castillo Playa that Thursday, under the name you know." A pause.

"I feel bad about this, *mi amor*—I feel separated from you. Where are you, anyway?"

He hangs up without leaving his name. He knows she will recognize his voice, but even in the early stages of their affair, when he could not make that assumption, he never left his name for reasons of security. He says if Sandoval found out he was cheating on his daughter he could easily have Miguel killed. Despite what everybody thinks, the death squads were never completely wrapped up; they just went to counterinsurgency school in the U.S. and took courses in "sensitivity." But Sandoval has only to pick up the phone and call Ochoa Campos and a dozen men will come for whomever he names.

Of late, though, Soledad suspects this is only a convenient excuse. While Miguel always made it plain he had no intention of leaving Serena, he wants that understanding to be backed up by a foundation of brute necessity, so he can allow himself the luxury of letting his emotions go, with a steel bulkhead to shield him from messy consequences.

She backhands the answering machine off the dresser. Its plastic cover cracks. She wonders why she did that—she does not feel particularly angry. Mostly, she feels tired, and hungover, and bemused. Because something is running inside her, like a long-dead appliance motor that suddenly starts up in the middle of the night so that you wake up wondering what on earth that noise could be. She does not know what the mechanism is—it's not the thrill of infatuation, which is old hat for her. It is not even the sense of having broken rules in a way she usually never does. She does not care to investigate any further right now. She gets dressed and walks to the Conservatory and works late. When she returns to the apartment she makes herself a cup of cocoa and goes to bed immediately.

She does not dream much at this stage of her life. But when the alarm wakes her the following morning it is as if she had undergone all the rigors of a child's nightmare, the kind of bad dream where you are locked in a closed space while something evil slowly and deliberately tears down the barrier separating you from it and you cannot escape and you cannot make yourself wake up, either. And when you do wake up, gasping and terrified, reality has taken on the gray and torrid tones of the nightmare, so that nothing seems as it should, and even the factors that once inspired joy appear fruitless and without worth.

She goes through the routines of the morning regardless: making coffee, the shower. In the little theater of hygiene, the rush of water loosening the hold of habit, Jorge's face enters her mind without warning: the way he was, not when he spoke his poems, but when he talked to her; the predatory nose, hair swept back as if by a storm. The deepwater green of his regard, the mass and tendons of his hands. Even after she dries herself the slight thrill of something running inside her continues, and it emits a squeak of parrot color, and fish smell, and complex emerald, as if the greater experience of the *cruce* had been captured and compressed into a music box inside her and she had lifted the lid a crack, just enough to start it turning. A tinkle of chord, of *Vallenato*.

She stares at the stack of student compositions she annotated and graded yesterday, realizing she has already completed her class work for next week. She should be leaving the apartment now to be on time for her advanced-technique seminar, but instead she pours a second cup of coffee and walks around the dark apartment, opening the dusty velvet drapes all the way to stare outside, at the stony balcony, at the windows opposite, the dark drapes of which shiver also as if in response, and then are still.

A third cup now. Soledad picks up the phone and calls the Conservatory. She is feeling ill, she tells the piano department secretary, a stomach bug probably. She will not be in today, maybe not even tomorrow.

She arranges to have the annotated compositions picked up later at the frame shop downstairs by a professor who lives nearby.

She does not reflect on what she is doing. To think about it would mean to analyze it, and analyzing would require triangulating back to every episode in the past twenty years that culminated in her feeling this way in this place, at this particular instant. It is a device, she realizes now, by which she preserves her inability to act. But just this once she is going to ignore that device; just this once she will see what happens without it.

And what happens is: She digs from her closet a small canvas rucksack she bought to go on hiking expeditions in Tayrona Park that of course never got beyond the planning stage. She stuffs in her sack her notebook of compositions (mostly unfinished), the Fischer edition of Dvořák piano works, a box of tampons, a toothbrush, hairbrush, three pairs of underwear, her cashcard, a thin crystal flask of Vengeance. Picks the answering machine off the floor and presses the RECORD button.

"I've gone away for the weekend," she says in a high, rigid voice rather unlike her real one. "I don't know when I'll be back." It sounds ridiculous, contradictory. She hesitates. The words she should say—she can visualize Miguel hearing them, not his face but his thin dark-suited form bent astonished over the machine—crowd inside her head. They are really the words others would have her say, the phrases of form to smooth out the harsh contours of the truth, which are that for one and a half years he has had his cake, *her,* and eaten it too, *her,* even if it took something out of him also to love her as he did, and he did love her—does love her—this she knows as truly as she knows her own name.

She opens her mouth to give shape to the feeling of sadness that wells up inside her at the thought.

Then closes it.

The little mechanism still hums inside her. If anything, it is running a little louder, and now she understands what it is, not intellectually but organically; as if it were the pitch of the motor that was familiar, a major chord of rotary motion that she is sure, from her professional glossary, represents excitement.

Excitement. Her mouth curves ever so slightly. She lets go

of the RECORD button. The answering machine beeps to itself, resets, and goes silent, waiting for her old life to call back.

She picks up the stack of annotated papers and her rucksack and goes out the door of her flat, locking it with ridiculous care behind.

FIVE

SHE WOKE AS IF she were lying in a pirogue drifting down a slow deep river that changed without barrier or frontier from a land of reverie to one of consciousness.

Tendrils of Bamaca clung to the sides of the canoe like the hands of the drowned. It was warm and soft in the craft, the Indians (she reflected vaguely, her thoughts still had the dream-generated ability to stretch to any length in all directions)—the Indians must have covered the bottom in fronds. She knew she was awake but was in no rush to open her eyes and come to all the conclusions that being awake implied. For now, the colors of dream were stronger and the *cruce* was alive and Jorge's *agobequis* cracked their calabash seeds and his pen was scratching among the debris of the party as she walked again through the hot breath of the Slave Market, although never had she walked through the market when no *Vallenatos* were playing and among a smell of such chilly, untropical neglect—

She opened her eyes.

A man stood over her, one sat beside.

They were backlit by neon worklights coming from behind a long blued window. Through the window she saw a low-ceilinged room that seemed as endless as an idea of purgatory. That room, in turn, had a long window on its far side, behind which lay an even vaster space where something was suspended that her brain casually but finally refused to process.

She noticed, also without deliberately registering, a third man standing beside an architect's pushscreen in the second room. But this was detail, wallpaper for what was going on urgent and in front of her. For a moment, reaching in memory for labels to put on these two men, she reached too far back and identified them as her dream might have—the thin tall one as Hector Ruiz, the man sitting as Haddad, he wore a half-sucker after all—but then even wishful REM fell apart, for this last one was totally bald and his skin was yellow and he had the crumbled posture of degenerative nerve disease. Also he sat in a sort of wheelchair with dozens of different contraptions attached to it and she had never seen anything like that before.

Now, as her pupils expanded to scavenge what light they could in this dark place stashed inside a lighter space inside another dark place, she made out their features, and they were gringos—worse, gringos she had never met.

And she was fully awake then, short-term memory dropping over her like a net, the huge thing with fire dripping from its snout and red and green eyes coming for her on its neat round feet—

"She's conscious, this time," the crippled man said. He was not watching her—he watched the top of his half-sucker screen. He moved a thumbstick and clicked once.

She sat up carefully, pushing herself backward on the bed, which was hard to do because the bed was soft as flan. It rolled and gave to her efforts like a huge blister. Her left thigh hurt like hell. Her lower back, which had gotten so much better during her trip north, ached once more, though not as badly as when she'd first twisted it.

"No shit," the other man replied.

"Wild theta patterns," the sitting man commented. He had an extremely handsome face, smooth as a woman's under the goggle sheen, padded but not distorted by fat. The man standing held himself as rigid as a Sierra Division paratrooper. His hair was short. His features were pointed, clean-shaven, still. He wore a faded jumpsuit, work boots, and a moldy forage cap with the words USS DUBUQUE SSN-61 printed across it. Various tools—baling wire, pliers, a jambook computer as up-to-date as any she'd seen in San Francisco's business district—hung off a thick leather utility belt.

Music thumped gently from a speaker behind her. She recognized Eastern beat, mouth music, didgeridoo, riffs from all over: Shift-shin.

"You wanna call Stix?" the man in the wheelchair said, glancing at the window.

The third man, though farther away, was easier to make out under the neon of the next room. He was of medium build, stocky, a little pudgy even. He had unkempt reddish hair, a short, concave nose, a tuft of whiskers bristling between lower lip and chin. He wore the same belt as the man standing beside Soledad, but the fashion parallels ended there; the pudgy man wore a black suit of iridescent cloth under his tools, as well as spats and a high-collared frill shirt and a black bow tie. All were cut in a style that last was fashionable in the era of flappers and three-stack ocean liners. He was tapping at the keys of a jambook, shaking his head; as Soledad watched, he walked to the long window and peered out. Her various perceptions had been coming in discrete packages ever since she exited her dream, and she figured it had something to do with self-preservation, coping with an overload of new and weird data that her brain could deal with only by chopping it up. For a fractured second, she felt as if she had been miniaturized, shrunk into a tiny room placed inside a separate box inside a bigger box, all of them set on a magician's table—for the pudgy man was looking through the outside window of the farthest chamber at a *bird,* a bird suspended on a thick steel cable in the outside box; a pterodactyl the size of a small cottage, a bird from horror movies with a giant beak and red eyes and huge black plastic wings and tailfeathers of more colors than a Bamaca parrot.

With no warning, a blob of something white and viscous, the size of a giant beach ball, plopped from under the tailfeathers where the anus would be, and vanished past the borders of the windows.

The man in fancy clothes swiveled and punched one fist in triumph into the air.

The wheelchair man flipped out his half-sucker mike.

"Stix."

"You see that?" The voice came loudly from a speaker behind the bed, and Soledad jumped.

"Yeah, beautiful bird-doo."

"A little loose. Diarrhea."

"Stix—"

"But can you imagine?" The well-dressed man punched the air again. "When we dive this sucker—"

The tall one said, "Our visitor's awake."

The other one peered at them through the grime smearing the inside window. Then he unplugged a cord from his jambook, limped leftward, out of sight, to reappear through the nearest door and stand beside Soledad's bed.

"Well," he said, looking at her curiously. "Had a nice sleep?"

Close up, the clothes were even more incongruous. They were antiques, made of thick organic fibers no one used anymore, velvety and almost blue. The smile on his face was understated but definite, as if he were reexamining some obscure joke, getting ready to mark the punch line.

She stared back at him. Her various wedges of visual reality did not really make sense together and her stomach was moving around in sympathy, if not synchrony, with the liquid underneath her. She was absorbing more of the room she was in: The stretch of wall beside her was interrupted by two ship's portholes made of brass, but the wall itself was cement, so she could not be on a ship. A piece of cardboard taped to the wall showed a strong black-ink sketch of what looked like an Italian pastry on wheels. Beside it someone had stuck a giant image of Winston Churchill, on which was printed part of the "We shall fight them on the beaches" speech. A photograph of a catamaran-frigate shooting missiles at a warplane had been heavily defaced with spray paint. A little engine clung to the flange of a thick steel tram track overhead. Around her, videocams stood on tripods, wires and insulation drooped from steel beams, faded naval bell-bottoms hung on masonry nails.

Her *cuto,* her pathetic kitchen knife, lay on a concrete shelf beside the bed.

The Shift-shin stopped, started again.

Something shook the building, gently, once.

She wondered where in hell she was. The smell of mold was still strong. Now she noticed another smell, like rotting jungle, with undertones of long-dead carcass. It didn't settle her stomach any.

The man who had come in both mistook and understood her silence.

"Ya don have to worry," he said. "We gave that armored car, the one that gassed you, a little bath."

"Stupid thing to do," the taller one said.

"They were off-limits," the man in the wheelchair said. "If it ever came to a court of law—"

The tall man laughed, without finding it funny.

"I wish it was the courts we had to worry about," he said.

They were all silent for a moment. The shorter man raised his eyes to the ceiling and said, "Bah!" Then he looked at Soledad again.

"Did you really know Jorge Echeverria?" he asked curiously. "You said something," he added, and actually blushed a bit, waving his hands sideways, "in your sleep."

She moved, at the mention of Jorge's name, and then at the greater shock, that she had said anything at all, when for three weeks she had been unable to force anything but the most rudimentary grunts out of her throat. Because of being unable to seek refuge in the complex stratagems of speech, she had recently found herself translating more of her emotions by way of movement. So it was not just the surprise, or Jorge's name, that forced her to stir—she moved as a physical reflection of her overall need to assemble the bits of reality again, find out essential data such as: Was she a refugee or a prisoner? Was this really the Oakland *cruce* she had found? And how had these men in odd clothes stopped something so terrible as that fire-car without selling themselves in the process? And was she happy or disappointed that they had saved her life?

But moving set off further motion in the liquid underlying the rumpled layer of blankets and sheets beneath her, and this in turn resonated with and further amplified the unease in her stomach. For the second time in two days she greeted her waking with a rise of vomit, leaning over the concrete lip of the bed to deposit it quickly and almost in ladylike fashion on a pair of filthy feet sticking out from the steel underpinnings of her place of rest.

———

A LONG-HAIRED MAN DRESSED in jeans and a tie-dyed tanktop crawled out from under the bed, groaning something of which the only recognizable component was the words "seminary school." He pointed a trembling and accusatory finger at Soledad, then turned and stomped away, mumbling, "You *cannot* petition the lord with prayer!"

The smell of rotting faded in his wake.

"Fuckin Mojo," the taller one grunted.

The short pudgy man did not fool around with sponges and buckets—he got a fire hose and washed down the floor and the parts of the wheelchair Soledad had splashed. This was his room, Soledad decided. The bald man fussed until a splatter had been removed from the footrest of his wheelchair. The taller one asked her civilly if she was well enough to walk, because they had to take her to Dr. Zatt's workshop, it was something they did with people they were unsure of, refugees from broken-up nodes—or *cruces,* he added, reading her unfamiliarity with the gringo term. He glanced at the shorter man as he said this, and shrugged. The cripple was happier now that his footrest had been hosed off. "Never introduced myself," he said, with an opera-bouffe slap at his own forehead. "I am Lafcadio Zatt. Welcome," he added, finally answering the most urgent of her questions, "to the Oakland node." Then he hit a switch, and his wheelchair buzzed and took off so fast it did a shallow wheelie before vanishing through the steel door. The men followed him without looking back. Soledad climbed out of the bed. Her inner thigh now throbbed sharply where the haptic suit had cut it. She was light-headed but her balance was OK. She was also dressed, even to her plastic sandals. Her tights were crusted with dried blood.

She grabbed the *cuto* and tucked it in the waistband of her tights. Then, after a brief hesitation, she followed them out.

The building she was in was bigger than she had thought. The room outside the first set of windows extended for twenty meters in either direction. The gray-painted chunks of outdated computers, the control panels and relay boards and haphazard circuitry it contained would have filled up a good-sized house on their own. The control room was so decayed and encrusted with dust and spiderwebs that, wherever they moved, clouds of debris floated around their feet and subsided slowly. She did not look through the windows at that bird of bad dreams she had seen earlier.

They boarded an elevator as big as half her apartment in Bamaca; it wheezed and sighed grudgingly downward and deposited them on the ground floor of what looked like a factory even grimier than the control room. This factory was fifty meters high and almost a hundred long and the shafts of metal-colored light thrusting down from serial skylights spotlit various pieces of unnameable machines parked along the shop floor—half-disassembled tubes full of gas cylinders and wiring, with multiple propellers on one end, attended by rusted machine tools. Broken forklifts, cannibalized diagnostic computers, and other, darker, mechanical constructs of which she could make no sense at all.

It seemed to Soledad, shocked as she was by accumulated loss and remembered fear and the particles of a more current terror, that this factory was like her soul—great spaces of artificial silence in which historical objects that together might make a terrible but at least logical sense could be kept apart, dismantled if necessary, so they would stay silent and not drive her mad. The analogy grew in realism because, as she started to get her bearings in the violet gloom, she realized that some of the machines were moving.

A thing that resembled a life-sized metal Jesus crawled on aluminum elbows, dragging its useless legs down the long far side of the factory.

In the corner, a much bigger machine—a combination of gallows and a carousel—repeatedly swung the giant and bloody carcass of a horse into a cement wall. It made flat, liquid splats, very unlike the deeper thud she had heard earlier. Nausea rose again, and she turned away, hand over mouth.

"Stix's toys," the man in the wheelchair commented, pointing at the shorter man.

High above her and to one side, the dark rectangle of the control room they had just left appeared small and isolated. The giant bird swayed slow and lonely in the air currents beside it. Her feet at one point sloshed through patches of something gluey and white. She realized these were the "droppings" it had vented earlier, and wiped her sandals automatically.

A pushscreen, framed by wildly welded scraps of military steel, switched on next to ventilation machinery. Unlike San Francisco, where it would have shown a trailer for *Pain in the Afternoon,* or a themeworld package, this one featured only a dim room where what looked like moss wired to banks of cheap jambooks did absolutely nothing on a Formica bench.

She was glad when Stix opened a door marked YOU ARE NOW LEAVING A LEVEL D AREA into the scour of colder air and a breezeway made of rusted corrugated iron. A railing separated them from a giant pit of cement, half filled with water of a cold, greenish brown, littered with old pilings and seaweed and the swamped skeleton of a barge. She looked at the far end of the pit, feeling a deep hunger in her, aware from this how much she wanted to see the ocean again, to friction her heart against its absoluteness, its eternal ability—something Jorge had invoked in his poem the night they met—to ram home a reality of most pure loneliness.

She wanted also to see something that was the same in this cold place as it was in Bamaca, because even gringos and their power could not do away with blue sea and straight horizon.

The end of the pit, though, was blocked by a warehouse and the workings of a lock.

Zatt was far ahead in his speed-chair. Fifty paces behind him, his two companions walked beneath a row of giant cranes of the same type as the one she had seen looming over warehouses last night.

Soledad followed them without thinking much about where she was headed. Waking up as she had, with unknown events and new people thrusting into her brain before she had time to analyze them, had somehow filed down the spikes of her earlier emotions—ground them into a kind of see-what-happens mode made up in equal parts of her habit of coping and that same melting surrender, that sugary death-wish that overcame her once more when the fire-car roared down the alley.

She did not have energy to cope; yet she had gotten just enough sleep to render giving up less attractive.

Anyway—her obsessive intellectualization blipping on briefly as she followed the men—the surrender of will and independence was something that had been decided when she fixed the terms of her search.

If this were indeed the *cruce*—the "node"—she was looking for, then it followed in some sense that whatever happened here was what she sought. Obviously continuing fatigue and the remnants of nausea and backache and the wound in her thigh informed this theory and finally it sort of drifted away in the effort she made to keep up. The ache around her wound in particular was growing worse and she had to restrict the swing of her right leg to hold discomfort within tolerable limits.

Now Zatt had reached the third and most gigantic crane, a mechanism thirty meters in height with a twenty-meter-long Meccano boom hanging its hook over another basin. Its three-story control cab was thick with aerials and satellite dishes. He rolled up a ramp, opened a steel door, and engaged his chair in a sort of paternoster lift at the base. The lift ran up the inside of one of four vertical legs of steel that rolled this crane on twin rails along the basin's side. The men guided her by the elbows as she ventured aboard. Zatt pulled a lever, the section they were on grabbed hold of a moving cable, and they were lifted sickeningly up the cavernous tube, rust and gobs of old tallow showering them as they rose in utter darkness. Then, just as abruptly, the elevator jolted to a stop, and they were released into a sudden square of white electric light.

The cab of this abandoned crane was not significantly different in style from the naval workshop Soledad had woken up in. Ancient, grease-caked machinery, thick cables, giant, half-seen arcs of shivs, gray paint peeling off the bulkheads. The cab, of course, was as cramped as the workshop had been spacious, leaving the cripple only a few pathways between lift machinery, cables, and a bench almost broken by the weight of twelve or fifteen B-Net terminals all illuminating in the coded hues of software the wedge of space allocated to them. Another difference was this: the artwork, instead of sketches and Churchill posters, consisted of pinup centerfolds from "touch" magazines—publications with names like *Epidermis* and *Feather* aimed at people who, fearing the Second Plague and other diseases of sex, confined themselves to rubbing, massage, and nonpenetrative contact.

The cab also had a view of the outside through thick gray gridded glass behind the crowd and hoist levers: a warehouse roof, the summit of a giant heap of scrap rising to one side, a broken pier thrusting through fade-outs of mist into pastels of ruffled green-gray that had to be saltwater. And overhead, where the mist was thin, a sky of a different gray, like the metal of a howitzer, but shifting, complex in a way that the works of men, for all their fractal intricacies, could never match.

The cripple wheeled around the engines, adjusting ultra-thin wireless terminals set in floating, helium-filled balloons in apparently random locations. One hung over a coffee machine. Its screen showed the intro file of a 3-D game: patterns, dynamic, a flow that coursed loosely then seemed to seize up, congeal into the single Greek word ΠΟΛΙΣ—and then flowed loosely off again. Another displayed a purple label reading VECTOR HOLDINGS/ALGO INC. over a two-headed freak-thing in a field of lines and squares. The heads had birds' beaks, sharks' teeth, three eyes, a horn.

As Soledad watched, the creature's leathery wings enveloped one of the squares while its tail, spiked with hypodermic needles, lashed into and tangled one of the lines.

The screen changed, and a different monster appeared, a giant snake's mouth with four huge fangs, grafted on a human hand, walking sideways like a crab. It squatted and gave disgusting birth to tiny clones of itself before moving on again.

MICRODYNE SYSTEMS CORP., the label on this one read.

From the keyboards, the cripple said, "OK, Stix."

The shorter man—his name, then, was Stix—held an object of matte plastic the size of a felt eraser. It was attached to a long phone cord. He said, "It's like a sonogram, a do-it-yourself CAT scan—you won't feel it. OK?" He looked at Soledad curiously. "You can talk to us, you know. If you're really from Bamaca then you're with friends—*amigos*," he added in a terrible accent. "*Les amis.* But we just need to make sure you're not carrying a wire."

He passed the sensor rapidly back and forth across the rear of her body, then the front.

"Why doesn't she talk?" the taller man asked. "Is it just 'cause she doesn't understand English?"

Soledad watched as an image of her built itself across a green grid on one of the screens beside the cripple. While the matrix spread, a thinner and less substantial grid that was Soledad's anger constructed itself across the front of her mind; anger that she, who had been spied on without cease and reported on by informers and attacked with fire not only in Bamaca but here; she, whose life had been gutted and ravaged and who then had to suffer the humiliation of running from emptiness to preserve her hold on the dubious status of living, should be suspected of being a spy.

Despite the sleep she'd had the fatigue was still huge in her and she did not have the energy to fan anger higher than a flicker. Other thoughts kept getting in the way—for example, her delayed realization that the cripple was the "doctor" they spoke of earlier; he was "Doctor Zatt." Lines appeared from the image of Soledad on the screen, linked up with fragments of green text. A red cone flashed at her waistband.

"Six fillings, all solid. The blade we saw earlier, she picked it up, nice move." He grinned. "No impedance, no standby charges, no backup even. She's clean. Told ya," Stix added, pressing buttons on the scanner.

Soledad sought their eyes, one by one. They did not look away, or pay much attention either.

A bell jangled.

"That's not exactly proof," the taller man said. He climbed on a drum of lube oil, and peered out a porthole. "It's Link. You know what I'm saying," he continued, hopping off the drum and pointing at Soledad. "I have no agenda with you, I don't even know your name. But no one knows exactly what happened in the Bamaca node. One minute it was there, and the next—" He leaned over one of Zatt's keyboards and punched CONTROL-ALT-DELETE, causing two of the screens to go black. Zatt hissed furiously at him. "No C-prompt. The assumption is, the death squads came back."

"You don't *know* that, Will," the shorter man said. "By definition."

"It's our responsibility to guess," Will answered. "We don't know who she is. She could be BON's way of finding out what's going on here. They'd figure we'd welcome her after Bamaca went off-radar—'specially after a show like they put on last night. But you know damn well what the death squads do; they don't just off people, brother. They burn down houses with the whole family and uncles and acquaintances in them. You think they'd just let one of 'em run away?"

"Will—"

Will looked at Soledad's face, and the muscles of his face slackened. "I'm sorry," he said, "but it's what I think. I gotta go," he added, turning toward the lift, "we're plugging—"

"But it's circumstantial," Stix interrupted. The smile remained on his face. His eyes were fixed on the taller man, and his tone pleaded a little. For the first time Soledad noticed that the two shared the exact same concavity of nose and a similar, slightly slanted cast to the eyes. Brothers, she thought, or at least close cousins. "We can't send her away," Stix added, "just on—"

The taller man, Will, turned back. His features too bore the same expression they usually did—a kind of Boy Scout concern—but his irises suddenly seemed hard as marbles and his body curved as if a leaf-spring had been bent that could send him in one vault into the other man's throat.

In competition with such anger, Soledad's own shock from hearing someone describe so clinically what had happened in the *cruce* piddled out and was diluted to almost nothing.

"You're not listening," Will said softly. "Did you *look* at that armored car last night? Did you *look* at it?"

"It was a new one," Stix replied, "I—"

"It's the Mark Eleven. A patrol saw it. We've never seen a Mark Eleven here before, Stix. They never sent Area 51 stuff here before. There's something going on, bro, only you're blinding yourself to it. You're blinding yourself."

The two men watched each other for four or five seconds. Finally Will turned back to the paternoster and stepped onto the waiting platform. He pulled the lever. He looked at Soledad as the clamp engaged and the platform started to descend, so the last she saw of Will was his smooth eyes drilling into hers, and then the peak of his cap that read SSN-61.

Stix rubbed his chin with one hand. He still had not

stopped smiling, but Soledad got the impression of something happening behind his smile that felt to her like the blizzards and empty prairies of Canada.

Finally he folded the plastic scanner and tossed it beside one of the bubble terminals.

The cripple glanced at him.

"Take it easy."

"I'm fine."

"Will Grammatico got his thing," Zatt said. He had turned back to the keyboards and was tapping almost absently, watching the patterns flow and check, blending from one color to another and sometimes back.

"We are under pressure," Stix told Soledad. "Nothing like you guys were, of course."

"We have ways of measuring it," Zatt added, still booting up computers Will had crashed.

"They'll clean up some angle," Stix said. "The Putamadres, probably." He was watching Soledad. "Or the jaggers."

"The Proto-Panthers."

"The hackers. The Ludd-Kaczynskis. The point is," Zatt continued, "Orgs been doing groundwork for months, on the Flash. We're a lawless area, they say, got to clean us up. I think we should give her the M-test," he added, looking at Stix. "You?"

Stix nodded. "Can you really not talk?" he asked gently. "Are you, like, mute? *No puede hablar?*"

She nodded, then shook her head, confused by the rapidity of his questions. But if mute meant the same thing as *muette,* then yes, she most certainly was.

Except, apparently, when she slept.

Stix lowered his head to stare directly into her face.

"You just don't *wanna* talk?"

He had very clear hazel eyes; they reminded her of pools in the coral, south of Santa Maria, where she used to catch crayfish with her father during school holidays. She felt a sudden and less-than-rational urge to tell him about what happened—tell him how often, and how badly, her emotions were broken and dragged through acid by what happened to her *cruce*. It was a contradiction she had already experienced and absorbed: in order to explain why she could not speak, she had to tell a story as intricate as the *cruce* itself. She felt tears surging, and pushed hard to control them; mildly surprised because it was the first time she had gotten near crying since arriving in the north.

She shook her head.

Zatt was back at the keyboards. The monsters on four screens changed into different creatures. The various labels shifted beside them. The short man was looking at the screens. The half smile was still on his lips but less humor was in it— Soledad thought it was a fake version of his face, put on to maintain continuity when something shook him up enough. She wondered what had gotten to him.

"Well," he said finally, "let's go see Molly."

———

STIX HAD A MOTORCYCLE but, as Soledad was beginning to expect in this place where factories were bedrooms and cranes, apartments, it looked nothing like the motorcycles she was used to. Four long, arachnoid "feet" had been bolted high on each side of a Yamaha 650; two big yellow headlights were mounted like eyes on a fiberglass beak, with a big hollow "abdomen" of the same material fastened over the pillion seat. The interior of the mantle was filled with cushions and extremely comfortable. Soledad could lie back inside—there was a Plexiglas windscreen to protect the top half—and look out on the road coming at them and stay almost invisible in the gloom of the spider's body. Stix put on a head-sucker, and coughed, and speakers inside the mantle clearly relayed his cough to her ears. And then they were off, so much wind cavitating inside her nest that she had a sudden, weird illusion they were taking wing on the nacred mist drifting in banks around the node.

They thundered out from the breezeway the bike was stabled in onto a road that had once been asphalted but now was more cut and rutted than the road she had used to get to the node. Down another alley, this one carpeted with drifts of dust—not ordinary dust but dust the blue of peacock feathers. Cadmium, she thought, or some other by-product of acid and copper. She recognized the towering wall of junked automobiles, people in half-suckers sitting in rusted vans on top; the long, rectangular warehouses; but those were the only similarities with what she had seen from outside. The warehouses looked like Kemp's real thing, compared with what San Francisco was trying to achieve, because almost every gray facade had been cut up into a "skin of life," full of balconies, windows, and Kempian "daily-drama spaces"; and all of them crawled with flowers, tomato vines, laundry, or hydroponic marimba drying on racks.

From ground level, between forests of jury-rigged pushpanels that flashed further homemade images of people doing something inexplicable, you could tell the walls were mostly open, revealing dozens, no hundreds of tiny workshops making (Stix reeled off a list) Wildnet encryption programs, Shiftshin recordings, hydroponic kohlrabi, Wildnet 3-D games; or services, such as the repair of bike-carts and face-suckers.

They roared down a ramp to a market filled with stalls and tents. According to her pilot, what was sold here tended to be less legal: jisi yomo, high-amp tazers, jagger triage, copied Clam Fetish spindles. Lots of black software as well, dark vindictive programs spiked with Trojan Horse viruses, Nobot assassins, logic bombs, Wildnet torpedoes. Big sections of this mist-fuzzed forum, however, seemed to offer nothing more controversial than strawberries, red potatoes, homemade crullers. All of these were the things, the objects, of the Oakland *cruce,* Soledad realized, and the quantity and diversity of what was made and traded among the condemned navy buildings and mobile walls of mist were impressive to her. Because if you put the barrio workshops of the Slave Market, Bidonville, and Ensevli together, you would barely have filled up ten of these warehouses of which there had to be twenty or maybe even thirty in the Oakland node.

What impressed her most of all, though, was the number
and activity of artists. They were of all ages and colors and
types. Some wore the homespun tunics that she already knew
from San Francisco were Ludd-Kaczynski garb; some dressed
like Will Grammatico, some wore gear like the jaggers at the
Nirvana. Yet they seemed to be present in every crease and
fold of the humming, undirected engine that was this node,
welding exploded sculptural pieces on three levels of factory,
painting in groups on wall-screens, drawing alone on old-
fashioned easels, filming videos in groups on balconies; video
that, in one case, was displayed realtime on a pushwall on the
next block.

There had been a clique of visual artists in the *cruce* also.
But the Bamaca variety hid out in their studios and corners,
whereas here everyone seemed to be posturing on a highly
visible cornice. Or, if the artist was not directly visible, he
wore a jambook hooking him up to a pushscreen that bill-
boarded his work, or linked him to another group doing something similar.

Musicians lived here, and this was similar to Bamaca. In
the *cruce* they had dominated the creative community by
their absolute numbers, by the way every level of population
tended to play its own music, and by the sheer volume and
energy of what they produced. This node, however, held far
less of them compared to the number of visual artists. Also,
very few played to open air. Instead they directed their
riffs into electrical pickups, blowing saxes into microphones,
singing back and forth in a session jammed through cordless
headpieces and face-suckers. Slowly plucking mandolins on
one pushpanel while on the next somebody keened a bagpipe.

There were exceptions. One man whanged bells on his
rooftop, a girl played a piano under a tent covering the depths
of a gigantic pothole. Soledad caught a glimpse, inside a warehouse's loading dock, of women using steel bars to pound cables that spanned the entire breadth of the building, creating a
deep, almost subterranean vibration. And once she heard a

deep, rhythmed breathing, as of someone blowing across the top of a giant bottle, that might have been music also; but in general the tunes were cut off from her, directed to a wired audience.

Later on, as she learned more, understood more about this huge gringo *cruce,* Soledad figured—because familiarity always bred awareness of difference—she would focus on this: How much more ascetic, segregated in detail and taproot, were the tunes and rhythms stemming from the Oakland node compared to the readily recognizable traditions and styles of the *Vallenatos, Cumbia, Lantos,* merengue, and megasalsa of her own *cruce;* how much more vivid and at the same time weaker was the effect of music cropped and roped into the bright dimensions of pushpanel video. But for now— maybe because she missed Bamaca so much—what touched her were the similarities: the ubiquity of effort; the attempt at, if not the realization of, a lifestyle highly imbued with rhythm and rhyme. And that correspondence was like a crack in the revetments of exhaustion and sleep and silence and caution that she had built high around herself, through which snuck an irresistible and specific awareness of what was forever gone.

And then Soledad was crying, wiping her cheeks the way a car's wiper blades flicked away rain. She caught a glimpse of her hands. The wetness stained her index fingers and the crotch of her thumbs a deep marine blue. A quick astonishment stopped her sobs. She realized, then, her tears must have been dyed by the indigo dust this spiderbike had roared through earlier.

Stix did not turn around, did not notice, although he had told her there were mikes as well as speakers in the mantle, and she was sniffing loudly enough for him to hear. This was a man, she reminded herself, amusing herself coldly by her own triteness—he drives fast, describes objects you can see for yourself, does not listen. But he was slowing down by a half-burned security post, a sign with a faded blue dolphin

insignia reading SUBMARINE GROUP INDIA—LEVEL E CLEAR-
ANCE REQUIRED, to enter a black square of tunnel and proceed in growing darkness down a shallow, garbage-strewn
slope. The spiderbike's noise tripled as it echoed back and
forth in the tunnel. In the twin fuseaux of the headlights, the
concrete was furred with algae and moss. The smell of sewers
was strong, bringing back unwelcome associations with the
Kundura men, though in truth they had helped her, not tried to
hold her back—had led her *out* of a place like this. Up a ramp,
into a stink of salt, strong as a slap. She caught a glimpse, below and to her right, of a long concrete bay filled with black
reflections of underground water. Pushscreens lined this tunnel, framed in old tires and driftwood. They showed public-
access talk shows, a classroom, a green naked woman; they
sent fey reflections across the curved roof.

Halfway down a smaller shaft the shit smell was fully
taken over by the breath of sea, of iodine and fish and rotted
things. And fingers of mist flicked through the headlights, and
gray light grew on the cracked walls and hunks of garbage
Stix was swerving around. Then the stench of seaweed and
the roughness of cold air was all around them, and they were
outside. The motorcycle half rolled, half skidded into a slope
of grayish sand among the black pilings of a giant pier towering above, like the mother of all factories suddenly spawning
its noisy and gasoline-stinking young.

The wharf skirted the shore of a tiny cove. Walls of rust-
stained concrete protruded past a silty strand into the greasy
black water on all sides but one. To the left, the enormous
hulk of a Los Angeles–class attack submarine lay canted away
from the left-hand pier, torpedo-loading racks angled uselessly from topside hatches, its port hydroplane half buried
in silt. The single view of what Soledad presumed to be
open water was blocked by the enormous black sides of a
Malaysian car-carrier anchored in the narrow channel. A half
dozen boats—smugglers' craft, she recognized them immediately by their sharp lines, their huge exhaust vents, their camo
paint—were anchored in the lee of the derelict sub. The

rubber dinghies that had ferried the crews to shore were pulled up between the ruined warship and the wharf, almost under the limbs of an enormous willow that, through some freak coincidence of mutation and freshwater seepage, had taken root and prospered among the farthermost pilings. And, in the intersection of those details—next to the willow, by the dinghies, shadowed by the vast rusting carcass of the sub— someone had built a small restaurant, using driftwood for planks and bits of old warship for walls and roof. A line of navy-issue portholes gave off a cheeky yellow light. A waver of thick, greasy cooking smoke rose from a stovepipe. In a scavenged window beside the worm-eaten door, a sign in orange neon reading

MOLLY'S DINER
FRESH COFFEE
HOMEMADE PIE

blinked among the platoons of mist that crawled on their bellies from the harbor and slunk unnoticed past the cove into the pilings, and inland.

———————

THE DINER WAS HOT and crowded. People lined a green Formica counter, packed booths upholstered in red vinyl under the portholes. Kitsch putti and cheap china featuring U.S. presidents lined the plywood walls; thin and rangy-looking cats lay as close as they could safely get to stoves, coffee machines, humans. A miasma of real tobacco smoke drifted around the booths, mimicking the fog coming in from the sea outside. The smoke smelled good to Soledad. She realized it was because she wanted a cigarette, and also because it reminded her of home—in California it was illegal to smoke in the streets, let alone in a restaurant like this.

A lot of people knew Stix, acknowledging him with a wave, a word. Some, especially the women, glanced at Soledad with a casualness, a lack of great curiosity, that recalled her own *cruce* to her and brought back pressure to the chest. This time the tendency toward grief was swallowed up by the need to carefully plan one's footing among the tangle of chairs and feet that lay between them and the corner table Stix was aiming for.

The table was empty except for a very thin, dark adolescent with hair like an Indio's. He was working at a jambook. In the seat next to him was an animal. It stood on its hind legs, grasping a dish of milk, holding it to its mouth to drink. Periodically it put the dish down and wiped its whiskers with elegant, long-fingered paws, looking around the diner with a stare both senatorial and interested. The black mask across its eyes, the alertness, the thick fur, gave it the look of a bank robber in ski clothes. A coati, she thought. She was to learn later it was in fact the animal's gringo cousin, a raccoon.

Stix smoothed the boy's hair with one hand, and gave the animal a quick pat, which seemed to annoy them both. Two women and one man at the counter slurped coffee and grabbed from each other's hands a much-handled journal with the words SMUGGLER'S GAZETTE MONTHLY UPDATE printed across the top in greasy Garamond. "A tad final, dontcha think, Ahab?" one of the women said. "To be shot outta the sky by a Warthog, in an antique seaplane in the Celebes?"

"Such a thing as crash landings," the man said. He had a ragged gray beard and filthy yachtsman's loafers parked over a rusty single-barrel shotgun.

"Ever think the *Gazette* could be written by somebody else? I heard his daughter was doin' most of it, even when he was alive."

"Who sez?"

"Onyx said. Even weed-pirates like you listen to Onyx."

"Hawkley ain't dead," Ahab muttered stubbornly. "I kin *feel* it."

Soledad stared at them. The talk of Hawkley and his smuggling theories was another link with the *cruce,* but somehow it seemed unreal and different here, two thousand miles north and in English. She had always assumed Hawkley was a

South American with an Anglo name, like Soledad herself. A woman came around the counter and headed for their table. She was tall, in her mid-forties and, to judge by the shapes under her apron, had once possessed nicely rounded breasts and buttocks. These now sagged but in a way that was comforting, rather than unpleasant, as if age and fatigue had imparted a softness previously denied them by energy and youth. Under the apron she wore a frayed jagger's tunic, dungarees, work boots laced halfway up. She had graying blond hair that hung around her cheeks in untidy forelocks. Her mouth was large and so were her eyes. The latter were of the same very deep blue as the cadmium dust Stix had driven through earlier.

They were quick, too, those eyes, in the sense that they made connections fast, moving instantly from Stix to Soledad, staying on Soledad just long enough for the message to be precisely drafted and sent: "I knew this man before you, and though I make no claims on him now, I have his welfare at heart."

Soledad looked back for a while, then lowered her gaze. She was too tired and devoid of territory right now to play the complex games of womanhood, even to the thin extent of denying claim on the man beside her. The woman placed two mugs on the table and filled them. "The specials are quince, pecan, and strawberry-rhubarb," she announced, looking at Soledad as if saying something more significant, "but I'd avoid the strawberry-rhubarb, I were you. It came out runny." Coffee steam drifted to Soledad's nose, filling her with a powerful lust for the dark liquid. "Quince," Stix said, wrapping both hands around his coffee mug and adding, "Molly, meet Mystery Woman. Mystery Woman, Molly. One of the armored cars was stalking her," he added, glancing at Molly to see if she was impressed.

"Mystery Woman," Molly repeated, brushing a forelock out of her eyes.

"Doesn't talk," Stix said. Molly's gaze changed color. "You need some pie," she told Soledad, "you look bushed.

Fat Zeenie!"—yelling toward the counter. "Two quinces for Twelve." She threaded her way back through the diner, refilling mugs as she went. Stix took a sip of his coffee and said, "Shit that's hot." Then he leaned toward her.

"Gotta admit," he said, "Will could be right. I figger it's a fifty-fifty chance you're a narc for BON, though why the fuck they'd want another one . . ." He sighed and added a third spoonful of sugar to his java, stirring it around.

"But that's not the point, either," he went on. "Maybe you are one, maybe you're not. Real point is, for us to find out for sure we'd have to get as obsessed by security and narcs as they are. And if that happens, then the node's finished anyway. You understand what I'm saying?"

The raccoon finished the last of its milk. *"Chirrrr,"* it said. Then it picked up a spoon, stuck it in the sugar pot, dug out a heap, and licked it off. The boy tapped a key on his jambook; a detailed landscape disappeared from the screen, and was replaced by a word in Greek characters. *"Tienes abastante açucar,"* the boy told the animal, and pulled its tail. The animal whipped around and growled. The boy grinned. *"Tranquilo,"* he said.

"So I'm not gonna ask you what your name is, or who you are," Stix continued. Soledad looked up at him in surprise. "I'm not gonna push," he insisted. "But there is one thing I need from you, something I gotta ask." He looked down at his hands, which had let go of the mug and were lying on the table in front of him, half clenched, as if waiting for a tool to fill them and give them purpose. He cleared his throat; he is embarrassed, Soledad thought. "See, BON—the federal Bureau of Nationalizations—they were in touch with the government down there, in Bamaca. Well, it's not like they could do the same thing here, but we still want to know what exactly happened, it could tell us something about their tactics.

"You're the first person we've talked to from there, since it happened."

She looked at his face now. She had been trained by Maria

Gisela not to look at men so directly but that training had been eroded in the *cruce,* where people were usually too busy for such sensibilities.

Stix returned her gaze. His eyes now were like the second or third layer under the *selva* canopy, a dappling of browns and leaf colors when the sun was not directly overhead.

He glanced down at his hands again. She found she wanted to tell him something, anything, she had no idea what he was looking for. She could tell him some of what happened, though the real secret of that violence was that it had no meaning or message.

For no good reason she wanted Stix's hands to find the direction they needed. And she needed to talk about the *cruce,* longed to trust someone with the bloody car wreck of her feelings after three weeks of being among people whose trustworthiness could be accurately measured by how much more you could pay them than the next man.

But something had happened to her in the convent, and after that she could not remember, let alone comprehend, how everything ended. And although she could work her throat muscles, open her glottis, flutter her tonsils, pump air in and out, ever since fire came to the *cruce* it had been absolutely impossible for her to combine the different elements to create speech out of them.

She tried again, without making it obvious—an "ah" that came out like a soft retch, which she covered by taking a sip of coffee. The coffee here was the usual watery gringo stuff. Perhaps because of watching Stix, or the *coati,* she had put too much sugar in.

Suddenly she felt like she was going to throw up. The smell of cigarettes, which before had tasted so good, now seemed vile and rough as an emetic.

She stared at the coffee, willing her gorge to subside, to do something it was supposed to do. The coffee looked the color of San Isidor deep in its ash gullies, before the sun reached them. And that simple association somehow both tempered the nausea and triggered in her the stirring of memories she might tell this man if she could talk. It was no hypnotic reflex working here, let alone a do-it-yourself version of Fernsehen's video therapy; it was simply another way of saying that she had not come to terms with the transition of the *cruce* from a place outside of her to a geography inside; and telling the story of how it had been before the attack would allow her both to avoid addressing that change, and ease it—by going back in her mind, and back and back until the diner and all its gringo talk and unfamiliar smells faded around her, and there really was no barrier at all.

SIX

SHE IS WORRIED AT first that the apartment will be rented to someone else before she makes it back to the fishing harbor. But when she does get back and tracks down the owner, who is loading ice into wooden boxes so as to ship out six hundred kilos of giant yellow eels with black spots and reddish eyes, she learns it is still available. He takes her upstairs and she understands then this is not a great bargain and in fact no one else has even looked at this place in some time. The three rooms are heavy with dust, there will be no heat in the rainy season, and the smell of fish, though mingled with other and more pleasant odors of the fishing harbor, is too powerful to justify the high price (for the *cruce*) he wants for it. She has a strong and, as it turns out, accurate feeling that she could do far better elsewhere. But she slaps down a month's rent in advance, partly because it is still absurdly cheap by Walled City standards; partly because, like any good bourgeoise, this flight from her old life is justified only by the availability of real estate and the possibility of a job; and partly because the view of sea from the front room is as open and full of light as the view from her apartment in the Walled City is closed and skyless and dark.

He gives her the key, shows her how the water works and where to place the bucket when it rains, and leaves. She sits on the floor, staring in some wonder at the sunlight streaming through the dust she raised in the front room. But she cannot let herself think—the possible implications of this (albeit tentative) step she has taken are too terrifying to address casually, in an unfurnished flat, without the protection of personal objects as votive and bulwark against her own weakness. So she goes straight out to the Slave Market and buys a bed made of bamboo and rattan, two wooden chairs and a kitchen table; also a plate and cup, some cheap silverware, a towel. She is still bemused by the absence of the objects that surrounded her in her old life, by how necessary, it now appears, some of them were. She is beginning to wish she had brought some along, instead of choosing to start completely afresh, if that is indeed what she's doing.

Almost under Lo Pano, in a stall laden with earrings in the shape of parrots, among a gaggle of Military-green and Spix's macaws, she spots a pair of birds with the same indigo wingfeathers she saw at Jorge's. She asks the vendor what kind of bird they are, and he says they are macaws from Los Altos Province, under the southwest cordillera, but he doesn't know their name. She buys the earrings and puts them on immediately. After that she hires a man at a stall labeled HANDCART DELIVERIES—there is, she thinks, a service for everything in this market.

Once the furniture has been delivered she arranges her music in a neat pile, goes to a Cadillac around the corner, and carries home two cups of *tinto*. Drinks the coffee. Smokes a Galaxy. Reads through Dvořák's opus 85, the "tone pictures," her fingers tapping rhythms against the rough mangrove tabletop. Looks out the window, at the orange roof of the *pilotis* houses below her, at the clean blue of the South Atlantic. The wind breathes in and out the window like a contented dog.

An explosion sounds, muffled, from inland, briefly rattling her new forks. She does not think of Miguel. She wishes her accordion were fixed. She does not think of Miguel.

Now her fingers drum exercises on the table—it is what they always do, when they have been deprived of work for too long.

She thinks, I am going to need an instrument of some kind.

———

SHE SPENDS TWO NIGHTS in the apartment and one and a half days: reading, smoking, drinking coffee, and eating hot *butifarras*—a spiced ball of fish with coconut, ginger, and garlic she buys from the stalls outside. No one bothers her, almost no one notices her. She meets a woman downstairs, with three children. The woman repeatedly offers her *tinto*. The apartment grows around Soledad, the empty rooms symbolizing the space that has grown in her life over the two years since she left the Conservatory in the capital. Since she met Miguel.

She still thinks of Miguel, but only a little, and only in small details. These are all she now can recall or, possibly, handle. She is aware of the proximity of Jorge Echeverria, especially in the room she has chosen to sleep in, which faces south and west in the direction of the volcano—you can see the Barrio des Anglais if you look to the right. Strangely, his proximity in the *cruce* feels weaker than his nearness in her mind, as an anode of opportunity that were she to complete the circuit might come to life, electrically speaking.

She tells herself the opportunity he represents is not primarily emotional, or even sexual. And she is only partially deluding herself, because the feeling she got from him was real for her, the sense that in the force and lyricism of his words, in the mixing that went on in his apartment, in the overall shaking-together of previously unmatched verbs and rhythms, lies a chthonic strength that not only powers this offbeat and smelly enclave but can also serve to recharge her own worn-out batteries; enough anyhow to give her life a boost, maybe even a real change in direction.

————

ON THE MORNING OF her third day in the *cruce* she wakes early. Only the very tip of the volcano has been touched by the gilding of light. She does not look to the right, though the pull of des Anglais has been growing every time she looks out this window.

She likes the feeling of being awake before the sun, before

even the fish dealers are up with their calls and boxhooks. Without turning on the lights, she walks naked into the tiny kitchen and sets water to boil. The gas flame turns her fingers blue, and the thought comes to her, They are suffocating for lack of music. She turns from the stove and catches a glimpse of the alley separating this building from the row of *pilotis* next door. She is fairly certain the building closest across the alley is a whorehouse—furtive men at any rate go in and out at all hours, and the clothes of women only flap from the drying line, and always an oil lamp shines over the door, as if assuring the men who must resort to this service that the comfort of rented women will never be denied them, at least while they have cashchips.

This morning, though, there is no movement. Just to the side of the cone of ocher light cast by the lamp stands a broad-shouldered man dressed in a baggy jacket, of the kind that would not show a shoulder-holster strapped underneath. He stands motionless and very straight in the partial shadow, his face turned upward—eyes aimed directly at the windows of her apartment.

F2, she thinks, most likely; but it is a practical certainty. The codes of the man: his build, the angle of his back, the coat, the fact that he is here at all, allow only a tiny margin for error.

She slips out of the kitchen and gets dressed, keeping to wedges of her apartment that cannot be seen from the street. It does not surprise her they found her so quickly. Miguel telephones every day, and after the second day without contact he would have called the Conservatory, and then F2. Only a few interviews—no one wastes time lying to F2— would have led to the *basukista* and then to Haddad, and here. For she gave Haddad her new address, so he could send the accordion when it was fixed.

What does surprise her is the breadth and depth of her fury. Her hands shake as she buttons her dress. She breathes in sharp explosions. She collects her music papers, drinks coffee till the fish market opens. The man is still in the alley.

She goes downstairs, knocks at the shop's inside door and, making some excuse, leaves through the fishmonger's front entrance, out of sight of the watcher in the alley.

———————

IT SHOULD BE HARD to find Jorge's house among the incredible warren of jury-rigged dwellings that have grown up in the cracks and frontiers of Barrio des Anglais but somehow she, who is not notable for her spatial memory, kept an accurate picture in her mind of the relative positions of volcano, convent, and the section of slope his house was built on. She only gets lost twice before happening upon it, from uphill. The combination of old sugar mansion and the rickety towers of plywood and cardboard surmounted by the two VW roofs sticks out, even over the crazy skyline of this place. She picks around the raucous sense-impressions of a cockfight going on in what once was a marble reception hall. At the top of the stairs she hesitates. But the fury is still strong inside her, as is the hunger in her fingers—she can see quite clearly in her mind the chewed up Mason & Hamlin that squats in the room beside the grape arbor. She knocks, too hard at first, then more politely.

Silence only behind the door, or at least, absence of sounds from human occupants. An Umbanda-Cargo axhead, wrapped in burlap with various spells and herbs that are supposed to protect this place from evil spirits, hangs on a nail over the lintel.

Vaguely, through cracks in the door, comes a glitter of guitars from a neighboring building, the slop of sea wind.

The floor shakes once, gently. She has noticed that these explosions, or whatever they are, occur regularly in the *cruce*.

Without warning the door scrapes. He is standing there, his hair pointed in a dozen different directions, wearing only a cotton shirt that drops as far as his knees. He looks curiously childlike in that getup, despite his salt-and-pepper stubble and stale breath. She will always remember, even through the bad patches, how childlike also is his reaction to her, an open-eyed wonder that she should be standing there, paired with an utter lack of curiosity about the mechanics of her arrival, as if he still believed in Father Christmas and magical transport and so did not have to waste time on the irrelevance of motivation and maps.

"You," he says finally, "the accordion player," and opens the door wide.

On the way up Teton she made sure she had her explanations ready. They are true, after all, he mentioned teaching jobs and she needs work and most of all she needs an instrument. But the ease of his welcome allows her to put off that awkwardness, and finally she forgets it almost entirely. The apartment helps, it is so much a parcel of what the node is coming to represent for her at its best, a higher form of the view from her own place—a representation of openness and possibility, of refusal to close off, or profit from such a closing. The place looks bigger under the sun's regard. It is also cleaner and less cluttered than she remembered, though that's only to be expected. The presence of the sea at one end—its horizon making geometrical union of a political impossibility, between the City of Boats to the northeast and the towers of the Customs building in the Walled City to the east—is of course more pronounced, now that everything is more than a half-tone shape in moonlight.

What strikes her now, in the light of day, is how the olive green of distant mountains, the brash blue of sky, the secret indigo of the Bahia, seem to carve this suite of rooms into corresponding domains of light. And in those domains, the tones of Jorge Echeverria's life—the scumbled shades of paperback books, the scoured mahogany tables, the expensive azure ink and cheap ivory paper, the draftsman's pens and filled ashtrays and cups empty of *tinto,* the blue macaw and black-billed *agobequis,* the mawkish figureheads and candles, the Qabalistic qophs and zayins of Umbanda votives, the musty cushions and bright-stringed instruments, the eroded yellow stucco—are stacked and nailed and propped into some kind of coherent whole.

She could easily have gotten spooked that first morning. Partly she is terrified at this brashness so unlike what she expects from herself in general. It hints at something even more frightening, which is the scale and viciousness of the situation that caused her to do what she did over the last few days. She is mortally distrustful of her own motivation.

An aquatint by Joachim Boaz. A photo of Jorge, with his arms around an overweight balding man, a dedication: *A mi compañero de corazón—Pablo Neruda.*

Everything about Jorge's flat speaks of the kind of openness and productivity that she could not deny without denying the part of herself that longs for the black-and-white building blocks of tune, the sweet meshing of chords. She is too self-aware not to recognize the circularity of this argument, and too intelligent not to recognize that circularity sometimes highlights links to other structures of logic you haven't gotten around to recognizing yet.

At any rate, except for one more thought, she does not annotate herself further that morning—drinks *caffe con leche* under the arbor and listens to Jorge and is more convinced than ever that this odd man sees no important distinction between speaking and reciting, and none at all between reciting and the crafting of verse, or at least highly charged prose.

And here is the last thought she remembers of that morning: if this state of acceptance is like a circus act, a series of graceful figures doing impossible things in thin air, then Jorge's verse-talk must be the big tent, the lights, the ringmaster and tigers and trumpets and clowns that weave it all together.

And she falls for a circus every time.

He starts off as soon as he has made the coffee, waving his cup and spilling a good quarter of it. "This *tinto*," he says, "I get it from an albino who runs his own pirogue, and it carries the burn and rasp and fucking corruption of the *terras pretas* that spawned it."

"It's not as sweet as Antioquia," she replies, mentally kicking herself for trying to keep up, "the pocket valleys."

He brings out mangoes, papayas. He fries breadfruit, the *friapen* no one in the Walled City ever eats because it's supposed to be peasant food.

"I liked your party," she says.

"I'm sorry about the fight," he replies. "Dolores—my daughter—has a thirst for danger. When she risks her body she submits to this illusion: she can cut the throats of her parents for losing interest in her."

He looks away, almost for the first time.

"It's an evil thing not to have someone interested in you, as a child," he continues, "it guarantees you will, in turn, become uninteresting, perhaps out of spite."

"You lost interest?"

He laughs without laughing.

"We abandoned her in our minds. We thought the stories we made up were more colorful—or that's what the Fernsehen man said. The video-therapist." He grunts, jabbing a finger at the Zenith squatting like a Buddha on a coffee table. "That was his first screen—Fernsehen's. I bought it at an auction. Our idea was, we could make up for parental lacunae with therapy." He sighs. "But it was a good party, nonetheless."

Still talking, about a friend of Ruiz's and also about Dolores, she thinks, though she won't pick him up on it.

"Sometimes the sky is full of fish, and they come down to swallow people on earth, their bodies, their thoughts, even their music, and these people do not know what kind of life they have been living until the fish vomits them out and they look back and say, 'Oh, a pike with golden scales, or a stingray with a bad liver that burrows in the mud.'"

It reminds her of the fish shop she lives above, that aphorism, further proof of the unity of everything that has happened to her—not real proof maybe, but the continuation of a certain spin.

"You really are full of shit," she says.

He laughs, and this time he means it.

"I am full of shit, but it's like the river, *chérie,* or so I like to think—in the shit sometimes are flakes of gold, at least a productive dirt."

Of course he is aware of his pretensions, he's aware he is performing, and at the same time the performance is so much a part of his craft that, as with any good actor, the lie becomes the reality of the man.

And she stays all morning, she and Jorge talking almost as easily as they did at the party. She is high on the rough tobacco of Galaxys as well as on too much upriver coffee, which skims her as high in a different way as the buzz of *tafia* did three nights previously. In this high she does not feel devoid of music because among the warrens of Bidonville surrounding different songs and tunes are starting up, like larvae hatching in the ever-increasing heat—here, an a cappella *lanto* from an old man in a cracked voice; there, a gaggle of kids banging on homemade *requintos* and tin cans; downstairs, a boom box playing Jasmin; a group of *Vallenato* singers rehearsing. The cockfighters take a break and a bunch of them troop off to cheer, and then join in, a sequence of *Vallenatos* particularly lurid in pornographic details. A scarlet flash blooms on a hill in the distance behind San Isidor: army units firing on Adornistas, or Adornistas feuding with *guaqueros.* It is followed seconds later by a faint and abstract "snap." Later she cannot separate any of it. The different tastes of music straining through the wind and smells around them, the rhythm of his voice, the near-murderous intensity with which he looks at her, are blended like different juices in a good *batido* with the thrill in her own esophagus, the words she uses to describe the *Vallenatos,* what she thinks of *Vallenatos,* or the work of Gabriela Mistral.

Then, it stops. Or rather, Jorge stops talking, as the bells of the convent echo. She counts backward in her head, in the chamber of their sudden silence, twelve chimes. She has been talking to this man for three and a half hours.

"I have to go to work," he says, rubbing at his stubble,

looking at her sideways, almost furtively. "But you don't have to leave, if you don't want. Help yourself to coffee, I—" He pulls at one earlobe. "I like talking to you."

She smiles at this. It is so typical of this man, already she can see that, the combination of deceit and generosity, the use of one to enhance the other, a stage-management justifiable only by a smile and the sense, as she apprehended earlier, that the whole performance is carried out for the sake of a more graceful construct.

"I never told you," she says, "the reason I came."

"You want to start teaching, but that is easy—"

"That, and I hoped—"

He raises his hand.

"You hoped to find me here, already you were bowled over by my Dionysian magnetism."

She does not smile.

"If you let me finish . . ." she says, and her fingers stretch of their own volition, like the claws of a cat extracting as he thinks of a clean leap that will land him on the spine of a mouse. "I hoped to practice on your piano."

———

ONLY A MONTH OR so later she will think back to that day and feel sure that she did not leave the apartment for a week after going there the first time. In fact, on the day concerned, she is not certain she will stay, because she isn't convinced she'll be able to play there at all—in her plans for the piano she had always assumed he would be gone much of the day, working in a studio the way people at the Conservatory did or doing readings perhaps or meeting a publisher; the reason his absence is important lies in the modified panic that has been the most profound curse of her professional life.

She worked on it, of course. She, too, went to a Fernsehen clinic, this one in the capital, for treatment (hours of movie clips featuring performances, or soap operas based on the lives of Chopin, Schumann, Brahms). And things improved to some extent, because now she can play stuff she has not written—even highly technical stuff, the more technical the better in fact—for strangers in highly formal surroundings.

But the music she writes falls apart in her fingers like overfloured dough if she plays it for anyone else. Even for her father, even for Miguel. Thus, when Jorge opens the French doors for her and watches her sit uncomfortably at the Mason & Hamlin, she plays a few scales and a Russian piece that ripple with technique and an utter lack of real dynamic.

But then, as if sensing her discomfort, he says, "I'll be in my study, you can play as loud as San Isidor erupting, I don't hear anything when I'm working." It must be some measure of the hold he already has on her that she believes him without thinking about it.

She plays through the hot part of the afternoon, takes a cigarette break during which she can hear him mumbling to himself on the porch. Between mumbles, his pen scratches audibly at the cheap foolscap.

Back at the piano she practices again, scales, trills, more scales, a Saint-Saëns exercise. Her fingers are clumsy and slow from disuse. After that she works on a Dvořák humoresque she has focused on mastering. It goes all right despite her fingers' stiffness, except for an adaggio movement with a rollicking left hand, chords switching rapid-fire over three registers, that she never was able to get the hang of. When she is sick of that she goes to her notes and does improvs on details of tune for the *Concerto de la Selva,* the project she has been working on since her second year in the Capital Conservatory, the one she has been unable to complete or even work on except in details of tune so minuscule she has no idea how they possibly could fit into the overall piece.

It goes no better nor worse than usual. At least, she reflects, it is possible for her to work on her own music when someone else is working in the apartment, and this is new—she could never play *Selva* except in soundproofed rooms in the Bamaca Conservatory. And she always stopped, at the *estancia,* when her father came back from the mine.

The room has bruised red and brown with sunset by the

time she is finished. She goes into the main room. The indigo macaw whistles. The sea is the color of Jorge's ink. A note in the kitchen reads "I had to go out. Help yourself to dinner: *macapa* stew in the icebox." A key—the front door key, it looks like—holds down the note against the breeze.

She is worn out from work. In the planed-off emotional surfaces of fatigue it suddenly seems dead wrong that she should be in the apartment of a stranger who leaves her notes full of implied information, the meaningful ellipses that normally would be built up only over months of intimacy. She finds also that she is vaguely upset by something else not-said—his lack of reaction to her playing. The Fernsehen therapist saw this immediately, and maybe this is the real secret; under the diffidence of stage fright, she is in her own way as much of a prima donna as Jorge is. Although she does not like to perform, especially on the piano—and this is one reason she only attained the rank of assistant lecturer in the Conservatory—when people do hear her play she is used to them complimenting her technique at least.

And she did not want Jorge to listen to *La Selva*. But she cracked off that Dvořák so nicely, fitting together the different allegro movements with real skill, that she would have liked him to admire her for it. She can feel her jaw grinding, out of fury, not at Jorge but at herself, for requiring approbation from this man.

She gathers her notes and leaves without writing anything down beside his words.

She also takes the key, putting it in her shoulder bag, and quite aware of herself as she is doing it.

———

WHEN SHE RETURNS THE next day—fairly late in the morning, she doesn't want to wake him again and she is also a little less anxious to get to work early, now she knows she has access to an instrument—he is already out. She can tell he has been back in the interval by the remains of breakfast on the writing table, but there is no note.

Her usual timidity floods back, as if her audacity in coming here, staying here, playing Dvořák for him the day before, had been only a fluke, a cryptic holdback of the tide that must always engulf her. And the timidity suggests, That key was a paperweight only, you had no right or reason to presume access to this man's house, and your gall in doing so will cost you what little friendship and alliance you have built up thus far.

She ambles aimlessly around the flat. The sounds of breeze, of birds, of outside music and commerce seem as dead and isolating as yesterday they felt comfortable and right. She feels empty. She senses she might be working up to a case of diarrhea, probably the water in the *cruce* is dirtier than that in the Walled City; sewers not maintained, wells contaminated. She remembers the open latrines of Ensevli, the smell of urine in the market. The occasional explosions that shake the ground of the *cruce,* she has been told, are set off by government engineers building a new sewer tunnel for the Walled City; of course it will not serve *cruce* residents.

"What the fuck am I doing in this place?" she whispers to herself.

A sheet of paper rolled in his typewriter reads:

> *No! The canyons of dust*
> *in which semen runs will not*
> *slow*
> *this taxi* (crossed out)
> *Onibus* (crossed out) *from*

She makes up her mind to leave, and puts the key back on the kitchen table. She checks the piano to make sure she did not forget any papers last night, no scraps of her concerto abandoned as hostages to a misunderstanding. A bowl of soursop is set on the piano's closed cover. Her cheeks stretch. The feeling of diarrhea leaves as abruptly as it came. When she lifts the bowl to open the piano, a spill of paper falls from the chinks between the fruit in which it was stuck.

> *this truck from running*
> *down the greenest roads of October*
> *through the nave of a cathedral*
> *dry of music*
> *"Ave, ave"*
> *gone hard, no soft, as desire.*

The words obviously typed on the ancient machine on his worktable, and stained yellow by juices from the fruit.

She picks up a *guanabana,* and licks a drop from its green skin.

Abruptly, she drags the bench over, organizes her sheet music, and begins to play.

———

AFTER THIS SECOND DAY of practice her fingers are starting to work reliably again and she has figured out a technique that suddenly breaks the back of the adagio left hand in the Dvořák. For the first time ever she runs through it with only two technical faults and a kind of mastery in timing, an ease with the overall hydraulics, that has eluded her so far. After doing that with the concerto she takes a break, pulling a book from his table—*Contraband,* it is called, *A Primer of Hawkleyite Smuggling Philosophy.*

> The jury is still out on whether *cruces* can maintain the thirty-seven percent-plus threshold, where almost half the activities of its inhabitants are fulfilled either within that *cruce,* by trade with a *cruce* outside, or by independent contracts brooking no commerce with Org or Megorg. It is not even clear whether the few *cruces* that have achieved that level of independence—Sixth Street/Nueva York, Manila—can maintain the essential level of activity without . . .

She goes back to the Mason & Hamlin. The small success she achieved with the Dvořák buoys her, gives her the courage she needs to pick up her own concerto, in particular a detail early on that always made her feel desperate in her throat, what she calls "The Sunrise." It describes the way the jungle around Glen MacRae seemed to fall silent, hold its breath in that short instant between thick night and no-holds-barred daylight—every one of the millions of creatures in the *selva* stopped in awe at this intrusion of time into their layered vertical space, this basic reminder of mortality and conception both, like the hesitation before orgasm, like the breath caught before dying. She has always written it as minor but today she decides to trim it with seventh chords, avoiding all tremolo stops in her Fourneaux (*putain,* she wishes she had the accordion!)—a progression of uncertainties, 6/8 and held beats, a final pause: and then a single held note, folding finally into G-major and the warm crowding of themes and secondary melodies as every last one of those creatures still alive and not actively dying or fucking greets the usual and extraordinary arrival of day.

She picks up a pen, scribbles the changes. Not bad, she thinks, not bad at all. When she puts down the pen the sound of rustling paper continues.

She walks to the porch. Dusk has fallen. The running lights of a cruise ship carefully approach the Las Animas channel. Jorge is lying in one of the hammocks, yellowed by a kerosene lamp, scribbling in a notebook. She says, "I didn't hear you come in." He says, "You were busy. Do you want to stay for dinner this time?" Dinner in Bamaca will not happen for another three hours, but he means more than dinner. She thinks, Do I want to have dinner and whatever else that means with this man with grimy fingernails who sneaks in and out of his house and listens, presumably, to my most secret music and then has absolutely *nothing* to say about it?

She shakes her head, recognizing the gross vanity underlying that thought. More important—checking back in the cavities of her mind—is the lack of blockage in her, the lack of the stopping anger she once would have felt because a man, a stranger, anyone, had heard a piece of *La Selva*.

And stronger than that, and yet a part of it also, is the excitement, the sense of having the energy needed to follow different paths, to make concertos (even flawed), to accept the flaws as part of the process and not be thrown by them like a rider off a fence-stumbled horse—the energy so huge she entertains a sudden fancy that she could fly, if need be, from balcony to balcony across this surreal barrio. This apartment feels to her like a cockpit where she might be able to grasp the controls, here, now, and rocket into the sun, or skim the sea like a bird, all the way to Africa if she wanted.

Some of the feeling comes from the good work she put into *Concerto de la Selva*. She recognizes that even more of it comes from this man with eyes like a jungle well, filled with objects of previous sacrifice. Whatever the details, he has listened to her music, and not been warned off by the agents of her psyche. And she has denied excitement for so long that she has no choice in the matter, none at all.

———

JORGE'S COOKING IS PURE Bamaca, which means it is like the Creole spoken here, a base of French from the Cayenne gold-panners who migrated to the Delta, and some Spanish, with accents of Portuguese mixed in. It reminds her of her mother, and this does not seem so bad or Elektra-oriented, only correct in the way all objects seem to mesh when the underlying conditions are at peace. He makes *lamohue,* cakes of salt cod mashed and fried with onions, peppers, garlic, coconut meat, jalapenos, and ginger; a salad of mangoes, avocado, and *friapen*. They drink a *vinho verde* from the northern hills. It's a watery wine that, when other wines would flood and wash them away in such quantities, goes down the way soda would, simply floating them like bathers till they touch bottom only with their metaphorical toes. They kiss like an extension of eating and drinking, the taste of garlic and young grape on their lips; they take off their clothes as an extension of the intimacy of lips. Making love should be a conclusion of that, as well as of the far deeper intimacy of stories they have told each other already, in tiny sidebars, around turns in conversation.

His touch, diffident, almost reverent, confirms a provisional assessment of subtlety. He takes out a condom without her asking. At the last minute, she asks him not to make love, not yet. It feels wrong—she has not had time to mark the passing of Miguel, of what may, or may not, be her old life. She touches him with his hand; he touches her, between her legs, as if he were polishing a tiny stone, peeling a muscadet, his big hands sure in small movements. They come in silence, one after the other. The fever moves at the speed of light and makes her hair and toenails glow serially like spark plugs. He locks his ankles around hers as he goes to sleep. The *cruce* makes noise from every direction around them; bursts of laughter, a radio playing merengue, mototaxis revving, parrots chuckling, a gunshot. His liquid is first hot then quickly cool on the lower mesa of her stomach.

———

SHE STAYS AT THE apartment four days this time. When her clothes grow dirty she wears his long shirts. He has a dozen of them, mostly old patched cotton, soft as a second skin. She thinks she has now shed not only her old life, but her new one as well—by staying at Jorge's and living in his shirts she has taken on an illegal identity, an alter ego that is older and vaguely masculine, with all the perverse independence that implies. She has no schedule, no appointments. The man from F2 still keeps watch at her darkened windows, telephoning the Customs House with increasing frequency to warn them of her bizarre lack of movement. The accordion repairman, Haddad, leaves unnecessary notes on her apartment door; twice she has caught him following her, always four or six people behind, pretending to do something completely different as she shops in the Slave Market; but Haddad has never followed her here.

She does not even think much about the Fourneaux-Dallapé. All of this is the symbol and surveyor of everything

she no longer is attached to. Nothing around Soledad can link
her, positively or negatively, to obligation or a fixed pattern of
hours.

She rises just after dawn, makes herself coffee, goes to the
piano. Between pieces, between riffs even, she lies in a hammock by the porch and listens to the *cruce* wake up around
her. Returning to the instrument she finds those shouts and
rooster crows, those arguments, songs and plumbing noises,
working their way out of her through her fingerpads, inform-
ing not only her approach to the Dvořák but the notes she
writes for *Selva*. She wants to keep them out of the concerto—
this is, after all, about the jungle, and her father's geographical stand against it—but the change in rhythms, the life in
these new sounds, is too strong and basic to exclude. Jorge
doesn't help because the poems he recites to her—he does
this frequently, unlike her he is a performer at heart and no
audience is too small for his art, if he has a meter problem he
will declaim the piece at her, over lunch or rum, pounding at
the words till they change or fit—the poems are at least as
strong as the *cruce,* fueled by a rhythm that draws its strength
from exactly the same source.

"Of what use is a root" he recites—it is part of a new cycle he is working on, the *Desdichado* cycle he calls it, grum-
bling it out through a snack of *vatapas* and coffee.

> *Of what use is a root*
> *that does not reach the volcano's sex.*
> *Of what use a love*
> *bound by the shadows' track?*
> *Desdichado*
> *Desdichado*
> *This land is sad as a wound*
> *though chained in terror your birds*
> *fill my eyes with sun*

And without realizing how or why, when she goes back to
the concerto, the words will scan inside her as she plays,

parched in cobbles still
I gulp your rivers whole

causing her to waste pages of paper and hours of work in writing it down and then eradicating it.

The problem grows in scale. The dawn passage on which she worked the other day preserves the feel of *selva:* what it was like to wake up alone behind the mist of mosquito netting and look over the pastures to the enormous trees rising out of a second mist from the river. But everything she wrote since has too much joke and talk in it for a place in which human life will always be a footnote. Just as the Manopani are footnotes, living as footnotes, breechclothed in their tiny clearings under the great canopy, praying to jaguars, monkeys, magical ants.

She explains her problem to Jorge over lunch one day. It is raining, a histrionic downpour, an ozone shower drifting over the cordillera from the Pacific and thudding so hard on the veranda that every drop lifts the dust ten centimeters in ocher spurts like the smoke of shellfire. Their ankles under the table are twisted around each other; it has become a habit with them. "There is nothing there but the forest for me," she says. "He loved me, my father—I know he did—but his love came out in projects, usually something to do with the mine. I could go to the forest but I had to have protection, even then there were guerrillas hiding in the edges. Just time to pick up an egg, or a feather, the shed skin of a branch boa. I loved those things but I never found what I was really looking for, which was why my mother could not love the forest as I did, and why she never came back from the mountains the times it mattered. I think—"

"I think you know," Jorge says.

"Why she didn't come back?"

"No. That was not your question."

"No—"

"Or maybe it was, yeh. But the question—"

"About the concerto. You mean—"

"You know."

She pauses. In any other man the pompous ellipses of such a conversation would drive her to fury. It occurs to her that she is filling in blanks in what he says, implying wisdom he may not have. But the fact is that she does know and she knew from the first how to solve the problem. For it involves not moving or changing the concerto, but shifting her own position in it so she is not working on something static, a set piece, something she at some level already conceived and finished in her mind—but rather a dynamic work that includes what came before, what comes now, what might come later.

"It has to do with the *cruce,* too," she says.

"Who knows?" Jorge puts his fingers to his lips and whistles through them, softly. "It's your piece. All I know is"—he stabs a finger at her—"*you* already know."

"Facile," she accuses. "Regurgitated Fernsehen."

Freeing her ankles, she walks onto the porch. The rain instantly soaks her and the shirt she is wearing so she is as good as naked through the thin cloth. A boy in the uphill *favela* calls to her appreciatively. She pays no attention, she barely notices. Maybe she can let the notes come now? she thinks. Fernsehen or no Fernsehen, she can make the concerto as long and varied as her life. She can change the name. If the notes don't work, she can wait until they do. She can turn the concerto *into* her life, and vice versa.

The feeling of broken handcuffs is as strong and total as the rain, which is actually increasing in power. She tilts her head upward and opens her mouth, it fills in a matter of seconds with the cool, metallic water of clouds.

———

A MORE FORMAL EDUCATION takes place during that time—a time that now has gone beyond the first four days, into the period when she has established a more normal rhythm, returning to her apartment two or three nights in the week for rest, for solitude. Though the epiphany she reached the second day is still active; the sense that she can allow this man at least to listen to the music she writes, as long as he is engrossed in his own writing, or as long as she doesn't know he is listening; she is still uncomfortable when she stops playing and doesn't hear the scratch of his pen and does not know where he stands physically. This feeling is mutating also, as it becomes part of a growing effort to preserve a minimum of independence from the great diesel of Jorge's life and influence. Anyway, the bulk of her days and nights she still spends at Jorge's, even teaching there, pupils Jorge has found for her, on the Mason & Hamlin she composes at.

They are making love now. It started the fourth night, just as she was about to leave. It was too quick, over too fast, it had been too long for him, he said, coughing, apologizing. But it was fine for her, not to let the fever get too high, let it lift slowly from the length of her body. Speed kept her thoughts clear. And, as if to compensate for the missing colors of orgasm, he enumerates for her—lying back in the stale tumult of the couch—the colors he saw in places he used to live. He had been a consular officer, like Durrell, like Neruda, a poet disguised as a bureaucrat writing advertisements for a government he did not believe in from places she has never visited. London. Barcelona. Shanghai. "They were the distillation of my cowardice," he said, "those press releases I wrote, and it showed. But it was all so subtle, nobody got the joke." He chuckled harshly.

The poems, of course, came out under a different name. If they had taken on some of the gray-brown tones of the Home Counties, the smoked tonalities of the Bund, the harsh terracotta repression of Catalonia, at heart they were always about Bamaca, and Bamaca always must include in its fiction the bone-cement structure that kept infants, in some villages, in many *favelas,* crying from a dearth of milk. "When the violence came," he tells her now, "I found that even if I'd once had the guts, in the grayness of my soul I bartered away the ability to live the way I wrote: Yeh, I had become a diplomat. I took on a new identity at that point," he said, "the hidden rebel, the secret plotter. But though I believed in the plots and the ideas behind them, the *force* here"—he slapped the table beside them with the knuckles of one hand—"the force was a diplomat, yeh, changing character to suit."

The deception saved his life. Writers who supported the Frente and then the Morena government were picked up before dawn and shot at the bottom of emerald mines, or forced out of planes high over the South Atlantic.

She gets the odd but distinct feeling that while he remains a performer, while he is far more open with his emotions than she could ever be with hers, he might never have told her this if she had come or even faked an orgasm with him.

———

IT IS A WEEK or ten days after they have first made love, during one of her increasingly rare nights in her own apartment, that she is woken by a noise she cannot place.

She lies still, aware of the noise by its reverberations, by the fact that it no longer exists; waiting for it to repeat itself.

She is naked under the sheet. Since about a week after she first went to Jorge's apartment she has taken to sleeping without clothes. All she wears is the parrot earrings, because she is so used to them now she forgets to take them off. She thinks of sleeping naked as a recognition of her own body, of the delight she takes in its pleasure, of the joy Jorge finds there as well, for he likes to see her naked or even what he calls "invisibly" nude—simply imagining her with nothing on under a shirt, he says, is as exciting to him as the real thing.

She knows, however, that her fledgling naturism is really based on something quite different. Making love with Miguel, while pleasurable enough, always included a tinge of embarrassment, of furtiveness because of the secrecy he employed to make their encounter possible. It was part and parcel of the excitement at first; later, it became part of her boredom. Whereas here nothing condemns what she is doing, neither in the gaze she directs upon herself nor in the eyes of others who know what is going on, in other words Hector Ruiz and a couple of other friends of Jorge's. So what she truly celebrates in her nudity is this: the ability to be a sexual egoist, without the moral opprobrium of the Walled City, or of Dona Serena, or the perpetually slamming influence of the One Holy, Catholic, and Apostolic Church glowering from its black cathedral in the heart of the tourist town.

The sea wind cools her breasts. The *cruce* is heavy with music tonight, more so than normal. Various drums compete for mastery of rhythm. Two men sing the same *Vallenato,* one of Jorge's:

> *Si mou estoma fue un chien*
> *je le promenerais parmi les cuartos*
> *oú tu estais*

The sound comes again. It is sobbing, hopeless, uncontrolled, of the kind so deep and damaging it can only come in waves that allow the mourner to breathe, and thus survive, in between. So close that for a moment she imagines it might even be herself, or the self she vouchsafes to dreams, crying in the parallel reality of unconsciousness. She rises quickly, puts on leggings and a shirt, and walks downstairs.

The door to Cloodine's apartment is ajar as always. Her children sleep in twin hammocks slung at one end of the living area. The infant too is asleep, in a swaddle of none-too-clean blankets on the tiled floor. Cloodine is slumped on a bench at the indigo window, her head cradled on arms which in turn are entwined on the window ledge, two meters below Soledad's window, which is why it sounded so near.

Soledad hesitates. Cloodine's dark brown hair is unfastened. It covers her face completely from this angle, like a deliberate affirmation of privacy. But Soledad finds she cannot listen to sobbing such as this without doing something, because doing something means dealing, directly if clumsily, with whatever makes Cloodine feel this way; while listening passively means she would have to understand such sadness through the prism of herself and her own history.

Her ego again, Soledad thinks, feeling its own way to op-
timum health through the debris of someone else's dharma.

Cloodine jumps when Soledad touches her. The fright
shuts off her sobbing. Then, wiping her face with the edge of
her forearm, not looking at Soledad, she gets up, walks to the
stove, and starts heating water.

"Tinto?" she offers, when she can make her voice work
right. The strain of that effort makes Soledad's chest ache.

"Cloodine," Soledad says softly, "what is it?"

"I can't remember how many sugars you take?"

"I want to know what is wrong, what makes you cry like
that. If you really don't want to tell me, I won't ask anymore.
But if I can help—"

Cloodine tamps black powder in the earthenware filter.

"There is nothing you can do. Did you tell me how much
sugar?"

Soledad does not take sugar. She has taken to drinking her
coffee black as a moonless night, the way the smugglers do
at the Cadillac Hawkley. But the ritual of coffee-making—
the pressing of the powder, the wait as steam forces itself
through the grounds, the pouring and serving—seems to have
calmed Cloodine. Whatever made her sob has cooled down
to the level of talking, where words can shift things around
a bit.

The story she pulls out, chunk by chunk, separated by un-
even breaths and occasional chips of crying, is an old story—
old in that seeing your man leave as soon as you gain weight
and then refusing to pay for the child and not having enough
money for food until finally you have to watch your kids go
to bed with stomachs growling most nights of the week is as
old as these poor volcanic hills, old as the metal hearts of the
Conquistadors—and yet surprising because Soledad in her
ignorance had thought the *cruce* built on some of the dis-
carded notions of the old Left, stuff the Adornistas espoused
in theory but never delivered on in fact. The propaganda, in
the Walled City, refers to Adornista splinter groups and other
violent types in the *cruce* who at least seem committed to

eradicating through utmost bloodshed a misery such as Cloodine's.

Sitting with the coffee humming inside her, stroking the woman's knuckles with one thumb, it seems as if the music she hears outside, dwindling now in the cool heart of the night, has been revealed to contain a core of deception, of something gone impure and soft.

"BUT THE *CRUCE* WAS never built on that," Jorge tells her the next day. "Even in theory, especially in practice, the idea was to get away from that kind of static social mercantilism."

"How can you sit there?" she flares up at him. They are drinking wine under the arbor, a little too much as usual and the slide of *vinho verde* makes flaring easy. It is a hot day, with promise of further heat to come. "How can you sit there and spout words like 'social mercantilism' and defend your, your high-flown theories, when a woman cannot feed her three children? Do you—do you?" She can barely speak from rage and, it must be admitted, *vinho verde*. "Don't you *see* how that fact, that one fact alone, how just one baby going hungry one night takes all your beautiful oh-so-stylized work, your *foutus poèmes*—"

"Soledad," he protests, putting down his wine.

"All the music, the words, and makes them worth shit?"

"Soledad."

"What."

"I have something to show you."

"Why don't you answer my question?"

"I am answering you."

She makes some comment then, nasty enough not to remember later. She is aware of being excessively influenced by this man. She is falling into the older man–younger woman trap, a sexual power struggle pitting her youth against his knowledge, the benefits of which will probably never outweigh its psychic drawbacks. She knows she gets less out of this affair than he does.

But when he slips on his sandals and waits for her at the door she follows, with only a small *tik* of the tongue to convey her disapproval of herself for giving in to that dynamic.

————

THEY WALK TO LO PANO. The Slave Market moves slower in the heat. A man plays a bass made out of an old oil drum, sawing his bow listlessly across the string, producing notes so low they sound like they are played underwater. People live like scared minnows in the sepia shadows of stall canopies. When they move they float like cuttlefish, swiftly propelled by their concern for cool, from dark shelter to black. The numbers and names of products on the various Udine boards flap spasmodically in the slow air. Jorge enters the square of shade under the tower. The desks here are all empty. Jorge climbs the ladder, taking the rungs two at a time for Soledad's benefit. Not for the first time she realizes how acutely aware he is of their difference in age.

Once they are inside the Flash Shack and the hatchway closed behind it feels like she has been transported to a different country, or world even, a place out of time, chilled by ancient Fedder air conditioners and so crammed with snaked wires, modems, overflowing desks, network ports, ledgers, card files, typewriters, and the yellow green blue black screens of archaic computers that she can barely make out the hot overexposed colors of the *cruce* blasting through the windows of this rickety structure. Phones ring in random patterns. A young man and a younger woman—the same woman, she realizes, who directed her to Haddad's workshop only two weeks before—sit in niches dug out of the paper and hardware, making connections between phone, computer screens, ledgers, index cards; keeping track of such connections with ballpoint on scratchpad.

"Four cases, twelve hundred units of Pornosoft, fifteen gigabytes," the woman remarks laconically, *"claro."*

Jorge turns on a coffee machine and serves a couple of *tintos* without asking permission.

"We have an urgency," he tells the man when the activity dips. "Or rather, she does"—jerking a thumb at Soledad.

The man digs around the heap of papers, futilely, for a good two minutes, muttering curses at absent filers, at the inefficiency of Hawkleyites in general. The woman clicks a mouse and pulls a ledger from midway in a stack of books, the rest of which totter and crash, raising a cloud of motes to obscure the sun. The words LEVY CASES: OCTOBER are marked on the ledger in red felt-tip. She hands the ledger to the man without looking at him. He tells her to go fuck herself and she laughs, pleased.

The man asks Soledad, "Who?"

"A woman in her building," Jorge tells him.

"I can talk for myself," Soledad says, and describes what has happened to Cloodine, at lengths she is not really qualified to address, while Jorge hums infuriatingly, looking over a traffic ledger in the corner, and the woman gabs in pseudo-casual fashion to a barrio cooperative selling T-shirt designs online from Valparaiso.

Finally the man slaps the ledger shut. Without looking at Soledad he says, "We'll check up on it, and if it's as you say, well, don't worry, we'll figure something out."

"Is that all?" Soledad asks. "You'll just 'figure something out'?" She is irritated now. The casualness of it all—the mislaid file, the offhand way she is treated—jars against her sense of emergency. "What does that mean, anyway? You'll send her a fruit basket? Those children are *hungry*!"

"We have done this before," the woman comments patronizingly, and sucks on a ballpoint.

"She'll get work if she needs it," the man says, and starts rummaging around his desk again.

"Nestor Prin's boat is looking for a hand," the woman says.

"You know Prin?" the man asks.

"Sure," the woman replies with that same fake casualness. "My sloop's moored next to the *Fumiste*."

The man nods approvingly. "Prin's a cigarette smuggler, in the City of Boats. He pays well."

"The *contrabandistas* have child care," Jorge puts in, "believe it or not."

"A cigarette smuggler," Soledad insists, looking from the woman to the Lo Pano man and back again. "Even in the Walled City they have professional social workers, people who keep track."

Jorge, who has been watching her, grins. It's a grin so wide and free of guile that Soledad knows instantly it has nothing to do with what she has just said—nothing to do with Lo Pano, or this problem even. It disconcerts her momentarily, because she wants to grin in return, but won't let herself.

The woman throws her hair back. It is medium-length and bottle-blond and she uses it as a prop.

"The idea is to avoid creating an org," she says, glancing at Jorge for approval.

"I didn't come here," Soledad replies, "for warmed-up IMF-ismo from the last millennium."

"It might be IMF-ismo," Jorge says. His grin lingers in the corners of his eyes. "If it happened in a context where the big bureaucracies still had a lock on power."

"But this is the *cruce*," the woman agrees, glancing at Jorge again, "this is a completely new way of organizing."

"And?" Soledad replies, more aggressively than she meant to, but this woman is so obviously flirting with him.

"And a *cruce* cannot get so big," Jorge says, "that the pathology gets out of control. Ten thousand people, yeh; that was the limit Hawkley worked out."

Without consciously meaning to, Soledad throws back her own head of hair, which is its own color and twenty centimeters longer than the other woman's.

"It's a *cruce, chérie*," the woman continues. "We rely on people to notice." She throws her hair back again. "If not at the workshop, then at the market. If not at the market, then at school; if not school, then in the barrio."

"But that's exactly the point," Soledad interrupts, her voice hardening in the relative chill of this dark tower. "No one *noticed*. That's what I'm trying to tell you. Cloodine is scared, and she's not the type to speak out, and what do you do with people like that?"

"Oh, but she knows somebody," the woman replies with a backtaste of sarcasm, "somebody who knows how to speak out for her." She points her ballpoint at Soledad. "Cloodine *knows* someone."

A yellow phone clangs, and she picks it up.

"Lo Pano," she announces in that same put-on cool accent, *"j'écoute?"*—leaving Soledad vaguely furious, mostly deflated, and with a hot and sudden craving to go back to that bottle of *vinho verde* and finish it down to the last drop.

SEVEN

SHE WAS AWARE OF eyes fixed on hers. A pair full of
fauna colors, another that felt like home to her, maybe because they were chocolate as the river near its delta. A third
pair small and black and curious and not human.

The pudgy man, and the boy. The third set of eyes be-
longed to the northern coati. As she watched, the animal
stretched across the table, opened its long digits, and broke
off a piece of her piecrust, eyeing her to see how she would
react. There was only a small piece of her dessert left.

"Paco," the boy sighed reproachfully, and did nothing to
stop the animal.

"You're crying," said the face with hazel eyes—fair,
freckled, its lines bunched in concern. *Stix,* she remembered,
as if she had only just met him. She had gone that far away
in the story she was retelling in her head. Stix. She touched
her cheeks. They were greasy with tears, and her nose was
clogged with mucus.

"You okay?" Stix continued, pushing his hand out almost
to her shoulder, then withdrawing it again without touching.

She shook her head, then nodded, contradicting herself.
Got to her feet, shoved the stool back with her knees. An
aluminum-paneled door in back read HEAD, which meant
nothing to her, but it was the right place for a toilet. Getting
there required a convoluted slalom between chairs, and shoving through the stares of people obliged to pull seats out of
her path.

When she got to the bathroom she closed the door and slid
the bolt, feeling a sudden and intense relief. Those people

were so American, she thought—so big and clumsy and
open-faced and loud-talking. It was as if this diner was too
full of their volume and drive, although possibly 20 percent
of the seats were empty. Whereas a Cadillac at home could be
twice as full and not seem half as frequented by bodies.

She really needed to pee. She registered sadness from
the memories that had just flooded her, but nothing like the
troughs of misery she had sunk into with some frequency
over the last three weeks. The primary emotion was something stretched between admiration, because her *cruce* had
been so complex and full of detail and her memory of it
so vivid; and disgust, that something so strong and colorful
should also be so weak as to be disappeared by thugs like
Ochoa Campos and Sandoval.

Despite the blood crusted in the fabric her tights were not
stuck to her inner thigh. The bandage was fresh; someone had
changed it while she slept. Soledad could smell herself, smell
the sweat and grime of her escaping; she had not had a
shower since she arrived at the motel two days ago.

She thought of the three men who were in the factory
when she woke up and waited for the automatic embarrassment, but it did not come.

At any rate, whoever replaced the bandage had done it
with skill.

Once she had wiped and pulled her tights back up she
took a paper towel from a pile on the sink and wiped her face
thoroughly. Tears still seeped from under the eyelids, despite
the fact that the daydream was receding with the ever-
increasing acceleration of a departing express. The mirror in
this bathroom was cracked and small and high, and she had to
stand on tiptoe to see herself. When she did so she gasped,
and her chest went hollow with dread; it was not the face,
which was the same only more so because of exhaustion—the
shallow *V* of her mouth a little flatter, the fold on each side
where the corners of her lips disappeared gone deeper and
darker, the nose like a keel of teak dividing the mahogany
planes of her cheeks, planes she had always resented, in the

reflexive racism of her country, because they were so broad
and Indio-looking.

What was new, and horribly strange, was the thin tracks of
tears running through those planes. She had grown used to
tears after Bamaca, but the thing was, these streams were the
wrong color: a deep, almost lilac blue where they pooled in
the lines around her eyes and nostrils, and a skylike azure
where they spread and shallowed.

It was not the dust. She had sponged the cadmium off
thoroughly enough that this possibility could be ruled out.

Her hand flew to her mouth. She found space in the back
of her mind to sneer at herself, at the clichés hidden in reflex,
the *telenovela* recoil in which she, who despised soap operas
and other stereotypes of femininity, took refuge like all the
rest.

She watched her image for half a minute. Paradoxically,
now she was interested in them, the tears had stopped. She
walked back to the main room, to Stix's table, and held out
her left hand, with the index and thumb curled to trap a quick
cry of water in the center.

Stix hit his forehead with the palm of one hand, a clown
gesture.

"Shit, shoulda told ya," he said.

The boy leaned over, dipped one finger in the pool. He
brought its thin blue humidity to the coati, who sniffed it,
then lifted one paw and made a strange circular gesture, as if
polishing a mirror or making an *O* in the air.

"They put something in the water," Stix continued, shrug-
ging and smiling at the same time. "Phthalein, probably, like
the stuff they put in Kool-Aid, only genetically shrunk; it
goes right through the blood barrier. Their psy-ops people
think it'll make us neurotic or something. Truth is, most of
the people in the node are too crazy to be neurotic."

"Don't listen to him." It was the diner chef, Molly; she
moved around the table, topping up coffee cups.

"Wait till you see your pee," Stix added.

"He's an *artiste*," Molly continued, as if Stix had not spoken. "He thinks that entitles him to speak for humankind, or this part of it anyway. You want," she added cryptically, "to taste the cream? You said you were gonna do that three days ago so I busted ass to get it ready then, and it's just been hanging around since. Stix, honestly—"

Stix stood up, apologizing. The boy did not move. The coati grabbed the last piece of pie. Soledad stayed where she was. Something inside her rebelled at the thought of getting up and following this man whom she barely knew and who so clearly expected her to follow him.

On the other hand, she'd had more contact with him than with anyone else in this barrio. Or this country. Not like—she made the comparison automatically, it had become a habit of grief as well as a way of maintaining memory, unless these were the same thing—not like the *cruce,* where she would have known half the customers in a place like this. A pulse of self-pity opened inside her, warm and sticky as the caramel coating on fresh flan. She bit the inside of her lip—she had no wish to cry blue again. And the habit of sorrow, even if she could do little to stop it, had long ago become boring to her.

But Stix was not expecting her to come with him. All he did was wink at her once, then turn and follow Molly to the door.

Soledad sat there for a few seconds. Then she got up and went to the door also. The irritation in her for following a man so blindly was divided and cut aside by the overarching reality of the fact that, for a while at least, she was relying on Stix to show her the ropes in this place.

No sign of Stix or Molly once she stood outside the diner. The mist was thicker, and the boats of smugglers in the cove morphed vaguely between different shapes: buoys, seals, sea monsters. Across the cove, the radar masts and periscopes atop the sub's conning tower were rubbed out by the eraser of gray humidity. Something banged behind the diner. She slopped through the silt, slipping in her soaked sandals. Two shapes bracketed a forty-liter cardboard tub at the entrance of a walk-in refrigerator. Stix lifted one finger to his lips.

"I still say it's—"

"Main thing is, it's stiffer now. It's not like anyone is gonna ask for seconds."

"The taste is important."

"It tasted better three days ago. If you could just be on time, for once in your life?"

Molly turned, sensing Soledad's shadow in the background.

"Wanna taste? It's whipped cream."

"Yeah," Stix said. "Tell her it needs more vanilla."

"He's only gonna bomb people with it, anyway," Molly said, fitting the cover back on. "Who cares how it tastes." She elbowed Stix out of the way, then slammed the reefer door shut and walked back around the diner. Grease from frying burgers blew out of a fan beside Soledad.

"You look like you could go right to sleep now," Stix said. "How about I take you back to the shop?" He didn't wait for an answer and disappeared behind the willow. Soledad stood in the silt, staring at the refrigerator door, still racked by both her unwillingness to go where he led and her lack of other options. The sound of the spiderbike's exhaust boomed monstrously among the loomed pilings and concrete panels of piers rising above them before the bike itself appeared around the corner of the little restaurant.

When she climbed in back he belted her carefully into the mantle. Then he gunned the vehicle around the willow and into the tunnel they had come through earlier.

———

BACK IN THE BED she had woken up in. "A test tank for torpedo models," Stix told her, not smiling. "The tech captain filled it with emergency flotation bladders and converted it to a water bed for screwing his WAVES."

Whatever that meant. Soledad felt weird but not uncomfortable in the long bed. The fatigue was indeed great within

her, as Stix had guessed—she realized he had in effect
told her she looked tired, which was something she always
hated. The people who knew her, starting with her father
and Maria Gisela, would never have said anything remotely
like that for fear of getting snapped at, or worse. But she
had not reacted, by gesture or expression. Maybe she was allowing for his ignorance, Soledad thought in light bewilder-
ment.

She lay back and the bed gulped and made digestive
noises beneath her. This time her stomach stayed where it
was. As soon as she closed her eyes, though, the fatigue was
run over by voices and inchoate forms surging from the back
of her brain like people stampeding to get off a bus into
which the guerrillas had thrown a live grenade. Her eyes
snapped open again: that was not a simile. It was something
that really happened, in a village outside Bamaca. Three people had been killed, a dozen injured.

She rubbed one eyelid at a time with her index finger,
smoothing it in a circular motion that reminded her vaguely
of the coati. She must have slept a good seven or eight
hours in this bed after the armored car attacked her. Yet it was
clear that the secretions of fatigue, from three weeks–plus of
traveling and living on the run, had built up to the point
where it would take more than one night of sleep to wash
them away.

Equally obviously, fatigue had hit levels that induced a
countercurrent in the psyche. Past a threshold of exhaustion,
her sleep grew crowded with dreams and dead people whose
unwelcome attentions actually had tired her further by the
time she woke up.

Perhaps a safety device that kept Soledad from seeing the
cruce while her grief was too fresh had shut down now that
she was in relative security. Despite the rigors of her journey
here, she had never experienced dreams of the *cruce* so enduring and vivid as the ones she'd had in San Francisco and
Oakland the last two times she slept.

She thought that a part of her was already growing reliant

on those dreams. The rubbed-off memory of what she "experienced" asleep—the colors and flowers and songs, the warmth
and security of her *cruce*—called to her the way *basuko*
called to the addict, compelling and lethal as a Greek en-
chantress.

In a corner of her mind she knew for certain, without the
flimsiest shred of evidence to support such knowledge, that if
she dreamed too often of Bamaca it would end up sapping
her, not only because it tired her out, but because the emotion
it summoned would erode her will to keep going, to survive—
to escape, if escape was required. And her experience of these
gringo lands so far had taught her that the ability to run away
was something you definitely needed to preserve.

So Soledad sat up again, wincing slightly as she heaved
her legs over the bed's concrete rim. The long control room
next door was empty of life, if you discounted the moving
colors of the architect's pushwall. SAN FRANCISCO CHRONICLE
EXAMINER *REALTIME,* its logo read, then wiped to reveal a
headline: THIRD LIFEJACKING IN THE SOUTH BAY IN TWO
WEEKS, followed by a vidclip of a jowly man in Neodisko suit
sobbing as he embraced a woman in split-screen makeup.
"The jackers held every part of Ed Vacek's life hostage," an
expert intoned. "At times it seemed they didn't just want his
tax-free memory margins—they wanted to *become* him, with
his heated pool, and his customized MicroCom lifebot, his
eight-million-dollar home in the San Luis hills."

Behind the fizz of telechat, water dripped steadily. On the
other side of the pushwall was a large bathroom with six
shower stalls. A quote had been roughly painted on the wall:
"We must learn to be equally good at what is short and sharp
and what is long and tough—Winston S. Churchill." She used
the toilet and took a shower. The water was lukewarm and it
felt wonderful. She washed out her underpants and leggings
and hung them on hooks to dry. She padded back to the bunk
room in her blouse and tried on the bell-bottoms. They were
loose around the waist and too long but she rolled up the cuffs

and tied the waist with string she found in the control room and they were fairly comfortable.

She could not locate the lift controls, and looked around till she spotted an EXIT sign. The door underneath led to the rafters of the factory proper, a cool and shadowy space into which a metal catwalk unevenly protruded. A segment of railing and even part of the gridwork had corroded and fallen into dark emptiness. Soledad hesitated, then started to walk, holding on to the undamaged rail with both hands. The catwalk paralleled a thicket of roof girders and changed into stairs that, doubling back on themselves every floor, descended through acres of humidity, pigeon shit, and the accumulated rustfall of steel girders to the floor below.

Soledad, who did not care much for heights, felt relieved when she got to ground level. Stronger than her relief was her visual curiosity, because the mechanical bestiary was much more visible now in the cones of newly switched-on spotlights.

The bestiary had changed somewhat from the first time she had seen it. The legs had come off the enormous carcass being splatted by the gallows-carousel into the wall. Sinews and bits of flesh flailed on the backbeat. She became aware of the corpse's stench, it was almost as bad as the old-socks smell that had greeted her on waking, and turned away quickly from the shattered horse.

A new sound made echoes in the hard space. It came from a particularly dark corner on one of the factory's shorter sides. A shadowed figure, occasionally booming words in military tones, moved convulsively there at odd intervals.

Power tools whined from her right, behind a rack of the long, complex tubes she had seen earlier. She picked her way through rainwater puddled on the concrete, rounded the rack, then a tall piece of plywood half painted in geometric patterns, a stack of *chō* parlor takeout boxes—and caught her breath.

A pastry; a cream pastry.

It was a yellowish tube of crust stuffed with a deep, thick filling of whipped cream. The top was smothered in a layer of deeply whorled foam, in which three vermilion-colored maraschino cherries were stuck. She had seen pastries like this before, in Italian cafés that composition students frequented in the capital; they were called cannoli and éclairs. She was pretty sure this was a cannoli. The cakes were so sweet and rich they made her feel ill after only a few forkfuls.

The thing was, this "cannoli" was as big as a truck, three meters high and at least five in length. The "cherries" were the size of wrecking balls. The cream, lovingly painted, looked like it was made of heavy rubber. A plunger, laced with hydraulic tubing, protruded from the cream filling at the far end. The "dough" was fiberglass. A panel in the bottom was propped open, revealing caterpillar treads and a mess of wires, filters and tubes. A man she did not know crouched by the wiring, holding a lamp. Beside him, Stix grasped a detail of machinery with one hand as he pulled on a ratchet wrench with the other.

"Ah, crapola," he yelled, and yanked out a section of copper tube. The broken end gushed pink fluid. He punched the machinery, which only increased the flow. "Piece o' shit!" he yelled. Then he stoppered the tube with a rag. Looking around for a more appropriate tool, he spotted Soledad.

"Mystery Woman," he said, "I thought you were asleep."

She shrugged, still staring at the giant pastry.

Stix grabbed pliers from his gear belt and slowly bent the tube in a deep *U* until the broken end, twisted upright, stopped leaking. Then he got to his feet, favoring his bad leg, wiping his hands on the thigh of his jumpsuit.

"You need me?" the other man asked, putting down the lamp and stretching.

"I'll need you later," Stix said, "we're two days behind on the mini version." He turned back to Soledad. "Is there anything you—" He followed her gaze, upward again to the monster cherries. When he looked back at her, he was trying not to smile.

"So it's a big cannoli," he said.

She rolled her eyes, then caught herself. She did not know this man well enough to express quick sarcasm, or criticism of his obviousness. He was smiling now.

"So what's it do?"

He was predicting her question. She liked people doing that even less than she liked being told she was tired. But in the great mystery of this place, in the greater puzzle of her own inability to talk out loud, she found she was prepared to let him speak for her until she got her bearings.

He pointed to the caterpillar treads.

"It moves. It's remote-controlled." He tweaked a series of little antennas protruding out of the skirt then, walking to the pastry's narrower end, pointed to the middle of the "cream," which bulged realistically, as if it had truly been pumped into its shell by a giant chef. "It shoots foam. Is there—I mean, what do you want to know?"

She shook her head. In a way, there was nothing she could logically ask. It made no sense—or it made a lot of sense, if this man was loony as a swamp-wader. For an instant the enormity of where she had been and what she had been doing overcame her: chased by fire machines, stabbed by a transvestite, prostituted at electronic remove, sleeping in test tanks, taking refuge in a military base with a flock of renegades who based their community on the worship of dessert. In context, perhaps the giant pastry was not so crazy after all.

She glanced upward, where the oversized bird hung motionless in the gloom beside the control room windows. She noticed for the first time that it bore indigo wingfeathers. A ripple passed between her skin and the tissue beneath.

Then she turned back to the sheet of plywood, and the pots of paint and brushes lined up beside it. Swiftly she picked up one of the brushes, dipped it in a pot of red paint, and drew, under a splattery diagram of what looked like a stork driven by a bicycle, the single word: WHY?

Stix shrugged.

"It's what I do. I stage . . . events, I guess you'd call them."

Shook his head at the lack of comprehension in Soledad's face. "Things that happen. I have a sort of, of company—it's called Apocalypse Planning. People come to watch. . . ."

He moved to the side, out of the pocket created by plywood, rack, and giant pastry. Pointing at the various incomprehensible constructs she already had seen.

"I stage 'em where no one is supposed to go, don't you see? Ah, crapola. Sniper art? I hate that term. Performance art." He was shaking his head as if in anger, although a thread of smile still looped around the corner of eyes and mouth. "I hate that term too. It's not art, I don't believe in the word, I think it's horsedung. But—ah."

He swiveled, glanced at the carcass-swinger, then up at the bird.

"Look up there," he whispered. "AutoRodan. I got echoes of Godzilla flicks, of what Tomoyuki Tanaka really wanted, a bellwether—what Hawkley says nodes are supposed to be. What Gustave Messmer was drawing toward." He pointed at another panel, where ancient drawings of bicycle-powered flying machines were tacked next to newer blueprints. "What I *do,*" he went on in a louder voice, and his hands clutched at air in the same tool-hungry way she had noticed in the diner, "I *involve* people in making these—these things. People who've never made anything in their lives. Totally bloody useless objects that still function in a kinda beautiful way. Ah," he added, punching his thigh in frustration.

"I can't put it any better 'n that."

She pointed toward the narrow end of the warehouse, where the Christlike figure, dragging itself on its stomach—responding to who knew what sensors in its beard, its barbed-wire crown of thorns—tried to negotiate an obstacle in the corner.

"Religious impulse, man." He was talking oddly, in a way that reminded her of some of the New Hippies she had heard hawking marimba on Eddy Street; he was making fun of himself, and this made her frown, because it was something few men did very well. "The belief trigger, the point where you decide you'll trade logic for faith. Eventually I'm gonna have Marx and Mohammed, Moses and Hayek, all following each other around like lemmings. Like I mean—"

The Christ figure made high motor sounds as it struggled to get past the obstacle. Now the problem was obvious—the dark figure she had seen earlier in the corner had sortied to block the dragging contraption. As it serially banged into Christ she defined the dark automaton as a four-square male figure, life-sized but broader than average, painted to resemble a military officer. Its right arm shot out convulsively every twenty seconds or so, describing roundhouse punches that failed utterly to connect with the supine, struggling prophet. The disproportionate violence of those lost blows, for some reason, made her think of the time long ago, in her apartment in the Walled City, when she had flung her answering machine to the floor.

While the "officer" punched, words blared from its loudspeaker mouth, and at this range she could hear them clearly.

"Front and center! Now hear this! Get that galley squared away! Four days in the brig, swabbie! Atten', *hut*!"

She dropped the paintbrush in the pot, still watching the confrontation between the figures. Stix sighed, reached into one of his jumpsuit pockets, pulled out a remote control, and pressed a button.

Nothing happened.

He lifted one eyebrow, then smoothly flipped the batteries out of the remote and replaced them. Tried again.

"Not the battery," he said. "Loose contact. Anyway, it's kind of the point, see?"

She continued to look at him.

"Action stations! Captain's muster! It's the *Navy Way*!" the blue-uniformed man shrieked.

"What?" he said.

She pointed at the corner.

"You mean, Navy Man?"

Soledad nodded.

"I wish you could talk, Mystery Woman. Or whatever your name is."

She shrugged. He turned away, watching the figures. To Soledad, who had observed in Jorge, in Miguel, in her own father, an encyclopedia of tropisms aimed at stopping her from probing certain areas, the resistance in him was obvious. This was not a question he wanted to answer—which of course made the answer that much more valuable. Abruptly she picked up the brush again and started to paint words on the plywood but he interrupted before she finished the "W" of "Who."

"It's not important," he said, without looking to see what Soledad was writing.

She moved closer to him, pointing extravagantly, the brush dripping red latex on the concrete.

He frowned, and slipped the remote in another pocket.

"You don't wanna hear that soap opera," he said. "Everybody has bad parents. Sometimes I figure it's the role of parents to be bad; it's what makes the kids do something different."

She shrugged again, irritably. Already she was sick of her own limited lexicon of gestures. And she was sick, even at such an early date, of Stix's restricted vocabulary of avoidance. He glanced at her sideways, crossed his arms in front of his chest.

"All right," he said. "*Not* my father."

She crossed her arms as well.

"My mom married again. A chief petty officer, OK? Navy brats. Newport, San Diego, Guantánamo, but not here—that was a coincidence. You satisfied? My stepdad. Just like a soap, huh?"

But the curl of smile was quite gone from the cradle of his lips.

"Well, you can imagine," he continued, gesturing, "from that, how everything was rules, and that was all there was. You fucked up twice, you got the brig. The brig was the kitchen closet. Thing is, I didn't fight him, maybe 'cause I was the younger one. Oh sure, I did passive stuff, like always being late for everything; that really got him hot under the collar. But Will—my brother—he resisted to his face, all the way. Finally Will duked it out with him. Got the shit knocked out of him, too, but somehow I was the one who spent most of his time in the brig. Used to read the contents of detergents to pass the time. Wanna know what's in Tide detergent? I'll tell you. Anionic surfactants. Nonionic surfactants, too, all biodegradable. Enzymes. They don't really tell you much about the ingredients." He cleared his throat, still not looking straight at her. "Any more questions?"

She hesitated, caught between her instinct, which was to find out as much as possible about this man on whom her well-being depended, and a sentiment, growing in power, that the cost to him of disclosing this information was quite high. And as she hesitated, the concrete shook slightly beneath her feet.

A deep thud, that seemed to come from everywhere, pudded against her eardrums, faded slowly.

It was not the carcass-swinger, which made noises that were softer and in a different rhythm and not strong enough to shake this factory in any case.

It was stronger than the subway rumbling she had heard across the bay, in the tunnels of the Kundura men.

The blood fled her face. Her hands splayed like the talons of some bird coming in for the kill. Her eyes popped. She could do no more about this reaction than she could slow the pace of her heart, which pumped as fast as if she'd been running pell-mell down Teton Hill (as she had done once, though she could no longer remember why, or when).

Stix looked at her, opening his mouth, about to speak. Then he dropped his arms and held them toward her. His face changed from a remembered anger to a concern—mouth open and forehead creased—that might have seemed comic had it not been so welcome.

"Easy," he said, and gently placed one hand on each of her

shoulders. "It's just drilling, babe. Test bores, a BART tunnel to the old San Francisco airport."

She stared at him.

"Just drilling," he said, "and a little blasting. That was a bigger charge than most, is all."

His thumbs rubbed her flesh almost imperceptibly. It did not feel like aggression, or the patronizing caress of a stranger. It felt friendly, and affectionate, and soft.

It had been a month at least since Soledad had been touched by someone who did not want to hurt or patronize or fuck her without feeling, and she knew that in other circumstances she would have started grieving again, but crying was impossible for now through the deep freeze of panic inside her.

"Mystery Woman?"

The concrete had stopped shaking twenty seconds ago.

"It's been going on for a month," he added, taking his hands from her shoulders. "I guess you get used to it."

She moved her legs first. They worked fine. Her hands and arms also had function as she surfaced in the lake of panic. She walked back to the line of paint pots and, selecting a finer brush than the one she'd used earlier, dipped it into a pot of forest green.

MY NAME IS SOLEDAD, she wrote and under that:

YOU BELIEVE WHAT THEY TELL YOU?

He watched the words she had written for a while. He seemed to be oddly interested in the characters she had fashioned. The detail of smile had returned to Stix's mouth. She was starting to get annoyed again when he shook himself and said, "Soledad. I like that name."

She shook her head, then underlined YOU BELIEVE twice.

"Soledad," he repeated.

She started to redip the paintbrush and he said, "OK, *OK*. But you got to understand something."

He squatted next to the pastry and began putting his tools in order. It was as if by doing such work with his hands he could do the same thing with language, because while he did it the words came out much more deliberately than usual for him, and in more orderly and complete fashion.

"This is not your country. I don't know why you were chased—probably they had wrong information on you. Maybe they thought you were Adornista, or involved in a coke run or something. Hell, maybe you were. But like I said, this is not Bamaca. You know what orgs and megorgs are, Soledad?" He glanced up briefly. She nodded.

"Big corporations. Or big agencies. Huge living entities—life-forms, according to Hawkley. One life-form, sometimes, the way they interlink." The wrenches clinked as he gathered, then slotted them one by one into a cloth carrying-belt.

"Of course," he continued, "they run this country just like they run yours. Hawkley got that right. But here, the control is covert. You know?" Another glance up, and down.

"What Hawkley calls 'negative information'—the surface stuff: congressional elections, agency hearings, news programs—they pay attention to that. Only issue gets people really interested, though, is regulation of the B-Net interactive rates. . . . You get what I'm saying here?"

She shrugged. They had negative information in Bamaca also, she wanted to tell him, though she would have to qualify that too. Because everyone always knew what was in the shadows, besides the big companies like X-Corp Sur and TransCom-Brazil; the army, and Ochoa Campos, and Sandoval, and the execution squads that would remain disbanded only as long as the General Staff approved of what was going on.

The fact that everybody knew never prevented bad things from happening.

Stix had not stopped talking. "They can't do what they did in Bamaca here. There would be envirocams all over the place, too much coverage, eventually it would affect the Flash and you'd get repercussions. And there's more."

Stix had his wrenches gathered now. He rolled up the

carrying belt tightly, looped a length of twine around the roll, and tied two hard knots. The way his hands worked reminded her of Jorge; or did all men grasp so strongly and without fuss? She could not remember Miguel's hands at all. Stix got to his feet, placed the roll of tools in a milk crate full of other neatly arranged tools, and looked at her again. "Can I show you something?"

She shrugged once more, then moved in his wake—like a barge following a tugboat, she thought, using similes both to amuse herself and to keep from getting upset because she was following him again. Like ducklings swimming after their mother, like a caboose hooked to a train. Into the shadow below the control room buttresses. And outside, under signs reading CONDEMNED and DO NOT ENTER (*PER ORDER* U.S. NAVY) and CHEMICAL HAZARD and APOCALYPSE PLANNING (*VICTIMS WELCOME*), across an alley, through a second warehouse, this one filled with hunks of black machinery obviously too big to salvage, past another sign reading MARRIED OFFICERS' QUARTERS: ENLISTED PERSONNEL KEEP OUT, into rows of three-story wooden houses—white-painted, green-shuttered, pitch-roofed, picket-fenced, like geography-book illustrations of Yanqui suburbia. Only this was not suburbia, because a good third of the houses were blackened by past fire. And hundreds of makeshift gangways, bridges, and tangles of looped wiring linked them up and down, diagonally, any which way, same floors, different floors. It looked like Dick and Jane's street had been taken over by a spider big as an aircraft carrier, which had cocooned the structures alive in the paths and webways it spun.

Inside, the houses were as incongruous and thrown-together as the outside. Mazes of parlors, kitchens, nurseries, and bedrooms—many still charred—had been opened up or sectioned off haphazardly to fit the activities they sheltered. A smell of burning underlay fresher odors of chemicals and warm circuitry. A majority of the cut-up rooms were filled with computer equipment lined in complicated ways and attended by people, generally young. They were dressed in varying combinations of split-screen, Goth gang, post-plague, proto-hippy. A few of the bigger parlors had been converted into labs turned stale by the flavor of chemicals. Some juddered and hummed with electric motors, or old-fashioned off-set presses, or vacuum molds. At every corner a pushwall glowed, usually showing nothing more than another work-room, or a digital notice-board, or someone adjusting an electronic instrument.

They climbed up and down ladders—even, at one point, slid down a rope through a hole to the next floor. As Stix met people he introduced them, mispronouncing her name, saying "Saul-ee-dad" instead of "Soul-ey-dahd"—but he said it with such evident pleasure, as if happy to be able to wrap his concept of her around a word, that she didn't bother to glare or run her hands back through her hair even, as she did usually when suppressing irritation. He invariably followed up the intro with a quick sentence or two on the work. A deeply tanned man with blond hair wearing a Neodisko suit that would not have looked out of place on Grant Street was washing dishes in a combination of miniature TV studio and kitchen. *"Jake's Cakes,"* Stix said. "He's syndicated in twenty-six B-Net markets; he's the one who invented that pancake mix with edible syrup globules inside."

Down again, sideways. A bunch of teenagers of both sexes were crowded around a bench sagging under glass jars filled with bright green algae growing on thin wire. The teenagers wouldn't talk to them but Stix said the jars, which were electrically spliced to a bank of cheap jambooks on the shelf beneath, were organic microchips bred wild in a salt marsh in Rhode Island. Each millimeter of seaweed, he said, contained over a billion more connections than the most powerful Intel-Samsung equivalent.

Not that this was new or original, he added, X-Corp had been developing similar algae for years. But the teenagers, working with Doctor Zatt, had patched into another group that in turn had wired their chip-grid directly into the marsh itself. They had discovered that the connection exponentially boosted the capability of each individual strand. Apparently a bioholistic feedback process was going on that they were only now beginning to sort out.

A couple in their sixties, who Stix said were former TV writers, were working on a logic germ package that killed a "supersniffer" search program BON was using to track Wildnet users. The software masqueraded as an illegal transmission, bleeping out complex and fictitious stories, waiting till the 'cookie stuck itself on with all its algorithmic suckers as well as the data it had picked up on the transmission's course across that particular Wildnet. As the false program and its parasite sped across the Web to a bogus destination, the logic germ slowly poisoned the supercookie with random versions of ancient Kenny Loggins music videos.

Soledad was losing ground. The bandage on her inner thigh had rubbed her skin raw. And the fatigue that perversely wired her earlier had slowed, stopped, flipped from forward to reverse spin. She was exhausted enough, in a healthy physical way, that she felt she could sleep now, and never mind what dreams might come.

She found herself leaning against walls to support herself. In a converted kitchen, a graceful twenty-year-old woman was teaching two coatis, who looked like brothers of the one she had seen in the diner, how to use American Sign Language. "All they want to say today is 'crayfish,' " she complained to Stix, wiping the back of one hand across her forehead. The animals chirred, and held up one paw curled in the shape of a crab.

Stix led her across a courtyard to the largest atelier they had visited so far. This one was crammed with sea smells and fish tanks. Most of the tanks, in the relative gloom of the sliced-up rooms, gave off a soft, unearthly glow. A pushpanel showed a dozen people dressed in animal masks playing bagpipes, harps, tambourines on a stage of a dozen separate platforms cantilevered on top of each other.

Exclusively women in this workshop, all in their twenties and thirties. They listened to a heavily made-up redhead wearing a tank top and jeans so tight the frontal wedgie caused Soledad to squirm in empathy. "Noctiluc," Stix whispered, also trying not to stare at the woman's crotch, "this is where it came from, and the licensing revenues from that—" He shook his head. "What I'm trying to tell you is, OK, nine-tenths of these ideas don't work or sell, or else they're downright illegal, but the other tenth—well, the orgs want 'em. These kind of people, though—" He waved his hands at the women. His whisper was getting stronger, and a couple of them glanced in his direction. "They don't *wanna* work for X-Corp or Whampoa-Teledesic. See, the reason they think the way they do is exactly the same reason they want to live *here*—in the node."

Stix's face was flushed, and he was hitting one hand against the other for emphasis. Soledad half smiled, watching him. She had not suspected him of this force of attachment.

"People here are illegal, they don't conform to state or federal ordinances—" Stix was talking loudly now. Someone in the group shushed him, and someone else entered the workshop from behind a bank of aquariums to the right, presumably to demand quiet. Stix paid them no mind. "They don't pay insurance, they use jisi and hot software and other stuff smugglers bring in, they pay each other in node barter chips, and that's exactly the point—they do things differently, which is why nothing in Xerox PARC or TV City or Belmont comes close—"

But Soledad was no longer listening. The new presence had moved in front of the swarming noctiluc plankton massed in glass cases. The silver-green light flooded over a nondescript blue Neodisko suit, a formal shirt, half blue half white like every other business shirt in the Bay Area. And the glow also brought out his features, or rather his lack of them. For, while a rim of gray hair grew around the top and a semblance of ears and chinbone and neck defined the limits of his head, where his face should have been was nothing but an opalescent, shifting mass of chaos, like a trillion bits of visual data tracking too fast to apprehend. In this "face," streams of digital noise switched on and off, one and zero, in superfast random sequence. Sometimes they approximated a fat long nose, a blue iris, a pursed mouth, jowly cheeks; sometimes they shifted to black eyes, a short nose, fat cheeks, sunken eye sockets; but never did they settle on any one detail for more than a fractured second. And even for that second they always left the rest of the facial area to that swirling, slightly numinous vortex of nothing.

The gringo of the End.

The Yanqui with no face.

She felt her hands moving to her throat, felt the stupid, hysterical reflex happening again.

The Yanqui stopped beside the pushpanel, his thin frame nicely backlit by the bubbling aquariums. He opened his hands, one to each side as if to say *Voilà*. It was an odd gesture, Soledad thought, but in the flat stomp of shock at seeing this man who could not possibly exist, that thought was as transient as a globule of water sputtering across the surface of a red-hot griddle into vapor.

"They needed you too," he said, "didn't they?" He had a voice like all frequencies playing at once; a million lost radio messages, Maydays themselves gone missing, high-megahertz low-megahertz hissing into the ether, unreceived except by her. "They needed a black harbor. Where else could the government import the embargoed substances it never could buy legally?"

"Not coca," Soledad found herself replying, in her mind at least, she had no idea why she was answering this apparition at all let alone tracking into his conversation, it had to be conditioning to authority, from school, from her father—"not the big stuff?"

"No, not coca," the Yanqui interrupted. "That was always the Twelve Families, and the guerrillas, and the army of course. But the hot encryption, the stolen music, the proprietary fashions that fueled your workshops."

Ochoa Campos's speech, Soledad agreed in half of her mind, while the other half reacted against this; I mean, she thought, Maria Gisela was one thing, in the hypertension of flight and attack, so many molecules of endorphin and adrenaline caroming into each other, you can understand illusion. But this is out of the blue, an illusion of illusion. Which means either my chemicals are seriously out of balance and I am going crazy; or I must go mad in another way, in the sense that I will have to accept a reality totally alien to the one I function in.

"Ochoa Campos." The nonface nodded at Soledad's last statement. "Where else," he went on, "could the smugglers live? What other barrio brought in so much Cayman cash-chip from contraband and piracy of every nature that it made up half a percentage point in the national product, and who knows how much more in multiplier effect? They could never live without you—or so you thought."

In the tank, the plankton swirled faster, and glowed more brightly. Soledad's grip on her own throat grew tighter, as if she were trying to strangle the man, and the image, by cutting off her own air.

Suddenly a spark of noctiluc leaped out of the tank, across the intervening space. It settled on the hem of the Yanqui's left blue pants leg. It made a ring of ember that widened, then burst into flame.

The fire was conventional, yellow and orange. None of the women in the workshop noticed it, just as they had never picked up on the gringo. Stix, still yammering in Soledad's direction, was oblivious. Flames quickly consumed the left pants leg, spread to the other, rose to the level of jacket and beyond, leaving skin puckered like moon craters and russet in its wake. Soledad shook her head, repeatedly. She could not scream, this was hardly new, but she could not breathe either.

"And there was something else."

The Yanqui's head was surrounded by a halo of fire. His bad-radio hiss seemed twice as distant, made metallic by conflagration. His legs had vanished, and now the heaving mass that was his lack-of-face disappeared behind the smoke of its own immolation. "Something that scared the corporations, and the army that worked for them. Something that even scared the Bureau of Nationalizations."

"What?" Soledad whispered. It was all in her head but she whispered it anyway in the silence.

". . . something else . . ."

Only smoke was left now, smoke black and gray as the volcano's, that faded into the nonlight of noctiluc and the shadows of the atelier's ceiling.

Soledad's knees gave way. She crashed backward, and her spine skidded down a bookcase full of manuals to the floor; still clutching her throat with one hand, staring at the remains of fire.

But the smoke was gone, the Yanqui was gone. In his place stood only a pushpanel that showed a dozen people playing instruments under a banner reading CLAM FETISH.

That, and a girl, no older than nineteen, in a badly stained lab coat, with brown curled hair straggled in all directions around her face, standing where the gringo had stood—staring at Soledad, ignoring a tray full of vividly burning dots made of cold and silver fire that she held in both hands like an offering.

———

THE WOMAN IN TIGHT jeans brought Soledad a cup of gin. It tasted like formaldehyde and set her coughing, which finally forced her hand off her windpipe.

Stix kneeled beside her, looking angry, which made her mad, too, and stupidly sad, until she figured out he was really angry at himself for letting this happen.

By the time she had fought off the ministrations of the noctiluc women the sleepiness spun off her earlier fatigue had like metastasized cancer made so many connections throughout her body that nothing else could challenge it.

This time she didn't bother pushing Stix away when he

took her arm. She just followed meekly, after all she had been following all day; out of the MOQ, through the warehouses of unnamed machine hunks, up the cargo lift, to the concrete test tank with its soft rubber interior, and the warm navy blankets of bed.

EIGHT

ONCE, JORGE SKETCHED OUT a quick diagram showing how cohesive was the reality he wove for himself out of his poems.

Beside it he made a second diagram for comparison, showing the cohesion he saw in dreams.

In both there was a percentage—roughly 10 percent in writing, 5 in dreams—that instead of being given over to the world of "reality" at hand, dream or verse, was what he termed *"cafard,"* or "staleness": a state that, while it was not consciousness, at the same time was not devoted to maintaining the fantasy either.

So she is not surprised to wake up in the hours before dawn one morning and realize that not only is Jorge making love to her but, though she has been dreaming of something very different—a city on a high mountain, a town of stage sets piled one on top of the other in which animals dressed as men played out a Calderón de la Barca farce—in some 5-percent layer of her mind she has known what is going on.

Her body, certainly, is aware. She is drenched between her legs, she comes much more quickly than she usually does, and the pleasure, washing over her like an impressionist painting, uses the same palette of hues as her dream.

Afterward, as he grows in weight on top of her and shrinks in dimension within, he tells her he loves her and—more to the point—he wants her to adapt part of *La Selva* to the *Desdichado* cycle. They can perform the result as a mixed music-poetry piece during the Frum-Oxum festival; in doing so they can be as united in their work as they are now in flesh

and everything else. What with the warmth of his semen and
her own juices mingled and gliding down the arroyo of her
buttocks; with the first warmth of sun touching the flank of
her left shin; with all the warmth of what she feels for him
and the hot feeling of what she has accomplished so far on the
concerto, she can conceive of nothing coming between her
and what he has asked her to do, not even the fears that once
prevented exactly this.

Haddad by this time has finished repairing the Fourneaux-
Dallapé. He has even slacked up on following her—now it is
only once or twice a week that she turns to find him standing
on one leg twenty paces behind as he looks in every direction
but hers.

He sends her the manuscript of a novel he has written. It is
called *The Wormgear of Deceit*.

She does not read it.

The F2 agents no longer stake out her apartment building.
She keeps the accordion at Jorge's anyway, which makes it
easy, that morning, and the next and the next after that, to fall
the way her musical mass is pulling, out of bed into *tinto*, out
of coffee into the long shirt, Jorge's shirt, and finally into the
piano room with its card table and the paper stacked and pencils sharpened, the way she keeps them when things are going
well.

Later in the day, when the scrawled outlines Jorge gives
her to work from start to hold her back—by the difficulty of
reading them, by the way words can interfere with sound—
she will walk to the room where he writes to the accom-
paniment of the indigo-feathered macaw and the jade parrots
and the black-billed *agobequis* and the southeast wind lisp-
ing through the louvers and truck backfires and the thuds
from the sewer tunnel and the different snatched songs of the
cruce outside.

The process of welding together words and music is not as
hard as she imagined it might be. Generally she will play a
movement, knowing from the outline the general drift of his
piece, and he recites to it the details of verse he thinks will fit.

Both change the details, he of words, she of notes, chopping or expanding to match, or bringing in phrases that smile if the music smiles and vice versa. She cannot judge what that does to his poems—they sound lovely to her, even cut up—but it doesn't hurt her music much. In fact some passages drastically improve because she is forced to bring changes she made recently to their logical conclusion. That is, she has to complete their conversion to *cruce* themes and weed out a lot of the minor lines: the loneliness, for example, the five weeks she spent searching for her mother in the high plains. Or not weed them out, perhaps, but concentrate them in the places they belong, in short movements she is starting to call "The Mines," "The River," "*Chanson de Los Altos.*"

She wanted to make it all more structurally intricate anyway and the *cruce* music, with its two and sometimes three or four melodic lines always going on at once, is perfect for that.

Scribbling, scribbling on the cheap vellum Jorge stocks in ten-ream boxes under the piano.

She runs out of pencils at one point. Instead of going out to buy more, she borrows a pen and a pot of ink, and that happens to work better for the movement she is concentrating on. The pause to dip the nib into aquamarine ink, the ritual three taps on the caked rim of the bottle, the splatters when she has let too much collect in the nib's well, the side-cut of pen, seem to mirror and emphasize the call and response of memory hawkers in the Slave Market that she is trying to reproduce by heart.

She will discover later that dipping for ink holds her back from the "storm" section in "The River." She will have to buy new pencils for that. But at this particular position in time, the change in handwriting pace is salutary, and it heightens the appreciation she has for new tempos, for the rhythm of her meeting with Jorge, the aptness of this hiatus in her life, the way these changes manifest themselves in her craft. All of it deepens the sense that working with Jorge can only bring out pleasure and other, less obvious, items of value.

Not everything is smooth sailing, of course. Music is too complex for that. She has to discard movements that come too much to resemble Manuel Ponce. And another movement is far too Villa-Lobos (the guitars took control there). But in the main the back-and-forth is, she believes, quite good: her right hand describing *Vallenato* ballads, her left the calls of fishermen below her windows, or the story-rhythm of cock-fights, the dialectic of bargaining in the market, the cycles of excitement among the artisans selling and buying at Lo Pano.

Even the older passages of *Selva* have their use because Jorge's *Desdichado,* too, has parts that wander far afield from the *cruce.* He writes a little about Barcelona and Shanghai, mostly about other places in this region—the delta to the south, the high plains southeast of the capital, the mountains to the west, the *selva* itself.

But it's the *cruce* that is the heart and lungs of his work, and the task of matching the depth and complexity of both his poem and the people in it taxes her technical abilities to the limit and beyond, forcing her to use, or at least consider using, every glissando, tempo change, grace note, seventh progression, trill and rumble and wheeze the accordion is capable of. Using allegro to counterweight adagio, pianissimo versus sforzando, exploiting the keyboard as far as her right hand can go to simulate different instruments—the syncopation of *bombo* drum, the scrape of *requintos* and *bandolos,* the thrill of *pito* flutes.

Juggling the rhythms, the compound duple, 6/8 against a loose 3/4 triple for the *Vallenato* lead. Bringing in hints of other dances, the 12/8 of *Cumbia,* the straight 3/4 time of waltz.

And then, when her education is used up and the well of her inspiration gone dry and her technical resources washed away and she has to suck further, further, out of the water table of her vocation for this stuff—yet she manages it, pumping out rills of song from deep reaches of her memory, Jean-Philippe's melodies, the songs Maria Gisela taught her behind the cookhouse at the camp, and further even, to her nurse Louise and the Indio lullabies about sick manioc and the spirits forever trapped in macaws.

Though they are short, she thinks some of these passages the best she has ever written. They surround the core verse of *Desdichado,* the *"Souche"* part that will be taken up later and made into an anthem of sorts by the *crucistas;* surround it like a hearth protects a tiny flame.

———

THE CONCERT, ARRANGED BY Ruiz and the Office of Fiestas, is part of a festival held in honor of a sacred date three weeks hence in the Umbanda-Cargo calendar. It will take place in the Slave Market, the center of both *cruce* and festival, on a makeshift stage lit by Lo Pano. For ten days ahead of time different barrios prepare giant papier-mâché statues of John Frum, the god of contraband, and Oxum, the deity of change and practical jokes. These are the spirit of the *cruce,* Hector Ruiz tells her one night, they are all drunk at Pytagoro's after a meeting of the storytelling society Jorge leads. John Frum and Oxum (Ruiz continues) together represent the freedom that comes from inventing your own story about the world, and forcing it, in a rush of wine and dancing and spicy food and hot sex, to come true. Soledad always takes what Ruiz says with hefty measures of caution but the food part of his description, at least, is true. Starting a week before, the whole city—specifically the combination of Ensevli, Barrio des Anglais, Teton Hill, Bidonville, Slave Market, the City of Boats, and the fishing harbor that constitutes the *cruce*—is perfumed by the smells of *lamohue, vatapa,* and *boudincocho.* The cooking that fills the three days leading up to the festival will nourish everyone in the *cruce* for a week.

The rhythm of music rises in volume from every direction your ears can name. As the fiesta approaches, a greater and greater proportion of people in the streets wear fancy dress.

There are clowns, devils, Punches and Judys, mandarins, conquistadors, ghosts, and all the pantheon of macumba-Cargo: Saint Sebastian, Yemanja-Marie, Jake Navy, Xango, Guinea Isac. An increasing number of pedestrians weave from the effects of *pinga*. A few, mostly the younger stratum of black-market memory dealers, walk in elsewhere-rhythm from the jag apparatus strapped around their waists. One night she sees Haddad performing a slow, slow dance on the parapet of a Cadillac built over the fishing harbor, egged on by a crowd of inebriated revelers in costumes mainly representing Death and ballerinas—and she thinks, coldly, It's lucky he fixed the accordion before all this started.

Such a sentiment is typical of the way she thinks, almost to the first day of the festival. Part of her is cold with the freezing technique she will need to apply as precisely as a surgeon to make the concerto function. Part of her is feverish with work, and warm as she felt the morning he asked her to do this; hot as her attraction to Jorge, and beyond that, and beyond him, warm as what she feels for this place so full of rhythm and the easy grace of work done by choice over compulsion. Cloodine has already crewed two trips on the cigarette smuggler's boat and she has enough barter chips for food. As a matter of fact she has twice invited Soledad to dinner, though she must refuse all invites until after the concert. Soledad has even canceled all her lessons to give herself more time to prepare. She does not have the leisure to worry about how she will pull off what she has never managed before: playing her music for a crowd of strangers. She rehearses with the orchestra, of course, but rehearsals never bother her, they are not the real thing and thus are unattached to any real worries. Anyway, for the three weeks they had to prepare this, it has felt like allowing such worries to surface would be anathema to the high-temperature holism of her initial drive.

Seeking in some measure to mark the force of this change in her—trying at the same time to affirm its reality—she cuts her hair short. This brings out her cheeks and neck in ways that please Jorge, he says he can see her tendons work. She doesn't stop to consider how big a step this is, for since she was a child she never once did anything to her hair beyond trimming it when it touched her buttocks. She is, frankly, in love, and the chemicals of this state costume her habitual monsters into beings as harmless as the Polichinelle motley the kids wear on the street.

And then, with less than thirty-six hours to go before the concert, sitting on the balcony and drinking chilled wine with Jorge and Ruiz; looking to the west where the sunset bounces rays of light off the squat cone of the volcano; the blood abruptly drains from her face and neck. The evening air seems as chilled as ice water. All of her is cold now. She drapes a blanket around her shoulders, and switches to *pinga*. Neither dampens the tiny, constant trembling that starts up inside her at that point.

She knows exactly what it is. She ignores it stubbornly, although fear keeps her awake much of the night. She keeps expecting the continuation of the emotion that created warmth in the first place to jump-start itself, now her work has rolled so near its musical conclusion. And every time she looks at Jorge, or hears women arguing about something unimportant, the way they love to do in this place, their voices clear as lawyer-birds', it feels like her warmth, her courage, could rise again, keep her skimming over the fear, like someone running faster over a patch of quicksand.

Twenty hours before the concert she is colder than ever, and her fingers tremble, and she cannot get up the energy to walk—all the old symptoms of stage fright. "I can't do it," she tells Jorge that night. "I know the signs. I won't be able to."

"Of course you will," he tells her.

"You don't know that," she replies passionately, "you don't know me, how much I've struggled with this." She feels like crying but will not let herself. "You'll have to ask Ruiz to sub for me."

And he does, he asks Ruiz, who agrees with little grace. But Jorge does not alter the concert schedule and Soledad, for her part, now she knows she has a way out, perversely spends the night before the concert practicing the *Desdichado* over and over, working out the dynamics and the impulsion to climax, the part where Jorge asks "Of what use is a root"; pounding at the keys and chord buttons till her fingers bleed.

When the sun comes up on the day of the concert she knows she is going to at least try, and for one very simple reason: because this is probably the only way the music, the songs she has bundled and pounded into a whole, will ever reach an audience bigger than herself. She will probably fail—at best, play meekly and weak. At worst her fingers will jumble into a mess of technique, the only way out of which will be a lethal and also merciful silence.

But at least, in the act of failing, she will have given birth to something. And maybe she can hold out long enough— pale, shaking, fucking up, losing her place—to achieve life for part of her *Selva;* enough, anyway, for Jorge to use as a base, to continue alone or with Ruiz. And she feels a partial warmth, thinking this through, and it is kin to the uterine warmth she feels sometimes looking at young children, as if it were the latent mother in her seeking to bring this process of creation to its conclusion, though she might sacrifice her own life in the process.

Her fear sharpens. Preparations pass in a blur. Sunshine rolls orange and finally violet as evening approaches. The lighting of red lamps. Putting on her dress, dabbing contraband Vengeance on her wrists, clipping on earrings; her good-luck ones, the indigo macaws. Gathering sheet music, checking the Fourneaux-Dallapé. Going downstairs, walking down the hill toward the glare of Lo Pano. The streets are full of hands and firecrackers. She hears everything as if she were listening underwater. Jorge touches her often, on her neck, her upper stomach, and even this feels at one remove, as if layers of silk separated her from stimulus. Smells, mannequins, a broken-off tail of parade, men and women attired like skeletons. People dance, the men zigzagging around the women, who shuffle, laughing, hips aswing, to face their partners, raising high bunches of lit candles held in scarlet handkerchiefs. *Cumbia.* And then the massive lake of people in the Slave Market, purple as night and pierced like starlight with the candles they all use to invoke the spirits of Frum-Oxum. There must be ten thousand people here, she thinks. The stage is set under the Flash Tower, next to a ritual airstrip—a cleared "runway," marked with candles, on which the spirits of Umbanda-Cargo are to land their darkened, treasure-laden DC-3 at midnight.

Everything colder, everything accelerating. A curl of tune, an Afro-Peruvian *lanto* from the act preceding hers. She cannot talk to other performers in the makeshift greenroom. Applause. Her knees are weaker than ever. They assign a boy to carry the accordion. She has to clutch the railing as she climbs to the stage. Two stools, only two stools, each with a mike, one much lower for her; the cellos, drums, and mandolins are locked in with the dark magicians in the orchestra pit.

Applause rises again, mingled with the usual catcalls and whistles. The spotlights and lasers of Lo Pano swirl sickeningly above. Higher in the darkness, where the distant hills would be if she could see them, a yellow ring of napalm rises silently to mark the different ballad of violence.

They sit. She is busy for a moment, adjusting the Fourneaux. Playing a heavy accordion for twenty-eight minutes straight is no laughing matter and she has to strap it on exactly right.

Jorge looks at her. His eyes are very green in the spots. She wants to throw herself on him and hold him as hard as she can to keep things from happening to her, to them—freeze this instant by the force of embrace. The space inside available for holding her feeling for this man is in that moment as limitless as a galaxy. She does not touch him though. She tightens the final strap and immediately nods, she cannot wait, she knows waiting will only augment her terror. And Jorge starts, alone, the spoken intro to *Desdichado:*

> *Before hawk made night,*
> *before bone made hawk*
> *before I made you*

The crowd goes silent as a city of ghosts, except for the throaty barking of a dog somewhere in Ensevli. She feels sick, it is all she can do to hold her fingers lightly against the keys she will sound first. She sees Dolores in the front row, her arm around a thin youth who reminds her weirdly of Jean-Philippe. Pytagoro is seated next to Dolores, and beside him Ruiz is watching her—waiting, she realizes; he is waiting for her to fail.

And then Jorge says, "Yet I have breathed a couplet of this sun," her cue. She responds like a soldier to an order after all: the long and simple sostenuto, the major chord, the seventh; ah, and on the seventh she misses the G, stumbles, makes a clumsy recovery. The cold in her becomes white heat for an instant, a flash in vision and brainpan, from the head-long madness of which she throws herself violently into the next chord, the run-up to a long A with her right.

Then something else happens.

Specifically, the faces in front of her blur, become a wash. The sharp candlepoints of the audience turning into a Milky Way of haze. A wisp of moon retreating down a tunnel of night.

And as all this occurs, the power of the audience, the power of her past, the power of stage fright, seem to dip slightly inside her; and at the same instant, like a connected engine, the slowing of which must result in speeding up its twin, the vitality of what she has to play peaks just enough to achieve a frail dominance.

It's as if her fingers were released from a small but impregnable steel cage. They take off, it's the part early on where Jorge says

sparking in a gap of air
tigers prayed around our feet like doves
we lived in rooms under the sea
lit by smoldered algae

and with the pulse of violins she brings in softly the held-breaths of *Vallenato,* and the climb of lyrics (careful to keep a rein on her excitable left thumb) and then the first climax, notes tumbling like jugglers, trembling like lovers, teaming together like an expert *fútbol* squad—she is warm now; she is more than warm, she is hot with the fever of it; she looks at Jorge, sweat streaming now down her cheeks, between her breasts. The violins and marimbas chime in, the music, *her* music, swells around her. Soledad's dress is soaked as if she had been making love in it for hours. And she smiles so hard that every millimeter of her lips is separated, which does not happen often, and never out of bed.

————

THEY ARE DRUNK FOR two days after the concert; drunk on *tafia,* high on grass. Ruiz brings fine high-mountain cocaine paste to make the party last; they are smashed mostly on the praise of almost everyone, and the adulation of the fiesta, which like all good festivals has become its own dragon, in the process electing her and Jorge as the heroes to whom it annually vows its fire and breath. Dancing on the terrace, alone or with others, laughing occasionally at nothing. It is the sweet run home of a sea voyage, after rough weather, hearing the fiesta wind down as the different kinds of street music diminish and fade.

The second night, during what is only a four- or five-minute stretch, but seems like a month, all noises die away completely.

For the first time she can remember, she hears only silence in the *cruce*.

The hangover is proportionate to the poison. They lie

abed, too tired to make love. The pain of nausea for once silences him. The color of his eyes has faded to the hue the Atlantic takes on after a long storm. The wind picks up from the land, dusting the terrace with a thin, ocher dirt. The sun is like the titanium-brazed drill bits her father uses to penetrate deep basalt. Her brain is tungstite ore. Light, darkness, light.

Jorge recovers. Fueled by *tinto,* he retreats to his workroom. The sound of his pen scratching seems incredibly loud to her brain now unprotected by either fear or the shielding effects of *tafia.* They meet over dinner. He looks out the window, and barely answers when she speaks.

Late on the fourth evening after the concert, he emerges from the study and suggests they eat dinner at La Plaj. He is more talkative that night, though neither of them drinks more than a glass of wine. It is she, silenced by the formality of this pink-canopied restaurant frequented by people from the Walled City—silenced mostly by memories of Miguel and herself talking close and intimate at a corner table in this same place, in a part of her life that now seems as incredible and distant as Saturn's moons—who says nothing of consequence. He looks at her curiously. He must be conscious of being in a weak position himself, after the last few days, when it comes to the issue of keeping up a minimum level of communication with your partner, or mate, or whatever she is to him.

She fingers her earrings. He does not ask her what is wrong.

The following morning she wakes early. Jorge is already in his workroom. She bathes and dresses and lies in a hammock on the porch. Thinking she should get back in touch with her students, but loath somehow to do so. Jorge comes out, searching for something to eat. He is unshaven, and the wind has calmed. He goes back to his study and shuts the door. Over dinner he tells her something has been bothering him about *Desdichado,* nothing to do with her music but with what he wrote. "I obsess over it," he tells her, tugging on an earlobe with thumb and index finger. "It often happens to me like this after a reading. I have to figure out what it is and fix it before I can go on."

And of course that is all fine. She of all people knows how difficult it is to arrange the variables of time and space and mood in such a way as to produce something like music, or verse, that has no quantifiable link to any of those variables.

She is careful to leave him alone for a while after that. But she has no energy for work. It feels as if the performance; the *successful* performance, she has to remind herself; squeezed all juice out of the fibers inside her. It will take time to generate enough to conduct her creative currents again. She hears mostly the echoes of the *Selva* part of the concerto in her head—apparently the snatches of song from the barrio do not stick in her mind the way *Selva* did. Without work to keep her occupied, jealously aware that *he* is occupied with work, she becomes that much more conscious of how her contact with Jorge progressively and for no good reason seems to be dwindling beyond the natural downturns of romantic entanglements and creative obsession.

And then, three nights after dinner at La Plaj, Ruiz comes over. They drink too much as a matter of course. Jorge, becoming jovial, quotes a verse he is having trouble with: "A bird of such color amazing me by landing on my balcony, changes the polarity in my words, and I am afraid," he recites. She knows it's about her, and it pisses her off. Around eleven they decide to go to Pytagoro's, but Soledad is not in the mood for drinking, especially with Ruiz's night-colored eyes always seeking her out, she is never sure if he wants her to disappear or fuck him, or both—one thing that is clear is that the respectful protection a man is supposed to grow for the lover of his friend is not there and never has been for Ruiz. She does not go to the Cadillac. Jorge staggers in at three in the morning, blind drunk. She snaps at him when he wakes her up, and retreats to a porch hammock to sleep.

OH, AND THERE IS more of it, and it is by no means a clear progression. Over breakfast one day he talks to her the way he used to, even apologizes for being an old bear, as he puts it, and blames it again on his work.

"I understand," she tells him. "Believe me, you don't need to explain, it's just."

He nods, decrypting silence as he always did.

Their ankles curl around each other under the table as their hands spread butter on sweet bread.

Then he locks himself in his room all afternoon, a hot afternoon, and she finds she wants, sharply, urgently, to make love, but has lost the confidence she once had to go and touch him till he feels the way she does.

It amazes her how over the mere two months she has known him, she once had gotten so sure of herself, and so skilled.

She touches herself instead, lying in a hammock on the terrace, hidden in the grape arbor, warmed only by the paws of the sun; gasping quickly and alone the way she has not done since she came to live in the *cruce*.

The morning after that, she goes to her apartment. She is not moving out of Jorge's place—there is nothing definite to move out from. She buys a Cargo axhead in the market, the kind with the slips of paper containing the latitude and longitude of the *cruce* and Greenwich, England, and other important reference points, plus spells written in Qabbalistic phrases.

This she hangs on a nail over the lintel of her apartment.

But she also leaves the Fourneaux-Dallapé in the piano room and that, if you like, is a statement of conditionality. When she returns to Jorge's late that night he is gone, which does not surprise her.

He has not returned by the time she leaves the next day, and this has happened once before by now so she is not worried, only irritated, and fashed at herself for being angry, and doubly angry because she has let herself get in a position where she has to be fashed at herself.

So same routine next day, and she comes back and he is

still gone, and she is certain he has not been home in the interval.

She has only time to feel fear for him, rising like a tidal wave to drown all other emotions, before he shows up with Ruiz, and Dolores drunk and passed out between the two men; blowing in with the smell of mud and diesel and liquor and horse sweat and cactus, the smell of other places. That and a wild tale she hears out because (she later realizes) she wants to find in its very exoticism a compensation for the mundane disappointments she has been experiencing since the concert—and also because it's a good story and he is, above all, a fine teller of stories.

————

"IT WAS DOLORES, OF COURSE, she and her weakness for dusty tomb robbers and in particular one Diego—he was the fellow who pulled a knife on the terrace that night of the party—do you remember? He took her on horseback to Tayrona."

Tayrona the vast territory, a national park between Los Altos and the delta, a place long ago taken over by the Adornistas and the *narcotraficantes* with whom, they always claim, they never make deals.

"An unnatural land," Jorge continues, opening a fresh bottle of Delta rum and passing it to Soledad, who hands it to Ruiz. "The Indians saw it as sacred, mainly because they were convinced only gods could be so insane, and so *strong,* as to survive there. Pocket volcanoes and magma holes and lava runs like thick cables holding together the growth, and the trees all have spikes, even the grass packs thorns, the snakes so venomous, *putain,* you die just by looking in their ruby eyes. And then the cenotes—deep black wells where the volcanic rock has cracked and fallen into the water table— the fish in there are all blind, yeh, for these are holes where the Indians came to drown their virgins and their gold, and so much waste blinded the beasts. Even *guaqueros* proceed with caution.

"Diego's group did not hear the branches break. Night is darker there, as if light itself feared the spikes, and the Indians knew the way, which meant so did the Adornistas, who had made a deal with *fuego verde* and *fuego blanco,* green fire and white fire, emeralds and coca, the coinage of Tayrona, a mixed fire like phosphorus—yeh, bad simile." His smile. "I'll have to work on that one. Also, the Adornistas had Milan rocket launchers."

For an instant, something shifts in Jorge's face. It seems to fall in on itself, the eyes curiously blank, as if he'd had a stroke.

He clasps one hand around the wrist of the other, a life-saving hold, and pauses. Ruiz glances at him. Jorge takes a deep breath and, locating the rum bottle with his eyes, picks up the narrative again.

"One of the Adornistas used to work with the smuggler Captain Standle. He recognized her"—gesturing toward Dolores who lies in a broken position on the couch. And from that moment forward Soledad does not pay attention, not because the story varies in quality or excitement, but because the spell was broken for her by that facial expression of Jorge's, where the bravura of the professional poet suddenly caved in like limestone over the cenote he spoke of, exposing the man inside: a father made vulnerable by his daughter and his own lack of confidence in what he had done for her; potentially killed by the might-have-been.

And she thinks, with a clarity that reminds her of spring water, Because of that fucking *Desdichado* I have become part of his creation. And that has been good for me, because it is the best part of him and it has killed, for now, the stage fright; but it is also as dangerous as guns and terrorists because it ties me to him in the manner of a parasite. And ultimately my work must become his and he must take it over. Or else it will die—or else I will leave. Such are the choices left open to me. The truth of all this makes irrelevant the melodramatic circumstances among which she imagines it. In any event the dénouement of Dolores's adventure is as predictable as that of all journeys of quest: the negotiation, the safe conduct, the horses, the risk of double cross; the Jeep to broken highways and the implied cover of Ochoa Campos's paratroopers.

Less predictable is what happens later, when Jorge has passed out in bed, and Ruiz has left, and Soledad is the only one still up, gloomily smoking and cleaning ashtrays at the same time.

She hears a bump, and walks to where Dolores has slipped off the couch and is sitting on the floor, an absolutely amazed expression on what can be seen of her face behind a palisade of matted hair.

"My father," the girl whispers, and her green eyes looking up at Soledad's are like a child's, wide and dark with fear, although that might also be the jisi yomo Ruiz says she has smoked, opening up her irises.

"He's asleep." Soledad kneels beside her. The girl grabs her right arm with both hands.

"He left me on the *floor*?"

"You were on the couch. You don't remember."

"He left me." Now the girl, keeping one hand on Soledad's wrist, uses the other to stroke the inside of Soledad's forearm gently, obsessively, as if comforting a cat.

"Dolores!" Soledad, watching the girl's dirty hands, feels a vague distaste. She pulls back without meaning to. "He went to find you—he risked his life, girl, to—"

"Oh, Tayrona, yeh," she says. Taking her hands from Soledad's arm, she wipes the corner of her mouth with her scarf, as if to do maintenance for the increasingly voluminous flow of words now working themselves from her mouth. "That's so typical of him, that's his kind of attention. Like war, yeh? Ten months of boredom—then two hours of action, flags, trumpets, ta-ta-ra-ta-ra, attack, which is wonderful and I am grateful, but what about those ten months? When you are five or eight or fourteen and in a country that's strange, the ten months of boredom are more destructive!"

Soledad, looking down at the girl where she sits muddled in both clothes and thought on a rumpled Miskito rug, discovers in a millisecond of personal clarity that what happened to Dolores could happen to herself and Jorge; and either could be the one to initiate such terminal engagement.

Then she thinks of him, sleeping as he always does with his arms spread out like the man getting shot in *Tragedias de la guerra;* and the clarity vanishes, washed into oblivion by a great green wave of missing one who has not yet departed.

—————

SHE DOES A LOT of walking over the next two days, and comes to few conclusions. Only one of these stands out, and even then only as a hypothesis: that Jorge, on some layer of personality that he probably does not know exists, might have become jealous of their combined success. Parts of the *Desdichado* have been adopted by the nihilistic guild of musicians of the *cruce*. Almost everywhere she hears the tune she invented for the *"Souche"* passage, often without the lyrics, "The Sunrise" by *bandolos,* the "Bone Cement" movement by *pito* flute. Both she and Jorge understand what is happening here: what they made together has transcended the link to its creators, which should hurt them both equally even as it makes them proud; and also, given the greater affinity of music to adoption by a diverse population, the music must soon grow stronger than the poetry, which strikes her as irrelevant—but only, perhaps, because the music is hers.

On coming back from a walk that took her all the way around Las Animas to the City of Boats—a walk so long she found herself growing sickened, toward the end of it, by the smell of piss and garbage, and the ubiquitous scurry of rats—she finds a note from one of the Lo Pano message services stuck to her door with the red-colored tape that connotes urgency. She is sure it is from Jorge. Partly worried, partly excited—because the power politics of a crashing affair have been heavily in his favor ever since he was first to employ

rejection as tool, and this symbol of need from him is welcome, as a slight readjustment of a dangerous imbalance—
she rips it down.

45233
11/14
Mlle. Soledad MacRae
asd Pesceria Huet, Port de Péche, Barrio 3,
Cruce Bamaca/Lo Pano 177
text follows
I KNOW YOU ARE HIDING AND THAT
FINE. I HAVE NEVER QUESTIONED YOUR
JUDGMENT AS YOU KNOW

And now she knows who wrote this, without having to peek
at the "origine" box below:

HOWEVER IF YOU WOULD LIKE A VACA-
TION FROM YOUR COMMITTED AND
PASSIONATE LIFE WHICH MUST BE VERY
HARD WORK YOUR ROOM IS READY.
SPECIFICALLY IT WOULD MAKE ME
HAPPY IF YOU WOULD BE HERE TEA-
TIME TUESDAY 7 PM
text ends
dimanche 1803
origine; MacRae Mining SA
Glen MacRae
via Ruedo, Rio Chingado

She crumples the note in one angry twist although she is
not angry, or not much. She puts off thinking about the issues
the note raises, though they are thick and complicated, and
the measures she should take, were she to accept this invitation, quite pressing in terms of time.

She lies on her bed, smoking, watching the Barrio des
Anglais come alive with lights as darkness grows thicker

around the *cruce*. *I am starting to be defined by loss,* she thinks, and the idea comes as a surprise to her.

She knows that at a level almost as deep as Jorge's jealousy, on a layer of character most accessible by smell, and specifically by the flavor of travel coming off Jorge and Ruiz two nights ago — diesel, horse sweat, road dust, the metallic chill of night air — she has already considered the question, balanced the different elements, and decided to go.

NINE

THOUGH THIS COUNTRY POSSESSES a squadron (albeit used) of supersonic fighter-bombers, and access to Virtix links that connect it instantaneously to any point on the virtual globe, it takes as long to reach Glen MacRae from the coast or anywhere else as it always did.

Early the next morning, carrying only a *ruana* basket filled with necessities, she catches the Onibus from the Slave Gate to the train station on the other side of the Walled City.

The ride along the coast to the provincial capital lasts most of the day. At first it feels good to be "Outside," as the *crucistas* say; free of the urine smell, the noise, the inefficiencies of her enclave. But eventually the unrelenting poverty of the coastal region bores her. Surprised by a weariness that must have built up in her like an electric charge since before the concert, she sleeps much of the way.

She spends the night in a women's hostel and takes a bus for Ruedo at 6 A.M. The bus is crowded with Indians going home to one of their innumerable religious celebrations. Even today she finds herself dozing across the coastal swamps and the section of jungle after that. But as soon as the bus starts to climb it feels as though she has taken a hit of *basuko* for her senses are kicked and sharpened into alertness by the cooler air. She listens to the Indians talking of schools and floods and market prices, takes notes on a game-song their children sing. Even these low foothills are free of the coastal haze and she can see much farther. She recalls another story Jorge told her of his wife, Dolores's mother. "When she was young she had the body of a fine cello, and she wrote also, pretty romances, or short stories about doomed love and peaches. Of course we were prepared, after Dolores, for the disillusionment. When it came, like café au lait three times warmed over, it tasted bitter yet still we got nourishment from it and besides it kept us awake. Perhaps I was more prepared for our boredom with each other than she was—she left me twice when we were in Spain. What I was not prepared for—this was Barcelona; we had an apartment right under Monjuich, the ebony fortress where in the 1890s they held anarchists and freethinkers in granite cells and tortured them using implements five hundred years old—but I was not ready for my boredom with *myself,* in the context of the family we'd made. My senses were wound backward. I spent days on a rack of self-hatred, a pain so sharp I would scream for minutes at a time into a pillow in my office at the consulate. I was becoming a man who, spurred by the inquisition of duty, would make an argument of the most flagrant contradictions. You see, I did not leave Lydia in Barcelona then; yeh, I had left myself."

In the air like fine vodka that soaks these altitudes, Soledad understands that it is this aspect of Jorge she has most to fear, not because it describes Jorge but because it reminds her of how she herself deals with problems too big to go away on their own.

In Ruedo she sees the Jeep before the bus has come to a stop. Juanito takes her bag as casually as if she had never left; won't accept her kiss, but solemnly shakes her hand. New timber exploitations have turned square miles of jungle into smoking patches of black stick and desert. After an hour of progress the jungle takes over again. Two-lane road becoming one lane becoming red-rock track climbing through a forest of snakewood, acapu, and guava. A glimpse, over river clouds, of the blue-white peaks of the cordillera. Then the smoke from the tungstite workings over Cairn Dubh wiring into the sunset, and finally the glen, with the long white finca

and his Land Rover and, *merde!* a gleaming white Toyota
4×4 alongside an army deuce-and-a-half carrying a heavy
machine gun, the sight of which makes a fist in her chest, of
apprehension and embarrassment and anger—and worst of
all, of satisfaction, muted but real nevertheless.

She rounds on Juanito. Her control slips in the mud of
disillusionment—she had thought her father wanted to see
her, she never imagined the invitation to be part of a politician's trick.

"Why didn't you *tell* me?"

Juanito shrugs. His hair, Soledad notices for the first time,
is almost totally white.

"He told me not to. *Le patron.*"

It is dusk already and the *selva* around the glen resonates
with the calls of birds and monkeys and frogs and insects.
Despite engine damage to his ears he heard the low-ratio
whine of the truck, or maybe Marguerita warned him, and
he is on the veranda to greet her—the other, she observes
with fierce approval, having the grace for once not to intrude on the greetings, however compromised, of father and
daughter.

Francis Iain MacRae is balding, white-haired, and stooped,
but the lines of his face are still bold. The vulturine nose, the
long chin and squinted eye continue to force themselves outward into the world. His body is bent from prospecting, his
legs thick with climbing muscles. The hands fast to grab. He
wears the collarless shirt, waistcoat, breeches, and boots he
usually wears. She points at the Toyota, almost surprised that
her hand is trembling, she must be angrier than she thought
even.

"This was all a trick, then? It's no coincidence."

She speaks in English, laced with Scottish terms; the dialect they have always used together.

"Soledad—"

"I'm going back. There's no point in—"

"It's too late, it's almost dark."

He closes his eyes to hide how exactly he had predicted this line of argument.

"Anyway you wouldnae have come," he says.

She leans against a veranda post.

"Why could you no' invite me when he wasn't here? Once he told you where I was."

"He told me—"

"Then—"

"Soledad, *chérie*." The Scots accent growing deeper in the rumble of *r*. He opens his hands halfway. "I was going to wait to ask you—just you—for your birthday. But he convinced me this was a good idea."

"Why?"

"I'll let him tell you."

"I have nought to say to him."

"You cut your hair."

She stares at him, shocked by the irrelevance of his statement.

"I want you to listen to the *Sassenach*," her father continues. "He knows things—things you should be aware of. I want you to listen to him just once. I am no' going to apologize for that."

"Och, as if you ever did," she says, but then relents; the set of his face is close to pleading, which is not a pastime he indulges in often. His hands are now open all the way as if to catch some butterfly that evades him with ease. It's not true that he never apologizes, he used to do it all the time. She hugs him grudgingly. He smells as always of sweat and tallow and saddle soap and Rothmans and the smell of him has almost a chemical effect on her, makes her settle her arms around his waist and kiss him, once, and on one cheek only.

JUANITO SAYS MIGUEL IS hacking the roan gelding he usually rides with Juanito's son around the perimeter of the *estancia*. She has time to take a long tub in the rosewood-paneled bathroom that was her mother's. Afterward she dresses in a dress so long and old and frowsy she left it here when she went to the Capital Conservatory. She makes herself a *tafia* with Delta rum and takes it back to her room, to the screened porch outside, where she sits in a rattan chair and watches the parrots flying home in pairs as night completes its blitzkrieg takeover of the jungle sky. Trying to keep a lid on the thoughts and emotions she previously had held at bay with the drive of travel. But it's hard to do in this place that is both site and symbol of her childhood, a house whose every detail injects in her like a syringe the powerful neurotransmitter of memory.

And so she recalls the savage isolation, the arterial abandonment, the nights so lonesome that it seemed a meteor cutting out of the farthest reaches of the galaxy had to be closer to companionship and understanding than she. Nights she felt so worthless that it would have been a kindness to humanity for her to walk naked into the jungle only two hundred meters away and let the snakes or spiders or leopards or guerrillas cancel her puny hold on survival in this place, not that humanity would notice; so misunderstood that the Manopani, with their monkey gods and closed faces, had a better comprehension of her than did her father, or Dona Susannah, who took care of her during the day, or Maria Gisela, who did the cooking, or especially Mademoiselle Weill, who taught her lessons and did not always remember to avoid touching her father in ways no employee should when Soledad was around.

Letting the rum sear her tonsils. Taking another sip. Allowing the alcohol to alter her mood somewhat.

It was not unleavened misery either. Soledad remembered enough good times here, even after her mother did not come back, to honey the bitterness of Glen MacRae. The animals, mostly. Her dog Pirou, who succumbed to the infectious bite of a red tick; her horse Bolívar. The old player piano in the parlor, and the books full of diachrome drawings and nineteenth-century songs that she used to play and sing by the hour.

And her father, not when he was trying but rather when he took her out and they did things together that he knew how to do, like ride and fix machinery. And Maria Gisela, anytime she was not working, which was pretty damn seldom because people around here worked awfully hard—right now, even in the velvet absorbency of dark, through the fragrant shadow of lupines and viburnum growing around her little porch, she sees a squad of Indios repairing the electrified fence that is her father's second line of protection against hostage-takers and Adornistas. There is something odd about what they are doing, also—the mechanical rhythm of the men bending to lift a new mangrove post into place, the stiff silhouette of the foreman—she can't put her finger on it. Maybe it's the presence of soldiers that throws them off. The escort from the deuce-and-a-half is making camp behind the cane shed. The play of their fire and the scratch of their radio seem oddly soft against the leavings of sunset, the raucous birdsong.

The rum has warmed her lower half and is creeping up on her chest. She walks back into the room, having it in her mind to open one of the songbooks, and instead retrieving from the dresser a little cigar box full of feathers she collected on the edges of the *selva* with Juanito. Goatsucker, *uira puro,* Cuvier's toucan. The colors have not faded at all with time. Which is when he chooses to knock, diffidently but knowing full well she is there—he always does his little research into details such as these.

Miguel.

She walks back to the porch before calling, *"Entre."*

He stands before her, illuminated by the light of the door he left open as convention dictates. Very straight, the hair as usual not quite lined up, the face like some suffering seer cribbed from El Greco, the beautifully cut Italian suit that doesn't quite conceal the thinness of his limbs, the thinness overall—he has lost weight, she thinks, and crushes preemptively the spark of concern fanning into light within her. His eyes seem darker, somehow. The concern links up with another kindle of attraction: those thin hands once touched her with a knowledge born of too many hours of pleasure, of education among the bedclothes—

She grinds out, in a voice too harsh even for this, "Are you proud of yourself?"

He says nothing.

"It's a two-day trip to come here from Bamaca. Such a cheap little deception—to use my father in this way."

"He agreed. As you know."

"He was always impressed by your European manners. And your wife's family."

Miguel sighs, and makes a quarter turn away from her.

"Do you think you are the only one with a bone to pick?"

She swallows more *tafia,* too much, she has to fight not to cough.

"You were married," she says finally, and clears her throat. "I owed you nothing."

"My marriage was a given. I was honest about it. You accepted it. To use it now is unfair of you—"

"You, *you* talk of unfairness?"

"That's not why I asked your father to carry out this . . . this stratagem."

"Trick, Miguel. Call a spade a spade."

"Trick, then." He turns back to face her. "I have to tell you, Soledad, I knew where you were."

She shakes her head, smiling without humor, thinking of the F2 man in the doorway of the brothel.

"The black-market slums. The *favela* of that poet." He isolates the noun "poet" with a tiny half beat on both sides, to include doubt, and the entrance of contempt. She is about to jump on that, mention Jorge's awards, his publications; but Miguel holds up one hand and it catches the column of light shining in from the hallway, defining clearly the length of his fingers, the neat manicuring of his nails, the whiteness; she has a sudden, clear memory of those fingers like soft dry leaves sliding between her thighs, so thin they barely disturbed the labia and fitted with little space to spare on the diameter of the uppermost tip of her clitoris.

She recrosses her legs and leans forward, feeling herself go hot as a pampas wind. Missing Jorge suddenly and savagely, despite or because of this betrayal of mind. Trying to think of him now—his rough hands, so different from Miguel's, his face—she sees the length of his nose, the color of his eyes, green as a jungle pool. The cheekbones are heavy but Oh, she thinks desperately, oh, she cannot see him whole anymore.

"I understood what you did, by leaving. I granted you that injustice, because it was always there, in the structure of our—affair. I never went after you. What I ask now"—she has slumped a little in the rattan seat, and he folds his hands behind his back, acknowledging her attention—"What I ask now is only that you listen to me, because you are in some danger."

"Danger," she repeats, and picks up the drink again, shaking the ice to strike a high D against the crystal. She lets a wedge of mockery enter her voice then, which is fine and also for show. Miguel has a powerful if undefined role in the ministry his father-in-law runs, and Sandoval has lunch every day with General Ochoa Campos, and if anybody in this part of South America knows what danger is and who is apt to dispense the stuff, it is Ochoa Campos.

"That *cruce,*" he says, and turns to the window. "Believe me, I understand the attraction, especially to an artist. The absence of rules. The bohemian mystique. The folklore, the *contrabandistas,* the wild democracy of it. The hint of risk, which you always enjoyed, Soledad."

"I am not there for the folklore, Miguel," she tells him quietly. "Or the risk."

"I know that," he says seriously. "I also acknowledge that the *cruce* has a role to play. The way society works, the creative element surging with ideas and strange initiatives, versus the action element, always trying to harness the wild horse, tame lightning for the power grid—"

"You're mixing metaphors."

"Claro," he says, and smiles, and as usual the smile makes a sunrise of his face, and she looks down and narrows her eyes a little. "And you can tell I have read Hawkley, no?

"But always these periods are short, Soledad. They have to be. The *Assemblée Constituante,* the Jacobins cede place to the Directoire and, finally, the organizing power of Napoleon. The Mensheviks fall to Lenin, the cohesive administration of Lenin. The Jeffersonian idealists are reduced to begging for jobs from Hamiltonian bankers. And in this country, the days of your *cruce* are drawing to a close."

A lawyer-bird whistles once its single pure note. She looks up at him again.

"What are you trying to say?"

He does not look away. He refuses to seek refuge in movement, and stands like the chief cadet of a Catholic military academy, which he once was.

"I cannot tell you details. We think there are splinter factions from the Adornista—ah, I should not tell you this much even. It would go hard with me if anyone found out. I don't know exactly what is going to happen, or when.

"But I am asking you, Soledad, not to go back to the Bamaca *cruce.* Or if you must go, to pick up your things, or see Echeverria—well, turn around immediately and come back."

"To you?" she asks softly.

"No," he answers. "I do not go that far." Abruptly, he takes three steps into her room, three steps onto the porch. "I am trying to keep this above the personal," he says, irritation hardening his voice. "Believe it or not, I am doing you a favor here. I am not asking for something back because of what we have, or once had, together."

"A pity," she answers, and her voice is cool and nicely

tuned. She recognizes this as a defense against the rage that unexpectedly flares in her—rage at his complacency, at the sterile momentum for order and predictability he represents, at the fact that they used to sleep together yet not once did he consider giving up anything of real value for her; at his knowledge, also, that harm might come to the place in which she sought refuge.

That anger makes her as vulnerable as a sheep when a leopard finds a gap in the electric fence.

She sips *tafia*. The rum gives her throat something to do. The fury dwindles as she focuses on swallowing. She figures it goes so fast because what he has just said about his motivation is so clearly a falsehood, a dissimulation of self, and thus makes everything else he told her open to doubt.

Including his warning.

Especially his warning.

She turns away and straightens the box of feathers on her dresser, feeling almost let down by the desertion of anger as well as by the absence of that tiny thrill of nerves that fluttered within her when he spoke of risk.

———

THE REST OF THE evening passes the way, she imagines, her father hoped it would. Dinner is not silent—Francis is alone too often to let an opportunity for discussion pass, and Miguel is a conversationalist so polished that even she takes pleasure in listening to his stories of scandal and backstabbing in the *Casa Amarilla,* the National Assembly. Yellow linen tablecloth and mismatched china and oil lamps and the billion bugs committing seppuku on the screens. The far-off snarl of a leopard. The scratch of his Brahms records. Sloth steaks tasting of mutton. The pumps of the mine beating when the breeze picks up from that quarter, like a telltale heart, like the thuds of the Bamaca sewer tunnel, the thought of which drops an unexpected cowl of loneliness over her. Her father's movements growing steadily more helium-filled as he empties the bottle of Islay Mist that Miguel bought for him at six times the *cruce* price. The pleasure in his eyes increasingly evident whenever he turns to look at his daughter sitting demurely in a dress she last wore when she was eighteen.

She has an impulse, at that point, a very new desire like a tulip sprout, to go to the piano now and play a piece of *Desdichado* for him, specifically "Daybreak," to see if he recognizes the birdsong and noises; it is the part of her that enjoys acting eighteen for her father, she realizes, and always will, and there is nothing wrong in that.

But she is also reluctant because of an upfront need to protect what she gained in the concert, the fresh but still delicate confidence she regards as a gift from Jorge Echeverria. Anyway the presence of Miguel (and the guilt she continues to feel from that quick spark of libido earlier) thoroughly precludes the possibility.

After that, the shadows seem to grow for her around the sepia lamps, quenching her small enjoyment of the evening.

She slowly becomes convinced that in the gut of events, where the first lines of their reason for being must lie, this situation in Glen MacRae is wrong, even wronger than she first imagined; inspired by deceit, fueled by misplaced hopes, by the clutter of old mistakes. Until she can stand it no longer and, complaining of a vague sickness—deceit thus inspiring further untruth—she gets up, goes to her room, and sits on her porch, smoking, until she is sure dinner is over.

———

MUCH LATER, TIPTOEING THROUGH the parlor after visiting Maria Gisela's daughters, she hears Brahms, and her father coughing on the porch. She hesitates, listens for conversation and, hearing none, goes out to join him.

He says nothing. She sits on a chaise longue. A monkey whoops. The Symphony Number Four fades into silence on his ancient Victrola. The wings of bats slap quick, unseen.

This side of the finca faces a brook that sneaks out of the *selva* under the fence. The fireflies of the high Amazon blink their blue red green yellow lights as they dance with each other over the slow-moving water, creating a tiny window of festivity that he used to call "Christmas lights" in this place that has never seen such a fiesta.

He pours her *tinto* from the pitcher beside him. The pitcher rattles against the cup.

"You will go back," he says at last, "naturally."

She lets silence agree with him.

"Do you—do you ever hear—"

"No, Papi."

"I like your cutty hair. It took me a while to get used to it."

More clinks. This time it is Islay Mist he is adding. "The prospector's conversation manual," he calls whisky.

"Och, I know why she didna bide with me," he grunts finally. "I will never know why she left you." It is a lament so old he uses it the way she would employ a refrain in a song: to emphasize something else, to outline an overarching structure. But this time he won't leave it alone.

"I ask because you are like her. Leaving is something that comes naturally into your heart."

Another old lament, that she always equated with his loneliness. It is only at times like these, late at night, that he ever lets himself complain.

But as she goes to bed, around midnight, feeling the snakewood footboard limiting her toes, she finds that his last comment stays with her, rocking back and forth in her memory for all the world as if it were resonating with something different from Glen MacRae, something separate from the geographical impingements of childhood.

———

SHE GETS BACK TO the *cruce* three days later. She walks through the Slave Gate into a dozen songs from market buskers and the myriad arguments of a cockfight and the braze of sea-filtered sunshine unmarred by any cloud save a thin black smudge from a ship to the east. It all fills her up as if she had three extra lungs to inflate, and for a minute or so she is bursting with the kind of pure joy that she remembers mostly from the more compartmentalized, and thus more simply delighted, viewpoint of a child.

"I won't leave this place," she whispers to herself. She runs, though her *ruana* is heavy with jungle mangoes and presents from Maria Gisela's daughters, all the way to the fish harbor and up the stairs to her apartment—

And Cloodine's door opens.

And Cloodine says mournfully, "I was waiting for you."

Soledad stops on the landing. Her simple pleasure is cut immediately, and she feels resentment that people's problems should intrude so quickly into the rare clarity of her homecoming.

The resentment swiftly turns into guilt, because she is acting like a Walled City tourist. After all, though she has no ties of family with them, she abandoned Cloodine and her hard problems to go to the *selva* and drink *tafia* and look at fireflies.

And she left Jorge without telling him where she was going, and no matter if this is exactly the type of behavior he is guilty of, it doesn't justify her treating in such fashion someone she deeply cares for.

"What is it?" she asks, when she gets her breath back. "Are you all right? I've been away. Did the job—"

Cloodine opens the door farther. Behind her, in the corner kitchen, a pot steams on the stove. A braid of garlic and a chorizo hang from a hook nearby. A grubby brown fist sticking out of a roll of stained swaddling marks the baby, snoozing on top of a crate. The crate is full of oranges. So she is still earning a living, Soledad thinks, and feels a quiet swell of satisfaction that something she did, something the *cruce* did, should continue, quite literally, to bear fruit.

Cloodine, tutting impatiently, opens the door all the way. And in the new angle thus revealed, Soledad has a brief illusion that she is looking through time, past Cloodine holding the door—worried but fed—to Cloodine sobbing and hungry on the windowsill almost a month ago. The hair is longer though and the face, what she can see of it behind a crooked elbow, much younger, and with a brow so like Jorge's she has no need of the black silk kerchief and *guaquero* fatigues and waistcoat to cue her memory.

"Dolores!"

"I found her this morning," Cloodine says. "She was sleeping in the corridor. I gave her some *tinto* but—" She shrugs.

Soledad nods. She sets the *ruana* down, walks across the cool tiles through the smell of diaper and garlic. Dolores's mouth is half open and her nose makes squirrel noises. Soledad shakes her and she comes awake immediately, hunching a little as if to dodge a blow. She stares left and right, then raises her gaze to Soledad's.

"Oh," she whispers. "You."

"You're in the wrong *cuarto*."

"You were gone. Your door was locked. How can you live with this smell of fish?"

Dolores's eyes are bloodshot and the smell of liquor and sweat is strong on her. Her shirt collar is torn and stained. She gets up, holding the windowsill for support. Soledad leads her upstairs to her kitchen. There she puts water on the fire, glancing automatically at the brothel entrance, though the F2 man has been absent for almost ten days now. She thinks of Miguel and finds a relic of anger when she does so. A new amusement is present as well. It all seems so preposterous now—the rigid technocrat and Dona Serena and the fact that they once held such space in her life that she literally took it apart and bricked it in to fit around the thin arch of his adultery.

Dolores has slumped against the little table in the same position as she was downstairs. Soledad pours her the *tinto*.

"When was the last time you ate?"

The girl shrugs. She presses her lower lip to the coffee cup, dunking her tongue in and out like a cat. She has lost weight, Soledad thinks, wondering vaguely what drugs the *guaqueros* are using.

"I'll make some *bouillis*."

"I'm not hungry," Dolores says. "I just wanna go to sleep."

"You need something in your stomach," Soledad replies, "then you can sleep. I have to go to the market first. Can you stay awake?"

Dolores does not answer.

"Dolores?"

Her eyes are closed. The squirrel sounds come again. Soledad shakes her. A seam of worry opens in her chest. She shakes harder.

"Dolores!"

The girl's eyes snap open. Again she hunches, like a dog, Soledad thinks, aware of how much Jorge would hate the hackneyed image—like a *campesino*'s cur.

"Dolores," Soledad says, "I need to know. What were you doing, earlier? *Basuko?* Smack? *Perica,* what?"

Dolores smiles, and closes her eyes at the same time, squeezing a tear out of the corner of one of them.

"Jisi," Soledad sighs.

"Jisi yomo," Dolores repeats dreamily.

Outside, the sun is working itself down from the volcanic fury of midday. A light breeze deposits harbor smells in her nostrils. The ship she saw earlier is much closer, the string of its smoke unraveled by something new offshore. Maybe it has to do with leaving the *selva* and its eternal and limiting perfume of jungle, but everything here seems magnified by the sea haze so she feels she can reach out and touch objects many miles away.

She finds the macumba stall where she bought her axvotive and asks for something to counter the effects of jisi. The vendor opens a jackknife and whittles a handful of shavings off a piece of very light, hard wood. The shavings are sharp as flint and smell like lavender and wet dog. The man asks to look at her hand. "Boil up enough to fill half your palm," he advises.

"She is very sleepy," Soledad tells him, "she still has the emotion."

"Does she caress you," the man asks, "like a cat?" Soledad thinks of Dolores five days ago at Jorge's, rubbing her arm without pause.

"Not now," she replies.

"*Calme toi*," the man says. "She'll be fine."

Soledad goes to the vegetable stall and in her relief at what the Umbanda man said buys a kilo of *mucaja*, which is too much. She enjoys how the small coconutlike fruits roll around in the twisted newspaper the vendor gives her. She buys anise and tapioca and on her way home stops at the shop downstairs for *sarara*. The river shrimp are piled like tiny, swimming, antennaed opals next to a bin of oval fish flapping about in their own blackish slime, goring each other with giant dorsal spikes.

She needs only twenty grams of *sarara* and Patrice gives her a good deal.

Dolores is still sleeping and Soledad doesn't wake her. She cooks a pot of rice and another of tapioca, then grinds the *mucaja* together in a mortar and pestle with the tiny shrimp. The shellfish will cut the fruits' viscosity, allowing the mixture to turn into the smooth paste of *bouillis*. Finally she stirs in anise, rice, and tapioca, and sprinkles cinnamon on top. The milky smell of it reminds her, as it probably does every person in this half of the country, of childhood—of Maria Gisela, of her mother even, coaxing Soledad to eat another spoonful of something so sweet and smooth and nourishing only a child could think of reasons not to swallow it.

She grew sick of *bouillis* as a kid. She remembers distinctly a gesture her mother had when Soledad refused to eat, wiping strands of hair off her forehead with the back of a wrist. "Ah, *la vie*," she would sigh, as if the troubles of *bouillis* were a microfiche of everything that would eventually drive her to leave. "Life is so hard, sometimes."

Soledad measures the Umbanda man's shavings and stirs them in a pot of boiling water. The kitchen, briefly, smells of wet dog and lavender. When everything is ready she wakes Dolores. It takes longer than before. The girl seems vaguer and more dream-bound than earlier, but the advantage of such a state is that she does not bother to protest when Soledad gives her the cup of boiled herbs. And she likes the *bouillis,* at first anyway, taking a dozen spoonfuls of the paste, one after the other until abruptly she puts the spoon down, sits upright, and says, "I'm not going back."

Soledad chews a mouthful of *bouillis.* She is very hungry. On the bus and train she ate only a couple of bags of nuts and a single *butifarra.*

"I'm not going back," Dolores repeats, slurring her words a little. She focuses on Soledad's eyes, then closes her own.

"To your father's?"

"No."

"Does Jorge know you're here?"

The girl snorts.

"He wouldn't even know if I was *there*." Tracing a diagram with one finger in spilled *bouillis.* "The *guaqueros,*" she explains, very slowly and distinctly, as if Soledad did not speak the language well. "I don't want to see them."

"Why not?"

"I don't like Diego anymore. My father says I just like the excitement. It's true, he's exciting. They have fun. They're not what you think—some are rough, it's true, but some were archaeology students, they just got sick of the university and all the bullshit. . . ."

"But?"

"But it's not that different from writers, when you come down to it." Dolores's finger stops making diagrams. "It's just the games men play. Some use typewriters. Some use pickaxes. Some use rifles. I want something different, for me. For us."

Soledad combs her hair back with her fingers. She thinks, There is something in Dolores's little speech—the clear logical connections of it, perhaps, or the way she looked down at the table just now, or maybe just the fact that her finger stopped making diagrams—anyway, it sounds rehearsed. The manipulation happening is as solid and tangible to her way of thinking as those little *mucajas* were to her fingers.

She fingers the tiny macaw hanging from her ear as she watches Dolores staring down at the cheap teak. She wonders why she is not upset by this, the way she was when Miguel did the same thing. The technique is so similar, even if the aims are different. It's amazing, really, that the stupidity of the girl's plight—caught between a compulsion for flight and a need to be enfolded by a man—does not elevate Soledad's temperature into irritation, that Dolores should let herself get trapped like that, and by *guaqueros* and drugs into the bargain.

"Do you have *cachaca*?" Dolores asks, flicking at her a glance that is hot with desire for rum.

"I don't think you need it."

"No." She shakes her head exaggeratedly. "I shouldn't drink it anymore."

"Do you still feel sick?"

"I'm pregnant."

Soledad's expression doesn't change. The sense she had earlier in the market, that everything is closer and more tangible, multiplies again by a factor she does not know. She feels the iron stovetop poking like a blunt knife into the fibers of her buttocks; feels the thousand kilos of limestone wall and terra-cotta tile of this little kitchen exerting their weight on the sump of her stomach.

"Are you going to keep it?" she asks finally.

Dolores looks out to sea.

"I know all the wisdom," she says at last. Her skin seems transparent in the changed light of evening. "How you want something that's truly your own. That will give back with no conditions the love you give it. How selfish that is, when it's so fucking hard, even here, to bring up a child by your-self." She looks at Soledad again. "But the obligation to this thing inside me is greater than those problems. And I do want something of Diego's. He wants me to have it. I don't know what to do."

Soledad clears her throat. She picks up the *tinto* jug, but it is empty. She opens the coffee tin.

"You can make your own decision. There are abortionists in the *cruce*—"

"Don't tell me what I already know. That's not why I came here."

"Why *did* you come here, Dolores?"

"I'm not sure. Obviously you don't want me. I need—"

A rolling comes across the *cruce,* a sound of giant *pétanque* balls on marble, of thunder twisted on itself, of a diesel the size of Matto Grosso switching into life.

The house shakes violently. The roof doves, startled, flash past the window. The coffee in Soledad's spoon drifts to the tiled floor.

The shaking stops. The sound is gone as completely as if it never existed, which is a possibility Soledad considers for an instant, then discards. For the second time she can remember, no other sounds are discernible in the *cruce.* No talking, no dogs, no music cricketing up from different directions.

Earthquake, she thinks.

She puts down the spoon and looks out the window, but nothing has happened to the view of orange rooftops and laundry stretching to the City of Boats. The doves drift back to perch.

She walks to her bedroom. The window is open. Framed in its rectangle, a tight fist of blackness rises over Ensevli in the direction of the garbage dump. As she watches, the fist opens into fingers that grab a turn of wind and are lifted up toward the more subtle reek of the volcano. For an instant Soledad thinks she sees flames rising like a frieze of scarlet all along the horizon of the shattered highway and the dump;

but it cannot be fire along such a broad front, only a trick of the approaching sunset, a fancy of the optic nerve.

Dogs bark. A man yells. In the angle of fishing harbor visible from this window, people start to run in the direction of the smoke. A mototaxi takes off in the same direction. A man and woman gesture toward the dump from a nearby roof. Voices multiply below her, rising in a rhythm of interrogation.

"Not a bad one," she murmurs to herself.

Beside her, Dolores laughs. She has a pretty laugh, like scales plinked on a marimba. Major A.

"That was no earthquake," she says. "It sounded like PETN."

"Like what?"

Soledad stares at the girl. Dolores suddenly looks five years younger. Her eyes catch light. Excitement has tightened her face muscles.

"PETN. It's a dynamite the *guaqueros* use, and—hear that?"

A new element has bubbled to the top of the sounds of a stirred-up *cruce*. Tiny blasts, only more continuous and timed than the first explosion. Single shots. A rattle of automatic fire. The doves rise once more into the air.

"FN carbines," Dolores says in satisfaction. Her hands, Soledad notices, are folded across her belly as if to protect the newly quickened egg inside.

Soledad finds herself enthralled by the urgency of this spectacle, caught up in the tension of not knowing, despite the increasing feeling of weight at the pit of her own abdomen.

She watches with Dolores for twenty minutes more, bent over the ledge of the small window, her thigh and shoulder companionably pressed into the thigh and shoulder of the girl beside her.

The gunfire stops after only a couple of minutes.

The smoke grows denser.

To Soledad's eyes, the faces passing in the street below are not the usual tan hue of *cruce* features but pale, as if what was happening had somehow brought their white skullbones closer to the surface.

Then Dolores leans forward, waving at a figure on the Corniche, a boy with the black cellphone belt of a *crucista* whose other salient characteristic is that he walks in a different direction, *away* from Ensevli.

"Toni," she yells, loud enough to hurt Soledad's ears.

The boy stops and peers around till he locates Dolores, who is leaning so dangerously out the window now that Soledad grabs her shirt in case she should slip.

"What're you doing? What's going on?"

"The sewer tunnel," the boy calls back. "The one the government was digging, behind Ensevli. The *guaqueros* blew it up."

"Putain," Dolores replies, impressed, as if that was all the explanation she needed.

"But why did they blow it up?" Soledad calls.

"It wasn't a sewer," Toni says. "It was a hundred and twenty meters over the *cruce* border, and it was full of F2 and listening equipment and soldiers.

"But I'm not here because of the sewer," he continues. "I'm here because of *that*."

He points to the harbor, then turns and disappears behind the brothel.

Soledad, leaning almost as far out as Dolores to see the harbor, realizes that the ship she saw earlier has negotiated the sea channel. It is now steaming very slowly in a half circle in Bahia de las Animas, just beyond the fishing harbor breakwater.

With diminished distance, the vessel has lost the washed quality the sea once gave it, and is now as hard and detailed as everything else around her has become. In that new detail one can tell it is not a ship at all, or rather, it is not an ordinary *batiman*—it is a warship, a frigate perhaps, with sharply raked bow and a long low hull forested with missile launchers, cannons, and the intricate, slowly turning gridwork of attack radars.

Everything on the ship is uniformly gray. On the calm surface of the bay, now turning the color of magma with sunset, it looks like a poisonous by-product of smelting.

The frigate glides to a stop. Chain rumbles, a mini replica of the earlier explosion. Both anchors drop, making orange ripples that reach all the way to the fishing harbor and set the small boats briefly to rocking.

Soledad pulls back into the room and sits on her bed. She hears words in her head, Miguel's voice. *The days of the cruce are coming to a close,* he repeats. *I cannot tell you the details.*

For no good reason she keeps seeing the horizon of Ensevli the way she imagined it earlier, burning across its length; and under the flames, all the queer apparitions that must eventually haunt them: Black-armored knights who write with pens of red fire. Giant dark tanks that float on air. A mist that turns, so rapidly, to bone cement.

Dolores looks at her.

"Well," she says, "show's over, yeh? I better get going."

Soledad returns her gaze. The "yeh" reminds her of Jorge. Her stomach cramps with emptiness as she realizes how much she misses him; misses, even more, the time before the concert, not even a month ago, when her life was as simple as falling in love and making music and helping someone who needed food.

"Please," she says finally. "Please don't go. I want you to stay."

Dolores's eyes remain on hers for a moment.

Then she nods, as if it were no more than her due. Soledad thinks naively that Dolores, lulled by the jisi hangover, will go to sleep now without fuss, the way a cat would lapse into slumber at his accustomed place by the stove.

Instead it is Soledad, made drowsy by travel, by the

ongoing compulsion to avoid thought, who lies back on the bed and closes her eyes.

Her last conscious perception is of the black shape of this girl, one thigh wedged on the window's stone shelf, the dying fire of day making a hearth of her cheekbone as she stares at the lights that blink like jungle fireflies around the tunnel the *guaqueros* blew up.

TEN

AND THE FORM CAME out of velvet blackness, the figure so human in the way it folded toward what concerned it— toward the square in which people framed views they could control.

But the square was flat, uniform, evenly lit, in a way a window was not.

And the viewer was not Dolores but a man, fat and yellow of face, leaning toward a sequence of small screens hung overhead.

In most of those screens, caught from a top-down point of view, a woman lay curled in sheets, short black curls stark against the pillow, mouth wound tight into the roller of her cheekbones. Stiff and silent and eyes fixed on the thinscreens, as well as on an overhead camera lens that stared straight back at her, its red ON light aglow, completing the electronic circle.

And so Soledad came awake, in the most twenty-first-century of ways, watching herself watch herself come awake.

Her hand was being held, and this comfort was like a tactile bridge back to the world of dreams, of Glen MacRae and Dolores and the Bahia de las Animas.

But whoever held her hand stood to one side, close yet outside her field of vision, and this was different from Dolores, who had sat two meters away on the window ledge at the foot of her bed, in her flat over the fishing harbor in Bamaca.

Faced by this betrayal of dream, by the intrusion of a world she had no wish to inhabit into the world she fled to in sleep, Soledad yanked her hand violently free of the person beside her. Rolled sideways, using the lower back muscles she had pulled on the morning of the attack and thus further clouding the issue of what was now and what was not.

The scene to her right allowed no confusion except, perhaps, with memories of the first time she'd woken up in this room, with these men.

Stix leaned on the concrete rim of the water bed, his hand still in the awkward position it had assumed to clutch hers. The control room behind the near window was dark. In the window beyond that, only a slight fuzzy light intruded to edge with gray the wings of the giant bird against the blackness of the factory's main room.

Stix wore a half-sucker with the visor down. He watched her through the clear lower portion, but flicked his eyes up repeatedly to whatever was showing in the silvered half.

"Bom journée?" a voice said softly. The voice came from a screen beside the one featuring her in bed, where a small dark-skinned face was backlit against radios and round windows. A shiny snout poked repeatedly from the lower edge of the frame, trying to get the Afro-Peruvian boy's attention.

"And so, it becomes a little clearer," the cripple said. "Ask her about the armor."

"She's barely awake," Stix said. "Give her a second, Zatt."

Soledad looked at Stix again. She remembered Dolores giving her a present, weeks after she came to live at the fishing harbor, on a day Soledad had been missing Jorge particularly hard. It was a mahogany box full of cowrie-shell conjuring pieces bought from one of the Slave Market vendors. It was nothing much, but the gesture of kindness, by causing her to let emotions in from outside, had freed the emotions she kept locked within: it was as if the defenses were the same whichever way they faced, and when they came down the monster of grief could swarm out of its inner dungeon like a movie beast and have its way with her. Now even the slight generosity implied in Stix's words had the same effect. She shut her eyes against the sharpness of it, feeling her abdomen tense and split open in her mind to expose the fissures, the great absence within her—the missing of the colors and smells of her city and the overarching flavor of the people she had lived among. Her eyelids burned with the hot water pushing against them.

Stix's hand found hers once more. She did not respond, or pull away. An electric motor whined repeatedly. She recognized it as coming from Zatt's wheelchair. She wondered if these men planned to reassure her with similarity—for this scene was almost identical to the last time she had woken up here—and thus subvert her defenses in other directions. Zatt was clearly too intelligent not to have made the connection. A voice coming from a speaker behind the bed said, "This is all in Theta which is in the medium-term circuits. More than three minutes, they'll blank out on you."

Stix sighed in exasperation.

"Soledad," Zatt began. He pronounced her name correctly. His voice was soft as a cloud viper's slither. "Can you tell us now, about the hovertanks? And the 'nightcrawlers'— exactly where you saw them. It's—" His voice broke on the last syllable. "It could prove something—"

She opened her eyes again. Struggled to a sitting position. The ache in her back was no longer much of a problem, but it was hard to push against the water bed's squishiness. The feeling of void was replaced by a sense of embarrassment, that once again she had been observed in the most private corner of sleep by men who did not know her—who filmed her and held her hand while she talked to Miguel and recalled arousal and rejection and even greater vulnerabilities. The heat of embarrassment grew to the point of anger. Then it changed in quality as other memories moved in, tying in those words Zatt had uttered, "hovertanks" and "crawlers," words she had only *thought* of as she watched the explosion with Dolores. Someone had mentioned, recently, that she talked in her sleep; this had shocked her, because she had believed she did not talk at all anymore.

Now she was shocked, not that she had said something, but that she might have gabbed in such detail. She had dreamed of other small things—she waved one hand irritably, looking around for a pencil, paper, anything.

"Give her a keyboard," Zatt said. "She wants to write."

"Oh, *now* she's mute," the speaker-voice commented sarcastically.

Stix unhooked his belt and placed the attached jambook on the water bed's concrete border. He unlatched the keyboard lid and toggled a key twice.

She twisted farther to type. I HAVE TALKED IN DREAMS. Then she turned the screen so it faced the men.

"That you have," Zatt agreed, peering at the display.

Stix tapped another sequence of keys. Above Soledad, the vidscreens showing her image shivered, went black, then flickered on to the same scene as before—except that the woman in the frame was no longer sitting up next to a jambook. Now she lay sideways on the mattress. Her right hand pulled the sheets in wave patterns toward her stomach. She tossed her head and muttered something, then said clearly, *"Pas les caballeros, portant la cuirasse! Leurs yeux comme des porteplumes en fuego écarlate, oh le brouillard se moût en ciment d'os"*—speaking in Lanc-Patua, the lingua franca of Bamaca, the dialect of her region, her *cruce:* the French of Guyanese gold panners liberally shot through with Spanish from Afro-Peruvian immigrants, and Portuguese from Brazilians to the south, and even some Hebrew words from the local Umbanda priests.

"Not the knights yet, the ones who wear armor." It was the boy in the parallel vidscreen, translating. "Their eyes that are like pens of red fire, the fog that, that changes into bone cement."

"There," Zatt said, "*that's* where the Farnsworth comes in. They just didn't bring in nightcrawlers, in Bamaca."

Stix placed his hand lightly on Soledad's shoulder. She pulled away, then looked down, suddenly saddened by her own rejection of such elementary kindness. She was sitting on something damp and for a moment she thought, Oh no, I finally got my period, on top of all this I was bleeding for these men to look at and film and what kind of voyeurs are they—but she was sitting on her pillow, the dampness was on her pillow, which lay half under her right thigh, stained indigo in patches where the tears must have run in her sleep.

"Could be just dreams, anyone thought of that?" Stix commented, using the hand he'd been comforting Soledad with to pick up a half-eaten Vietnamese shrimp roll. "Nothing more."

"Or it could be a warning for us," the speaker-voice replied. Its tone was similar enough to Stix's that she recognized it now as Will's. "Someone told her to say that, the same way—"

"I don't believe that," Stix replied, and Will said, "Of course you don't, homeboy." He said it half in exasperation and half affectionately, almost teasing. "You're a hopeless storyman and the bitch is in distress and *muy linda* to boot."

The cripple reached behind him, pulled a half-sucker from its hook on the back of the wheelchair, fitted it over his head. He was already drumming commands on the keyboard of his right armrest, humming softly as he pulled the visor down. Light yellows and blues played on his cheekbones when the screen lowered. Music now flowed gently from the speakers beside the water bed: *Vallenatos,* not Bamaca *Vallenatos* but southward along the coast, something these men had brought in as sound track to watch her with. Probably it was meant to sharpen her dream memory. It should have sharpened her into irritation again; instead she had the opposite reaction, welcoming the familiar 6/8 beat like someone from home she had met unexpectedly on the corner.

Zatt's humming stopped. In a voice that was withdrawn one level from involvement, almost meditative, he said, "Philo Farnsworth spent seven years in seclusion in the early fifties, after he invented TV, working on the P-272 particle and the Bell-Everett Phase Entanglement model. He was sure the P-272 was really half wave, half something else, and that meant—well, the important thing is, his notes showed you could measure it, in the deuterium-oil capture tanks at Berkeley. And it *has* to be around, for her to be affected by other event horizons."

"See the future," Stix mumbled, his mouth full of shrimp roll. "Whyn't you say what you think?"

"Not necessarily," Zatt replied. "What the particle does, once the wave function crashes, is connect story-structures on a sub-particle level. So if she really tuned into a Farnsworth, then the number of possible event horizons is infinite, almost. But some are far more probable than others, you know? And some people are ridiculously sensitive to that, something to do with calcium ions, and the navigation areas, the hippocampus—"

Soledad glanced at him, and shivered. Though she had gone to bed fully dressed, it was damp in this room without blankets over her. There was something not-warm, not-comforting in the jargony talk between these men she did not know. Separation was strong even between them, and it made many times deeper and more obvious the gulf between Soledad and the chill abstraction of their concerns: the unapologetic voyeurism, the cynical use of her most sacred music to resonate further dreams out of her, the other cool preoccupations of this node.

Whereas her own concerns had to do with hot loss and warm cycles such as men like these could never be aware of.

The emptiness in her seemed wider and deeper than normal. The dampness on the pillow was from tears, not menstrual blood. She was sure now her period was well overdue.

She had bought tampons in Guadalajara when she expected it to come. And she had last been in Guadalajara, looking for a *coyote* to sneak her over the border—she counted it out—thirteen days ago.

Yet worrying about pregnancy was a familiar anxiety, something she had lived with all the way back through Jorge and Miguel and university and Jean-Philippe. It was a warm and innocuous worry and as welcome, in its own way, as the

Vallenato. Nothing like the fear—no, it was no longer fear, it was closer to panic welling up like glittering aluminum locusts in her third space. And she knew—

And she knew nothing, because the concrete rim of the water bed shook under her buttocks. Because a huge sound, like giant *pétanque* balls on marble, like a monstrous diesel switching into life, rumbled once, and then was still.

The *Vallenato* continued for a few seconds, then stopped in the middle of a bar.

Stix flipped up his face mask, then removed it altogether. Looked through the two sets of windows at his massive bird, swaying grayly under the I-beams. Beneath all her panic, Soledad recognized his reflex as being a key action, something that revealed far more about this man than he knew: that he should choose to pare levels of abstraction at moments like this; fine his perceptions down to feel and sight.

Whereas she, at such moments, could not devote the energy to visuals, but only to listening. Because her deepest level of comprehension and early warning was in her ears.

There were no sounds now, in this northern *cruce,* for far longer than the silence went on in Bamaca, in the dream she had just left.

And then came a humming. Soft at first, it grew out of the next vast room: three or four discrete and electronic tones rising in pitch and volume.

She glanced to her right, through the first window, into the big control room.

From this angle she could see a third of the room. Three of the giant, gray-painted computer terminals that she had noticed earlier—de-networked and mothballed cybernetic mastodons, so archaic they had probably last been used to machine torpedoes for the Taiwan crisis in the first years of the century—were stationed at strategic points near the windows overlooking the factory floor.

As she gazed, one of the ancient screens flickered. Then a second, and a third. The flickers coincided in time and space, the transmission clearly the same for all. Under the dust coating the screens, a pattern now emerged, shivered, and steadied.

A landscape. Broken buildings, their shattered beams showing like compound fractures. A woman's body folded like forgotten garbage over the rubble. Smoke, or fog, weaving thickly around the ruins. A man staggered from the left foreground, his legs working with difficulty, whether from fatigue or some invisible obstacle Soledad could not tell.

No sound besides the humming, or perhaps the thick plate glass prevented her from hearing the higher frequencies.

Will's voice again. His face now showed brightly on one of the vidscreens over the bed. His features tensed as he spoke of concepts that were no longer speculation or dreaming: barriers, observation posts, fallback positions. Two squads of Navigators to the Wall of Chevettes. Stix stared at his brother's image, the remains of shrimp roll forgotten in one hand. Zatt watched the landscape of devastation unfolding across the ancient terminals. "Interesting," he said softly, "there must still be ARPA downlinks in those machines."

Soledad averted her eyes. She knew what was coming in that movie, and wanted no part of it. She wished she could avert the other knowledge now surging over her like a storm wave washing over a kid's sand castle, but it was too big and too deep. Already it had flooded the great cracks of absence inside her, chilling her gut with the certainty of doom, no, more: with the certainty of the same doom, because this seemed to be a replay of what she had already lived through in Bamaca, that first casual probe of the *cruce*'s defenses. And the freezing horror rising in her now came not from the facts of the probe—it had been tentative, after all, and easily beaten away—but from the logarithmically rigorous follow-up, the process that must inexorably bring about the next step, and the tactical tricks, and the overwhelming savagery of that final assault with its claws and lusts of flame—

Convulsively, she pulled the jambook close. Words flitted through her head, she'd had thoughts just like this recently but nowhere near so specific, and not quotes—*"A survey of responses to carefully selected scenes from* Hogan's Heroes, Pain in the Afternoon, The Young and the Restless, *shows a positive correlative factor of 1.778 for American audiences (over three times the level of Creole). The correlation exists between those television scenes, levels of adrenaline (adjusted for weight, etc., see Field, O'Hearn, 2002) of 0.40 and above, and images of the womb, the controlling mother of American Matriarchy. This, of course, is a natural if regressive relinquishing of control to the first power-figure. . . ."*

She had no idea why her own reaction to stress should involve the summoning of Fernsehen in chapter and verse. However she did understand the associations her frontal lobes were making, and tapped out on the jambook BON ATTACKS THROUGH TUNNELS. She had to pull at Stix's scarf to drag his attention from his brother's face; curiously, when he looked down and read her words, he smiled.

"We've already been through this."

She stabbed the word ATTACKS angrily with her finger.

"Yes, it's a raid; big fuckin' deal. They've done raids before."

"You're wrong. It's a beta test." Will's voice came stronger now. She and Stix both turned toward the vidscreen that framed his face. "But even if it's only an amusement, Stix, this is no place for you, for the people who started this—"

"You're one of 'em," Stix observed softly.

"But I can handle it." On the vidscreen, Will moved, and his eyes seemed to grow brighter as the shadows around him dimmed. "I could always handle it. But you need space, man, you need *security* to do your stuff."

"You're saying I should pull out?" Stix's voice was low, yet it too sounded stronger, recharged with energy. "You want me to run, like last time. So you can take the brunt again? So you can be the hero, again."

"It's nothing to do with that." Will glanced offscreen, to the left, and said something about detonation. When he turned back he said, "I just want you to be safe, boy. You know that's all I want. I gotta go," he told the camera.

"Will," Stix said urgently. "Wait. What was that about—"

The screen filled with snow.

"Crapola," Stix muttered. He walked to the plate glass, watching the archaic terminals, where smoke billowed from ashen ruins. "Leave it," Zatt said, "it's just Will, there's no time." His wheelchair whined as he backed and turned, still watching whatever played at the top of his face-sucker screen. "I'll be at the crane."

Stix readjusted his scarf, his bow tie. He took off his own half-sucker and folded and stowed it in his jacket pocket. Combed his hair, watching his reflection in the window. Then he turned to look at Soledad where she sat, legs dangling over the water bed's rim. He appeared angry, Soledad thought, and at the very second the thought came he squinted his eyes and the anger fell out of his mouth- and frown-lines like water spilling from a collapsed awning. He smiled—not widely, but it was a smile all the same.

"You," he said. "You're the one's gotta get out of here."

———

TWENTY-FOUR HOURS LATER SOLEDAD would have trouble understanding why she once more followed Stix when he told her to follow. The first couple of times she'd had no choice—she was sick, worn out from alarum and flight, utterly dependent on these strangers. She barely understood where she was and had no alternative to proffer as her own choice.

This morning though, she felt rested for the first time in weeks. Moreover, she knew where she was; more than that, she was dropped into a scenario similar to one that she had lived before, and whose parameters and escape clauses she was familiar with, even if they had originally applied in a place far removed from this one.

The trouble was, the scenario, like a locomotive pulling

an endless sequence of refrigerated cars, hauled as its weighty psychic legacy a certainty of evil poised.

And that ice-water knowledge now filled all available space inside her, subtly and accurately paralyzing the chakras of individual will. So that now she was capable of only two things: to sit frozen in body as she was in mind and wait for the familiar attack to play itself out in the vertical battlefield that she knew, without knowing how she knew, had to be the principal vector of attack in this node—or else, to move on the rails of someone else's plan and story.

The decision was not a decision; not with one way blocked and cold as stone.

She slid off the bed, then moved after Zatt as hc wheeled and disappeared through the control room, conscious at that point only of the great loneliness of staying where she was, and thc relative comfort of going somewhere, even into rising danger, with company.

Stix did not use the spiderbike this time. Once out of the factory he led her down a wide thoroughfare, then left, between two of the huge warehouse structures with their crowded balconies and courtyards and workshops. The ground level of this alley was crowded with makeshift tents sheltering government-issue chairs and desks and hundreds of items of consumer communications. Men and women jerked quickly about camp stoves, watching vidscreens. In every case their heads and bodies were festooned with electronics both live and dead: headphones, full-suckers, cellphones, uploaders, beepers, cypher circuits, army radios, coils of purloined B-Net coaxial. And the alley was filled with the hiss of static, of a thousand different Flash *telenovelas*, cooking shows, even 3-D interactives, all going at once. "Teedees," Stix explained, "Teledysfunctional syndrome," which she knew already. "They prefer it outside—better reception."

The TeeDee alley ended in a sort of extended lean-to, down the side of a concrete wall. The lean-to was filled with hydroponic tanks, encryption booths, and benches selling what looked like fanciful jagger apparatus. She was reminded, with a wince that felt very close to nostalgia, of Haddad— remembering how her feelings about the technician had altered in the last weeks of the *cruce*. Well, her thoughts about everyone had changed; she would have given all the illegal riches of this alley and the node on top of them to see Haddad again, with all his black obsessions, if only the *cruce* he lived in could be returned to her as well.

Between the benches and hydrotanks, makeshift push-screens had been fitted, easy to spot because of teedees clustering around them, human moths around a digital flame. The first pushpanel (an irregular oblong lined with thousands of glued-on sequins) showed a typical thumbnail holovideo accompanied by overengineered sound effects of the kind the people in this node loved to play around with. A second started in the same genre—then the quartet of dancers, all locked in some post-post-Béjart stomp, shivered and vanished.

In their place appeared a huge face with large cheekbones and a wide, smiling mouth whose sides furled into the woman's cheeks. Her eyes were the color of northern seas. It was a face both familiar and unutterably alien in its connotations to Soledad. The eyes shifted and the mouth moved and the vision's voice boomed out of speakers concealed around the tunnel.

"Just plain *silly* to react at all" she announced, in a voice cramped by the vowel sounds of a country run through by the Dniepr. "The law officers of Oakland they are merely investigating jisi pushers, jag addicts, and spindle pirates in the squatters' camps in parts of the Oakland naval supply base formerly rented by the Chinese National Maritime Agency." She was reading from a script.

"These officers they are experts in sensitivity training and will be using nonviolent tactics and weapons only to arrest a number of drug czars and kingpins in this traffic. There is no cause for alarm."

Soledad felt her hand being tugged. She had stopped in her tracks by the vidscreen.

"Larissa Love," Stix grunted. He was smiling, not altogether happily. "She was a VR star. It's standard tactics, for the Bureau of Nationalizations." He glanced at Soledad. "You know, I never noticed before, you guys kinda look alike."

"Legitimate squatters should stay indoors and watch B-Net channels 87 and 112, currently showing reruns of *Pain in the Afternoon*," the actress continued, tilting her head in fetching fashion.

"Come on," Stix said, and limped off, around a bankful of chained-down balloon screens showing maps of the left parietal lobe.

But she's dead, Soledad wanted to say. The news of Lara Love's murder had reached even as far south as Bamaca, for many watched the dubbed versions of *Pain in the Afternoon*, translated as *Dolor en la Tarde*, on TV beamed from the capital. And the fact of that discrepancy—the sudden resurgence into life of a legend whose existence she had never been sure of to begin with—seemed suddenly as sad as any of the tragedies she had unwillingly witnessed over the last month of her life.

Stix was already twenty paces gone, however. Soledad put away her shock in favor of catching up to him.

They crossed a small, deserted market and an organic garden where the tunic-clad figures of Ludd-Kaczynskis scurried in urgent harvest. A team of Navigators trotted in the opposite direction, watching the readouts of tiny navigational computers. A group of Hoffaists asked them for money to make everything turn out OK. Then, at the end of a concrete down-ramp, Stix opened a watertight door into the womby warmth and dim light of—inevitably, thought Soledad, hanging back—a small tunnel. But the memory of the warren under the Nirvana Motel, and even the thought of the Kundurans, were not enough to break her new habit of following.

It was a short tunnel, anyway. After only a minute she smelled a mushiness of rot and salt. Shortly thereafter the beam of Stix's flashlight lost itself to the right, where a long black flatness of harbor water had been trapped by buttresses of reinforced concrete.

The submarine base. The flavor of fetid seaweed was accompanied by a stench of truck engine wound around a very low-frequency rumble; all of this, high-powered diesel exhaust plus filthy seawater, like a Proustian code spelling out "smugglers' boats" to her.

As they went through the next bulkhead she saw lit portholes, the port-side running light of the tugboat she had seen the last time she and Stix came this way, on his bike.

Seen from close up like this, the tug was clearly an ex-naval vessel; equally clearly, it had not been in regular service for a long time. Though the hull was the same dull gray as the tunnels, the superstructure and funnel were decorated with painted eyes and planets, all connected by lines and differential equations. A dozen old televisions had been stacked and chained down just aft of the wheelhouse, and an equally out-of-date workstation bolted to the wheelhouse roof. All these screens glowed softly, as if their "on" status were part of the rules of the nautical road. A mammoth loudspeaker perched on a bridge wing played Shift-shin, just audible over the engine's throaty idle. A news-zipper running around the upper deck flashed odd comments at twenty-second intervals: THE BRIDGE IS THE OTHER SIDE, TRAVEL IS THE DESTINATION, TIME: AN EXCUSE FOR CONTROLLING SPACE. It reminded her of Lo Pano, and deepened the black mood that had come over her on seeing Lara Love's face in the pushscreen.

And so up a gangplank to the aft end of the superstructure, past a stairway smelling of tallow, into a small saloon and kitchen. This area was brightly lit; cats lay curled in soft corners; an alcove circled by a green settee surrounded a table of well-polished mahogany, currently covered with torn-up cereal boxes that the raccoon—the same animal, Soledad was almost certain, that she had seen in the diner—was systematically tearing up and piling into symmetrical stacks.

Wedged in a corner of the settee, his long legs on the table, a half-sucker flipped down over his nose, the

Afro-Peruvian boy wielded trackballs, thumbsticks, haptic gloves. The precise movements of his hands were reflected in minute adjustments: to weather over a landscape of volcanoes, to lights shining in a crystal airport, to the activity of crowds and flocks of ravens showing on various LCD screens bolted onto a bookcase over the settee.

The boy glanced at Stix. His features were calm, though the half-sucker over his eyes must tell him what was happening at ground level. Stix peered up a ladder in the kitchen, then turned and said to Soledad, "You'll be OK here. The kid will take care of you. And Ahab will take you out of the harbor, if necessary. Or if you just get too nervous?" He nodded and smiled, but the smile and the eyes didn't connect. He was doing it again, Soledad thought, cutting her off, and the thought made her even lonelier than before, that he should abandon her at such a moment, in such a place.

All those jumbled feelings and thoughts, in revealing how small and vulnerable her sense of self had become, depressed her further and shamed her too, because she had followed this man for the third time in two days, as if she really had no choice—and then started whingeing because she had done so.

The refusal in her was automatic, directed at the closest obstacle, and she didn't mind the fact that in this, too, she was doing what she always did; because refusal in such a pass was an affirmation of herself at her most vulnerable, and also at her most basic, a tiny foot-stomping cry of "I exist!" that caused her chin to tighten and her fists to seize up and her head to shake violently.

Stix's eyes focused on her again.

"No. No, you don't want to stay?"

A headshake. Conscious of the growing impulse to sob, unwelcome and irrelevant, inside her. Conscious also of a whiff of treachery that was out of place in this situation, where Stix only wanted, he *said* he only wanted, to preserve her safety and peace of mind. Moving, in the fascism of such despair, toward the saloon table and the boy's keyboards— the boy shrinking oddly into the corner, watching her—to type out letters that appeared in yellow Gothic characters in a corner box on four screens:

I AM NOT YOUR WOMAN
I WILL NOT BE TOLD WHAT TO DO

She turned to find Stix gazing at the screens, a vague smile on his lips.

"But you can do what you like, Soledad," he said softly. "Big fuckin' deal. Nobody in this node's gonna make you do anything you don't want to."

Then he turned, limped awkwardly over the coaming of the door they had come through, and disappeared into the diesel-smelling dark of the sub pen, leaving Soledad feeling only more diminished, and sadder, and angrier at him for soliciting in her further emotions she had no desire to parse.

———————

BUT SHE DID NOT disembark from the tug. The thought of trying to find her way out of this underground base by herself was too tiring. Her previous panic was not gone, anyway.

Also, her revolt had apparently depended on someone to revolt against, and with Stix's departure she found that she had lost her will to do things differently.

After a few minutes she evicted a cat from the settee and sat down heavily, watching the raccoon and the boy. The boy finally coaxed a crowd of pilgrims into the airport and abandoned his interactive game. He had been watching Soledad from the corner of his eye, and now he got up and climbed the ladder. A few minutes later the diesel sound changed, and the hull shivered and rocked very slightly, and Soledad knew the tug was moving.

Someone else came to the same conclusion. A string of half-screamed curses rose from a door to her left. Then a tall, silver-bearded figure wearing only yachtsman's loafers and underpants staggered out the door and up the ladder.

The curses continued for another ten seconds. The boy said, "It is easy, Ahab." The weed-pirate replied, "Oh, if a *lady*'s involved." Then they both fell silent.

A pulsing red light grew slowly in the saloon portholes, illuminating the slimy sides of a massive tunnel. An alarm siren grew, honked painfully, diminished. Pores and cracks in the concrete moved slowly from the forward edge of portholes toward the back. The red flashing light was replaced by another form of light, this one coming through all the portholes at once as well as a skylight behind the kitchen: *daylight.* She was getting used to its difference, deep and cold where the other lights were flat and cold. Gears rumbled, the tug scraped on something hard, the boy yelled. Soledad got to her feet and peered out the nearest porthole. Still nothing visible but cement, cast in the shape of a dock; and the little coati, watching intently as Ahab turned a rusted metal wheel set in a pipe running down the wharf's length.

Soledad sat down again. For some reason the sight of that little animal trying to understand hydraulics made her want to cry more than ever. She decided not to look outside for a while.

The rumble of diesel ratcheted to a higher volume, and the saloon began rocking steadily. Stronger shadows shifted along the saloon walls. She figured they were in the bay now. She had not been on the water since a bunch of *contrabandistas* unaffiliated with the node took her out of that hellhole creek in the Tapon de Darien. Before that, the last time had been a joyride with Cloodine on the *Fumiste,* Nestor Prin's boat, almost six months earlier. The thought was grossly irrelevant, except for the fact that she had not been seasick then and thus, with luck, might be spared that agony now.

She watched the terminals the boy had been staring at, aware that the varied landscapes, of farms and trailer parks, dungeons and maps, changed very slowly over time, even when no one was playing—not worrying about it. Deliberately not worrying about anything much.

A Greek word blinked occasionally in the corner of each jambook screen. ΠΟΛΙΣ. She had seen it on a 3-D game in Zatt's crane cab.

An hour passed. When the tug's movement changed again, and the rolling adopted a longer period that affected her stomach the way the short sharp movement of Prin's boat had not, she got up without thinking of associations or consequences and climbed the ladder through which the boy and the weed-pirate had disappeared, emerging into a wide and well-lit wheelhouse that for a shocked moment she imagined must be the cockpit of an airborne craft, or the top of a high tower. For all around was silver-white cloud, not even sea visible until you approached the windows and looked down at the tug's hull making creases of waves running black-blue and solid out of the everlasting fog.

The boy stood on a pedestal next to a ramshackle computer, watching its screen as well as a giant, brass-enclosed compass. Ahab the weed-pirate leaned into a jury-rigged chart table, piled high with an assortment of used marine radios, walking a brass instrument across a chart. He was still in his underpants.

Soledad stood in a corner under a fire-alarm panel, out of the way. The men glanced at her, then calmly went back to what they'd been doing.

They kept doing almost exactly the same thing for the next hour, except that the weed-pirate also watched a radar screen. Occasionally, responding to a prompt on the terminal, he would type in identification letters, at which point the boy adjusted a dial and the tug's course shifted, never by more than a few degrees. "Coast Guard traffic computer in Duluth," the weed-pirate chortled at one point. "Hacked in the numbers for a Moran tow headed to Valdees. Thing is, they never *check*." Shortly afterward the wall of fog parted around the tug and she saw, well off to the right, an impossible landscape of dark green capes meshing like interlocked fingers with silver lochs that protruded into the landscape behind.

"We have visual," the boy said softly and the weed-pirate, with a muttered "fuckwit," grabbed another brass instrument, threw himself off the chart table, threw himself out the door of the wheelhouse, and, holding the sextant sideways, manically measured angles between capes. "Punta Reyes," the boy whispered to her, "but he'll never admit it until he makes the navigation."

Soledad recognized in the landscape to starboard the deep green of temperate trees, set off by the bluish tones of fog and the occasional column of milky yellow where the sun managed to probe its weak spotlight. On black rocks lay large finned animals that reminded her of schoolbook pictures of walruses or sea lions. On one headland a Victorian mansion with turrets and finials stood cheek by jowl with a modern house of vast horizontal planes and green-shaded plate glass. A wedding or large party was taking place on the lawn between the houses; women in long white dresses and men in long dark jackets moved very slowly till the fog dissolved them again. The pirate came back inside, shivering. He sprawled over his table, drew ruled lines on the chart, burped, scratched his head, then announced happily, "Point Reyes."

She went outside. The wind came from the left. She found a corner on the tug's right, behind the wheelhouse, where the stack of televisions, now tied down in shabby tarpaulin, kept her out of the draft and fairly warm. The news-zipper, the graffiti, had also been covered in old canvas, she noticed, turning this node vessel once more into an unremarkable and shabby workhorse of the waterways.

The fog lifted once more. The sight of vegetation, even of this dark and windswept northern variety, brought back the homesickness she'd felt earlier. She had been scared when the Ensevli explosion happened, in Bamaca, but she had not known what was coming then the way she did now. What was more, she had been home, with people she knew and cared for, the way she was not and never could be in this node.

Though she liked Stix; liked his obvious enthusiasm, his

apparent openness—liked, quite frankly, the way he seemed attracted to her. She hoped he was safe. There was no real passion in the hope. The movement of the ship, now that she was outside, was more comforting than nauseating. The view of hard sea and soft headlands folding in and out of each other through the lacy bedclothes of fog imparted a feeling of otherworldliness, of stageset and illusion, softening her awareness of tunnel attacks and marauding soldiers into the same dreamy unreality as those Marin County capes. The view also softened her memories of Bamaca (to complete the lazy round of her thoughts) into a state where even the recall of fear, and of the terror beyond that—a terror whose source she could not recall, which meant she must live in panic that she someday would—contributed to a more pervasive homesickness. *"When the worst danger threatens: a ten-year flood, or army deportations, or a new disease, things they could do nothing about; the Manopani revert to dream-life—"* It was her mother who told her that, long enough ago that Soledad didn't know any better than to accept it the way she accepted everything her mother said, without a hint of doubt. Watching those strange walruses, who surely could not live so far south, in a country without visible ice?

Soledad settled herself deeper into a fold of tarp, out of the wind. She wondered for the first time if Fernsehen had heard of the Manopani's dream reflex. The old psychiatrist had after all lived in the capital. He even helped establish the video clinic in Santa Karen. She closed her eyes, just to shield them from the reflection of light on seawater. And he had written somewhere, *"We do not make stories out of an overarching reality. Stories are our reality. Through them we make a liveable structure out of the multifarious and differently interpretable 'facts' communicated to us by our senses. And it follows from this that, if the facts are not to our liking, or even dangerous to us in some way, we can, within limits, arbitrarily change the story we made to something safer. This act, committed chronically and over a certain threshold, we call madness; but done with self-awareness,*

*humor, and as a means to an end, it is the purest expression of
our psychological resilience and our imaginative force."*

She could not have borne without hysteria or breakdown
the direct experience of another attack so similar to the
one the *guaqueros* had triggered in the sewer tunnel.

A large part of that inability, she now knew, lay in the fact
that she had tried once to be a character in a story she willed
to happen, and it had not worked. Not at all. Stix had known
this—perhaps he had even known that this method of travel,
with the ship rocking gently but purposefully beneath her,
and the occasional sunshine warming her face, was as soothing as a bedtime story, and ultimately as soporific, to someone fleeing the awareness of flame and bloodshed and of her
own overriding powerlessness.

ELEVEN

WHEN SHE WAKES, NIGHT HAS FALLEN.
(no one holds her hand)

Soledad looks where she was looking last in this room, at the open window, but its shape is unbroken now, a square frame for the violet cone of San Isidor detaching itself against the deeper matte of night, the shimmer of lights on the lower slopes, the rim of Ensevli.

It is hot, and the air is still. Sweat glues her shirt to her skin. She lies in bed for a moment, hearing the sparkle of sounds in the streets and houses, gauging them also—she has been here long enough to be able to judge what time it is by the level of sound, the nature of voices, even to some extent the type of music. On a tinny radio a man talks instead of arguing, not one of the *cruce* pirate channels, then; someone is listening to an outside station. A dog barks repeatedly. Two men, in fighting, howl at one another. A group of people pass on the Corniche, discussing something in quiet tones. A helicopter thuds back and forth in the distance, a door slams in the whorehouse, a mototaxi passes, a woman laughs, a baby wails, and the music: far away, a drummer beats hard, a frenzied rhythm; nearby, someone sings a *lanto,* slow and sad as so many *lantos* are, it's a man paying attention to the words and syllables, honoring each with melody in a voice also slow and sad. He thrums his guitar in a mountain rhythm, *rrruccha-bo, rrruccha-bo,* slapping the wooden soundboard between stanzas.

As Soledad listens, farther away another *lanto* starts up, this one sung by a woman.

The man falls silent. The drums continue. The woman's voice grows stronger. She is backed by a small flute only, one that matches her tune three notes higher, minor binary weaving delicately, mournfully through the purple night sky.

The man fraps his guitar again, changing his song to play counterpoint to the woman, starting the call and response. It is too rough though, his voice and style unsuited to her airy improv, he is too loud also and Soledad swings to her feet, annoyed as she always is by unprofessional production, thinking it must be 9 P.M. at the latest for this level of activity. She goes to the bathroom, then to the kitchen. She is hungry all of a sudden, and parched as well. She stops in surprise, for the clock over the stove reads 10:35.

She opens the shutters. A different arc of the Corniche is visible from this part of the flat. A couple sit on the hatch of a sloop, smoking, looking southwest toward the volcano. A gaggle of teenage girls skitter by; one of them swings a kerosene lamp. Two men follow, then two couples, all carrying instruments. Except for during the festival, she has never seen so many people on the Corniche at this time of night, and never do people walk this promenade in such numbers and with speed. Everyone so far has exceeded the normal pace for the Corniche, which is a lazy saunter aimed at seeing and being seen rather than at arriving anywhere. Instead, they walk with intent and purpose, as they did just after the tunnel blew up. For the first time the potential gravity of what occurred earlier is impressed on her mind.

The fact of this discrepancy between time and activity causes a tiny insect of discomfort to wake within her. It's an insect in unfriendly territory, though, because sleep has soothed her thoughts the way it was supposed to, like the tide smoothing over and absorbing gullies in a beach, leaving her with a memory of an incident that frightened her but then was absorbed by the complexity and resilience, not only of the *cruce,* but of her own existence here.

The fact that Dolores has come to live with her, Soledad realizes, gave her another measure of fool's confidence. It makes her feel needed and responsible, trimming the sense of loss she at one time felt was defining her. Also—with the perspective gained in Glen MacRae, she can face this uncomfortable fact—it renews her broken association with Jorge, even or especially at one remove.

Through the scrim of this illusion of family-renewed Soledad retains a calm sense that some police action has occurred on the *cruce*'s fringes but has been stopped, beaten back, wiped out. She has not the tiniest grain of evidence for the notion, and maybe that is also why the twee itch carries on within her, like a hint of indigestion at the end of a good meal. It could be just the disruption in internal clock caused by napping at an odd hour. Or the collapsing of emotional time zones engendered by that fast trip to the *estancia;* the sudden imposition of new spatial relationships within a personal landscape no longer obscured by the time requirements that this *cruce,* though in greatly diluted form, imposes through its own patterns of activity.

With quick deft movements she takes the bowl of *mucaja* out of the icebox, warms it on the stove, eats enough to calm her stomach.

She is a day or two away from getting her period. But she has always rejected this explanation for her moods, seeing it as an excuse agreed upon by men and women to maintain their safe division of labor, something to place the wilder swings of emotional forces neatly in the woman's domain.

One of the fighting men screams in pain. In the silence that follows, the radio sounds stronger. She can make out the words now. The voice is well modulated, familiar.

"*. . . and sisters, in the outlaw area of Bamaca. For we do not see you as our enemies. Or even criminals. The criminal elements have exploited you mercilessly for their own gain. Your legitimate enterprise and industry are models for the semiregulated free-market economy. This has been the goal of our administration from the very first day. The high-tech workshops will someday be the focus of a new enterprise*

zone . . . *and free port, that will be established in the pic-*
turesque streets of Barrio des Anglais and the Slave Market.
This our administration will fund, with the assistance of
grants promised by the European Union and the World Bank.
We make this promise to you now: We will fund it together."

Ochoa Campos. No one else speaks with that mix of volume, confidence, and short breath. She saw him once, at a
rally Miguel organized and asked her not to attend; she standing incognita on the outskirts of the quiet crowd that assembled behind the cathedral in the Walled City. Watching the
general and Sandoval and Bishop Thiers open a hospital
for the poor. Everybody fully aware that the hospital had
four floors of offices and only one of clinic. It was a clean and
efficient-looking building, though. Ochoa Campos, in pictures,
appeared thinner and gentler than one might surmise from his
voice alone. Miguel stood next to him, diffident and retiring
in his charcoal suit, keeping an eye on the roofs, where Sierra
Division snipers crouched feral behind dovecotes.

Soledad shakes her head. She puts her bowl in the sink.
In the bedroom she opens the drawer in which she keeps
her soaps and toiletries. A good half of it is now occupied by
earrings in the shape of parrots and macaws similar to the pair
she bought the first day she came here. She supposes she is
collecting them, though the concept of collecting, with its
anal concentration on order, is foreign to her; she has enough
trouble bringing attention to bear on important things. She selects a pair of turaco parrots, fastens them. She opens the bottle of Vengeance and dabs it sparingly on her elbows and
neck. Looks at herself in the mirror and flicks the parrots with
her index finger, causing them to swing madly for a short
while.

———

THE RADIO SOUND COMES from Cloodine's flat, Ochoa
Campos's voice high in Soledad's ears as she descends the
stairs; Cloodine must have left it on when she went out,

because through the half-opened door the room appears dark
and otherwise silent.

Downstairs, the fishmongers have set up planks and kerosene lamps across two wheelbarrows and play dominoes with
fierce concentration, while a box of very round fish with
golden fins and thick silver scales, and feelers twice as long
again as their bodies, flip weakly on the stall. Across the bay,
a blaze of high-intensity lights marks the frigate. A helicopter
hovers like a dragonfly, then moves back and forth over a defined area of the bay, dragging a circle of whiteness with it
across the water.

Soledad follows the Corniche around, ignoring the lights
and motion in Pytagoro's. The density of people on the
promenade grows exponentially as she approaches the Slave
Market. As she enters the vast agora through the harbor gate
she sees that the space is thick with people, not just the vendors and clients that are around at all hours but people clearly
on more pointed business, talking in loose groups, emphasiz-
ing urgency with hand gestures, their arms and shoulder
blades angled toward Lo Pano. And the tower itself pulsing with lights and activity, far more than it did even at peak
business hours; barter prices and calls as usual, classified
and personal notices—but there are also messages more specific to this time and place. One news-zipper reads MEETING
TONIGHT LO PANO TO DISCUSS BACKSTABBING INVASION-
TUNNEL AT ENSEVLI. Another flashes Hawkleyisms meant no
doubt to inspire, but actually rather weak and meaningless in
this context. QUALITY IS THE SKILL YOU PUT INTO YOUR OWN
WORK. TACKINESS IS LABOR FOR THE MEGORG. Two-thirds of
the way up the tower, a panel flashes barter notices. Heckler
& Koch machine pistols on sale, fake ID cards in eighteen
hours, homemade gasoline bombs specially discounted if
bought in bulk over the next day and a half. Colorful neon,
moving patterns of light animate the tall structure, and searchlights in its Meccano skeleton probe and blind at random.

The crowd is thick enough that people have climbed to

sit on the sinister orange-brick corrals at the side, where Cameroonian and Yoruban slaves were penned five hundred years ago. Soledad advances through the loiterers, the brawlers, the mildly interested, the drinkers, the half committed. She heads for the thicker densities around Lo Pano marking legions of the excited and prurient, the angry and scared, and the pickpockets who haunt such agglomerations.

Many of the groups contain a critical mass of instruments and musicians—this is the *cruce,* after all, where speech without music can only be half meant—and of course these groups are performing in muted tones, almost all *lantos,* slow and sad and pressed down. The crowd in aggregate makes much music and even more noise. A lot of the noise is sharp and emphasized in argument, and some of that comes from people taking turns to speak on a mike wired to Dolbys on the towers and pens and countinghouses surrounding.

And some of the noise is merely audience input, opinion exploded out of its bedrock of discourse; nonetheless the general volume is only a third of what it would be in typical circumstances, of concert or market or other celebration, and missing half its lyrical pith. Thus the overall effect, to people familiar with the *cruce,* is one of restraint, like a carnival deliberately organized to be the reverse of other carnivals, to *hold in* passion and emotion rather than push it outward—to sublimate it finally, not through the songs it generates, but through the music it does not.

The strangeness of this crowd increases the lack of comfort in Soledad. Eventually the spacey sleep hangover, that had created its own soft haze of optimism, a peach tinge of relief after waking from nightmare, is fully dispelled. She sees people she knows vaguely: the Umbanda vendor, a local eel-fisherman. They nod distantly and automatically in deference to this something-else that has taken over and weighted the air. When she turns to make her way around a particularly tight group she almost bumps into Haddad. She stares at him in surprise; it has been two weeks now since he last followed her around. He folds his grimy Arab robes around himself as if this might hide him better.

Stepping around Haddad, she sees others she recognizes—Cloodine, and the mate from Nestor Prin's boat, whom Cloodine slept with once quite noisily, just before Soledad left for Glen MacRae. He is a short thickset man with a bull-fighter's mustache who goes by the name of Jako. A crowd of faces from Pytagoro's, with the tightly curled head of Hector Ruiz at its center.

The university economist, with whom Jorge used to discuss Hawkley for hours on end.

The *mounchey* from Jorge's party, the one who predicted a doom whose details Soledad no longer remembers, stands at the outskirts. She wears the same white turban and overdone medallions and bare feet, and slips one hand into the side pocket of a man wearing the jeans and climbing shoes of a gringo. The crowd opens to reveal Jorge's face, intent and forward-thrusting, pounding the air as he does when he makes a point, addressing a dark-haired woman—whom Soledad recognizes, after an instant of blankness, as the girl who works in the Flash Shack at Lo Pano.

The one who lives on a sloop next to Nestor Prin; the one who got Cloodine her job.

Soledad turns away quickly from that sight. With all her newfound independence, with the increasing balance she brings to her life both in and out of the *cruce,* it's amazing how the sight of him still makes her feel like the ground has dropped from under her feet—a sensation both impressive and terrifying. She angles away, too fast for Haddad, slipping through the knots of crowd like a catadromous fish headed for sea.

Trying to slip away also from the feeling of panic, not because of Jorge, but precisely because of this muted quality to music, to conversation, to life. The muteness of it feels to her like a night-roaming hawk hovering high, its shadow printed by the stars over far too much territory—or the huge web of one of those poisonous female spiders the Indians call "baby stealers," that between sunset and sunup stretch cords thick as your finger from tree to tree to catch jungle birds in their sticky web and inject a cold paralysis into the fluttering creatures. It is nervousness, she knows; it would be premature and histrionic to call what colors this crowd "fear"—and yet the taste, the smell, the dampening of it are the same.

Finally she is standing only twenty meters from the tower itself, the tiny lasers moving dots across her face, looking upward like a virgin being electronically annunciated, as someone, a *guaquero* by his kerchief and knife and boots, stands on the first deck of the tower and speaks into a cordless: aggressive words, verbs full of action but poorly marshaled, like a regiment of rabble swarming in all directions. "Ah, you *know* it was a bluff," he shouts, sweeping arms too vastly in the direction of Ensevli. "They took no precautions. This is how Ochoa Campos in the capital, he does this." Whistles and catcalls from opponents or, more likely, friends.

"Last year, when we were in Santa Marta, his troops would play pop tunes loud in their compounds. They thought we would be scared by the songs of Jasmin. We, who excavated an entire Quichey village while the Sierra soldiers hunted for us. Their mining machine was too noisy; no one would do this for real." No one listens to him, though he will get his five minutes. Behind the glare of lasers and zippers, an orange fire grows in the cradle of hills, and then another; howitzers and high-precision mortars talking across a ridge. A lot of activity opposes army and guerrillas, or *guerrilleros* and gold smugglers, tonight. She doubts it has anything to do with what the army is planning for the *cruce*. Maybe it is the deranging influence of the moon, rising fat and almost full behind her to plate the cornices of countinghouses, the masts of fishing sloops, the bay. Only the frigate remains dark in this chrome process, as if its stealthy contours could absorb moonlight as well as radar beams.

Soledad wraps her arms around her body and shivers a

little, though the cold of this hour does not usually bother
her—or it never bothered her on those occasions she and
Jorge, drunk late at night on the balcony, shucked their
clothes and made love in a hammock in the shelter of the arbor and the perfume of frangipani. Of course they had other
factors to warm them at the time.

A woman follows the *guaquero,* endorsing his words in
a voice so soft she is quickly yelled off the tower. Then another familiar figure pushes toward the lit desk at the tower's
base. It strikes her as odd, at that moment, that there is no
queue of people jumping up and down to address such a
crowd; but this is her stooped parrot man, the one who sells
the bird earrings it seems she is now collecting. The *guaquero*
supporter retreats, trembling. The parrot seller's voice is louder
and far richer in tension than the *guaquero*'s. Oddly, though,
what he has to say is the opposite of defiance. It is, she realizes as she listens past the opening sentences and the re-
cap of what happened, the expression of that night-flying
hawk, that spider-poison, that freezing paralysis she felt seeping from this audience as she passed through it. And the
sentences her parrot vendor builds and structures—small stories about overwhelming might, the hardness of men like
Sandoval, the uselessness of defending a tiny soft portion of
city against tanks and rockets, the vulnerability of women and
children and market vendors—all nestle neatly into soft and
cozy tales about the ease of escape, the capacity to start
somewhere else, the overall preciousness of life. "Hawkley
himself said that not one principle of the *Smuggler's Bible* is
worth the life or suffering of the tiniest baby rat," the parrot
vendor cries, and as he gestures she spots one of his wares, a
Spix's macaw perhaps, swinging under the man's own left
ear. "The writing is on the wall. We must question the mo-
tives of those who would defy the army, when all they want
is to—"

The crowd grows noisier again. A group of *guaqueros*
shouts abuse. One of them throws *guanabanas* at the speaker,
but is too drunk to hit his target. Much of the crowd claps in

approbation of the vendor's words. A Lo Pano man walks over to the *guaquero,* and more shouting ensues. Jako and other smugglers stand silently in the path she took to get here; the smugglers tend not to get involved, since it is their religion and habit to take a cut no matter what direction others may go in. The higher the risk, the greater the percentage. She cannot see Dolores in their midst.

She hugs herself tighter, wishing she could block her ears because the words of the parrot vendor have three times more effect on her than did those of the *guaquero*. The real persuasion of the vendor's argument lies in the resonance it finds inside her, doubling, tripling in volume inside the echo chamber of her own personality—for she knows this freezing paralysis so well, to feel it is like meeting the old myrrh-smelling priest that baptized and confirmed you and officiates at every stage of your life.

It is the great anesthesia that happened twenty-four hours before the concert, and grew until she had trouble mounting the steps to the stage in this very square.

It's the rigidity that overcame her fingers every time she tried to perform, in front of strangers and finally even friends, pieces she had written and cared for.

It's the deadness that invaded her, so early, so very early, in all her days and months and years in Glen MacRae; the deadness that prevented her from ever rising and identifying and stamping on the treacherous creature that injected it.

It was her inability to move—despite her travels, despite what her father said—move out of the havens she had chosen and defended so well: the university, the various conservatories. Her apartment, her piano faculty. Soledad feels as if she herself stands up there, summoning with language the Soledad she was, the Soledad she is, the one always in control—the default Soledad, the shrinking timorous Soledad, the woman who would never, ever risk her comfort for what she thinks is right. The Soledad who will always win, always conquer at the last, the one who will be waiting for her in the shadowed corners of the room where she dies; the one who has always triumphed, with the single exception of that gossamer and jewel-bright event that arose like fairy lights out of this very place and music, when she walked in front of a crowd bigger than this and played *Desdichado,* and it *worked.*

She is the opposite of cold suddenly—she is sweating and trembling and breathing as if she were in a road race. She peers around wildly. God she needs help—not enough of her character is left, in this clash of feelings, to cast a coherent human out of. Spinning left, and yes, there is the Pytagoro crowd, there is Ruiz, no Dolores yet but there, just when she needs it, the womb-tightening vision of Jorge standing with one hand on the shoulder of the Lo Pano woman, his head and chin thrust forward. He is still beating out a point on the poor girl with the hammer of language. And Soledad's sweating freezes, her trembling slows, her breathing stops under the huge shock of a completeness, a rounded and total love for Jorge that wells like a gushing spring out of the moment—bringing with it, in a companion freshet of understanding, this certainty: *that she can love completely only that which she already has lost.*

And she loves this man, and the verses he makes and the whole vortex of his existence into which she so gratefully sank. Loves this man who includes in him the *cruce* entire, with its easy rhythms, and soft backdrop of tunes, and acceptance of those lost and with no homeland of the heart.

Something is still running inside her. Maybe it's the remembered brilliance of herself at the concert, the single sharp fact, *I did it once.* Along with that, the reluctance, no, the sudden impossibility of turning her back on the *cruce* that allowed her to be, for a few days, for a few hours, everything she had always dreamed of being.

Because if the *cruce* disperses—she sees this with absolute clarity, it was in Miguel's tone, it's in the blackness of that frigate and the increasing mass of their efforts to interfere—it will never be allowed to form again.

And for her to let that happen without resisting would be

like falling off a ship in the middle of a cold ocean, and some-one on the ship throwing her a line; and her turning away from that floating rope, and choosing instead the cold clasp of sea.

So she moves. Through a cluster of women listening in-tently to the parrot vendor, through a mixed group in the mid-dle of which a girl softly plucks a *requinto* in time, to the base of the tower where a man she doesn't know stands beside a ladder to the first platform, murmuring into a wireless phone, a clipboard and a *tinto* balanced in one hand.

She points upward with one finger, not trusting herself to speak. Yet how will she speak to a crowd if she can't utter a word at this stage? The man raises his hand in a gesture that means "Wait," which of course is what will kill this green and untypical impulse toward intervention, to wait while her fears grow and bubble inside and finally block her fragile drive. Luckily the parrot vendor has run out of words as well. He ends on a philosophical note—"We have built something good and right and profitable; we can build it again, as long as we do not fall into this trap of violence into which *they* wish us to fall." The clapping rises high and strong; his fear has rushed out and touched theirs with knowing hands. He swings down the ladder jauntily and drops the last three rungs, a larval politician confirmed in his occupation. The man with the clipboard nods.

"There's no one else?" she asks him, hoarsely. "Where is everyone?"

"*Putain,* they have been talking for two hours," he an-swers. "There has been no resolution. That's the problem here," he adds, and shrugs. "Talk talk talk, but in the end everybody does what they want, you know what it's like, anyway this is almost over, there's too much *pinga* around, and you—"

Soledad does not hear him out. She is already halfway up the ladder, herded by the pounding in her arteries. The plat-form is made of planks stretched between horizontal angle braces. The mike swings from a string hung on an imperfection of welding. She picks it up, straightens, looking over the black heave of crowd. There has to be more than ten thousand people in this *cruce,* she thinks vaguely, and doesn't this contradict some position of Hawkley's? The stars of oil lamps, the quasars of a bonfire, a row of trees at the south end of the market that Umbandistas have dressed in candles so that they look like trees of flame: Yemanja.

People stand at the lit windows of the countinghouses. A dozen different tunes, muted but alive, worm from guitars, flutes, voices, in different sections of the audience. High above the rooftops of the market, above the horizon of Ensevli, a starshell bursts over a skirmish in the very brush of San Isidor. Neon pulses the air green, yellow; a spotlight steadies on her form, destroying her vision of night.

She has to say something.

Even if she leaves, she has to say something. It would be too humiliating, it would be total victory for that killing silence to leave without a single word uttered.

"I want to say . . ." she begins. Her four words, picked up by the sound system, echo hollowly across the square. Mucus clogs her throat, and she coughs.

Someone applauds nearby. Bored people whistle around the fringes. The girl with the guitar fingers a trio of chords she knows well. "Soledad!" someone shouts good-humoredly, "play us the *'Souche'*!" It touches her, briefly, that she is still remembered from that concert a good two weeks ago now.

But what would she say, even if she could say it without coughing? What she really wants is to use words and arguments the way Miguel does, as elegant engines of logic, gleaming and metallic, whose every stroke of verbal piston is accurate and finely balanced and leads without possibility of error to a set conclusion. She wants to speak like Jorge does, bringing an army of sweating mules and storms and bridges and oceans full of silver mist, where the cries of seabirds mingle with the plaints of lovers to weave a spell over those whom she would convince.

She wants to speak as her father used to, plainly stating a problem and then listing exactly how many pumps or hoses or bags of bone cement—deployed where, by whom, and when—would be needed to solve it.

The panic is close to mouth level now. She clears her throat once more. The crowd is restive, but tolerant of her nervousness so far; someone shouts "Soledad!" again.

"I want," she says. And then, quickly: "I—I can only tell you about something. Something that happened—what happened to me."

She starts to tell them. She begins slowly, haltingly, using the wrong words often but throwing them in anyway, the way a shipwrecked carpenter throws in any damn driftwood to rebuild his boat. What happened to her. How she came to the *cruce* under house arrest from storm troopers living inside, where they kept her music handcuffed and barred shut in a life that was nothing but a series of half-successful jailbreaks from one soft refuge to another. How she found in the *cruce* a place so full of music and so friendly to those who wished to free the tunes crushed behind those bars that it allowed her, for the first time, to break out and perform; to play the music she had made by and in the *cruce* for those who lived there with her.

Her voice grows in strength. Telling a story like this, to these people, is not so hard after all. The crowd is fairly silent, the guitars ribbing on like air conditioners underneath.

"A place that is like this for me, and I think for you also," she says, "for most of us—well, I cannot abandon it."

And all at once the drab feelings, of weight and things off-kilter, of travel, lag and foreboding, of menstrual cramps even—all the mass that has been dragging at her since she woke—seem to dwindle. The angst and reluctance, the terrible deadening caution shouting "Stop! What of the risk? Think of the humiliation!" is amazingly quiet. For her words are not perfect but they are hot and they are more or less connected. And in that heat, all the terrors and gloom crust into a slag heavy and gray that falls off what she has to say, like clinkers scabbing off melted iron ore, so that her verbs and adjectives can run pure and orange and malleable into the mold of night.

"It is everything, this *cruce,* it is nothing specific. It's a story—this is what Jorge Echeverria would tell you"—she looks for him without looking for him, she would never see him through the lights—"it's a story we tell ourselves about who we wish we were. And because we *are* the story we tell of ourselves, we in turn become the story, the story itself. That is what the *cruce* is."

Someone shouts, *"C'est ça, chérie."* A drunk yodels raucously.

"In the *cruce,* I told a story to me, about myself." Is she repeating herself? She plows on regardless, sweat pooling under her eyes. "Thanks to the *cruce*—thanks to you—it allowed me to become as realized as, as a—a fire orchid in the *selva* in that moment of balance when it has absorbed the dew of night and is touched by the early warmth of the sun; open. Fully expanded. And what allowed that here, and only here," she continues, talking much more quickly and strongly, "is the almost-total freedom you have—to do what you want in this community, *as a community*. To act without the outside rules imposed by corporations and copyrights and the ministry of commerce and the church and the bishop and the *telenovela* fashions and all the forces of greed and insurance and overriding fear, yes, the ones that built that tunnel, the ones on that warship!"

People start to clap, and like a fire set in dry undergrowth, the clapping grows and takes over the northern half of the market, invades that portion of sky and city, coming in waves so loud it terrifies her, she only just restrains an impulse to cover her ears with her palms.

But the south side of the market is not convinced. Whistles and shouts and a manic "shusssshh" rise from there and finally extinguish the northern applause.

"We have bad problems here," she continues, more quietly, when her terror has subsided, after the echoes of applause have been absorbed by the night. "Families still starve, they fall through the cracks. Our streets stink, they are not safe, there are fights.

"But we have one another," she says. Her voice, though no louder, holds more energy. "We can do the work we want, we can live as we decide. We have music, we have this together. With music, with each other, with our ideas we can hold this town. Even against the army. Even against all the killing machines they could use—and do you know why?"

"No!" and "Yes!" and *"C'est ça, chérie!"*

"Because they—" She points at the Walled City now. "They are afraid." Her voice cracks on the "afraid." Her throat is drier than ever, she won't be able to speak much longer. "Ochoa Campos and Sandoval and his advisers and the navy—*they* have no story about what they'd like to be, because their lives are built only on what they do *not* want. They have only their own fear, which controls them and limits them until finally it is fear itself which defines them.

"You see, they are afraid of people who try to make something out of love and curiosity. It exposes them for what they are, little men and cowards. *Des lâches.* And that is why we can defy them—" Her voice cracks again, she has to rip the phrase through her vocal cords to finish—"That is why they can never defeat us in the end, though they dig their tunnels and send their ships and soldiers and try to force us with bullets and noise to become like them!"

And the Slave Market rises in a small but growing tide of applause and cries. *"Oui, si! C'est ça, chérie!"* Voices near her call "Soledad!" and *"Souche!"* In the south corner, near the flaming trees, another tropism of rhythm and clapping begins, and spreads like a cloud's shadow across the vast space, from north to south, from east to west.

Beside and under her, the girl on the *requinto* strums, adapting her chords to the meter of applause and then adding a grace note, and another, twisting it to fit the words she sings.

Of what use is a root
that does not reach the volcano's sex

The girl's group picks it up, and then the cluster of women and then the *guaqueros,* pulling it toward the center of the crowd; they stop their clapping so the words can fly, free of the tyranny of precision.

of what use a love
bound by the shadow's track

The clapping dies in the market as people strain to hear what is being sung, recognize it, and join in. Finally the whole crowd from the Slaves Gate to the flaming trees to the fishermen's harbor is singing, not quite in one voice, different parts of the crowd listen to themselves more than to the whole, but near enough to approximate a fleeting unity:

Desdichado
Desdichado
this land is sad as a wound

The song is so strong in their ten thousand voices, it feels to Soledad that she is being physically compressed by its volume, the way a woman is embraced by her mate, with strength and passion and tenderness. And the pressure inward causes an equal and opposite reaction, an outward surge that she can only define once more by the overused terminology of love: love for these people in all their impossible contradictions; so true and fickle, so independent and conjoined, so gentle and violent, so loud and musical, so angry and forgiving; love for what they make together and separately, this *cruce* that has allowed her not only to do what she just described, but to tell it as a story, a parable of herself, and in so doing confirm it like a marriage vow, to them and to herself, once more.

She is nothing if not logical, though. Her father taught her that and so did the math of music. Even Miguel in his own way taught her something.

Thus, as *"Souche"* swells and ebbs in the Slave Market, as she absorbs the great fact of her love for these people and this place, she also remembers the insight she had earlier—that she can only truly love what she already has lost. And because she must follow that thought all the way to its logical conclusion, she realizes that if she loves them in this way, then in the logic of her own emotions, it follows the *cruce* already is doomed.

The terror that comes then is far stronger (though cold, not hot) than the nerves that assaulted her before.

She swings, turns dangerously on the narrow platform, using movement to put it out of her mind. Finds the ladder with her toes.

At the base of Lo Pano people are already dancing. Haddad waits in the shadow of one of the pylons. She steps clear of the loom of tower and he steps forward—somewhere, maybe at one of the vendors still plying his trade around the crowd, he has found a fire orchid. The coincidence distracts her long enough for terror to loosen its grip somewhat.

"That was incredible," Haddad says, "you told them what I wanted to say, Soledad. But you said it—I mean, it was lovely." His eyes, beneath the jagger mask, are crinkled and moist. "There is a *cruce* in Oakland, California"—he stares at her intently, the reflected lights splash over his half-sucker screen—"even there they will hear of what you did tonight."

She takes the orchid from him, leans forward on impulse, and kisses him quickly on the mouth.

Then turns, slips into the crowd, dropping the flower into the crush of feet and cobbles, before Haddad in his adoration and shock can follow.

The crowd is as full of movement now as a storm sea. The *pinga* flows freely. Nobody ever remembers much of *"Souche"* beyond the first couple of stanzas and thus, as she predicted, all that's left now is her music, gaining in volume, changing, being improvised, riffed on, vulgarized, improved. She wonders, in the spaciness of aftermath, if music gains precedence only when words, for one reason or another, no longer work—or is it that words and their cargo of consciousness are never as strong as the emotions music summons? Men and women twirl in the glare of acetylene lamps. It's like the end or the beginning of a carnival, an impression furthered by the fact that some have adapted pieces of *Selva* to *dance de nègre,* which is a carnival step. Men crouch and whirl, holding wooden swords, demanding rum. One has even borrowed lipstick to paint his face blue, as tradition dictates. Sideways and step and bend the woman back, and turn her like a handle. Some of the dancers acknowledge her with a wave, a proffered bottle, a comment—*"C'est ça, chérie!* You said it!" A few, hostile to what she said, shake their heads or make some comment like *"Putain,* now you've done it," and smile anyway, if a little sadly. But no one gets in her way, no one tries to drag her into dance or party or discussion, and she is grateful for this discretion. In the end this is what she has treasured here above all else: the ability people have to be open, and curious, and hands-off in the same instant.

She navigates by San Isidor, by Lo Pano. With the volcano behind her, she is heading for the harbor. She is looking for someone—she actually has to think for a second to figure out who. Dolores, of course, her once and future tenant. Dolores, and the baby inside her, and the passel of potential problems they are likely to cause.

It will be pleasant, Soledad thinks, if those are the gravest problems she has to deal with in the next few weeks. She is deliberately not thinking about herself and her emotions; not thinking, obviously, about Jorge.

The crowd thins and breaks into small pieces around the Corniche. Soledad walks to the very edge of the water, where the moon slimes its trail across the bay. She lights a Galaxy and wanders north down the waterfront. A smuggling catamaran with giant outboards shows lighted portholes be-low her. A radio squawks against the music of *"Souche,"* al-ready broken up into a dozen party tunes in the market. A searchlight lances, thin as wire, from a fast patrol boat in mid-bay, grabbing in its tight white fist a dark sloop that thought it could get around the picket by stealth and local knowledge.

She thinks it must be hard for *contrabandistas* to keep in mind all the variables of tide and the changing sandbars of Cap Naufrage and now this frigate, and still keep the per-fect pitch they need to race across such perilous dark waters without fault, night after night—obviously, it's impossible. Just as it will not be feasible for her to maintain the level of courage—no, more, the level of passion, for she is certain at this point they are one and the same—the passion necessary to act as she did tonight.

Clearly, she is capable of feats like this if the conditions are exactly right. Equally clearly, she cannot act this way all or even most of the time. The weight of her days will be spent as handmaiden to the same kind of fear she accused Ochoa Campos of harboring. It's the average, though—this is what she tells herself now—it's the average that's important; bal-ancing her cowardice with an occasional bravery of perfor-mance.

It is not a balance worthy of the force of this *cruce,* or the grace of the *selva,* or the meter of Jorge's poetry, all of which she has folded into her own work. It is a poor story, at best, of a woman who tried and mostly failed. But perhaps, one day, it will be enough.

She turns south. The cigarette has calmed her nerves, slowed her breathing. The lights of Pytagoro's wink across the inner docks of the fishing harbor. She truly has no big desire to see Jorge at this point. But she would like to find Dolores, who sometimes winds up at Pytagoro's if the Tayrona is not lively enough.

Mostly she would like to see people she knows. Even Ruiz would do at this moment. The bay seems awfully cold and lonely out there, and she is still recovering from the four days she spent traveling by herself.

She lights another Galaxy, then throws it into the water half smoked. The sea breeze runs through her cropped hair like fingers. Stepping more smartly now, chin up, she follows the broad curbing stones of the Corniche around the inner docks, and enters the warm noise of the Cadillac.

SHE SPOTS RUIZ IMMEDIATELY, which allows her to turn aside, to the bar on the left, avoiding Jorge's group for now. Finds a corner between a *contrabandista* and a pair of regulars playing pinochle on the mahogany counter. The owner ignores people clamoring for drinks to grease over to her, eyes popping more than usual. "Dona Soledad," he whispers, just loud enough to be heard over the disc jockey; this form of address, used as an honorific in the Walled City, verges on insult here. "A *tafia*," she tells him, "double on the *pinga*," and does not add *"S'il vous plaît."* He hisses, but mixes it strong.

Turning aside to lean on the bar, Soledad finally sees Dolores, in the middle of a group of *guaqueros* of course. They too are dancing the *dance de nègre,* and briefly she wonders what aspect of ritual she is ignorant of here. Is this more than a carnival rite? Does it have to do with communal confabs, or the arrival of danger?

The bar is denser than usual with smoke and noise. The casse-co jockey is in full swing, leaning riskily out of the backseat of the Coupe De Ville bolted high on the stone wall in back, slotting illicit spindles of music downloaded from Wildnets or smuggled from Cayenne and Salvador do Bahia to the Bidonville workshops.

Watching Dolores again, not drunk but certainly high, being pivoted by her black-kerchiefed partners. Thinking, almost in satisfaction, that living with Dolores, trying to help Dolores, will probably be harder even than living with Dolores's father. Who appears almost as soon as she thinks this, opening a wedge through the crowd toward a reserved table, beckoning Ruiz and the Lo Pano girl and a thin man in a professor's suit with a white beard and gold glasses. The *mounchey* from Jorge's party follows quietly behind, towing with one finger the gringo victim of her earlier pickpocketing. The crowd closes around them, but not before Jorge glances up and spots her looking at him, and *putain* her gaze must be like the patrol boat's searchlight, it has been so long, in so many ways.

A few seconds later he is in front of her, taking her left hand in both of his, lifting it to his lips. The green of his eyes slips through the defenses of her own, then breaks on something harder within.

"Soledad," he says, "you stole my talent, yeh, and that was unfair, you ripped off my skill with words and never gave me your grace with music."

She nods, slightly pleased at praise from such a craftsman; mostly pissed off, because even his praise must be in relation to himself. Last week, according to Dolores, he asked Ruiz to turn one of his older poems into a song, and in a way that hurt worse than seeing him tonight with the Lo Pano woman. He shakes his head then, as if he'd heard what she was thinking and says, "No, *chérie,* only you had these talents, it was wonderful. You have built a city on the city that was already here." She wishes he would shut up now, people are listening and even strangers must be able to make out the component of manipulation in his voice, but he continues relentlessly, "If the *cruce* survives, you can tell yourself it was in part because of you."

"If," she says, and takes a nervous sip of her drink.

"I have to get back," he says, pulling at his earlobe. "I tried to see you—they told me you went Outside?"

"Yes," she says.

"Echeverria," Ruiz calls. "The game begins."

"The story group," he explains. "I have to go. But we must talk, soon; it's more important than weather, or the entelechy of rats." Before the crowd heals around itself again she glances in the direction of Jorge's group and catches the eye of the Lo Pano woman, who until now has been careful not to look anywhere near her.

The DJ announces a break; the music dims. Someone lights a half dozen Oxum votives. The conversation swells, fades. Pytagoro places a wireless mike in front of the white-bearded man, who adjusts his glasses, makes sure his cigarette is drawing, and begins.

"Krik," he says. It's the traditional Caribbean way of opening a story, and Bamaca is close enough to the Caribbean for most of the audience to know the response.

"Krak," they answer.

"He was a naval architect," the man begins. "He had many women and three wives. All of them hated him. He had lived in many strange and wonderful places. . . ."

The crowd is quiet now except for the clink of glasses, the occasional scrape of a match, the click of pinochle dice; all except for Dolores, who fidgets and whispers loudly. Even the *guaqueros,* who are proud of their mountain roughness and their ability to throw stelae around in the dark while dodging choppers and night-vision sights, cock their heads to listen. There is, in the Costeño tradition, a real respect for the dynamics of a story. "Krik," the white-bearded man repeats, and "Krak" the crowd responds, louder than the story warrants. Is it the African tradition that forges such attentiveness, the race-memory of griots sitting in the pounded-dirt center of the village, spinning tales of spirits and jackals? And is it the fact of Dolores's continuing fixation on her past—her fossilized adolescence, the continuing angst from her parents' separation—that causes her to reject the story being spun in Pytagoro's tonight? Soledad finds herself searching for Jorge's face, hidden now behind a row of listeners. She sucks at her empty drink.

"As Anne slapped his face, it struck him that he had engineered the whole thing to coincide with the new container ship he had to build in Finland. That it wasn't so much Anne he wanted to leave as the ship that was finished, the landscape he was sick of. Krik!"

"Krak!"

She has to say, this story is not much good. She could weave a better story out of thin air, out of nothing but what she's thinking about at the time. Which is, for some reason, a town 120 miles down the coast from here, a resort called Santa Maria del Mar perched over sandstone cliffs on the ocean, an early-twentieth-century beach colony of white villas and Bavarian cottages and Mediterranean-style arcades with big cool rooms painted pastel and the sea breeze pushing curtains that smelled of salt. Enormous casinos and hotels with dark lobbies and tearooms dank from mold and cigars; and seaside cabanas with tattered striped parasols scattered across the short orange beach.

They went there once a year, in the dry season, staying always at the same hotel. Her mother loved the place, with its plate silverware and china white as fish bones and stocky Germans dressed in brown reading the *São Paulo Deutsche Zeitung* on the porch. She loved sitting on the beach and would read there for hours, deckled books by Céline and Balzac, while Soledad walked with her father or played in the sand with other kids. Soledad also loved Santa Maria because of details that appealed to children—tall peppermint *batidos* at the casino restaurant, an abandoned cabana kids used as a fort, a carousel with ornate, if faded, horses, the hotel curtains that made her feel as if she lived in a palace and must therefore be some kind of princess.

"Krik!" the white-bearded man said.

"Krak!" the audience said.

But she has started this story wrong, Soledad reflects, eyeing the fresh *tafia* Pytagoro placed on the counter in front of her. She should have mentioned the carousel, right at the start. She should have begun with Glen MacRae, and the normal state of affairs: her mother lying in bed in her darkened room for most of the day; her father deep in the mine tunnels with his hands curved around the machinery he loved; all the elements that were the real foundation of her love for Santa Maria, all the things that made their escape to the coast such a pleasure for all of them—until the visit that sparked this story to begin with, in the early days of that vacation.

They had arrived late two days before. A mud slide delayed the train and the next day it rained, an unusual event in and of itself. None of them minded much. Her parents read and she skipped rope with a Guyanese girl on the vast porch, but she had not been able to go to the carousel and ride on the white-and-green horse that was her favorite. Riding "her" horse was a tradition, in Santa Maria; the ritual that somehow unlocked the reality of being there from the fantasy she made of it the rest of the year.

The third day dawned sunny and clear. Puddles steamed into blue oblivion past the porch railings as they ate breakfast. A tall Norwegian in a black double-breasted suit came over and with a mixture of diffidence and brio sat at their table. He was an engineer named Gustaffsen; he had blueprints for extremely high-efficiency gasoline pumps that would enable Soledad's father to open up manganese workings in the soggy soil by the Rio Chingado. It was clear her father knew him, and was not surprised to find him here.

It was clear, also, that something about him upset Soledad's mother. She refused to talk to Mr. Gustaffsen or shake his hand. Francis MacRae uttered words charged with an energy unsuited to breakfast. Soledad was sent to her room to pick up her beach things. When she came back, her father and Gustaffsen were talking to Herr Mueller, the manager, while the Indio houseboys cleaned up the broken china wreckage of their meal. "She's outside," her father said curtly. "Ye'll both go to the beach." "The carousel?" Soledad said. "Away!" her father shouted. ("Krik?" "Krak!")

Irena MacRae stood on the street in the full sun without a parasol. Though naturally dark of skin, she seemed pale in contrast to the staring houseboys and everybody else in the streets of that beach resort. She took Soledad's hand and marched her down the boulevard of hotels toward the carousel. She, at least, had not forgotten the traditions. The smells of the beach greeted Soledad like friends: barbecuing beef and salt and the rot of algae and sweet coconut sun oil. Presumably because the rains had kept them indoors the day before, a lot of children were waiting around the cast-iron gate that barred them from the swirling colors and honky-tonk calliope of the amusement. Germans watched, disapproving, from porches. Soledad's mother said nothing. The grip of her hand was hard, her face was set the way it had been at home. Soledad too was silent, not wanting anything to interfere with what was about to happen. She followed the line of children onto the immobilized ride, looking for the horse she always rode; she didn't even remember why she liked that particular horse, but now it was hers, with its gilt bridle and green paint flaking from the tail, and she would ride no other. She walked around the carousel twice, but the horse was not there. Ran back, the tears just starting, to the gate. Her mother picked her up, and all of the girl's tears and quick sorrow had not changed the iron cast of her mother's face. Though she did go up to the man who ran the ride, and asked what had happened to the horse.

"They took it for repairs," she explained to Soledad. "They take three of the horses every year. It will be back next season."

"I don't want it next season," Soledad bawled. "It's my horse, I want it now!"

Irena yanked her into the sun.

"Do you want me to buy you some *barbe-à-papa*?" she asked.

"I don't want *barbe-à-papa,* I want my horse!" Soledad screamed. She was not as upset about the horse as she had been only seconds before, but a tantrum had its own logic and obligations and she was not through with this one yet. She stamped her feet, crossed her arms, tried to cry again.

"Soledad," her mother said.

"What." Not looking up.

"You will understand someday. You will not always get the horse you want. In fact, most of the time, you get the horse you don't want. Or you don't get a horse at all."

"What?" Soledad said. "You mean I'll *never* get the white-and-green horse?"

"I don't mean the horse," her mother said, sitting in an odd position on the hot curb. "I don't even mean the carousel. I mean, you cannot expect good things all the time, like this." She waved her arm wearily. "Like Santa Maria. Mostly," she added in a softer voice, "life is just sad. Sad, and much too long."

Soledad stamped her foot again, less hard. She had no idea what her mother was talking about. She was young enough that the borders of her *estancia* seemed as distant as the ends of the earth, and the vagaries of her parents as incomprehensible as weather. Moreover, her father had a Presbyterian Scot's distaste for Catholicism, so the complex papist guilt that might have tied her own spoiled behavior to the grief and anger her parents sometimes betrayed simply was not there. The arms and songs of Maria Gisela had been enough until now to assuage the confusion of such times as these.

Her mother wiped the back of her hand over her face, not once or twice but six or seven times in a row, as if to dry tears that never showed up. Soledad's primary emotion on that perfect morning remained confusion; but, oddly, it did not go away, not during the strained remainder of this vacation (cut short five days later), or for weeks thereafter.

Though her father aborted the deal he had been about to sign with Gustaffsen, and pulled out of manganese mining altogether in order to spend more time at home, Soledad's mother gained no joy from her small victories.

They never returned to Santa Maria del Mar. And long after the details of the carousel horse had faded, Soledad would remember what her mother had said then, the dilemma it raised—about her parents, about herself—a question that did not fade, but remained as sharp and strong as the light in that clear beach town where the sky and buildings and sand were mostly as white as each other.

————

"KRIK?" THE WHITE-BEARDED MAN asks, sharply.

"Krak!" the audience replies, louder.

The naval architect is in serious trouble now, Soledad gathers.

She lights a cigarette. Half her memory circuits are still bathed in the sea light of Santa Maria. She still feels shaky because of adrenaline released in the Slave Market. She takes a slug of the fresh *tafia* and a deep drag of rough smoke and feels better. Looks around the crowd to see if they are really listening to the white-bearded one, and once again is struck by the extent to which these Costeños are suckers for a story. They will go along with anything as long as you keep the dialogue going. The *guaqueros* stand there, beers dewing in their fists, rapt as schoolboys. Dolores leans against the tall one, who is not Diego; her eyes are shut, so it's impossible to tell if she is listening or not, but her body at least is in repose. Jorge is hidden in the crowd.

The girl from Lo Pano is visible. She signals Pytagoro for a drink, avoiding Soledad's eye. Pytagoro puts the *tafia* on a waiter's tray and turns away. Soledad unscrews the top off a bottle of *diablo vert* pepper sauce and dumps a third of the bottle in the girl's drink. She feels both pleased and disgusted with herself as a waiter delivers the glass. She watches to see how hard the Lo Pano woman will choke.

The *mounchey* is in plain view through a gap in the people, and so is the man in Yanqui clothes she was pickpocketing earlier. Now, for the first time, Soledad sees the man's face. As if he could feel her eyes on him, or hear what she is thinking, he turns and looks directly at her.

"Krik?"

"Krak!"

The bar darkens. The words of the story, the sounds of the audience, the Lo Pano girl taking a first sip of her tampered drink, fade behind a rushing noise that seems to grow around the stranger. The rushing sound is appropriate, because it is a white noise, a sound of absence, of blankness, of negative information such as Jorge says orgs pump out to numb the senses of their human clients and victims; and what this Yanqui's face is, is nothing—or more accurately, within the stageset of a regular face outlined by scalp, ears, and jawline, it is a seething mass of data and motion—not nose or mouth or eyes, but only a roiling cloud such as you see when TV stations go off the air at 3 A.M., after the national anthem and the test pattern, when chaos rushes in.

She wants to move, to siphon her drink, do something normal, but cannot. She is transfixed, it's the opposite of how she was while listening to the story—for the white noise is growing in volume, and the bright chaos of light and dark where the man's face should be is getting bigger in Soledad's vision, swelling till it seems to touch all the boundaries of perception.

And now, amid the chaos, forms appear—shapes that at first seem as random and meaningless as the visual noise, but that all of a sudden click into things recognizable: different angles, like *telenovela* shots, like those video clips the Fernsehen therapists use: two men, one with a blue anteater tatooed on his arm, bending over another man slumped somewhere (next frame) a chair leg bolted to a massive ringbolt on the stone floor (next frame) the face of a man concentrating, his eyes narrowed to slits like those of a lizard (next frame) man in chair arching backward, his mouth open so far she has trouble recognizing him but the hair is Jorge's, the nose too, the lines in his flesh worn by gentler times, the shirt is one of his old linen shirts (and she pushes herself away from the bar now in Pytagoro's, the *tafia* fallen and exploded in an F-sharp chord of glass and rum on the tiles); both hands covering her

mouth as she stares at the nightmare face of Jorge's guest
(next frame)

The arm with the tapir pulling something raw and bloody
and still-moving out of Jorge's mouth, as he screams silently,
and she screams silently, on and on; and everyone else in
Pytagoro's goes calm and quiet as a mountain lake.

TWELVE

THE TUG WAS RUNNING in a different direction now, or perhaps the wind had shifted; at any rate her shelter in the lee of the tarpaulined TVs behind the wheelhouse protected Soledad no more. The wind picked up speed in the angles of ship and snapped around her curled form. Her mouth was open so wide it ached, the wind literally blew among her teeth. She wondered if its whistling had contributed to her dream of that long, silent scream in Pytagoro's.

She closed her mouth, got to her feet, staggered as the boat rolled, grabbed a taut rope for support. She felt thin and insubstantial; the wind was chillier now and more humid and she knew her limbs would start to tremble once they figured out she was conscious. From this perspective she could see over the tarpaulins, back into the white churn of the tug's wake, where enough fog had burned off to expose a smooth giant arching span, molten orange in color (orange as the feeling she'd had of herself, freed under Lo Pano from slag of doubt); a leap the size of sky, transformed into steel, that pulled a dark green headland to the tug's left side into contact with a headland to the right.

The Golden Gate Bridge. For a stunned second she wondered if by going backward in time in her dream she had been pulled backward in reality, too; they had passed under the Golden Gate outbound a good hour before she fell asleep. Then she realized the sun was at a different angle and direction and they were going back into San Francisco Bay—back to Oakland, the former Naval Supply Yard, and the node.

The node. She tried to whisper that name to herself; as usual, nothing came out.

Soledad stretched. She saw the weed-pirate on one wing of the wheelhouse, fooling around with his antique brass instrument. He had put a sweater on against the cold but his skinny thighs were still unprotected. Ahead, a huge flat-sided ship moved like a lost building out of a bank of fog that rose and lay down in the bay till it finally curled around the geological anomaly in glass and concrete that was downtown San Francisco.

She looked forward and left, where the new Bay Bridge led her eye, where Oakland should be, but it was obscured for the time being by the steep island supporting the bridge's midpoint. She was perfectly conscious of the fact that she had only this morning left the node while it was under some sort of undefined attack from the authorities; she also knew, with hindsight, that Stix had been right in bringing her to the tug, out of the way. It was clear to her now that, however tentative the attack had been, it would have resonated in her mind enough to stall her in some basic fashion.

She knew this, just as she knew that recalling the nightmare visions in Pytagoro's should have doubled or tripled her sensitivity to the potential horrors being visited on this gringo *cruce* she had fled to. Yet now she looked out over the tug's frothing bow wave with a fragile yet undeniable calm that, she reasoned, had to be built out of the sense of ease and rightness that touched her like a hot-water bottle when she dreamed of the people and tropisms of the *cruce,* of a love— she had used the word in her dream, and it had a right to be used—a love that could transcend details of horror, portents of pain, even when they must come as an ineluctable finale to the main experience.

Behind the salt-streaked windows of the wheelhouse, to her right, the boy tapped on a computer terminal, and the tug altered course northward. They were coming around Yerba Buena Island. Details of Berkeley and Mount Diablo, only slightly twisted by fog, marched into view around the island's rocky end, like cards dealt from a deck of distance.

The tug rolled gently in the container ship's wake. It had been good to get out of the node and the vast echoing factory she slept in. To breathe air full of iodine and Pacific and free of the complex information of human smells; to see green, even if it was not the bursting frothy joyous yellow-green of the *selva;* to feel the long and mysterious motion of waves, and to move to a pattern that was not made by others. All of it had combined into this partial serenity, allowing her to look calmly forward as more and more of Oakland came into view ahead.

"It was a probe only," the boy said at her elbow, and she jumped violently. "There was a message on the Wildnets. They came in the tunnels, but they could not break through."

Soledad stared at him. It dawned on her that he had spoken in Lanc-Patua. He looked back at her for a beat or two, then peered forward to where the first giant crosshatching of port area scribbled out of headland; where the exhaust flames on the refineries' stacks burned like shrines to a technological deity; where a single thin column of dark smoke now rose from beyond the headland, where the node should be—like a smoke of story, an ur-smoke that combined the trickle from San Isidor and the combustion of Ensevli and exhaust from the workings of Glen MacRae mine with whatever the American flics had ignited in the node before her.

———

STIX WAS WAITING WHEN, after negotiating the manifold of tunnels of the ancient base, they moored at the access tunnel's quay.

He found Soledad in the saloon. His face was smudged, but darker than soot were the shadows around his mouth and eyes. He confirmed what the boy had said. His voice was curt and unhappy. "I have the bike," he told Soledad, then added, disconnectedly, "Wanted to make sure you were OK. I'll take you back to the torpedo shop, if you want."

She shook her head, not sure of what she really did want

but certain, maybe because of that free air she had just sampled, it was not this.

"Whatever," he said, "I don't have time to escort you around." He brushed his hair back, tiredly. The gesture reminded her, for some reason, of Miguel. "I gotta go to Liteworld."

She tried to find his eyes. He was watching the raccoon, who had poked a straw into a closed sugar container and was trying to suck the crystals out. Watching the terminals around the settee, the ΠΟΛΙΣ screens in particular, where the pleasant scene of fields and crystal airport had been replaced by maps showing bunkers, and secret doors, and tunnels winding from castles to hidden color-generators. She waved, to catch his attention. When he looked at her, she pointed at her chest.

"You," he said. "OK."

She pointed upward.

"You want to go up? Sure, I can—no. Whaddya mean?" He shook his head. "I don't have time for this, I'm totally late. . . ."

She pointed at him, then at her chest again, then up, her finger stabbing fiercely. Stix sighed, and looked back at the ΠΟΛΙΣ scene.

"You want to go with me? Outside?"

She nodded. He pulled the jambook from his belt, jiggled the thumbstick, watched the display for a minute. He glanced at the raccoon, who was annoyed because it couldn't get enough suction to pull crystals over the loop of its straw. It was now lying on its back on a pile of data spindles, sorting flashcards alphabetically, then winging them viciously in all directions.

"What the hell," Stix said. His voice was not enthusiastic. "It's my show, right? Don't see why I can't bring a date if I want."

"Rrrreekeet," the raccoon said angrily, and tossed the whole stack of cards to the deck.

AN HOUR LATER SOLEDAD was on the lower deck of a bridge, riding in the front seat of a large, black, fish-smelling convertible.

An entire cow's skull was bolted on the car's hood, only partially obscuring the quad carburetor intake bolted underneath.

Inside, hundreds of warning lights flashed among a chaos of Malta cans and ripped Naugahyde. Outside, the setting sun was old marinara on the tablecloth of night. The bridge was the same one she had seen from the tug, not the Golden Gate but a long series of spans that jumped from Oakland, to a giant pylon that looked like a Speer monument, to an island; there, the bridge seemed to pause, take a breather, turn a little, gather its steel and concrete haunches beneath it, and then leap across the rest of the bay to the twinkling urban galaxies of San Francisco.

A panel at the city entrance warned all trucks, and cars more than two years old, to dive to the lower deck and the truckways below. But the smokeways were blocked as usual and the driver, a Putamadre with hair teased into question marks and the usual Goth clothes and giant circuitry medallions hanging off his neck, swung his ride off an exit and up, illegally, onto flyways running alongside the upscale Tibetan deep-fry cafés and Webware workshops and maté houses.

Two fuel-cell Daimlers immediately clotted in front of them. A third car held level with the Puta's window. It was a Ford-Volvo with an urban vigilante sticker on the door, driven by a young white man wearing the rank-tie of a Flash keiretsu. He screamed at them uselessly through the slipstream, stabbing his index finger toward a ramp to one of the truck-streets. The Puta, by way of reply, pulled a rusted, sawed-off hunting rifle from under his seat, pointed it at the three-percenter's face, then blasted his nitro-injected 408 into the lane reserved for VIPs and breakdown vehicles. He peeled left onto the Van Ness Flyway, evading the investment-scum ahead.

"Jesus!" Stix shrieked from the backseat, where he was

trying to keep the piled crates of his machinery from tumbling over in the curves. "You'll get us killed, you fuckin' crazy Puta!"

"Choo said choo were late, *maricón*," the Puta answered, holding his cigarette with one hand, the sawed-off in the other, steering now with his knees—and Soledad grinned, still in the grip of the irrational calm, the mental Jacuzzi of abstraction in which she had been metaphorically soaking since the tug.

Anyway, none of this was real to her; nothing, it seemed, could surprise her anymore. Not the too-quiet node that they emerged into from the sub base: alleys smelling of burnt chemicals, the vidwalls showing images of 1979 Saigon, or 1950s American *telenovelas* morphed to dress *El Beav* Cleaver in mourning, or wheel vampires darkly over Gilligan's lush island. Not the BOQ laboratory, where Stix picked up a small container full of glowing green seaweed, and tucked it in a shoulder harness; nor the hacker's hut behind a warehouse where she sat in darkness while an invisible woman scanned a laser over her fingerpads, retinas, and laryngeal ridges to burn her ID onto a fake UCC card, a twelve-hour rental that cost Stix such a high sum in barter-chips that she almost felt guilty about asking to come along. Even their method of leaving the node, in the face of all those checkpoints sealing off exits in the Wall of Junk Cars and the Wall of Ancient Mainframes, did not faze her: it had been a deceptively simple operation whereby Doctor Zatt, running a crane perched over the Fairlanes, the highest part of that wall, lifted her and Stix and three wooden crates in a cargo net through the thickening fog and down, past a giant cistern painted to resemble a toilet, straight into the backseat of the Putamadre's convertible—which took off as soon as they unhooked the net, blasting through a jungle of weeds along red-rusted railroad tracks, and so fast that the armored cars they glimpsed through gaps in the former Chinese shipping line offices had absolutely no time to react.

She supposed this haze of unreality was how she had learned

to cope with excessive information and violent change. It was as good a way as any, she reasoned—though Jorge would probably have preferred Stix's method, which was right in line with his own theories, or rather Fernsehen's. Her companion, fuming over his ever-increasing tardiness, had barely spoken a word to her as he rented the fake spindle, to the point that she wondered why he'd agreed to take her along. Anyway the off-road route down the tracks along Middle Harbor Road and finally through the tunnel under Route 880 was too bumpy for speech. But as they navigated the flyway into the clear lanes of 101 North he said without preamble or even looking at her, "I ran into Will six years ago, right down there, in SOMA, Market Street; I had lost touch with him, you know, after San Diego. I got a major wad of credit organizing a terror-art show for a gallery that catered to the Dead—exactly like the place we're going to now, matter of fact. Then I go outside with the public relations CEO and boom! There's Will, organizing a protest 'cause they're virtual-consolidating, software keiretsu sponsoring the show is closing all their shops in the Valley and subcontracting to Webshops in Uganda.

"I thought he'd despise me," Stix continued, watching the Moscone Center flash by. "Here I was, rolling in cash, taking money from the Megorg—we'd both read Hawkley in San Diego, though good ole Stepdad tried to beat us up every time he saw the *Smuggler's Bible*—but Will just grinned. We went out to Vesuvio's and got drunk and it just felt so good. We talked about girls, and music, and Joachim Boaz—we both loved his paintings. Talked about how to make performance stuff that would subvert the orgs even though they were paying for it, we didn't care so goddam much about the theories then. I mean, we still had major differences of opinion—like, I was always a big Road Runner cartoon fan, and he thought Road Runner was silly, Planet Blast was his thing—but brothers have those. Just then it felt like we were really brothers, we had just survived—everything. I wish—"

But he never told her what he wished. For the first time since he'd started talking he looked at her. His scarf made whip sounds out the open window. She stared back at him, unwilling to do anything to interrupt either his flow of talk or the almost Buddhist detachment with which she greeted it.

"Will booby-trapped the tunnel they came through," Stix continued in a neutral tone. "Him, his Navigators, what's the difference. Blew it up right after a squad went in; they were dressed as cops but they had UCC cards with all the data blanked out. Federal job." Stix picked at a piece of Naugahyde off the seat in front of them. "Just smoke-inhalation cases and blown eardrums and one guy had a broken leg, but he could have killed them like that." Stix snapped his fingers. Suddenly he was shouting: "Coulda killed them, just shit-ass McDonald'sland people join the special units to get outta Kansas, and anyway there was never a town meeting, do you understand?" Staring into Soledad's eyes now. "No one gave him the right to use amatol."

Soledad nodded because she did understand something important in all of this, which was, This was the second time she had seen him transmute his childhood into a story told to her. It was probably the way he defanged the snake coiled at the bottom of the pit of how he grew up. It was exactly the way Fernsehen's story theory went, and Jorge would have loved to see it.

Then she bit her lip, hard, because thinking of Jorge put just the thinnest crack in the glass bubble surrounding her sensibilities, and she was definitely coming to like that transparent distance, that crystalline calm the Pacific had brought to her like a gift.

———

THE GATE WAS TASTEFUL, made up of fantastic wrought-iron gargoyles and pagodas and large, leafy, iron sans-serif letters spelling CLOUD FOREST. It was also thick and laden with steel spikes and a massive set of bars that stayed shut in front of the rust-riddled hood of the Putamadre's Malibu. "Apocalypse Planning," Stix announced. "We're going to the gallery." Lenses moved over them, a randomly generated voice politely urging that they swipe their UCC cards through a slot in the gate; then the voice said, "Welcome, Apocalypse Planning, Mr. Stephen Xavier Grammatico and Ms. Consuela Magdalena Castro. We regret that the card of Mr. Leon 'Kukuman' Osorio has expired/carries felony violations/has a maxed credit limit; therefore we are very sorry to have to insist that it would optimize the comfort level of our security staff if Mr. Osorio did not enter Cloud Forest proper. However we would be delighted if he would accompany the vehicle to the delivery entrance."

"Fock you," the Puta said, without rancor.

"You're welcome," the voice replied. "Enjoy."

Cloud Forest almost lived up to its name, Soledad thought. Though Kempian in inspiration, it was clearly not original Kemp, which tended to be more rooted in the native materials of redwood and granite; maybe one of Kemp's disciples had turned the general theory into this extremely tall tower where the vertical component consisted of transparent tubes shot through from top to bottom with smaller tubes of noctiluc coiled around a core of I-beams. The horizontal component was thick cantilevered balconies hanging every which way, supporting the various jungles the condo owners were sponsoring, often with Sierra Club or NRDC sanction, on their personal ledge of concrete.

Behind the balconies, Moorish arches or giant portholes shone warm light into the vegetation and the skeins of fog drifting past. The top floor was divided between an enormous cantilevered balcony, topped by a wind sock and a parked tilt-commuter plane, and a glass penthouse picketed by tall trees. One of these was so big, Soledad thought, it had to be a giant sequoia or perhaps a baobab, cabled and lashed down in its own fifty-thousand-liter container of moistened mulch.

And that was where they were going, all the way to the

top: Soledad and Stix and the three crates—one of which she now realized was the source of that fish odor in the jalopy—in a freight elevator tucked into the I-beam spine. The doors opened on a long pantry where blond men and women dressed in Swedish national dress prepared trays of champagne and pastries and then carried them through a sliding door in a small Moorish arch. Another tall person stood waiting for them, wearing a suit that was like the rich cousin of Stix's, cut of cloth smoother and more supple-looking, with iridescent lapels.

Soledad was not sure, then or ever, exactly what this person's gender was, and thought of the person in patois as "elil," a designation that covered such cases: elil, in any event, had a shaved head and almost Egyptian features made up with a lovely shimmering coat of violet on eyelids and cheekbones and a way of moving that would be effeminate in a man and butch in a woman. Elil grasped a take-away QuikViet carton between finger and thumb in one hand. "I've decided," elil said to Stix, "that your atrocious tardiness is latent hostility; luckily I remembered last time, and budgeted for the delay—anyway, you always look so much more handsome off the Flash, so I'll forgive you. I'm Randy," elil added, turning to Soledad, "has anyone ever told you you're far, far prettier than Lara Love?" Randy's smile was wide and surprisingly open, for one of the Dead—Soledad slapped herself mentally for using a term only a radical *crucista* would use: the Dead, the Safe People, those who lived Outside. She had never agreed with such in-group/out-group categories; it was the way Walled City people thought, in reverse. Elil turned, led them past a vast kitchen shining with butcher block and Tuscan terra-cotta and through another door, up a set of stairs—and Soledad gasped.

The room seemed to take up all of the glass penthouse area, though she found out later it occupied less than half. Part of it, glass-floored, was cantilevered into space so you could look down almost four hundred feet under the soles of

your shoes past a diminishing perspective of stacked gardens
and balconies to the driveway and the pea-sized limos parked
along it.

On the other side, in the penthouse garden, the giant sequoia tossed in a gray wind over a forest of lesser trees as an
ozone shower dropped its quick fury on Pacific Heights, then
blew away.

Above Soledad, where she stood at this entrance, one
wall writhed with the curves and sinews of a dozen Joachim
Boaz murals, under the shadow of a minstrel's gallery loaded
with envirocams and supported by beam-knees of redwood.
The main body of the floor was also of polished redwood. Everywhere else, one saw mostly the lights of San
Francisco, only slightly diffused by rain and fog and the
bulletproof glass and the curved aluminum supports the glass
was fastened to.

"I will leave you here, maestro," Randy said, and handed
him the *chō* carton. "There's the *goi cuoc ton* you requested.
Sven and Rolf are wheeling in the, shall we say, mechanical
artwork?" Elil giggled. "Be as quick as you can. I'll invite
the honored guests in as soon as you say the word, although
with the Flash index down 870 points today—there's another
Infocrash on the way, you mark my words—they could whine
all night, bless their greedy little hearts. In the meantime—"
Elil giggled again and held out one elbow toward Soledad.
"May I introduce Señorita Castro to the party?

"I'm his sole dealer west of the Rockies," Randy said as
elil led Soledad through a hallway lined with fat Boaz diora-
mas. "I live in my gallery, you see, or maybe work in my
apartment, I can never decide, never mind what I tell the
IRS." Through the grandest Moorish archway yet they entered a room running the full length of the penthouse's western side, one paneled wall covered by three giant Boazes, the
other all glass, and the center occupied by seventy or so people dressed in various items of formal attire. A half dozen
transparent sculptures—similar to the ones she had seen
by the mall over the Kundurans' tunnels—shifted colors and

patterns, depending on both their software and whoever stood near. A series of vidscreens on portable stalks showed live envirocam shots of Jermyn Street, Rue de Seine, Unter den Linden, Ginza 4-Chome. Wheeled speakers, moving slowly to the commands of a dynamic sound program, produced rhythmic rumbles, explosions, tweets and trebles.

"There's the Pacific." Elil gestured leftward. "Can't see it, dark and foggy night heh heh, *pinus nordicus,* northern spruce to you, and the Presidio; then southern tamarack, and way over there to the left, that ridiculous Swedenborgian church, and all the way to the right—Temple Emanu'el; we're surrounded by faith, half this building is Hoffaist now, it just makes sense in a way. Everyone else works on commission, why not God?" (Another giggle.) Randy jinked right, past an oddly homey-looking couch, straight into the depths of the crowd, the smell of Vengeance, the noise of speakers, the lesser noise of conversation. "Sunspot storms on Jupiter," elil shouted, "the music I mean, it's programmed to the light display. They say you can predict hydrogen hurricanes on Io with this program."

Soledad, with her ear hypertuned to what she could not emulate, noticed that most of the conversation in this room seemed odd and shot with silences. Looking closer at the knots of people, she realized why: the guests, though often clotted in eerily social knots, mostly spoke into cellphones, or stared upward into the silvered half of their face-suckers, chatting animatedly to people not in the same room. "Junie L. Swayne," Randy whispered, nodding at a woman dressed in garish split-screen with earth-mother tones and dress on one side and a sort of Via Veneto post-post take on 1970s slacks on the other. She was arguing heatedly with her mask. "Leading memory broker on the San Jose exchangenet, has more money than Hoffa, *loves* Boaz. And Evan LaRude"—this a sleek black man with his hair lit in a half dozen colors, dressed from head to toe in Neodisko glitter, pacing thoughtfully back and forth with a cellphone, mumbling "Debentures." "Just the top psychogeneticist at JPL, that's all. Oh, the humanity, the hu-*man*-ity," Randy continued for no apparent reason, snagging two glasses of champagne and a pair of hors d'oeuvres from a passing Swede. "Try these, juniper-smoked Atlantic cod with macadamia tapenade, you just don't *find* cod anymore, and the carrier" (tapping the cracker) "organic millet, organic garlic. Most of us in this building have apartmentranches—I have one in Sonoma, only eight acres but it's enough—we grow all our own organic produce, it's *so* much safer don't you think? Although maybe in your country it's still organic, what is your country Señorita Consuela, if that *is* your real name?" Looking at her suddenly from quite close up through pupils that were a very light green and carried no giggle in them at all. "I'll be right back," elil added suddenly, and disappeared.

"Well, if you can't force him into court, attach his Bot!" someone yelled into a cellphone to Soledad's left; and was answered, in tone if not in fact, by a large man in an "urban waistcoat" of bulletproof Kevlar with thinscreen panels showing realtime broadband futures as well as thumbnail videos of Boaz's atelier, who said, "She wouldn't come in just for Swiss chard focaccia and a glass of Vacaville pinot grigio, now would she?"

Soledad took a sip of champagne—organic, she assumed—and felt immediately ill. "It's not funny," a voice said desperately in the crowd somewhere, "it's *Alison*. Doctor Stein said she has *classic* symptoms of TDF."

Randy, returning, plucked at Soledad's elbow, led her to a terminal set in the wall under one of the Boazes. "Off-list," Randy told the terminal, which caused a stack of prices and titles to vanish, and "Guests, Bots, current, directory."

A triple column including perhaps two hundred names, addresses, and UCC balances rippled down the screen. "Just look at this," Randy said excitedly. "No, not you, cancel voice," as the list magnified to 150 percent. Randy turned to Soledad, tapped elil's chest proudly with one finger. "These are the Bots, people's Web-constructs, that is. Maybe you don't have them yet in your country. . . ." Elil waited, and when Soledad still did not reply, continued. "Their Web profiles are all online through an envirocam and sound pickups in the main artspace. See, if they've got a 'sucker on it's as if they're really here, and *everybody* came!"

Randy's finger left elil's chest, as if to make a direct connection. It touched one name, and the screen jumped to the image of a bearded man sitting in golden steaming water in a tub carved in the shape of an ox. A tickertape of financial data streamed over the image. "That's Mickey Reisen, the push producer who bought *Pain in the Afternoon* reruns for international distribution. *Loves* adventure, you know, but he's worth too much to take risks, that's what Apocalypse Planning does for him." Randy sighed in admiration.

"Most of 'em don't allow the two-way link, though," elil continued. "In fact, some of 'em hooked up their Bots to lifeboxes, so it's as if they're really on the Net even if they're not watching, but that's incredibly dangerous too with all the lifejacking going on, so of course—look." Elil's voice broke. "Lazarus MoTief, czar of the infobrokers, and, omigod I don't believe it"—pointing at but not touching a screenname, LIFESKIN.COM, with a small star blinking next to it, one of the few names with no data attached. Soledad turned away; the guided tour of Stix's clientele had made her stomach feel worse, perhaps it stemmed from reading the tiny letters. She hoped she would not have to flee to the bathroom. Randy continued, in a jag of excitement, "Kemp. I don't believe it, Vanny *Kemp* was here, but the star means"—shaking elil's head mournfully—"not anymore but—" Frowning all of a sudden, elil whipped down the half-sucker's mikerod. "OK, d'you want"—("It's Stix," elil whispered to Soledad, "he says he's ready")—"OK, the east doorway. I'll tell them now."

Randy pulled a wireless keypad from elil's belt and tapped a message. All the people in half-suckers looked around, suddenly alert. "Kirsten," Randy muttered into the mike, "seven, four." One of the blond people who had been shepherding trays of champagne opened a set of studded doors in an arcade beside the largest Boaz. The half-suckers began ambling in, snagging extra flute glasses off the Nordics. The people on cellphones or those merely talking to each other, noticing the movement and scared that for the first time in their lives they might miss out on something important, began to move in the same direction. Randy put both elil's hands on Soledad's shoulders and ostentatiously planted a kiss on her forehead. "See you in there," elil whispered, and glided out of sight behind a light sculpture. Soledad put down her champagne. Watching San Francisco twinkle and fade and reappear as the fog was blown in and then blown away seemed to lessen the nausea. The slight buzz she'd gotten from a third of a glass of wine had rebuilt a small corner of the tranquillity she had felt earlier, on the tug, when they steamed past the glow of bridge and into the deep green only occasionally struck with light that had been the coast toward Point Reyes.

Then, with the last clot of spectators, she walked through the arch into the gallery.

———

THE SHOW BEGAN WITH the abrupt quality of a traffic accident. The guests, followed by dynamic speakers, had barely entered the glassed space when the door was sealed and the lights dimmed.

Only the peak of a noctiluc column, together with the sparkle of city lights, the flashing pencils of searchlight from police choppers over Buenavista Park, and the nearby blip of a red navigation blinker from the tiltplane illuminated what was going to happen. Among the audience, heads of "lit" hair glowed and bobbed. One or two people still murmured into their half-suckers. The ranked envirocams beeped on the minstrel gallery. And Stix sat quietly, almost invisible in his black suit. Two jambooks lay open on a horizontal easel in front of him; one hand was encased in a shiny black touch-glove, and his face was lit ghostly by the screens.

Suddenly, loud in the sound system, rose a jumble of kettledrums—cliché, thought Soledad automatically. However the drums were absorbed in a skirl of bagpipes that succeeded in surprising her. Boys' voices, raised in song. A piece of tune mixed with the crash of ocean waves, a hint of Gregorian plainchant, early eleventh century she reckoned, maybe twelfth. She grew intrigued, but had no time to analyze how deep her own curiosity might run, and by extension how facile or complex the music was, because little jade lights were switching on inside the three opened crates lined up under the minstrel gallery. And things came out of them now, black machines rolling at eight or ten kilometers per hour into the center of the drama-space, and were lit by Swedes lined up behind spotlights on the minstrel gallery.

They were Stix's machines, versions of what she had seen full-blown in his workshop, only reduced to a twentieth of the size, fifty centimeters high by a maximum one meter in breadth. The horse-carcass flinger, with additional arms and two big headlamps that made it look like a helicopter; the shitting Rodan pterodactyl, which shot off fast in one direction, scattering onlookers in waves before it crashed into the glass above the lights of San Mateo and basically did nothing for the rest of the evening. And two machines Soledad had never seen. One was a sort of mechanical dragon with a claw-nozzle, plus wheels for locomotion, and a concave bull's-eye target occupying most of its abdominal area.

The biggest machine consisted of a giant blowup sphere with a military officer's cap perched on top and a giant white plastic hand, digit finger extended, sticking horizontally out of what she presumed was the machine's front.

The machines whirred, reversed, accelerated in jerky circles within the larger circles of the spots, like dancers unsure of their steps and partners. Some in the crowd laughed; a few punched cellphones or jambooks, presumably to call friends and relay what was going on. Soledad moved around the outskirts of crowd to stand near Stix under the balcony. In this roomful of strangers who did not talk to each other, the urge to stand beside the one person she knew was strong. Her stomach still felt like it was close to heaving out its contents, and she thought that running to escape one of these mini-machines would make vomiting inevitable; but Stix, presumably, would keep the machines well away from his own controls.

One of the machines shouted suddenly, in a deep, crackling voice with a heavy British accent. At about the same time she realized that the giant hand was shadowing the carcass-swinger, the arms of which, instead of being fastened to a horse, were attached to fresh squid, which accounted for the earlier smell of fish. The arms were quiet at first. Then Stix pointed one gloved finger at a screen diagram and the giant sphere lurched close to the carcass machine and stabbed its own outstretched finger into a panel under the carcass machine's nozzle.

The eight arms of the carcass machine started to revolve. The British voice grew louder as the sphere stopped in the room's center. A flick of thumbstick, and the carcass machine began to follow the target-dragon, without getting too close. "And the great Liberal Party which in 1889 was vigorous, united, supreme, was shrunk to a few discordant factions of discredited stragglers, without numbers, without policy, without cohesion, around whose neck is bound the millstone of home rule," the carcass-swinger bellowed. *Churchill,* she thought. He loves Churchill.

Soledad's nausea was on a down cycle again, or maybe it was just that she was interested now. And so was the crowd, which pressed closer, trying to catch the pattern here—and then seeing it, as the arms rotated faster and faster, and one squid flew off, missed the dragon entirely, to nail an info-broker splat on the collarbone. Another ricocheted off the dragon's fuel tanks, soared into the air, and was fielded by a Swede. Another miss, smacking the plate glass over Point Lobos—and finally a hit, on the outer circle of the dragon's abdomen.

Which caused the target-dragon to stop in its caterpillar

tracks and shudder. A coin-sized feeler of flame appeared in its claw, then spewed with a roar into a fan of hot yellow. Soledad held her breath and moved behind Stix, fascinated and repelled at the same time.

The dragon began to move fast in an ellipse, pushed by its rocket nozzle, holding another smoking tube out in front with its own giant claw. The carcass-flinger, still hurling squid, backed and circled as it tried to escape the dragon. The crowd stampeded back and forth along the gallery's back wall. A few voices were raised in genuine fear, or pain when a squid connected. The claw-dragon backed the squid-flinger against the wall between two of the crates under the minstrel gallery (the Swedes above holding Bot-envirocams well outward to catch the action); the claw-tube roared again, spewing out a larger gout of flame.

By now, however, the squid-flinger had scooted sideways, out of harm's way, slamming a crate askew. The claw-dragon's fire simply scorched the paneling from which, so Soledad belatedly noticed, the priceless Boaz canvases had earlier been removed.

The audience was now in high excitement. In their daily transition from apartment to limousine to suite to commuter flight to limo to ranch and back, they never experienced this degree of risk, except through the medium of virtual gear. What this must give them, Soledad reflected vaguely, was an archaic frisson: the knowledge that, while VR was just as "real" in a sensory way, only in this gallery could they actually get their clothes singed or earn a raw squid in the chops. Stix was yelling over the noise of flamethrower and crowd, it took Soledad a few seconds to realize he was talking to her. ". . . was lying to you earlier. I had a manifesto once, it went like this: 'Antiproduct, antipractical, antiwar; this is a night of industrial-strength sociopolitical irony where humans have bit parts only, as operators and victims.' Catchy, huh? Meaningless, huh!"

Soledad looked around her. Her nausea was gone now. When you threw in all the data—her sickness on waking, the fact that her period was two weeks overdue—it added up to classic morning sickness.

So that's why I've been so calm all day, was her next thought. She was starting to get used to the idea of being pregnant, and it did not bother her at all. Touching her flat belly with one hand. She still felt an aura of sickness around her, but it had more to do with what was happening here, the gratuitous nature of this event, the fact that Stix took money from such people. She liked Stix, she did not wish to feel contempt for him.

The calm affected how she looked around her now, coolness summoning further clarity. In that clarity she interpreted easily the stance of one audience member in an urban waistcoat lounging a little bit apart, near the kitchen door, head canted as he talked to a mike sewn inside a Kevlar collar.

Another, a woman, also in urban Kevlar, stood by the east exit watching not the audience, not the show, but the artiste where he sat hunched over the jambook controls, slapping left fist hard into right palm, yelling with the squid-flinger, "There is no wanting those who say that in this Jubilee year our empire has reached the height of its glory and power, and that now we shall begin to decline as Babylon, Carthage, and Rome declined."

Still slowly, still calmly, she walked over to a Scandinavian waitress and, raising her eyebrows for permission, removed an order pad and pencil from her apron. Then she leaned over Stix's shoulder (". . . the vigor and vitality of our race is unimpaired!" he bellowed, then glanced at her). She put the pad on his back and wrote in capitals SECRET POLICE IN THE 2 EXIT DOORS NOW, and placed the pad on the keyboard of one jambook. He looked down, and did not visibly react. The squid-flinger had circled behind the sphere; it darted out and shot a cloud of pink foam the size of a tablecloth that quickly solidified around the knees of two women in split-screen dresses. Randy's mouth appeared out of the darkness, almost kissed Stix's left ear, whispering words she couldn't make out against the squid machine's sudden declaration, "Our flag

shall fly high upon the seas!" Now Stix, unaccountably, was
grinning. His eyes fizzed with excitement, he was having *fun*.
It made Soledad think he took her note for a joke and secret
police was no joke, so she grabbed the notepad to write another message.

Stix's fingers were working twice as fast. The three machines lined up more slowly across the parquet floor, as if
suddenly conscious of the magnitude of this event and ready
now to start the serious minuet they had come here to perform. The crowd watching anxiously, every fog bank in the
Pacific smeared across the backdrop.

Then Stix locked six keys down, grasped the jambooks
with one hand and Soledad's blouse by the other, and backed
away, while Randy pulled Stix by the iridescent elbow of his
suit.

Which was good, Soledad thought; that is, it was good
Randy was guiding them, for one thing because the door
elil opened under the gallery was invisible to the naked eye,
and for another because the three machines had now assaulted the crowd, barging toward them with foam spewing
and squids flying, but no flame, Soledad noticed; everything
moving at three-quarters speed, the squid-flinger screeching
Churchill at twice the volume as before but not loud enough
to overcome the screams of the crowd, which had, quite
simply, panicked. The once-elegant PR/CEOs, infobrokers,
Flash-journalists, trustfunders, e-commerce magnates, and
other Dead surged backward from the oncoming machines
screaming "Hoffa!" and "My lawyers!" and other epithets of
despair. Then, finding all escape room occupied by fellow onlookers, they tried to climb over, under, around, through each
other, using nails, fists, swung jambooks, until under the dark
gray banks of fog, among the circles of artificial light still
tastefully doled out by the lighting-Swedes, it looked like
an extreme-rugby scrum being played by an army of models
from the Von Lipschitz catalogue.

All except for three people, attired in urban Kevlar, holding UCC identification and tazers high above the worming

bodies, who fought to push against the crowd and churning machines, toward the open door under the balcony. But they had forgotten, or maybe they never learned, the lessons of the Coconut Grove fire, the Trump Bordello explosion: there was simply nothing one could do to fight a mob gripped by total panic.

And Soledad, Stix, and Randy moved down the hushed green-blue length of a corridor floored with noctiluc mosaic, into the empty kitchens; through a steel double doorway into the sudden slurp of wind and a whistle of turbine and the smell of juniper. Following Randy as elil hustled head-down through a close alley between box hedges and stacked refrigerator crates marked FREE-RANGE ANTELOPE CHOPS, ORGANIC MESCLUN, FARM FLOUNDER.

Finally elil stopped at the jutting mesa of heliport. The edges of roof were defined in noctiluc, the supply-tilt they saw earlier suddenly huge in front of them, door open and glowing in the fuselage. Massive twin propellers, almost as big as a chopper's, spun gently in hover mode. Randy turned.

"Scram," elil said.

Stix did not move.

"The guest list," Randy explained impatiently. "It finally spewed out their UCCs. They were blank, which means they're Feds—you didn't have an OSHA permit, remember?"

"I arranged it with the pilot," elil added, "far as he's concerned it's just a private gig to Oakland. I'll take it off your account."

"Wait a minute," Stix said, "you still owe me half the advance!" But Randy was backing away, into a grove of yew silhouetted by the glassy glow of the penthouse behind. Stix, watching elil, did not move. Soledad had both hands on Stix's suit. Picking a path between her own preternatural calm and the logical necessity of the next step, she let go of the fabric, grasped his left hand, and pulled him toward the plane, where a figure in airman's polyester peered out of the hatch, looked at his watch, held his cap against the wind.

Only half a minute later she and Stix were belted in seats

that sank three inches when you sat in them. The door closed. Their ears popped with pressure and the swelling roar of turbines. The plane jolted, rose, yawed sickeningly. Her stomach leaped, subsided. Stix, in the aisle seat, leaned into the porthole beside her, his glove on the jambook again, and she looked where he was looking, catching a glimpse, no more— a fragment of detail that she could never be sure about after the fact—but it *looked* as if, behind the confusion of escaping guests, flame had returned as a weapon of art to the gallery.

The claw-dragon brazed the squid-flinger in a gush of petroleum orange; the squid-flinger put out the dragon's flame in a spew of pinkish foam; at which point the giant sphere exploded in a flash of magnesium white, covering the huge windows and everything else in an even gout of thin and multicolored cream.

THIRTEEN

THE VTOL FLIGHT LASTED all of two minutes. Only ninety seconds after the propellers cranked all the way to horizontal and the plane was in airfoil flight, they were crashing back into a hover, over a blaze of light punctuated by more urban gardens and a giant neon Buddha holding a can of Zero Cola and letters spelling out EDMUND G. BROWN JR. OAKLAND ECO-MALL AND BHODIDHARMA THEME PARK. Stix hustled them out the door and down seven escalators to a taxi rank full of gleaming fuel-cell cabs. Soledad hauled Stix right back out of the queue, setting customers in Birkenstocks to looking at them, like, in shock; dragging him along the platform till she had located the bicycle exit, then hustling him past a security gate and onto a poorly lit access road.

"What're you doing?" he asked, frowning and crossing his arms. "I know that was all kind of weird and maybe you're upset but don't you think I'm kinda freaked, too, and anyway I got some stuff to take to Berkeley tonight and—" Whereupon she pulled out the waiter's pad, which she had kept hold of all this time, and scrawled quickly: NEVER TAKE THE TAXI THEY GIVE YOU. He shrugged, then grinned; the idea of such tradecraft delighted him—then again, he had never had to live under people who made tradecraft necessary, like Ochoa Campos and his buddies in the F2.

She had seen Clint Eastwood in the classic Dirty Harry films and she knew the Bay Area police were nothing like F2.

The cab they ended up hailing was definitely not "the one they give you." It would have looked more at home with the

Putamadre fleet. In fact it turned out to be a node vehicle, driven by a Proto-Panther from the revived Black Panther headquarters in Warehouse XVI. He was a furious youth, whose skin was lighter than Soledad's own, with a counterfeit transponder and Black Infopower stickers pasted all over the inside. He muttered about "sisters doin' the nasty with ofays" all the way to the address in South Berkeley Stix gave him.

Soledad let him mumble—she was too tired to whip out the pad again to reply. The burn of escape had pulled apart what was left of her hazy contentment after the wrestle with nausea in Cloud Forest.

Yet something had settled through the multiple filters of memory and desire during this day of travel and change.

She was not one of those people whose personal tumblers were turned by kilometers rolled off the odometer, else the two thousand clicks between here and Bamaca would have shifted her into someone different; she was not sure who, by definition, but certainly not this trembling, back-staring individual whose whole character, it seemed to her recently, was built on echoes of a previous life.

Still, it *felt* as if the tugboat, and that strange high-rise topped by trees, and the instant transport by VTOL, shook her up enough that now the real possibility of her pregnancy—that she was carrying a child, and the child was Jorge's—had gone from speculation to certainty without pausing around the "maybe" space at all.

They stopped in a quiet side street lined with shabby ranch houses from the middle of the last century, at a house more run-down than most. Paint flaked off its porch in the breeze, rectangles of vinyl siding hung askew at intervals on the walls, the grass in its yard was high, a FOR SALE sign from the Ohlone Realty Company ("Your Choice for Happy Homes in the West Bay") was pounded into the grass; but lights shone redly through russet curtains at the windows, and a thick arm of cable, signifying a high-speed Virtix link, looped between a telephone pole and the bungalow eaves.

A dog barked in back. "Broadband to the people," their driver hissed to Soledad, raising clenched fist to orange sky, "sistah."

Stix led Soledad around back. The dog, tethered in the depths of the yard, danced against its chain. A curtain shivered. Stix said something into a little speaker and the door clicked open, revealing a short woman perhaps forty years old in fedayeen slacks and a thick pullover and scarf. She hugged Stix so long and looked at his companion so intently that it spoke of some history behind and between—reminding Soledad, in feel if not in detail, of the way Molly had greeted her the first time she walked into the diner. Well, well, she thought, only partially amused, quite the Lothario, our Stix.

Stix voiced ritual greetings, then added something in a low voice in which Soledad caught the hiss of her own name.

The woman's name was Esther. Contrary to Soledad's first impression, she didn't seem much interested in sexual politics. Or perhaps, once she examined her, she didn't consider Soledad much of a threat, because she produced for the other woman a smile that was pure gringa, a rictus friendly and without meaning. They walked into the main room, the only room—kitchen, parlor, living and dining areas had all had their partitions knocked out on this floor to form one large untidy space framed by curtains and four different styles of peeling wallpaper.

An unmade double bed, Guatemalan hammocks, a giant freestanding wooden counter covered with automatic coffeemakers, coffee mugs, used coffee filters, hanging plants; a half dozen Labrador retrievers, and at least a score of signs that read NO SMOKING and PLEASE DON'T SMOKE — OCCUPANTS ALLERGIC and CIGARETTES HAVE BEEN ASSOCIATED WITH LOW FETAL BIRTH WEIGHT—all the appurtenances more or less separated by reefs of Moroccan cushions, apparently to differentiate between various modes of daily life. This formed the extent of the occupants' commitment to living in the world. Or this world, at least, if you distinguished it from the other-world of the Net. Because what was impressive and dominant about the room was the quality and quantity of Webware: five-foot-high tumuli of parallel-linked jambooks, modems, T-3000 routers, full face-suckers, consoles, haptic suits and other state-of-the-art gear, most of it piled on government-surplus desks that surrounded, or perhaps protected, a circle of moth-eaten, dog-occupied couches in the center.

"Hey Victor, guess who it is?" the woman announced, leading them around a high tower of circuitry.

A thin man in denim overalls and a sweater thicker than Esther's pulled a full-sucker off his head, bounced nervously out of a broken-springed armchair he'd been sharing with a gray-muzzled Lab.

"Stix Grammatico," he said, "you honor us with your presence, sir, though weren't you s'posed to show up Friday?" Staring at Soledad in the meanwhile with *sanpaku* eyes.

"Yeah, sorry," Stix said, not sounding sorry at all.

"And who's this?" the man continued, repeating for emphasis, "who's this, who's this?"

"She's a refugee," Esther said, "you saw the e-mail."

"And what does that mean," Victor said, still not taking his eyes off Soledad, "what does that mean, yeah. No offense."

"You could call Crip and Benny refugees," Esther said mildly, pointing at the dogs; "they came from the pound. You could call Ella a refugee." Soledad thought at first that Ella was another dog, but Esther's nod was directed at a human form huddled under unzipped sleeping bags on the most swaybacked couch of all.

"We're all refugees, in a way," Stix said lightly, meaninglessly. "You know that."

It was cold in the room. Soledad, feeling goose bumps rise, put her arms around her waist. The woman noticed. "It's way under sixty-six in here," she said. "Even the machines don't like it that cold." She leaned over a rack of cypher spindles and tapped at a keyboard. A tiny fanfare sounded, and air was forced out of the ceiling registers. A coffee machine beside Soledad hiccoughed and started to perkle. "Java'll be ready in two minutes," Esther said, "whyn't you get some blankets for her, she's prob'ly not used to this shit-ass climate as it is."

"Sure," Victor said. "Moles have thin skins, yeah. No offense."

He got up and clumped down wooden stairs to the basement. "Oh boy," the woman sighed, and charged after him. Stix turned to Soledad, opened his arms, palms up, as if to say, What can you do? What he actually said, in a voice hard to hear against the hot air, was "They used to have a friend living upstairs, friend of mine, too, named Charlie Rickle. Took a Newman exit last month.

"A Newman exit," Stix went on, answering the question in her expression, "named after the first guy to do this, in the 1980s. See, Charlie canceled his Bot, destroyed his Websites, his cyphers, his Liteworld ISPs—Internet Service Providers—even his Wild contacts. Also stopped all the credit and booking and online shopping stuff. Which of course automatically invalidated his UCC card, so in a sense he was already dead, even then, far as Outside was concerned.

"Now Charlie had started to put together a life-box—all the data of his life, I mean everything: stuff he wrote, his memoirs, letters from boyfriends, family data, and all of it hooked into a storytelling program—he had stored all that in hard drive. So he goes upstairs, puts on his 'sucker, jacks into Polis (or at least the domain in his hard drive), and spikes into a jagger program. Only instead of jis', mesc, MPPP and liquid psilocybin, he loads Seconal and White Lady heroin. And the works dose him till he just stops breathing."

Soledad shook her head. She only understood half of this, but even that she did not want to hear, not the way she felt now, cold and tired and in the withdrawal of contentment. Stix misinterpreted her reaction.

"We don't know why. He'd broken up with Jay, it was nasty, that was part of it. But also, these three used to live in the node, they ran a rogueware barter site out of a Wildnet of pirate cellphones that got shut down by BON. Charlie had to get a Liteworld job. He started getting hassled at checkpoints, by the credit cops, all that, so they moved out of the node. Which meant they kinda had to stop smoking, and I think the strain—"

He stopped. Esther and Victor appeared out of the basement, bearing macramé and woolen blankets that they dropped at Soledad's feet.

"I'm sorry," Victor said without preamble, watching Esther as he did so. "Really sorry, really sorry. Esther told me you come from Bamaca node, though we heard almost no one got out, not really, it must've been tough, to be the only one, or almost."

Soledad looked at him in confusion. The form on the couch stirred, peeled off the sleeping bags. It was a woman in her late twenties, with tangled hair the color of sunset and eyes gray as an Arctic horizon. She was pretty in a thin, elfin sort of way, though a scar marred the left side of her face. "Coffee," she said, peering around her with her nose almost twitching. "I smell fresh coffee."

"Ella can't sleep through coffee," Esther said.

"Ella can't sleep through the noise we make," Victor contradicted her. "I'm going back to work." He picked up a wireless jambook and headed for the basement stairs again.

"You can see," Esther said softly as Victor disappeared down the hatch, "it's not getting better, 'fact I think it's gettin worse."

"He needs out," Stix said.

"I *really* need coffee," the woman named Ella insisted, scratching her ankles. "Is it ready?"

"Funny thing," Esther continued, pouring coffee into mismatched mugs. "His work is getting better. Plug in," she urged, wagging her chin in the direction of a rack of full facesuckers, "we've been filling in fractals in Malindi, so you'll know where you are. You too," she told Soledad, "if you want."

Soledad shook her head. Stix said, "You ever seen Polis? I mean, ever been inside, full VR?" When she shook her head again he steered her to the rack of masks, found the right-sized rig, and sat her down on a couch. She looked at the gear, wide-eyed, thinking strongly about the man who had chosen to kill himself in this way. Stix put his hand on her arm.

"No jag," he said. "You'll see, the reason Charlie went into Polis was, it's a good place; or at least, it has good places in it." She started to shake her head again, then stopped and examined the mask.

"You don't have to if you don't want," Stix added quietly. His tone said he knew she was going to refuse.

I'm not scared of this, Soledad thought, *I'm just too tired, too shook up to play little boys' games in cyberspace;* but she was a little stung by Stix's tone and the assumption that she would chicken out. And enough doubt about her own feelings remained that to prove she could—to prove something was still left of the woman who had performed quite well at the Frum-Oxum—she nodded, and let him adjust the 'sucker to fit snugly over her face.

And darkness came over her, and an absence of sound filled her ears.

———

A COUPLE OF MINUTES PASSED. It seemed longer. Then Stix's voice, beautifully translated into stereo digital, said, "Ready? I'm going to pilot us, since you're not used to it. You won't be able to see me, but I'll be there all the same. Here we go."

The darkness diminished. Stars prickled out of the purpling black, so distinct and three-dimensional it was like night in a *selva* clearing, that same feeling of being able to touch them, if you could just reach a few millimeters beyond arm's length. When Soledad moved, the stars shifted; they were shifting around anyway, swirling into words that soon resolved into a Greek word, just starting to become familiar:

ΠΟΛΙΣ

"Password?" a woman's voice demanded.

The answer was not transmitted.

"OK," Stix said finally, "Malindi sector, uh, West Island; fourteen, thirty-three, one."

The Greek script disappeared. The rest of the stars began to move. It was a horrid, sickening sensation at first because Soledad knew, her body knew, that she was soaring through space with no clear idea of what was up or down, and no feeling of wind in her hair though they had to be flying at huge speeds for the constellations to shift like that. She also knew, of course, this was not real, this was virtual, but it was also so indistinguishable from concrete sensation that her body effectively told her brain "I don't care what you say, this is real enough for me and I'm going to react accordingly."

As her night vision improved she began to make out shapes: the curdled gray of clouds around her, a faded silver signature of river below, and far ahead, the smooth ebony cord of the planet's horizon. Just as she was beginning to enjoy this feeling of unseen and uncontrolled flight, the horizon plated itself in steel colors, which turned to salmon and red. The sun came up all fiery and set flame to the sky around her and to a continent below, a frill of pink sea ruffling a cliffy shoreline.

Then, she fell.

Icarus, she thought. Her breath seized in her chest. "I'm crashing—" The scream welled up from her diaphragm like bursting lava, it felt as if it would finally break down the barriers that had blocked her throat since Bamaca. Before something could change in her throat, though, the blur of speed resolved into ground coming up from below, but very slowly; either her speed had diminished or they had not been going as fast as she'd thought at first. A mountain, hills, a marsh. Docks, a village.

At length she was close enough to the village that she could make out wooden cottages painted in cheerful colors, a small square, picket fences, green lawns, vegetable gardens and, incongruously, not one but two QuikViet franchises. The perfect American village, she realized, like something out of the geography book Mademoiselle Weill used, except for the QuikViets. Doric columns held up a town hall, the shingled side of a wharf workshop blocked the sky, and they were *down,* stable and motionless on a cobbled street outside the workshop.

Through the workshop's open doors she saw an old-fashioned cast-iron stove pumping heat around a cluttered room. Stacks of boxes, each perfectly square and glowing with an eerie blue light, occupied most of the space. Victor was inside, taking clear blue spindles out of one glass bowl and dropping them, very deliberately, into another. A man with short black hair and a potbelly, wearing loose Indian slacks and sandals, lounged beside him on an ornate Roman couch, reading the *Smuggler's Gazette.* Soledad knew, without knowing how she knew, that this was Charlie Rickle. The theory was confirmed immediately.

"Hello, Charlie," Stix's voice said.

"Yo, Stix," the man replied, not looking up from his reading.

"One thing he didn't cancel," Stix's voice continued in her ear, and maybe she was getting used to alternating between the nonexistent contact and the light-speed connections you could make in this reality, but she knew Stix was talking about Charlie here, she even knew what he was going to say.

"His life-bot, of course," Stix continued. "I didn't mention some of the other stuff, there's so much you can't do a full list: video clips, med records, kid pictures, favorite recipes, CVs, notebooks, shopping patterns, choice of deodorant. Plus a servo-program that lets his life-site interact with Polis. Point is, he's alive, in this environment. And now he never has to leave."

"He shouldn't have let her in here," Victor said, "should he, Charlie?"

"I've gotten more mellow," Charlie answered, still without looking up. "I've gotten downright copacetic."

Esther appeared on the street beside them wearing

diaphanous opalescent robes, through the fabric of which one could easily make out the outline of taut and youthful breasts. "C'mon," she said, "let me show you the fractal."

"Snap," Stix said.

Daylight vanished, like switching off an electric lamp. But the village was still there, the skeleton of houses glowing around them, as if their skin had been turned to glass, revealing the noctiluc built into the roof beams and joists. And now geometric lines of different colors appeared, connecting the various buildings to a junction in town hall, then soaring into black space in all directions. The glowing lines multiplied the farther you looked, until in the distance space resembled a billion cat's cradles hooked up to each other, hooked up to the very stars. As she looked closer—or perhaps the space around them was being magnified somehow—Soledad saw that what she earlier thought were stars were, in fact, other townships; tiny villages like this one, for the most part, although here and there stood larger complexes—kasbahs, skyscrapers, cliff dwellings, fortified mountains embracing complex roadways. The lines thickly connected the villages; not a few of them were pulled in weblike to the bigger structures.

"The structure of Polis," Esther said. "The villages are *booming,* Stix. Even the rogueware is selling again. Our barters, our hits, are going up; we can check every day how close we are to the thirty-seventh percentile. That's what Victor's doing now."

"He's obsessive about it," Charlie Rickle commented from inside the workshop's structure. "Bad for his blood pressure, really. Me, I just let it slide."

"What she means," Stix's voice said, "a lot of people disagree with Hawkley. They don't think you need a node or a geographical component."

"That's not true," Esther interrupted.

"OK," Stix agreed. "Ten or twelve households, in the same area—but almost all your transactions are by Wildnet."

"Our necessary dependency is low."

"Ooooh," Charlie Rickle commented, "sixty-dollar words, watch c_ut!" Everybody ignored him.

"I ain't knocking it," Stix told Esther, nodding at a sort of pink neon gate into which a fat line of cable disappeared. "Though that looks like an X-Corp router."

"That was Victor. He had to buy another TransCom mother-board last week. Point is, Stix," Esther continued more urgently, "the Megorg is *changing*. With twenty-four-hour infomarkets, those orgs are shape-shifters now. They drop one arm in Calcutta, pick up another leg in Toronto, the electronic margin trades, the mergers-and-acquisitions, it's all so fast only servers can keep track—and all of 'em wanting to burn node ass because we're the only idea they can't control—well, we got to be able to move fast too. And the *only* way you can do that, Stix, is by shifting and changing and disappearing and reappearing the way they do."

She paused for breath. When she spoke again her voice was lower, but no less intense.

"We got a Wildnet now that doesn't touch a single Liteworld router, not one. The sleeper viruses never know our message was even there."

Esther, or rather her image in Polis, came back into Soledad's line of sight, posturing against the workshop's structure, her back against one vertical door joist. She had blond hair down to her buttocks, braided in amazingly complex patterns like a Rasta child's. This was one of the reasons people played these games, Soledad surmised: so they could enjoy in cyberspace the fashions, the lives they desired for real.

"Cool thing," Esther added, taking out a pack of cigarettes and lighting one, blowing the smoke out as if in illustration. "Before he offed himself, Charlie located a bundle of cyan-and dove-colored lines out of that Wildnet hub." She pointed at a spider's nest of multicolored cables below and to one side of them. "It was plexed with off-market T-3000 cables for West L.A. Had no idea what they were. He looked and found other places had them—I mean, Rockland, Maine; East New York. Even the node, homey—even the node."

"It was nothing, really," Charlie Rickle's voice whispered from behind Esther. "A bagatelle."

"Cyan and dove." There was a sarcastic tinge to Stix's voice. "I fail to see—"

Soledad felt her ankles itching. She wanted to scratch them; she knew that back in Berkeley, where her real body was, she could do that no matter what was going on in Polis. But because Stix was in control of her viewplane and her movements in Polis she felt as if it was impossible to move without his help, both in the virtual world and outside. So she tried to ignore her ankles, and concentrate on what Esther was saying.

"You know he did years of Fernsehen," Esther continued calmly, throwing down her half-smoked cigarette and lighting another. "Well, he tracked down the lines to their jack-in sites—cable and phone routers for the Liteworld Web, pirate transmission vans and black-market multiplex for Wildnet—all the way, in some cases. Found that when they connected one city to another, they always hooked into the exact same areas. Not something people chose, you dig, homey? Complex concordance it was, no doubt about it."

"Esther, this Fernsehen shit—"

But Soledad understood. Though her own exposure to Fernsehen in the capital clinic was limited and unsuccessful, Jorge had expounded on Fernsehen often enough. In any case the old doctor, who had practiced in the capital and once even opened a consulting office in the Walled City, was so much a part of the folklore of the *cruce* that to spend any time in the enclave was to gain a working knowledge of his essential themes.

"Complex concordance" was one of these, it was part of his "urban postulate," which claimed that cities—even Hawkleyite *cruces*—had distinct personalities. It followed from the concordance that beyond a certain level, as yet undetermined, of size and complexity a city would reach such levels of stress and repression that it would split, in ratios of behavior not unlike those of human schizophrenia. Foreground would hive off from background, frontal lobes from limbic areas, conscious from subconscious. The city itself would specialize in one form of behavior only.

But because no personality, whether urban or human, could function entirely as consciousness, or purely as subconscious, the broken city would eventually adopt another city: a town in the same vicious bind as itself, one that usually resembled it in certain quite profound ways, like the percentage of small chess clubs, the patois of the dock areas, the rhythm of stop and go, rush and hold, traffic and siesta. The big difference was, if 'ville "A" was loud and open about its rhythms, town "B" tended to hide them, push them back into its urban "id." Thus a "subconscious" city would start linking somehow with a 'ville that had chosen the sunlit road, in any continent or country, it did not matter as long as the deep rhythms were close and minimal trade and communication existed. It mattered even less with the Nets, whether legal or no. And soon images, immigrants, and more solid goods would start to flow harder between them, as each used the other to complement itself.

"He only had time to figure out West L.A.," Esther was saying. "That had major links with Maronite Beirut. Couple sublinks, too, with Yokohama Port. Had a theory about Santa Monica and Jaipur—"

"And the node," Stix interrupted. "Where did those lines lead?"

Esther did not answer. She was standing straighter in the doorway.

She pointed, and Soledad turned, and the view she had of the virtual village and the cobweb space on all sides turned sickeningly with her, allowing her to focus on a strong umber beam passing under "town hall"—and a bizarre, torpedo-shaped thing that seemed not so much black as made of dead light, sliding swiftly along it toward the junction with another gray-green track.

"BON sniffer," the Esther image whispered. "They must have broken through behind us." A smile grew on her lips. She threw down her latest cigarette, whipped out a chambered Nautilus shell with characters inscribed on its nacre, and touched a symbol. "Control torpedo," she added mysteriously. *"Watch."*

Something appeared from under the surface of the village. It moved ahead of the torpedo toward the junction. It was a yellow object, shaped like a beetle, with a pattern of square holes in its back. It reminded Soledad for no particular reason of the tortoise from the story of Lao-tzu. A fringe of cilia greatly augmented its resemblance to an insect.

The beetle reached the umber-gray junction well ahead of the government torpedo. It hesitated, and trundled leftward on the gray-green track. Suddenly it accelerated, fast, heading toward a shimmering agglomeration of lights that was the obvious terminus of that line.

The torpedo followed immediately, smoothly matching the beetle's acceleration. As it approached the beetle three thin blue feelers grew out of its no-light, reached out to touch the square holes in the beetle's back, then played them delicately, like a master safecracker picking a lock.

The two objects were now moving as one. Space blurred as Stix followed, and Soledad of necessity did too, traveling like a rocket at full thrust powering horizontal down the gray-green freeway so that they flew just behind and above the coupled Web engines; as the lights became a larger structure, growing in a matter of nanoseconds from the size of a marble to the size of a house. Her chest wall had gone rigid again as they braked from a million kilometers per hour to maybe ten in front of a huge, haphazard circus tent that looked one hundred meters high, made up of striped poles and luminescent guywires and millions of squares of varicolored silk, each of which gave off its own independent glow.

"A Wildnet hub," Stix whispered. He pointed at a flap where the gray-green cable, along with several hundred others, penetrated the tent, and from which came a faint glint of noise—cheers, the growl of lions, the trumpeting of elephants. "You don't usually see one this big."

The torpedo's feelers glowed suddenly, turned green, then yellow.

Something moved inside the flap of tent.

From the beetle rose a burst of music, commercial pop, only multiplied in its cheap brasses and Gibsons by a factor of six or seven hundred; soppy tune-lines and sentimental lyrics compressed and blown into circuits not built to handle so many cheap associations at such volumes.

"Look at that," the Esther image whispered. "Look."

"Dag." Charlie Rickle's voice came out of nowhere. " 'Tis wondrous strange."

Soledad did not wish to look. There was something about that tent—it was too loud, made of too many pieces, too many bits of clashing color; the noise coming out of it was too full of lust and the greed of jungles. It frightened her.

But her viewpoint was fused with Stix's, and he watched the tent as it collapsed, guywires parting simultaneously, the whole cockeyed assembly folding into itself, to the size of a house, a small car, a suitcase.

Then Stix looked away and downward, at the yellow beetle, which suddenly had shrunk to the size of a button against the back of the lightless torpedo.

And the torpedo itself was swelling, to ten times, fifty times its previous size, so big it was clearly bursting. And as it burst it turned hot hues of pink and lavender and mauve and puce that alternated faster as the snatches of pop from the last century, the cheap self-referential rubbish from names she half remembered out of music history classes in the capital conservatory, Michael Bolton and Billy Joel and Henri Salvador and Madonna Ciccone and David Cassidy and Raffi and Kraftwerk and Kenny G and Loggins and Messina and

Johnny Halliday and Joe Walsh and Jackson Browne and Don Henley, grew insanely, painfully, in volume and chaos.

Until all at once a crack appeared down the length of the torpedo.

It juddered to a complete stop.

Off to one side, the suitcase in which the tent had been packed was starting to move. It glided away down a single line of blue-white cable, and was swallowed in the dark.

All the light went out of the torpedo, and even the lack of light went, and finally the music died away, too, all except for a whiff of cheap jingle that rose into the black ether of Polis, hung for a second—

> *No I can't go for that*
> *no can do*

—and then was rubbed away by the emptiness.

———

ON THEIR WAY OUT the door of the rotting ranch house Stix unbuttoned his jacket and took out the vial filled with glowing weeds.

Shucking the retaining harness, he uncorked the vial and dumped its contents into a tiny aquarium warming on top of a stripped-down Aleph processor.

Only the red-haired woman, Ella, had unplugged with them. She poured more coffee, smiled at Soledad, but said nothing. She was scratching her ankles again. Soledad remembered that she still wanted to scratch her own. She did so, and it felt wonderful.

To Soledad's surprise, the Proto-Panther was waiting, V-8 idling, outside the ranch house. He greeted them enthusiastically. "Right on, sistah, take you to another honky joint? Sell your heritage, bruthas and sistahs, downrivah for bossman, yassuh yassuh." But he drove fast and avoided traffic and roadblocks and Soledad was content enough with the sensation of real speed, the speed that happened outside your brain, that she didn't mind his vaguely racist rambling.

She even liked the feel of the foggy wind, so much fresher and full of life than the miasma of hot circuitry and coffee and dog in the ranch house. She scratched her ankles again, hard; the dogs, apparently, played host to legions of fleas. Stix was talking under and over the cabman's lingua. "I don't know how long Esther and Victor think they can get away with it. I mean it's weird. Hawkley's geographical imperative was always a dated thing, you know? Or that's the way it seemed, once the Net happened, and especially the wireless, the Wildnets; but now the Net is so important, the orgs really cracked down on it, BON cracked down, they got sleeper viruses installed in every phone and cable router, every legal hub, it's classic Hawkley theory." He sighed.

"Now it takes two hundred grand worth of equipment just to travel Wild in any kind of safety, and even then there's sniffers like you saw, and you know how they patrol the whole thing, you think they're gonna let a BON torpedo get fried like that without doing something about it?"

"Casper boys makin' revolution talk, wanna cut into Afrika gene pool make cafay-oh-lay," the driver muttered bitterly.

Soledad leaned back into the cracked vinyl seats, watching the brightly lit "Jack London" theme park in Piedmont jam into the somber projects of North Oakland which then turned into Flash developments. The new buildings came to a halt where the navy, so Stix had told her, reclaimed the Chinese shipping docks in the old Supply Yard during the Taiwan miniwar. The cut in her thigh was stinging again. Even her back complained about this position. She was calm, but not in the same Zen zone as previously; this calm was built of fatigue piled on fatigue, and the desire to sleep. It also hiked off the underlying knowledge that she would not be in immediate danger while under the stewardship of this plump lame man still mumbling about sniffers beside her.

So for the balance of this evening, at least, she was content to follow Stix, without questioning it as much as she usually did.

And she found, when they got back to his control room, that the willingness to follow had turned, through whatever alchemy of exhaustion or loneliness or information overload, into an odd reluctance to be without him. As he made ready to leave it crossed her mind that she did not know where he slept when she took his bed. Did he rely on a standby, a girlfriend in some other part of the node, as Jorge had relied on the Lo Pano woman once they split up?

Or did he still sleep with Molly?

She did not think he was in love with anybody—there was none of the preoccupation, the gaps in his routine. Ignoring those issues and the memories of Jorge they raised, she took out her waiter's pad and scrawled quickly, STAY WITH ME PLEASE?

He looked at her. He had believed she carried some info, she remembered, data someone in the *cruce* wanted her to bring to Oakland. Maybe he would ask her about it now. To preempt that possibility she quickly jotted down I DO NOT WANT TO BE ALONE I DO NOT WANT TO DO ANYTHING. Underlining "anything" twice. JUST SLEEP?

She could see the desire stirring like a reptile in his eyes— and just as clearly, like a leashing expressed at the level of the optic nerve, his effort to direct it. She hoped she had judged correctly, that the kindness in him was strong enough to overcome the male compulsion.

"Just sleep," he said, and smiled wryly. "Whatever." But he unhooked his jambook belt.

For a while, as they lay on the weird gulping surface of the water bed, scratching discreetly at fleabites, not even holding hands, an unexpected longing for the touch of another body, for the nerve-thrill of lovemaking, for the absolute if temporary eradication of the loneliness that had tormented her since the *cruce* died, for a reproduction of the

physical closeness she last had felt with Jorge Echeverria—
all of it almost drove her across the intervening sheet space
into Stix's arms.

She could hear him breathing so calmly and regularly that
she knew he, too, was awake and tense.

But the absence of Jorge lay as thick as a roadblock between them. And for some reason, the face of Charlie Rickle
also flickered in her mind, a small charge of almost theoreti-
cal sadness to add to the losses she was already acquainted
with.

The continuing inertia of exhaustion also made that first
tentative move in the direction of sex hard to initiate.

And then, too quickly even for surprise, she slept.

FOURTEEN

THE TWO MONTHS, MORE or less, following the assembly in the Slave Market are among the most peaceful—no, when Soledad thinks back to that time, they *are* the most peaceful and contented time she has ever known. Almost every morning starts for her in the haze of waking up—which is hardly unusual, for her or anybody, except that the haze is so warm and relatively free of doubt or trouble. Only a few dark factors and fears remain to cast shadows even in the morning, and one of these fears is the flip side of her continued happiness: that it must inevitably disappear.

Not the least unusual aspect of this state of grace is her awareness of what's going on, and the fact that she is conscious of her contentment even while in the midst of it. Always she will recall the surprise in her when she wakes up, alone, in the bed looking south and west toward the high cone of San Isidor, and realizes she is happy, and that what lies before her, as far as she can predict, is another day of happiness.

Of course memory, tuned as it is to filtering out washes and background noise in favor of breaks in pattern and sharp events, does not do a great job of recording the particulars of day-to-day contentment. By contrast, her lead memory of that period lies in her continuing knowledge that since the Frum-Oxum concert she has come to evolve totally in relation to loss: the loss of Jorge, but also the possible loss of the *cruce,* which Miguel warned of, which she herself sensed when preparing to speak at Lo Pano—the loss of Jorge's daughter and the other people in it and her place and role among them.

The disappearance of her new self, yes; that is the greatest possible subtraction she can conceive of.

But Dolores turns up at noon the day after the Lo Pano assembly, blithe and uncontrite, carrying a "house gift" as she calls it, a fired-earth proto-Chibcha head of the twelfth-century A.D., the provenance of which Soledad carefully does not inquire about.

The day after that the two of them already have started to work out a routine. Soledad gets up with the first trucks and roosters of dawn, brews *tinto* and walks to the market for milk and whatever supplies are needed that day. Her fingers dry-running Dvořák on the instruments of thigh, of countertop.

Then, when Dolores is awake, she takes the Fourneaux-Dallapé to the tiny living room and does the exercises for real. The run of technical passages allows her to preserve the agility of her fingers without having to cope with the epiphany of her performance. Nor does she have to address the related dread that, despite how she has reasoned it into her scheme of things, as one pole in an acceptable spectrum of behavior, her public playing was after all a fluke, something that could happen only once; something that could happen (she dares not dwell on this thought even to herself) only when she was with *him*.

The Dvořák exercises are worthwhile on their own, of course, as a way to work the Taoist trick of hitting distant targets by focusing on proximate goals. And as the days go by, they allow her to edge into fibers of music that came to rest in her brain from the constant Calypso contest of tunes happening at all hours in the *cruce;* and also to preserve the sprouts of melody generated in the deeper cortex, whether by osmosis, imitation, or some more covert process of description and interpretation.

She spends all morning playing that game, knowing it *is* a game, and also knowing she can take away from it more than one item of value. Rippling trills, chords, working on the bellows rhythm till her shoulders are on fire and her fingers start to bleed a bit. All to capture, like tiny birds snared among a vast and complex netting, the dynamics of a melody that will eventually become one of the *Onze Chansons du Marché*.

Late lunches of salad in the deep cool of kitchen. A lesson or two in the afternoon, earning sufficient barter-chips for food; the cashchips she has left over from the Conservatory will pay her rent for another six months. Later she drinks two glasses, no more, of *vinho verde,* then walks with Dolores through the market as the evening melts light into tones of amber in which they are trapped like the fly in Jorge's poem. Dinner after that, listening as they eat to the merengue, *Vallenatos, Cumbia,* and other wildsound that the cooling breeze bears in like bits of straw flitted home by sparrows to construct a nest of song.

Other dark tones to this pastorale are present in sufficient strength to balance what could be too much, to cut the sickly sunset colors with solemn gray tones and darkness.

Dolores makes an effort, after that first night out, to stay in the apartment and avoid the *guaqueros* whose rowdy all-night sessions at the Tayrona Cadillac can sometimes be heard through the kitchen window when the wind is from the west.

But after three weeks her stomach starts to swell noticeably, and as she grows visibly pregnant she becomes more restive, and as she grows more restive her drinking and smoking start to increase, even though she and Soledad discussed this and the effects on the baby right from the start. Soledad remains silent for as long as she can stand it, until finally she makes a comment that is tense with the effort she makes not to be offensive. And Dolores snaps back, and it all tends to escalate into a row that usually ends with Dolores storming out, slamming the door behind her, not showing up till late or even the next morning, with *pinga* and tobacco strong on her breath.

Soledad has accompanied Dolores to the midwife who is taking care of her, thanks to Jorge's money. The *sage-femme* backs up Soledad's arguments, and Dolores does try. And eventually, after the third month, her cycle seems to slow, stop, even reverse itself. The bouts of restlessness come at shorter intervals, her reactions also start to grow shallower, as if this were indeed a matter of wavelength—their arguments less vicious, the smokes less numerous, the drinks often less strong than *tafia*. Soledad rations her own Galaxys to three in the morning, and seven for the rest of the day.

One afternoon, on a day Soledad has no lessons sched-uled, Dolores comes in to listen as she runs through the open-ing bars of what she is now thinking of as a *chanson,* a song. She listens all the way through, uninvited, absently winding a strand of cormorant-colored hair around her fingers. Soledad says nothing and feels absolutely no brake or slowdown in her work—an absence of inhibition that is greater than what she felt with Dolores's father, as one compares absence, by reading a sort of internal pressure gauge, obviously and eter-nally subjective.

That same evening, Dolores's *guaquero* shows up and treats them for free to the same kind of dubious buffet of Delta rum and cigar smoke and tales of pointless machismo that Jorge and Ruiz generated after their own Tayrona expedi-tion. Dolores starts to drink and smoke with abandon and returns Soledad's unspoken comments, glare for glare. The *guaquero*—presumably the child's father, though Soledad has never asked and Dolores never tells her—throws up on the tiles, passes out on the couch. It may be contrition that causes Dolores, two mornings later, to show up with the man's *ban-dolo* and, again without asking permission, to provide a rough but quite musical percussive strumming to the same *chanson,* the second one, which she clearly favors.

Other little incidents occur to mark the seascape of her happiness with the channel buoys of time passed. One day she spots de Weick in the street—de Weick the cocky first violist from the Conservatory. He looks frailer than she re-membered, and glances fearfully behind him as he trembles through an alley near the market countinghouses where jisi sellers and jag craftsmen call out provenance and gigabytes in a mellifluous singsong that Soledad is struggling to transcribe in a notebook without looking too much like an F2 spy.

She remembers at that point that de Weick was the jis' addict who recommended Haddad to her, it feels like years ago now. By some trick of fate, only two days later Haddad himself shows up on her doorstep to ask if she has read his manuscript. She has to confess that she has not. He looks so crestfallen and lonely then that she promises to look it over before next weekend. "I don't know why you want me to read it," she tells him, and he replies, "Because you see clearly." All the time they both know he is still infatuated with her and this is simply a way of achieving an intimacy greater than either jag-works or reality can provide. She starts reading the manuscript in the bathroom one afternoon, and to her shock discovers an hour later that she is still reading and it really is quite good. *The Wormgear of Deceit* is a prose poem in raw and violent language. In it the tortured protagonist walks a kind of infernal calvary through a *cruce* that to him is rotten with pretension, bloodshed, and conceit; an overloaded, unstable half-city perpetually on the verge of tumbling into a final apocalypse of consuming guilt, followed by a white-hot redemption, a redemption that does not heal.

She does not know what to make of it so she passes it on to Jorge, who is now visiting on a regular basis until they are all growing quite at ease with each other in the same apartment.

———

THIS MEMORY WORKS IN linked sequences, though, the ease they have achieved with Jorge leading backward to the initial stress of his first visit. Which starts off quite stiff and constrained as they all figure out how they're supposed to deal with each other in a context that carries no set goal or agenda. He tugs at his right ear with the fingers of his right hand. He uses the formal *vous* or even the third person for the two women as he paces nervously across the living room— two paces one way, two back. "I have no requirements for my daughter or for the woman I still love but apparently have no more hope of living with than a male spider in the crevice where a fast lizard lives" is one of the statements he makes, to which Soledad replies, "Rubbish, your terminology is so completely loaded, Jorge," and Dolores adds, "It's pathetic, you use your poetry like a bashful girl keeps one hand between her legs, thinking, no hoping, she'll be fucked at every corner." Which makes all three of them laugh.

The visit improves after that. Soledad never mentions her gut certainty that Jorge is sleeping with the woman from Lo Pano, the one he was with on the night of the Ensevli attack. It hurts that he's having an affair, but it is also protection for her. Anyway, by effectively leaving Jorge, she has made it none of her business.

She is certain, for reasons she would be hard-pressed to explain, that it is an *affaire de peau,* a physical involvement only.

She hopes, quite altruistically, that the Lo Pano girl is getting more out of the relationship than she did.

That evening, their first evening together, she buys the makings of *vata: dende* oil and coconut paste and bonito fillets. They pull the kitchen table into the living room and eat by the window, and this time Soledad does not count the glasses of wine Dolores or she consumes. Even with the dark silhouette of the frigate and the flashes of mortar fire from the hills behind the lagoon—for the fighting in the hills seems to be escalating, toward what climax of destruction and high explosive Soledad dares not guess—she remains aware, almost to the exclusion of all else, of the hope in this.

Because by the end of that first visit, and in subsequent calls, never mind whether it's in the *vous* form or in more personal address, Jorge seems once more free in his ability to talk to her, to weave odd imagery into stories that might not always hold up narratively speaking yet are fun to listen to nonetheless. Once in a while, an obvious multilevel longing kindles in the shadows of his irises as he watches Soledad; perhaps this is what makes her so confident where the Lo

Pano woman is concerned. Then he visibly catches himself, and looks away, usually at his daughter, or at his daughter's belly.

He is volubly and thoroughly delighted at the thought of a grandchild "to spoil and corrupt without the vexation of having someone talk back," as Dolores puts it, not without a certain wry affection. She is learning to talk about herself to Soledad—it is not something that comes naturally. "It's because I grew up in a household where the women were supposed to listen to the sparkling brilliance of poetry. Yeh, but only the poet was allowed to make poetry. The roles were strictly defined. . . ." This is one of the sparse details she hands over to Soledad, usually accompanied by a gravelly bark quite unlike her usual unguarded laughter. Soledad is certain this is a laugh she practices to make herself sound like the *guaquero*'s moll she knows her father does not wish her to be. "I'm sure Diego was very respectful of the poet in you, in between stabbing people and drinking and digging up the tombs of dead Indios," Soledad says, to which Dolores replies, "Don't you get it? At least he didn't pretend to be anything different from what he is." Soledad, for her part, talks more about herself than usual, perhaps hoping to make the girl feel more at home with intimacy, the way one might train a wolf child, she thinks—the way one might train a wolf. She tells her, for example, about Mademoiselle Weill, and that is a story she has never told anyone, not even Jorge, or Jean-Philippe.

———

"I NEVER HAD A lot of affection for Mademoiselle Weill," she begins one day—they are both taking a break after a session on the *chansons*. "I suppose it was because I suspected— no, I knew deep down, without even understanding what it meant—I knew they were having an affair, they'd been having one for years. At first, when the biggest thing I could dream of was spending a day at the mine with my father, I just resented her. Having to do homework and geography and math just to satisfy her. She was stern looking, though she had beautiful brown hair, I guess the kind of woman you'd call handsome, with all that implies.

"But as I got older and bored with Glen MacRae, we became friends, of a sort. It was not a personal thing; it was based precisely on the books, of geography and mathematics, that took us out of the *selva,* the feeling of being suffocated there. And she taught me piano, until finally I played better than her. She wasn't musical but her technique was good."

Soledad looks away from Dolores at this point. She has held this memory for so long it feels like a betrayal, or at least a fire sale of something precious, to hand it over free to a girl who sits there tuning her boyfriend's *bandolo* and thinking of something else.

"What had to happen, happened in due course. I went for a ride, and Napoleon shied at a snake, and I fell and tore a liga-ment in my ankle. So we were home two hours early. Juanito carried me to a chair in the hallway, then went to fetch Maria Gisela. I often wonder if he knew, if he wanted it to happen; Maria Gisela barely spoke to him afterward. . . . That was when I saw her, coming out of my father's bedroom. She wasn't wearing a stitch of clothing. I can still hear her gasp. Then she ran back in, which was a mistake.

"They yelled at each other all night, the way he and my mother used to yell. And when I woke up she had already left, Juanito had taken her to Ruedo, and all her books—our books." Soledad finds her voice trembling now and notes this coolly, a strange detail, evidence of unusual excitement.

"I didn't speak to my father for weeks after that. Maria Gisela didn't speak to him *or* to Juanito. It was a pretty silent household. The next governess he found was old and ugly. She did her job, but that was when I found out, by hindsight, that Weill had really loved those books, and the new one didn't. You see," Soledad added, looking out the window now and not caring if Dolores was paying attention or not, "I think it was the confusion I resented most of all; being put in that position to begin with, as a teenager who worshiped her father—and then both wanting Weill to leave, in some ways, because then there'd be no competition for his attention—and also being desperate for her to stay. I have hated confusion ever since."

Dolores does not comment on the story. She does not respond with equivalent openness. Thinking about it later, though, Soledad realizes she herself has learned something that makes it easier to understand and maybe live with Dolores. Because she and the girl, at different times, wanted the same thing from their fathers—an openness, a clarity in the most complex and hidden relationships, that could be summoned on demand. And it seems to her in the wake of her own storytelling that the deep drama of adolescence might come from a child's need for similar openness, and the fundamental inability of the world, and especially the world's fathers, to supply such a rare commodity.

———

SOMETIME AROUND THE END of September the weather turns. The temperature, which has hovered around a comfortable 29 degrees Celsius during the day, rises to 33 and higher. The humidity climbs till the sheets of music Soledad works on are soggy with atmospheric water, and Dolores's hair curls like the metaphorical wormgears in Haddad's book.

Then the wind starts in off the ocean, carrying a fine reddish dust that gets into Soledad's face cream, her coffee, even the accordion case.

But the wind brings no relief. Though the temperature dips a couple of degrees, the humidity actually gets worse. "They call this wind La Loca," Dolores tells her. "The crazy one. Up north it brings hurricanes across from Africa. That red dust you see is from the Sahara Desert, it's carried on the jet stream."

Everything starts to rot and mold. People grow irritable. The *cruce* clinic on Rue Ravachol fills up with pistol wounds and pus.

Soledad finds herself less able to concentrate on work.

A low-grade headache starts on the second day La Loca comes; it will only go away on one occasion while this wind blows. The smell of dead fish and garbage grows unbearable. Milk spoils within hours. It is too hot to go out during the day for any length of time. She and Dolores snap at each other. Downstairs Cloodine bitches at her kids almost incessantly. Dolores, despite the palpable tension in the small flat, does not break and run for the *guaqueros'* Cadillac; perhaps, like all native Costeños, she is used to La Loca, and knows instinctively how to make adjustments. Soledad sticks to her old routine for two days and on the third it is she who cannot take it anymore. Jorge comes over that evening, is insulted by something Dolores says to him, it does not matter what, La Loca makes the slightest departure in tone, or a misused word, gravely suspect. He turns to leave and Soledad says sharply, "Let me come with you, walk around, whatever. I need to get out of here for a while."

Jorge's way of being affected by La Loca is to reduce the volume of his talk by about 10 percent. "I was going to Ensevli," he tells her as they walk up the Corniche, "I need a dose of absolutes."

"The *mounchey*," she says, remembering that the Umbanda priest he frequents lives in Ensevli somewhere. Remembers also the last time she saw that *mounchey*, and the memory of the man beside her, the gringo with chaos for a face. "I'll walk with you until the market."

"Are you sure you want to?" he asks. "You look tired, Soledad."

"I'm fine," she snaps at him. "Let's go."

The last glimmer of sunset, red as persimmons behind the haze of Sahel dust, is being extinguished by night. She is sure she does not want to visit an area as crowded and rough as Ensevli while La Loca blows.

The Slave Market seems more crowded than usual. The Umbanda stalls are doing a lot of business, perhaps selling nostrums to people affected by headaches like her own. Jorge says he is in no rush since the *mounchey* won't start incantations until one hour after sunset, and they walk slowly through the memory hawkers, the fruit stands, the outboard repairmen, the merchants of video. A lone mulatta sings *Puta Rosa,* strumming sadly on a *requinto*. A knot of gold smugglers play African chess, serious and concentrated as philosophy students. The cafés in the Moorish arcades behind the slave barriers are ripe with people laughing too boisterously. The bands are mostly *Cumbia* ensembles, fast and noisy, or straight *batuque*—a half dozen men and women pounding on drums shaped like mushrooms, hourglasses, tree limbs.

Jorge, Soledad notices, stays well clear of the brassy lights of the Flash Tower. He talks about Haddad's book which, like Soledad, he admires with reservations. He even quotes from it, he has a poet's memory for language: " 'Y. was still prey to the feeling that, in the very process of discussing her conversion, she had sliced open the skin under his sternum, clamped the cut vessels,'—ummm, how does it go—'took out his spleen and, without detaching it from a single nerve, nailed it with a dozen bright needles to the mahogany balcony of her house, in full view of the women dying clothes below—their scarlet washes mimicking the blood that would never flow from him.' " Jorge shakes his head. "That has power to it, yet there's a dishonesty at the core of this book, I can't put my finger on it. The narrator lies, of course, but it's more—he doesn't even believe in the process of lying, and how in Exu's name can you tell stories that way?"

He has posted a chapter of *Wormgear* on his story-group's Wildnet site nonetheless.

They buy *butifarras,* then amble toward the northwest corner, where a series of tents and stalls, facetiously called *l'Université du cruce* and grouped around the farthest cafés in the arcade, are traditionally devoted to teaching or just sounding off. People stand or squat, slapping at mosquitoes, listening to lecturers inside the tents, yelling or applauding as they choose. A tobacco-voiced woman dressed in the lab coat of a Fernsehen theorist talks into a megaphone while behind her a satvid on a shelf nailed high in the coral wall shows a three-year-old segment of *Tristesse dans l'aprésmidi,* the VR *telenovela* from up north. The star, Amy Duggan, has just been told she has teledysfunction, which is OK because Lance Martin, playing Docteur Graves, has invented a vaccine for it—but then she is lifejacked, and cannot be treated in time. The Fernsehen theorist freezes the satvid on an establishing shot of Bayview, the mythic town where *Tristesse* takes place. "Bayview is only five miles from Glendale," she announces, "separated by a river—symbol of hidden forces, underwater barriers. Both towns are built on the prostituted fables of the people who live there. Look—the Melrose Tower in Bayview, where Amy, symbol of evil, has an apartment. And look: Central Hospital, in Glendale, which is the nexus for subconscious force-flows coming over the river, out of Bayview; a classic case of concordance. Fernsehen also wrote," the woman continues, "that certain 'vortex cities' tend to converge around the stories they collectively build of themselves—tales of the streets, myths of the laundromat. What city," she asks rhetorically, "have *your* stories built?"

Two stalls over, a very short young man with a bullfighter's mustache talks of monsters. "Not fantasy monsters," the young man shouts, "real monsters, of bureaucratic teeth and tentacles—you can represent them visually, each tentacle an independent and rival arm of Mitsubishi Baring Holdings Limited or Pricewaterhousecoopers-Deutschebank. Its size and length are precisely calculated according to Hawkley parameters: number of employees, degree of goal-occlusion, and so on."

"You're insane," an elderly man shouts from the edge of this crowd. "You, like all the Hawkleyites, think we are persecuted—but it's your *paranoia* which causes the frigate to be here, not the other way around!" A lot of people whistle and clap. The younger man remains serene.

"That's not what I said," he announces, picking up a glossy business magazine, and waving it so the pages flap. "X-Corp/TransCom, ThomsonSiemens/Aérospatiale. That's what we're up against," he continues in a voice that is both softer and more intense, "aliens: huge life-forms that woke up and took control of this planet seventy-odd years ago. Orgs, ladies and gentlemen: giant banks, provincial agencies, any bureaucracy where the traffic in information has reached a threshold beyond which humans start to lose control and an org-consciousness has evolved to assume it. Those orgs are as alive as ant colonies. And they are far more hostile to the human species."

Jorge turns away, finishing his *butifarra*. The young man, still talking, watches him go. "Oh to be white-green and full of sap," Jorge says in a loud and melodramatic tone, "and all your fernlike illusions intact."

For some reason this annoys Soledad intensely. She knows it is because of her headache, her pent-up irritation, the days spent cooped in her apartment. Also, the *butifarra* gave her a stomachache. None of this knowledge has power over her specific annoyance. "Oh, it's so easy to use your clever words," she tells him.

"Is it?" he cracks back. "You should try it sometime, see how cooperative words are—yeh, days when they are clumsy as bone cement, or broken tools, bolts that don't fit the nut."

"Like the prudish girl," Soledad flings at him. "What Dolores said, oh you protect your virginity?"

"I lost my virginity a generation ago," he replies. "It is innocence, yeh, the philosophical hymen, the rose-petal political cherry I was talking about, girl."

They leave the Slave Market by the south gate, headed toward Ensevli. She should turn around, leave him to his snide comments, cut off her irritation, withhold oxygen from the fire. By going home she could also dodge the aura of deep uncertainty that surrounds the idea of the *mounchey* for her.

But at this period of her time in Bamaca she is still buoyed by the fact that she twice managed to rout her fears by forging a battering ram of her innermost desire. So the idea of the *mounchey* and Ensevli is not as worrisome as it might be otherwise.

Anyhow it's hot and La Loca continues to blow and she wants to finish this argument with him.

So she accompanies him into the alleys of *pilotis* houses that swarm close-packed in this section of Bamaca *cruce* where it skirts the old causeway to the Walled City and cuts between the vast *pepinador,* the garbage dump, and the lagoon beyond; choosing verbs she can use to prod and poke this anger inside her to reveal the scarlet coals of what they are really trying to inflame in each other.

Children and dogs scamper ahead like sand crabs; this is the part of town where the Afro-Peruvians live, and the children are fast and very black of skin. A half Chevy pulled by a mule almost runs her over. A cockfight takes up most of the alley twenty meters on; dead roosters, yesterday's champions, have been tossed carelessly in a heap to one side, blood thick and black on their matte feathers. Kundura survivors walk sideways through the shadows, pulling kerchiefs taut around deformed features. Dark silhouettes crawl like crabs over the great hill of the dump, scavenging for saleable junk. A doorway opens in a small *pilotis,* revealing a flare of Coleman lamp and a group of girls, clad in fatigues and rifles, crouched around a low table that is carpeted from end to end with the green smolder of emeralds.

Two doors down from the *esmeralderas,* red votive lamps and a rumble of voices mark an open-air bar under the porch of a condemned *pilotis*. The house across the alley has fallen down, allowing a slice of view: black lagoon against the even blacker battlements of the Walled City. Overhead the night sets off here and there an errant star, lights from an apartment near the cathedral, the torches of eel fishermen, the cigarette of someone walking beside the still water.

Soledad tugs at Jorge's jacket.

"I want a *tafia*," she says.

"We don't have enough time."

"We have plenty of time."

She lights a cigarette and drinks the *tafia* too fast, watching the lagoon, wondering what to say next. As usual Jorge says it first. To her surprise he sounds just as angry as she.

"I would call myself a Hawkleyite," he begins, "otherwise why live here, yeh? But at heart it's a revolt against the mythic father, something textbook and cheesy, a wish to come to terms."

"Talk about simplistic," Soledad cuts in, breathing her words out in smoke. "Talk about—"

"He started young," Jorge interrupts her in turn. "Hawkley. He manufactured lysergic acid. He fell in with smugglers, he saw in them a political structure, maximum freedom—maximum revolt. An adolescent fantasy, attainable absolutes, like fast motorcycles."

"You." She stubs out her cigarette. "You—"

"Later he wanted to fold himself back in with the father archetype, like egg white folded in on itself to make mousse— then you had the creative-collaboration theories, the thirty-seven-percent minimum, the compromise workshops. Even this new idea, which for my sins I have taken seriously, written about even—these cyber-*cruces*."

She is sweating with heat and rage. She finishes the last drops of *tafia* and lights another Galaxy on the coal of the last, thinking irrelevantly *I'm going to have to give up cigarettes if I keep smoking like this, I can't afford it.* Very wary of what she might say out loud. The *tafia* has not helped her stomach. Watching the lagoon, she notices it being cut as if a knife had sliced the skin of black water, allowing taut flesh to peel back on both sides; a huge waterbird, in taking off, is silhouetted momentarily against the son et lumière of the cathedral. With a high croak, it disappears.

"The real question," she says at last, "is how to achieve balance in a life. That's all Hawkley—"

"Balance," he begins mockingly, "like the symphony of—"

"Tais toi," she says loudly. "I'm trying to say something, let me finish for once."

He sighs, and hunches into the counter, rubbing his side-burns into his cheeks as if this might protect him against her speaking.

"I meant that Hawkleyism isn't that different from people—what we are, what I am anyway, it's built on the same dynamic. I mean the limitations, the strictures that are imposed on you as a kid; then later, what you make of your-self *despite* them, what you can do once you've learned to use them even, to make your own music out of life."

He turns toward her now, triumphant, lifts his rum as if to christen her with it. "Music versus politics," he says, "now there is a distinction ostrichlike in its very nature; elitist, antipolitical."

"What are you talking about?" she responds hotly. "The Adornistas use it"; stopping then because Jorge's features in the puce glow of a votive lamp are so drawn that paradoxi-cally it makes him look young, like a child yanked out of sleep.

It's more than his face, though. She gets the feeling that if maturity is the crafting of a consistent personality, then somehow over the last few weeks he has grown less mature, while she has grown older. Soledad, thinking back, sees how his artistic insecurities, his political doubts, his flight to voodoo, are of a piece with that idea. And she wonders if the Pygmalion dynamic between them was turned upside down as a result; whether that upset might even have caused their separation.

Yet he *is* old, at least in years. He is only seven years younger than her father. And all this talk of fathers and chil-dren, not to mention this sapping damp of La Loca, must wear him out even more than it does her.

She reaches up, anger gushing out of her like air from a cracked bellows, to stroke his cheek. Then her movement stops, frozen by a surge of voices in the alley, male voices shouting, screaming out of nowhere, the rasp of a scuffle that reaches climax almost immediately, without the usual slow crescendo during which men talk themselves out of really wanting to hurt each other and risking getting hurt in return.

Everyone in the hole-in-the-wall pours into the alley. Someone waves a flashlight around. Between the legs and shoving of onlookers she catches a glimpse of a body lying motionless on the dirt. Liquid, black and wet and dark as the depths of the lagoon, pools deeply in the rut beside him.

A woman sobs. Half the people in the bar encircle a thin man, very young, not far from boyhood really, who holds a *cuto* loosely at his side. He looks at the men with wide dark astonished eyes as they twist the knife from his hand and frog-march him down the alley toward the market until he is lost behind the crowd and the *pilotis*.

"Where's he going?" Soledad whispers. "What will they do with him?"

Jorge shrugs, and sets off in the opposite direction, looking at his watch again, moving toward Ensevli.

"Well, what?" Soledad insists.

"If he's lucky," Jorge answers finally, "they'll take him to Lo Pano and ask the Webmasters to judge him. If he's less lucky they'll beat him senseless, then cut off an ear or a finger to mark what he did.

"If he's not lucky, someone will find him in the lagoon to-morrow." Jorge's voice is rough, indifferent, but he walks much faster now and sweat darkens all of his shirt, whereas it had only soaked his armpits and stomach before. Soledad knows that this has affected him, and that he is like other men in this also, that he tries to lose feeling he cannot absorb in the rhythm and burn of movement.

FIFTEEN

"ENSEVLI" MEANS "BURIED." It was once an area of machine shops, garages, and agricultural depots called Villeneuve. It lined the main highway to the capital, which curved on concrete stilts across the lagoon and around the northwestern flank of San Isidor.

But twelve years earlier a level-three hurricane had dropped such torrential rain on Bamaca that it caused part of the volcano to slide off in a giant wave of soggy ash, crumbled lava, and mud. The Walled City and the main body of the *cruce,* separated from the volcano by the lagoon, were not touched, but the surf of slurry, fifteen meters high in places, rolled unchecked toward Villeneuve and the highway. There was some warning—a group of *pilotis* residents and workshop mechanics, former Central Province peasants who had seen this kind of thing happen before, had organized an evacuation—so relatively few were killed as the wall of former mountain engulfed the neighborhood, covering it entirely in slurry which, as the rains stopped, solidified to a texture as hard as chalk.

Since then, the previous tenants of Villeneuve, now called Ensevli, had tunneled into the substrate to salvage what possessions had survived. And when the salvagers left the poorest residents of Bidonville moved in, to dig out a warren of rent-free caves in the new ash-lava cliffs under the concrete of the buried highway.

Jorge's *mounchey* lives in one of these, a large cliff-dwelling with a roof of steel and tarmac holding up the tons of slurry above. You reach it by climbing a series of ladders in the angle between two well-burrowed embankments. It reminds Soledad of pictures in Weill's geography book; the villages of Pueblo Indians in Mesa Verde, Colorado, or the temple of Petra in Jordan.

The ladder ends on a tiny balcony of wooden joists and earth planted with medicinal herbs. Beyond, massive iron I-beams from an arch of the old highway buttress the walls and roof of a warm burrow. Part of a metallic sign, reading

BAMA
0.8 KM
VILLEN

with an arrow beside sticks out of the ash-lava to the right. Between the I-beams are makeshift supports of thick bamboo and plywood, and lots of shelves. Each shelf is thickly loaded with Umbanda-Cargo votives, various saints done up in the gaudy blood and hieratics of the Catholic syncretics: Guinea Jack, Yemanja, John Frum.

Among the saints are scattered odd objects: Indian adzes, Tayrona masks, terra-cotta tiles with Hebrew characters chalked on their surfaces. Twenty or thirty candles and a half dozen oil lamps—Ensevli has never had electric power—cast shimmers on a massive horsehair couch and a row of unevenly matched chairs on which sit three women in the white flowing robes and scarves of Creole peasants. There is also a Walled City couple, the man overweight in a tropical suit of fine tergal, and the woman in slacks and pumps which must, Soledad thinks, have been hell to walk in through these unevenly hewed canyons.

A *batuque* of seven drums—hourglass-shaped *parlays,* the deep gourds of *courges,* the tripod *bombos*—are lined up at the deepest end of the cave, partially obscuring an opening veiled by a bead curtain that looks pathetically suburban in this environment. From a corner beside the drum, among a collection of feathers, emerald chips, and concrete bones, a radio from the 1930s, wired to a motorcycle battery, puts out loud static.

Jorge walks in and helps himself to a glass of water from a pitcher beside the couch. Soledad chooses a chair and sits, hands between her knees. The white-shawled women stare at her. The Walled City man—a civil servant, she figures, or a banker—nods uncomfortably. She nods back, and turns her eyes once more to the ranked saints, trying to breathe normally. The fast walk and climb winded her but what really has screwed up her rhythms was the killing by the lagoon, and its aftermath. She is sure, deep inside, that the boy with the *cuto* is dead by now, as dead as the man he had just stabbed. She cannot put out of her mind the look in his eyes, as if a sequence of tiny mechanical movements in hands and brain had astonishingly culminated in an outcome much bigger than any he could have foreseen—like her exercises, she can't help but think, her small trills working toward a song or concerto so much bigger than the sum of its parts. And what does this mean, she asks silently, for herself and her role in what she had believed until now was as close to paradise as she might find on this earth?

"A fool's paradise," she mutters. And she herself was the fool; for she sees now what it means to live in paradise ("*Paradise,* from 'an enclosed park' "—the words, from Mademoiselle Weill, coming unbidden as if out of her subconscious; "from *peri,* Greek for 'surrounding,' and *telchos,* a wall"). To live outside the law of civilization. For here the music is free and copious and vibrant and you can get anything you want, with no restrictions; but you can also get taken away and drowned in a lagoon by a crowd of strangers for making a mistake.

Admittedly the mistake the boy committed, if in fact he did it, was a particularly vicious one. But it deserved to be analyzed and the punishment meted out soberly and in the sharp light of reason. And even if the boy was taken to Lo Pano, as Jorge said he might be, she could not envision Jorge's girlfriend or the others she had met there measuring up to the task of life-or-death judgment. The Lo Pano people were supposed to negotiate with the Walled City power authority and the phone company, keep the Wildnets and electronic barter links up and running, and adjudicate in matters of commerce—check out who sold rotten cola nuts, or short-weighted fish—that sort of thing.

She presses her knees tighter against her hands. Her elbows compress her stomach to dull the ache there. She feels sick from complicity. This *terreiro* suddenly seems to her wrong and full of powers that should not be allowed out of their dirty, subterranean hiding places.

Even Jorge, fingering the votives now, seems a stranger to her, a man overly fleshed in behaviors he has allowed to grow beyond their natural size. Men who have no children are spoiled, Maria Gisela used to say, and for the first time she sees this spoiling clearly in him. Dolores is not his child, he long ago put the girl behind him, behind his writing, raising her in the lee of a series of nursemaids until she was old enough to leave home.

She misses Dolores—and suddenly this seems to her the only pure thought she has had this evening—misses the girl and the shady sanctuary of their apartment. She would get up to leave now, except she knows she would lose her way immediately in the rat's maze of ash-lava alleys outside. And Jorge would not help. He would say she consented to come, which is true enough. He looks pale—her concern, in the midst of criticism, comes as a surprise. He pulls at his ear-lobe, his back is twisted as if it hurts.

Shortly after that thought the bead curtain rattles and the *mounchey* appears, followed by three men dressed in white slacks and shirts who take their places behind the drums. A bottle of *cachaca* rum is passed around the group. Her first instinct is to refuse, she doesn't like this kind of pressure, this push toward getting high. But when the bottle reaches her she takes a small hit, and the rum is so fiery and somehow different from her sick doubts that she swallows another. The

priestess lights platters full of dried herbs. The smoke coils
around, forms a solid licorice-smelling cloud that builds
steadily from the ceiling down.

Now the drummers start slowly, a 6/8 beat, then a 3/4. The
mounchey squats by the Walled City woman, whispering
questions, nodding at the answers, throwing cowrie shells in
the dirt, counting them over like a monkey picking its own
dead fleas. First one, then all three of the white-clad women
sway and dance in the beaten ash-lava of the cave's center.
The *cachaca* is passed around again, and again.

The women start to moan. One lifts her voice in song, and
the others follow suit. The song is odd, clearly Costeño in origin, it includes all the West African traditions of held rhythms
and varying beat, but a lot of inland is thrown in as well:
lanto, Pasillo. Parts of it remind Soledad of the plaintive forest tunes that the few town-adapted Manopani used to sing
for coins in the market square of Ruedo. The words are
mostly Lanc-Patua, with some others she can only guess at—
"Moma," which she thinks is Witoto for "moon god" and
"elohim" which is Hebrew, and "yamungu" which sounds
Bantu, and others that ring no bells at all. It doesn't matter,
though. What does matter is the beat, which is almost insanely catching, impossible not to stamp your feet to, or
maybe that's the rum and the herbs. She realizes at this point
that her headache, which she was coming to think of as permanent, has disappeared. The licorice smoke smells good to
her now, like the pure cool air from the high cordillera,
though in fact it is so strong and thick the dancers have become a visual scale of clearly distinguishable brown feet to
hazy midriff to heads well distorted by the descending fog.

Two more men come in, carrying mandolins, and the rich
strum they add to the music gives subtlety to the force of
voices and drums. They break the rhythm, start a new tune.
This one is almost pure *Vallenato,* full of the typical *ponte*
stanza, the transition between happiness and sadness, major and minor, fast rise and slow fall. She still holds in the
back of her mind the preeminent darkness of what she was

thinking earlier, but what the fog seems to do is build a bulk-head between the part of her brain where somber thoughts live, and the clear chambers where music reigns unchallenged. Before she is fully aware of what she's doing Soledad is tapping her heels on the dirt floor, rocking back and forth, imperceptibly at first, then with increasing abandon. A hand reaches out of the fog, a woman's slim wrist, thick with cowrie bangles. It is one of the dancers. By this time Soledad is too locked in to the dancing side of her brain to resist. And she is up on the floor, feeling the dance tension, tight inside her like a hurricane-bent palm, start to release in rhythms of toes and fingers, ankles and wrists—till it flows more or less without let from the center of her abdomen to every single cell of her. She is twisting like a vine in rain, turning like a waterspout, reaching higher than the volcano, imitating floods and ants and the syncopated breath of her own music, feeling above all the huge power of many living beings, working by some miracle in concert together, welling in a vast upsurge from her own untrammeled gut.

The *mounchey* takes Soledad's hands. *"Envoutée!"* she cries; "possessed." Soledad is not possessed however, not the way these women are who spin like bobbins and lace their wrists in fey patterns while their eyes turn so far up in their sockets you can only see a quarter moon of pupil. What is strong in Soledad is of course the music, but underneath that it's the spirit of her own raw openness, the newly discovered ability to cut the three-inch-thick steel cables that lashed her down inside—the knowledge that cutting those cables of her own childhood is only half the struggle.

Because the true freedom, in her, in everyone, lies in the ability to use the steel tension stored in such restraint to power something new out of who she is and what she must become.

The music slows, turns minor overall and mysterious, accent on *bombos*. Her legs take wider steps to match. Jorge watches without expression. The *mounchey* kneels beside the Walled City woman, who lies prone on the ground, crying hoarsely, frothing at the mouth like a dog. Great theater,

Soledad thinks. But this observation doesn't dampen her joy
from the movement and the associated epiphanies within
her—including the clarification of something she has known
all along, but never so perfectly, which is that the engine of
her music lies in this co-opting of tension locked in deep; and
that the power of music generally lies also in its ability to
both use the tension and *hide the process,* exactly as the mind
seeks to hide such bloody and finally intolerable forces from
the crucial anesthesia of everyday living.

That is why music, which continues the dissimulation, is
so much more powerful than words, which do not work if
they do not elucidate.

Which is truly why Jorge could not live with her, after the
concert.

She starts to laugh, knowing how frothy this thinking is,
how dependent on the false connections of exoticism and
smoky herbs and physical release. Figuring also, What the
hell! Another of the white-clad women grabs her around the
waist. She kisses her on the mouth, and snakes her tongue to
touch Soledad's. Soledad spins free and shrieks at the joy of
her discovery about Jorge; then, as if to balance such abandon, sees a fleeting image of the boy-killer disappearing down
an alley behind the drummers. *Fickle,* she reflects; so fickle to
forget the boy almost immediately like that, in favor of wild
thoughts like the one that follows. It's at this point that she realizes more is at work here than the *cachaca.* The herbs the
mounchey burns must contain hallucinogenic elements, possibly sap from the jisi-yomo vine which grows wild in the
swamps of the *selva.* Making wild leaps now across the floor,
she has not danced like this since those first liberating post-
adolescent parties at the Capital Conservatory, with everyone
playing Ruiz and Jasmin and talking Adorno. But her recent
epiphany is summed up in the name "Adorno" because now
she has remembered the perfect argument to rebut Jorge's
earlier accusation, chapter and verse from the anti-elitist, ul-
trapolitical philosopher himself: that art, and aesthetic illusion,

can provide an ideology-free mechanism to realize a small utopia; and music is the most powerful form of art. "Concentrated social substance" is what Adorno called it. Her dancing slows as she remembers how driving this truth home to Jorge can only have one outcome, which is to isolate him further from her life.

The music grows more somber as her steps slow and the final sadness of that last conclusion soaks through her. She will never be sure, when she thinks about it later, which was chicken and which was egg in the process; did her thinking dismal thoughts make the music seem sad, or was it the sad music and so forth?

Yet from any perspective this music is not only slow and somber but disparate as well, gathering a loud riff from a drum, a keening snatch of mandolin, that do not fit the tune's logic at all.

Soledad's energy leaves as if holes had been drilled in the soles of her feet to drain it. One of the women in white yells shrilly, and falls to the ground in a faint. The drummers are confused; they play more rolls and thuds that don't match each other. The Walled City woman is fast asleep. The *mounchey* gets up, feet splayed for stability, looking wildly left and right, yelling at the musicians to stop; but their eyes are fixed on the cave entrance. Slowly, their beat comes back into line, a heavy, thudding, animal sound. And they shout in unison, *"Exu!"*

The two dancers, standing rigid now, add their voices to the chant. *"Exu! Exu!"* Louder and louder, almost screaming.

Soledad shrinks against the wall. This music is not good, that's the only way she can describe it; it is wrong, the beat has gone stupid and violent, the mandolin's chords are jangled and discordant and at the same time make a kind of sickening sense, a logic ultimately dark in nature and full of things that begin with the murder she just witnessed and then go on from there into as-yet-unplumbed canyons of deceit and brutality.

The smoke eddies around the mouth of the cave. When it lifts for a second, someone new has entered the circle of reddish light.

He is short and pale and shrunken in on himself. His eyes are dark, nose and cheekbones even and fine, hair slick and full. His mouth is pulled wide in a grin. He looks wild and extremely seductive, as if by merely touching him you would at once locate the knot of your most secret inhibition and slice it away forever. He wears cheap shorts, a T-shirt, no shoes, and a single *saquitel* medallion. He moves fast on bowed legs into the center of the dance floor. His feet are large for his size, with long hairy toes that seem to grip the ash-lava. He stares at the *mounchey*. She has grabbed two of the votives off a shelf, a Yemanja and an Exu, and is holding them crossed in front of her as she mumbles, over and over, *"Malcadi"*—curse—her eyes fixed on the bent pale man.

The visitor remains motionless for a moment. The musicians, their faces registering nothing, multiply the power, speed, and wrongness of the music.

Soledad glances at Jorge. He is seated in the same chair, writing in a notebook. *Writing,* at this juncture. I love him, she thinks dramatically, I love him anyway—and completely loses that thought as the little man starts to move.

He lifts one foot high, stamps it down.

Lifts the other, stamps it.

Moves in a circle that will bring his too-dark eyes to bear on each of the audience in turn. Stamping harder, faster, for the intervals he has chosen shrink as the music accelerates.

The *mounchey* starts to sing a completely different song, invoking Frum and Guinea Jack, repetitive as her competition, louder and louder. But when the little man's circle brings him round to face her she gives one great cry and falls backward, as if felled by a machete, into the *bombo* drummer, knocking him and his equipment over with a crash.

Soledad feels her exhaustion swell as she watches the little man circling to the dark music, so fast that he seems to make a personal hole in the cloud of herb smoke graying the *terreiro*. His movements and features start to blur. Now he is singing too, words she does not understand and that she knows nonetheless are *quimbanda,* a summoning of the killer shades, everything the Umbanda-Cargo people strive and work against, this ode to pure violence, the diseased flames of sacrifice, the black gods of Tayrona, the celebration of blood ritually spilled.

For the first time she cannot see Jorge through the smoke. What she does perceive, growing in clarity, are giant shadows that seem to point toward the vortex of smoke surrounding the little man. Evil figures in wigs and robes, all black; writhing forms that are cold and would be impossible to resist once they clearly demanded something of you. And on the slick ebony surface of those shadows, something else. The hands and eyes of violent men as they grip and stare in battle's rage. Knuckles white on the smooth black plastic of automatic rifles. Bullets opening flowers of blood in the stomachs of women. Purple-black puddles forming behind a dam of bodies in Teton Road's smooth-worn gutters. A child . . . She cannot finish this vision, she closes her eyes and screams to stop it—which works, because when she opens her eyes again the vision has skipped like the needle on an old vinyl record, picking up on another track. Dona Serena; this is really weird—she has not thought of Dona Serena in months. But now she sees her closely, holding Miguel's child by one hand, watching Soledad with brown unreadable eyes. The flush of shame barely has time to heat Soledad's cheeks when there is another skip over the record of her brain, another image, and she is back to the war she saw earlier: a man, seen from behind, who directs other men into the doorway of Jorge's building, she can tell it by the blue seahorses painted on the sill. She knows who that man is, knows what he must be, just as surely as she knows Jorge will never survive his attentions. For the killer shades have arrived, the F2 have come—the F2 who work so closely with Dona Serena's father. They are here to suck out the soul of Bamaca *cruce* and Jorge is as close as the place has to a soul and she puts her hands over her ears and shrieks bleat out of her like the draft of bombs as she tries to blot out what she knows must happen—

Someone grabs her around the waist and drags her violently sideways, toward the *terreiro* entrance. She knows by the smell who it is, a nanosecond before she twists away in panic at the thought of the cliff below.

They are on the wedge of balcony just outside the *terreiro*. The evil music cracks dully on their ears. A pall of russet smoke now obscures everything inside except for a vague whirl of dance.

"Down," Jorge grunts. He is pale as cut turnips and sweating more heavily than before. A control in his voice reeks of emergency and danger; it's welcome to her because it is so different from the power of that creature inside, and with wonderful ease it gives her something else to obey.

Trembling, she gets on her hands and knees. Jorge, one hand on her shoulder, guides her toward the ladder, and then hand over hand down the rough rungs. As her eyes descend beneath the rim level of the balcony, she sees a crowd of tiny glowing lights shooting out of the *terreiro* entrance, like fleeing birds or forest spirits, which according to the Manopani are the same thing, pretty much. And she hears a final word, yelled by the whirling thing in the cave—a word that means nothing to her then or for a long time after that night, and this is, in itself, meaningful; because if that little dark man makes any sense at all, it is in his *lack* of logic, his celebration of suffering without reason, death without warning, words shorn of human dimension, notes without the sanctifying resolution of chords.

————

JORGE TAKES HER HOME, hailing a mototaxi when they are out of Ensevli. He holds her tightly around the shoulders. Neither of them says a word. In Soledad's eyes the night is full of half-sensed creatures that came into being in the *mounchey*'s cave. She is certain Jorge, for all of his note-taking, sees what she does.

When the driver steers right, toward the Slave Market, she touches Jorge's knee. "Wait," she says, "tell him to wait."

"Stop," Jorge shouts into the Hyundai roar. More softly he asks her, "You want to go somewhere else?"

"I can't," she says. "I mean, I don't want to reopen—any misunderstanding. But I can't be alone tonight, not in my own bed. I mean—"

He is silent, his body still.

"And don't tell me I will be with your daughter," she says. "That's not the kind of company I mean."

"We never talked enough," he begins.

"We never had to," she retorts, "and besides, I don't want to talk, I just want to hold you, oh God, Jorge," and her voice breaks, she punches at his vast and somewhat flabby shoulder and he jerks in surprise, "when did we ever need your bloody fucking *words* to tell each other these things?"

He waits a beat, as if this scene were a poem he was going to read, the pauses clearly marked with a pause symbol the way he does. A pinpoint of orange burns briefly in the hills to the northwest, followed, seconds later, by a far-off pop. Jorge leans forward and says, "Barrio des Anglais." The night is filled once more with the blat of a two-stroke engine.

They get to Jorge's house ten minutes later. She narrows her eyes to screen out details of this building, like the blue seahorses on the stucco that she saw in that *terreiro* vision—slopes in, eyes downcast, holding on to Jorge's elbow. A cockfight is chaotically winding down in the lobby. This reminds her less of Ensevli than of the first time she came here, it seems like years ago now. The warm humidity of La Loca has the effect of magnifying the aroma of frangipani blossoms on the terrace, as well as the slight symphony of megasalsa and *Cumbia* wafting off the stacked slums. Together with the chill of *vinho verde* and the croak of his macaws and the rumble of his voice it all acts like a poultice to quiet the pain—for yes, it is an actual physical pain she feels in her stomach and intestines, the *butifarra* ache she had earlier, like menstrual cramps only worse. It must have been deepened by bad herbs and cheap rum and the overriding horror of the vision that creature lit up within the small caves of her mind.

Since she left, Jorge has gotten someone to wire the Fernsehen TV set to the lights. The blue flicker of its screen brings in chaos, which she knows is the point, though here and there you can make out ghostly shapes, characters from *telenovelas,* perhaps, or *Tristesse dans l'aprésmidi* appearing out of the electron snow like an Antarctic rescue, then disappearing again.

He proffers one hand and leads her to a couch in the arbor. He undresses her. The piratical lust within her is a force enhanced by the dampening of noise, the salve of memory.

They remember how to do this, too. It was probably the one truly egalitarian act they shared, each of their bodies being aware of how nicely it drew pleasure from the other's satisfaction. It takes her longer to reach orgasm than usual; he has to work at it, sweating and grinding until she cries out. The pleasure is not the greatest she has ever had, the sensation of enveloping oneness is nothing to what lovemaking has given her before. In any event, this was always far less than what music could offer. She does not smile in coming, not all the way, as making love with him caused her to do in the past.

Still, for now, it is enough that their ankles lock strongly around each other as they used to do, because such energy presses away the memories of far more vindictive forces that come out at night in other parts of this sweltering town.

SIXTEEN

THE DAWN WAS SILVER, shiny, and great as the sperm of whales.

Soledad stood at the entrance to Stix's torpedo-repair factory, leaning her cheek against the oxidized side of one rolling aluminum door. Watching the light change.

She had never seen a light quite like this before, even in this region where light was always translated and leveraged by water—water of the Pacific, water in the fog, water tainted and dyed in underground pipes. Everything had become a sliding scale of saturation, from the dark bay to the wet streets and the nacre of clouds where the sun must be rising, there, leftward, behind the crane where Zatt lived.

The giant mechanical pterodactyl perched on its landing gear on the factory floor behind her. The cartoon beak pointed outward as if it, too, were silently observing this light that flowed in waves as the Pacific wind pumped it over Oakland.

She had no idea when Stix had winched his flying creature to the ground. In the strange formlessness of dawn, in the strong psychic hangover she always woke up with because of those dreams of Bamaca that were not true dreams, nailing down events on a time scale seemed less important.

She looked behind her, over the autoRodan to a pinpoint of electric light high in the gloom of the abandoned factory, where she had left the bird's Frankenstein snoring in a tangle of navy blankets on his water bed. The cold from the gate ached in her cheek, in her cheekbone even. It connected with the chill of fog and wind flipping off the ruined tarmac and cobbles of the Navy Yard streets.

She shivered, and started walking, not to go anywhere in particular, just to warm up with exercise. If she had looked for direction, she probably would have turned right or left for the fishing harbor or Lo Pano, so thoroughly was her mind locked into the story she had just told herself in sleep. She stamped her feet a little on the cobbles, to emphasize the fact of the here and now. Not that it mattered so much, she supposed, to be dreaming in her head as she walked in California, but a basic discipline had to be maintained. The primal connection between outside facts and inward calculation was something that in theory had value. Her plastic sandals were hard and loose. Stamping hurt the soles of her feet and reminded her coldly that she needed new shoes, not to mention new clothes, and had nary a cashchip to buy them with. Reminded her also that she was not home in any real sense of the term, was here on sufferance, always and forever a refugee; a tropical anomaly, ecologically speaking, in a place where cold would kill, albeit slowly.

A ship's siren groaned to her left. Drum-driven music, a clot of sound, rose above and to the right, and abruptly switched off. A vidwall up the street showed a man in a ninja outfit standing absolutely motionless on a pile of molding potatoes.

The smell of garbage was strong. She turned right, away from the coldest light and the sound of ships.

This alley led between three-story warehouses so old and derelict that the original node squatters had practically rebuilt them, substituting for entire panels of supporting wall a network of balconies, catwalks, and courtyards. It reminded her a little of Jorge's quarters, the tower of Volkswagens; but once again her prime reaction had to do with Vanny Kemp. For this was what the architect had been really trying to achieve, the "living skin" of human and animal life featuring the dramas and concerns of its inhabitants across all dimensions of a building's surface; vibrating with such abandon that it ultimately broke through the boundaries of walls, growing like a flu virus, including the next-door structures in its rhythm.

The music started again, louder. It was accompanied on bass by the weird, breathy sound she remembered from her first day here. A loudspeaker overhead picked up a rip of Stratocaster through a rumble of distortion. The left side of this alley was practically all pushwalls, the usual oddly shaped phosphor display pinned in frames of junk mosaic or painted wood. A number of screens showed close-ups of musical instruments—a pink sax, a washtub bass played with cello bow—worked in synchrony with the sound above.

The rest of these patched-together screens, however, were uniform in their dark content. A slow pan across a plain that from horizon to horizon was filled entirely with headstones, and women draped in black. A sequence of buildings burning—she did not linger on that one. A Satanic ritual, but so contrived and Hollywood that it did not bother her despite her recent dream of what had been virtually the same thing; people wearing bloody goats' heads, drinking cups of blood, bathing in scarlet; subtlety was not the strong point of vidwall directors.

There was a scene she recognized from a classic of early cinema, *On the Beach,* when the female lead watched the submarine of her lover diving in anticipation of the nuclear poison that was engulfing Australia. And one screen featured the famous death tape of Joachim Boaz, where he stripped, doused himself in ink, took ten cc. of Sodium Pentothal, and printed his body on a series of canvases, all on video—not that far from what Charlie Rickle did, she thought. The canvases held stream-of-consciousness imagery: ghosts, crying boys, ravens, storms.

And then, just as the images were about to drag her out of the strange peace that had suffused her from the second she woke up in Stix's bed, a giant vidwall showing Dick Shawn, in faded technicolor, speeding a sports car in search of his mother.

She smiled, and that act reminded her of Stix's smile, which he had used a lot last night—a function, she supposed, of the effort it took not to do what his body so clearly wished to do in bed with her.

It had felt good to wake up with a man asleep beside her in that water bed, and not a single envirocam to spy on her treacherous dreaming, no uplinks or downlinks translating what she had muttered in Theta stage. Stix slept with one arm thrown over his eyes, mouth slack like a child's. Waking up and seeing him 'here, when she had just dreamed of lying in Jorge's arms, seemed both strange and normal. The dream hangover allowed irreconcilable events to coexist, even after waking—and it had been good to love Jorge, it had been good to make love with him even when the love part was over; it was good to sleep with a man who was kind. And Stix was kind, she was a good judge of body language and the outward codes of behavior, she was certain of that much.

Just as Jorge had been kind, around and above his terminal egocentrism. He had gauged her distress after the *mounchey* and hastened to reassure her, saying, "That creature, Soledad, I know him. He lives in the City of Boats, he believes he is a descendant of the British Satanist, Crowley, he gets paid by bored Walled City teenagers to set up black masses, yeh, and inflict pain on cats and chickens; the pain somehow makes an altar of the bitter repression of such bleak fantasies." But they were both shaken by the episode. Both looked around anxiously, where they lay naked in the arbor, checking the lights of their *cruce,* and she knew Jorge was thinking the same thing she was: These are the first days of the end of the world. He was subdued and attentive and for once did not run over her conversation with the eighteen-wheeler of his eloquence. So she told him about the Manopani, who believed that when a person died, his soul got thrown back into a communal spirit pool, like chucking a bucket of water back into a well, to be drawn again by another body. This was a notion akin to that of early Provençal Qabbalists and it had worked a kind of reverse flow, so that

Qabbalists had started taking an interest in the Indio tenets adopted by Umbanda-Cargo *mouncheys,* who repaid the compliment by including some of the Seffiroth in their pantheon of texts, and Qabbalistic symbols in their amulets, and so on.

And then there was *el reb sagrado,* a Qabbalist rabbi who had lived in the *selva* and worked miracles, so the Indians said, curing children of bilharzia and typhoid fever. Consider also—Soledad was talking faster now, using words to repress her mounting sadness—the strange coincidence of the word *tikkun,* which to Qabbalists meant the rebalancing of a disjointed world, while to Central American Indians the same word meant the opposite, an infernal chaos.

"It is dangerous, though," Jorge had interrupted at that point, "the coincidence is meaningless. As Frost the poet said, there are only so many word tones, and even *telenovela* actors like to dabble in Qabbalist symbols—it makes them appear deep. But for people who think religiously, yeh, for those who need to *stop* thinking, a coincidence can become a symbol of power. In times of trouble the temptation to trade thought for symbol is overwhelming."

The dark wind grew bloody in the light of a La Loca dawn. They held each other closer. He grew hard against her, she clasped her legs around him and he entered her, not bothering to use condoms, of what use were condoms when the world was about to burn up? Though she had definitely made a mistake there; life had a way of cracking the rigid notions of historicism and millennial dog feelings, the way these weeds under her feet had cracked the massive slabs of concrete paving the streets of the Oakland Naval Supply Station.

Soledad, skirting potholes, touched her belly with the fingers of both hands. For the third time in two days she got a sense that there truly was a life in there, a little glow like those phosphorescent algae in the noctiluc workshop; flame created by the spark of Jorge and the tinder of herself—the personal fragment she had brought to these shores from the ruins of her city.

The thought did not make her happy or sad. It did make

her feel useful, in a strange way; as if she could waste time as much as she wanted today and still be doing something useful. Perhaps this was the secret of that quiet purpose she had noticed in the eyes of expectant mothers on Bamaca's streets.

The music grew louder and changed in quality. The breathy bass now dominated the rhythm, augmented by another low-register element that was as much vibration as note. A sound like a hundred pianos had invaded the melody, and the rhythm was scratchy, almost casse-co. Soledad's fingers stretched, it was pure reflex, the effect keyboards had on her brain. Now the sound was transmitted mostly by air or fog rather than by scavenged stereo.

She turned right at the next alley, toward the sound. A *chō* parlor created steam of noodles and fish. A tazer booth displayed its wares. Two girls sat quietly in the purple innards of a jag shop. On a third-floor balcony, a woman stood beside a locust tree, looking down. She wore a fancy blouse and a campesina skirt. Her hair was curled in elaborate Germanic braids, her strong chin jutted out, brooding eyes sheltered in deep sockets, a book grasped as always in the left hand as if for comfort.

Mademoiselle Weill. Soledad's heart beat a little faster but she did not avert her gaze from her tutor's, just kept walking until the apparition was screened from her by a line of washing strung across the alley.

Dreams, sleep, visions, waking were all starting to feel the same. Partly this was because her unconscious rhythms had been so distorted by fatigue and flight. But this node also shared with the *cruce* the ability to constantly surprise, to churn up weird details of life from the fecund swirl of human currents in its womb; until reality became relative, and events that might seem impossible in the Walled City or San Francisco became, if not normal, at least unremarkable here.

The music was still getting louder, and at the next corner she had it located—always that breathy bass, overlaid by a deep throbbing beat, coming from an area she had seen before between the open-air market and the Wall of Chevettes.

The composer threw in a Mozart pivot point, pure treble, over low ballads from American urban mythology that had been popular with avant-garde string sections in the Capital Conservatory. Then the melody veered to include chants of underground dwellers, similar to the drone she had heard coming from the lair of the Kundurans. But the music did not stay long in that vein, and this fickleness was the agent of its intricacy; instead, on that platform, it built riffs of Shift-shin, and Crank, and what sounded like joke songs, and odd samples too, stuff she could only guess at: muon counters perhaps, the squeak of avalanche fields, the fracture stress of exotic metals, the rumbling lead-in to the Honduras earthquake.

The bass faded, returned. The harmony came suddenly back to a 9/8 casse-co, then went off on a tangent again, screaming tearing rampaging acid-rock chords and psychedelic beat on a scavenge of pop from the last century. Lyrics here: lizards, blood, blondes, beer; shamans incest Spaniards surfboards. All of it mixed up in a kind of film-school orgy, a stew of overheated short-takes.

A giant triangular tube and bellows stood over an open manhole beside the warehouse. An overweight woman, manipulating the bellows, cut gouts of steam into vast breathy notes that were half of the bass.

Soledad supposed that, in some other part of the node, a pump jammed air and steam into the tunnel's far end, turning the entire sewer into an organ pipe.

A row of truck-loading docks stood open at ground level. Now she recognized the rows of cables strung taut along the inside length of the building, the lithe women in pajama bottoms running athletically up and down catwalks to strike a cable with iron bars and produce the uncannily deep thrums she had heard six blocks away.

She clambered up a loading dock and leaned inside. The warehouse had been gutted, then lit with rods of neon the color of alpine brookwater, all hung haphazardly in the air; thus the factory floor resembled the inside of an iceberg, and the people in it azure and fingered fish. The sound was immense and acoustically richer than anything she had ever heard. The floor and walls trembled. Somewhere, glass broke.

Then the sound ebbed. Under the serried cables, a filthy pit lined with at least three dozen pianos of all shapes, ages, and sizes, from honky-tonk uprights to a massive Steinway grand, were serviced by musicians who hammered or stroked or kicked at the keys from every conceivable position. Various staircases and catwalks provided a stage for guitarists, three violinists, a man with a pink bass sax, an oboist, four bathtub basses, two tubas, and six dancers moving around a half dozen jambooks networked via wireless.

One of the dancers, a tall man in bell-bottoms and beads, was the fellow with smelly feet—Mojo. Spotting Soledad, he stopped whirling and attacked a jambook. The thinscreens in front of most of these players changed colors. A fat man in bathing trunks mashed a Steinway, snagging the lyric part. The music swirled back to 9/8. "You!" Mojo screamed, pointing to Soledad's left, "pick it up!" Soledad glanced left, to whomever Mojo was yelling at. All she could see was a pile of junked instruments, Suzuki violins, banjos, electric pianos filling an entire bay from floor to ceiling. "The Hohner!" Mojo howled. "You pick it up!"

She approached the pile. Her fingers stretched again. An accordion, a Hohner, hung by one strap halfway up the pile. She clambered gingerly up the broken instruments and dragged it down. Then looked at Mojo.

"Well, get it *on*!" he shouted and, tossing a mike in her direction, went back to the jambook.

She screwed in the wireless, strapped on the squeezebox. And a mandolin spotlit by blue kliegs began the lilting, syncopated, thrummed intro of a *lanto,* 6/8; the beginning of "Chantal." Without thought—it was a natural progression, like a smooth railroad switching, from the stoned acceptance of tune in her previous spaceout to a hole in a melody that she, as a professional musician, was obligated to plug— Soledad mimicked the mandolin's chords with her left hand, sounding the lyric with her right until she was seated in the tune as firmly as a good rider on a familiar cob.

She freed her right hand a little at that point, lengthening the stanza—*"elle traversa la foule du marché,"* "she came through the market"—adding trills and returns that were followed by the mandolin, an alto sax, and half of the pianos, raggedly at first, then more smoothly as the other musicians began to realize that she knew what she was doing and where she was leading them; smoothly, that is, except for the pink sax and a horn, which both seemed reluctant to follow, playing wildly a half beat behind, but not so loud that she couldn't ignore them for the moment.

And back, strongly into the main refrain, letting the girls on the cables, the woman at the sewer bellows, do their work. The combination of that vast breathing and the thrumming of taut three-quarter-inch steel strings was awe-inspiring, it made the pit of her stomach crawl with rhythm and excitement. So she asked for it again, just for the hell of it, and then once more; building slowly, a practice run toward a height she was not yet ready for, something she was tickling though with her right hand as she played "Come with me, you who walk so fine"; glorying in the depth of sound those massed pianos could provide, all crunching the deep chords underneath her.

She moved down the loading platforms, then recklessly along a rusted catwalk over the greasy pit of pianos. And caught sight of the vidscreens. They were lined up like a messy portrait gallery against the wall she had been standing under, and while half of them showed other parts of the node—people waking up, jalopies braking, clips of *Zorro* or *Viva Maria* and other bullshit images the gringos associated with *lanto*—the other half were focused on her, through the middle step of six cameras bracketed at various corners of the music workshop. Soledad twisting, throwing her shoulders into the heavy Hohner bellows action, her face contorting with strain, with not-talking, with not being able to say the words to a melody she was trying too hard to ignore. And while it caused an unkillable revulsion, to see herself as others must, she was having too much fun to be depressed by the visuals above her.

So she dropped her eyes, and led the instruments into the final refrain of "Chantal," still dogged by the horn and sax. But she knew how to trap them, using the same weapon they employed, holding the beat a half beat the way they did, and then holding back again as they held back, until the whole warehouse was locked into a deepening tension, an adagio 4/4, then a 3/4, waiting so hard for something unknown that the pink sax and the horn had to struggle even harder to retain their individuality; so hard that when the backbeat came, stronger and stronger, one musician, then three, yelled from the sheer joy of expectation; *waiting* so forcefully now that all anybody listening could think of was release: the first drops of rain after a month of drought, the first slide into sleep after two nights of wakefulness, the smile of a child you thought for a year had been lost. And when, at the end of the longest refrain, she let it go

> dropping
> far
> deep

into the sweet swinging flow of the opening bars of *"Souche,"* the reprobate horn and sax could not keep themselves separate from the crowd, and joined into the bittersweet mesh of major-minor, minor-major.

> *Of what use is a root*
> *that does not touch the volcano's sex*

Of course it should have been Jorge she thought of then, for his words haunted the *Vallenato* the way he had haunted her dreams last night.

But because dreams worked in backbeat and side angles,

it was not Jorge she saw but her mother, looking exactly as she did in a photo Juanito took of the new wing of the finca, the one that was struck by lightning. Irena standing, dressed in white party clothes, in the aftermath of fire, in the crash of rain, in the center of what was to have been the music room, gazing calmly around as if the roof still stood to shelter her. Her mother's face somehow had been captured very clearly in the light of the last flames, and this was the photo Soledad eventually chose to take with her to Los Altos three months later, because Maria Gisela said she had been spotted boarding a bus to Los Altos at Ruedo station (hold on the refrain, deep in the heart of *"Souche"* now, allowing a flute to move the way it wanted, she should have been a conductor).

Soledad, at fifteen, clutching the photograph hard in increasingly grimy hands as she asked people in hotels, at bus stations, if they had seen this woman.

> *those like you and me, my friend*
> *cannot see clearly close*

Leaning into the chords, she felt the strain in her shoulders; *putain,* it had been so long that her accordion muscles had softened, and so they came around the word-bend:

> *the shale for the fossils*
> *the waltz for the woman*

An involuntary glance at the vidscreens. The clips of gringo flicks were gone. In their stead flashed an MTV pastiche of cityscapes, many of them dated: Times Square on V-E day, the Houses of Parliament, Calcutta Fort, the tombs of Luxor, Jack London Square, even—she gaped at the sepia shot—Bamaca's Walled City. These alternated with crowd scenes. German shells exploding on Warsaw, Depression breadlines, the grieving mothers of the Plaza de Mayo. But such images were soundless and weak compared to the

sounds she wove out of her own hands, and the images
they somehow evoked in her brain: the flic who led her
to a convent that first night in Los Altos because she looked
so out of place, wearing schoolgirl clothes and a Scouts back-
pack.

> *ah but we have our ships, our jets,*
> *our midnight trains*
> *to show us what we lost*

It took her three days to figure out she had to rip the dress,
abandon the pack, grime up her face and go barefoot so she
resembled the Indians and Romany children panhandling
around church steps and bus stations. By the time her father
and Juanito caught up with her in Chamonville, they literally
walked right past her, so much had she become a part of the
scene, so thin and motherless. And it was no coincidence, this
was the soft, slow part of *"Souche"* as Jorge whispers

> *how dark the hyacinths*
> *how violet the mountains' peak*
> *from such a distance*
> *how perfect the circle of this harbor*
> *how much you loved me*

The chords groaned on, slower, slower, like Tibetan
monks, like the souls of the dead, like the agonies of those
still alive, darkly. In that shady quiet she could conceive a
new song, not part of *"Souche"*—she was god after all, she
was Yemanja and John Frum and Oxum rolled into one—
she could bring in that *pito* that was a bird waking up in the
very first part of *La Selva* and pull it back, to even earlier;
patting down air with her left hand to tell the other musicians
she was aiming toward the greatest quiet, to the first flutter of
wings.

Patting down further, losing the horns now, the fucking

pink sax, the honky-tonks—back to the increasing clarity of water, holding thumb and index apart and then narrowing them down, feeling the power, the love, that came always from such symbiosis with professionals—

To the first three photons of sunlight that touched the river mist—

But she missed Jorge's words, the end of *"Souche"*: "five thousand leagues away/warmed by a foreign wine/still, we remember." The thought passed through her mind, What I am doing is dangerous, for music without words has no restraint; and then the thought was gone.

Her finger touched her thumb. The last violins vibrated to silence, to that first round hole of silence that was the beginning of her song, and the beginning of the day, and the beginning of *Selva* all rolled into one— And as she stood there, her fingers not touching the keys, in that great noise that was the absence of noise, the word that came to mind was not one of Jorge's after all. The word around which silence had accreted, like nacre around the first grain of sand in a pearl oyster, was

maman

Not the first word she had ever spoken

maman

The first word she ever said was "Papa," like most kids, but first was not necessarily most important

maman

Her lips touched each other, twice, forming the word.

Behind her lips, the silence, which was also absence, had stretched all the way down her throat to her lungs, her stomach, and nothing else was there. Thus the sound could return, clambering back up the channel silence had already hewn, stomach lungs throat mouth lips ears

maman

She could *hear* it

maman

She felt the breath rushing through her open glottis to make that closed *a,* she could *whisper* it. *"Maman,"* harsh and weak in her ears.

And for her *"maman"* was the only noise. The concert warehouse, the anarchic vidscreens, the awakening streets of the node itself were all utterly quiet, as they had never been before, as they would never be again.

The musicians waited.

Overhead, vidscreens showed Soledad, thrown around her instrument, hands held like frozen birds over the keyboard, face in close-up pursed around lips framing a word no one else could hear.

Other screens showed node shots, two-way links of people in the alleys, in their ateliers, in Molly's Diner, in the jag market.

Everyone was still, frozen in the act of listening to this death of tune. Even Stix said nothing as he sat up in the water bed, grinning at the envirocam he had pointed so often at Soledad when she was the one asleep and in his bed.

SEVENTEEN

SHE WALKED WITHOUT PLAN or direction for a while, moving fast, getting lost in side streets, trying to avoid people. Though she couldn't avoid them entirely in that crowded half city, and felt churlish trying.

It had been hard enough to drop the Hohner and get by Mojo, who had gone daft at the end of her riff. Chased her across the catwalk screaming "See it! See how we made it come alive, we stopped *time* then, man, don't you see? *The node controlled its time!*" She had grinned and accepted his smelly *abrazos* and the hugs of other musicians, even the sax player, and then slipped out—only to find that many, many people had been tuned in to whatever pushscreen channels her music was broadcast on, and they all seemed to have liked it. In any event they clapped as she went by and called "good work" and it reminded her a little of the *cruce,* the night of Jorge's concert, which made her both sad and happy.

But she needed to be alone for a while. She wanted to clear her throat gently, to keep practicing the audible rush of breath, to preserve that consonantal hum, the vibration of air against locked lips, the complex sound that was the first word she had spoken since Bamaca, since—

Since the time when all words (she realized now) were buried and lost for a reason—

So they could not speak what they must always have known—

She was down by the jag market by then. An ozone shower wetted her briefly before scooting off toward Santa Clara. A crowd of Hoffaists ritually ran their UCC cards through a preacher's credit scanner on the corner. They ignored her. She turned abruptly, breathing too hard, and headed down an alley that she was pretty sure Stix had used once to get to Molly's.

At the diner, everyone would treat her like someone who could not speak. Maybe that would rub off, until she forgot the word *maman* that had shattered her complicitous silence.

Perversely, with the prospect of such retreat, her panic subsided a little.

Until, after a minute or so, she could try those larval sounds again, very softly, while making her way to the harbor.

> mmmmmmmmmmmmmmmm
> aaaaaaaaaaaaaaaaaaaaaaaaaaaaa
> mmmmmmmmmmmmmmmm

more quiet and ineffectual than a kitten's hiss.

Her lower back hurt. The crooked way one used one's shoulders in working an accordion had woken the ache again.

The recent wound in her thigh, perversely, did not bother her at all.

She needed another shower. She smelled her armpits, and grimaced.

A trio of weed-pirate launches made their way out of the little cove as she came out of the tunnel next to the diner. The launches were unlovely and efficient as sea ducks; their diesels burbled in friendly fashion, their wakes made black lines in the water that pointed at the boats long after they had disappeared in the fog.

On the half-tide mud, a squad of Navigators aimed brass instruments at what would be the horizon if you could see it. They ignored Soledad, as the Hoffaists had done.

A dozen Putamadre jalopies were pulled up under the massive dock. When she opened the diner door the wash of talk and smoke and clinking silverware was like a thick hot wind pouring from inside out.

And again it felt like the time after the Slave Market, and also it felt different. A few people smiled at her, touched her elbow, said "arrright," as Yanquis did. The gangbangers and a Proto-Panther were more effusive, going through their complex dance of welcome, the fake handshake pulled back, the assrub, the crotchgrab. Vidpanels among the kitsch putti showed her pit pianos now riffing off a tango rhythm based on old Piazzola film scores. And, incongruously, a view of autoRodan, with Stix's assistant half hidden by the engine cowling.

But other vidpanels showed Liteworld footage of microwave feeds. A financial anchor jabbered beneath a logo screaming INFOCRASH? Live coverage of San Francisco Airport.

Will stood amid a knot of Navigators conferring with a Putamadre jefe. Most of the other customers were tensed inward, people leaning into the steam of their coffees as if for warmth, for privacy, talking in low tones about what scared them.

All of it made sense to Soledad. Bamaca, which was so focused on sound, so frivolous, so isolated in its sunny party mode, had the spare time—it came down to that—to obsess on musicians and popular tunes.

Whereas this big gringo *cruce,* surrounded by the massive tech of superpower, must occupy itself with matters of moment, and heavy equipment.

Which suited Soledad down to the ground. She had pulled it off, after all; only now, with the multiple spikes of adrenaline slowly diluting in her bloodstream, did she dare think back on her own performance. She slipped into an unoccupied booth, savoring the slick feeling that she had performed well. More, she had gone beyond her own music, into a wild improv which—despite the audience of strangers, and the perverse feedback of watching herself on video playing and watching herself—she had still pulled it all together till it worked *better* than the one at Frum-Oxum.

She wondered whom she could ask for a spindle of her performance. She grabbed a paper napkin, but having no pen to write with, went back over it in her mind, humming the main tune and beat so they would fix themselves on the blank paper of memory. For the first time since the concert she truly understood she had *talked*—formed the first consciously driven word she had spoken in a month.

"Maman." She whispered it again. She could barely hear the sound she made now. Maybe it had all been her imagination. It seemed so pathetic, if altogether logical, that she must go back to a word of early childhood in order to jump-start the interrupted process of speech. She would have to try something more adult, to see if that worked. Looking at a vid-panel for inspiration. The autoRodan. "Au," she began. The word broke on hoarseness in her voice.

She cleared her throat. "Ro-dan."

The huge metal pterodactyl, shining in the gray mist, filled the screens that featured it. Someone, she thought, had pulled it into the light.

"You play awesome."

Molly folded onto the bench opposite. Soledad, startled, drew herself upright. Molly, as if to mimic her, slumped forward onto crossed arms, then immediately sat up again.

"Coffee? Want an apple turnover? They're fresh." Her face looked older, Soledad thought. The lines around her mouth and eyes were more deeply defined, as if the muscles there had to work harder to keep her focused on the world. Molly's eyes didn't stay in one place but flicked around the diner, quicker and more nervously than usual. She brushed back a blond forelock with one hand. Soledad opened her mouth to speak. Molly, not noticing, said, "Right back—"

She was gone. Soledad, looking after her, smelled other people's smoke and thought of cadging a cigarette. Following the strain of that concert, a cigarette would taste really fine. Then she remembered, with a jolt, that the baby inside her might suffer from tobacco.

So she would have to give up smoking. In fact she would have to think of herself as two people from today forth, the old Soledad and the new baby, both occupying the same territory;

each having to adapt to the other. For a few seconds the world changed color around her. The sense of bright fresh life within her contrasted so oddly with the puce thrills of performance, the overall wash of doom that hung over her from the *cruce* dreams and sense of drama in this diner—*the sense of enemy,* she thought, riffing off the way everybody in here moved and sat this morning.

But they would have plenty of time, if the attack had been just a probe. It would take weeks for their army or police to mount a real assault. Realizing, at the same instant, that she could be wrong. The overlap with Bamaca was not perfect. The logistics were so different here that exponential change might be effected without her knowing a thing about it.

Molly was back as suddenly as she had left, sliding coffees onto the table along with a hot tart that smelled of cinnamon and apples. It reminded Soledad of the fact that she was very hungry and also, for the second time that day, that she had no money to pay for anything, not even a diner breakfast.

She shrank back instinctively from the meal. Molly, expertly reading Soledad's movement, slid into the booth next to her, put her arms around the younger woman's shoulders, and squeezed, unexpectedly hard.

"It's on the house," she whispered. "Free, *comprende*? Stix says you're OK, I say you're OK. You're welcome here, baby." She wiped her forelock with the back of her hand again.

It was odd. Only twenty minutes after the greatest impromptu performance of her life, during which she'd uttered the first conscious word she had spoken in a month, it was odd that the biggest impact on Soledad that morning should come from a hug.

It was also true, thanks in part to Stix's forebearance while sleeping beside her, that Soledad had not been embraced like this since Ensevli began to burn.

And while Molly had a distinctive embrace, with arms strong from mixing dough and a smell of sweat and deodorant and coffee and vanilla all her own, the hug acted as a sort of gearshifting medium, changing the ratio of Soledad's emotions in such a way that, for a second, she imagined it was she and Dolores who were clutched in each other's arms this way.

The weirdest part was that—perhaps because Molly was older, and the consoler here—Soledad felt as if suddenly *she* had become Dolores, and Molly had altered into Soledad, thus neatly flopping the memory she carried within since her flight from Bamaca.

And it struck Soledad with sudden force that she no longer understood why she fled Arapa Province after the *cruce* was destroyed.

She remembered the logic of flight, that it was better to keep moving, best to have a direction in mind, and that made sense as far as it went.

But what made no sense at all was the calculation that triggered such logic in the first place. Fleeing was the best solution when you had lost everything. Yet Soledad had not been certain, and to this day could not be sure, that she had lost everything when the *cruce* was taken.

Oh, Jorge had died, she knew this from her gut as well as from two women who saw his poor torn-up body in the *pepinador*. And she had talked to enough survivors, in those fear-soaked days of aftermath, refugees who had seen no trace of Dolores, but had on the other hand witnessed the Caterpillars shoving whole ramparts of the dead into hastily ripped trenches beside the lagoon.

All the proof was negative, however. All it said was, Dolores did not show up afterward among the living. Too much of it was based on the opinions of people as clueless and terrified as herself, that no one else could have escaped the viciousness that killed their neighborhood.

Neither did it prove Dolores was still alive. Yet in the curve of Molly's hug Soledad simply could not comprehend what had possessed her, in that lack of certainty, to abandon a girl who had become far more than just a ward of her apartment. For Dolores had finally turned into a surrogate child of hers and Jorge's. Just as she'd also become a surrogate sibling to Soledad to compensate in some measure for the loneliness of Soledad's childhood on the *estancia;* even an embodiment, in her efforts to mother and take care of Dolores, of the comfort Soledad missed out on between the day her mother left and the day she herself had quit Glen MacRae for the Capital Conservatory.

"You're crying again," Molly remarked.

She touched Soledad's cheek with one finger, then glanced at the dot of blue on her index nail. If she lived to be a hundred, Soledad thought, this gesture of catching tears would always mean the node to her.

"Fait rien." Doesn't matter. It was somewhere between a whisper and a croak. It was automatic. Molly didn't react for a few seconds. Then she cocked her head, like a dog listening for a new whistle.

"Soledad, you're—you're talking?"

Soledad shook her head, inanely, then nodded. Used the napkin she was going to write music on to wipe her nose instead. Molly moved closer, to bring Soledad's neck deeper into the cove of her elbow. "What happened?" she asked. "I thought, well, like you couldn't?"

Soledad shrugged, but gently, so Molly would not interpret this as resistance to her hug. It didn't matter if Molly thought she had been faking or not so long as the hug continued. Maybe Molly did not think it mattered either because she held that position for almost two minutes, rocking ever so gently from side to side, as Soledad tried not to think about Dolores. And then, perversely, *tried* to think of Dolores, because the missing of her and Jorge had built up to a point where she could not hold it in anymore without damaging herself.

"It can do it to you," Molly said softly, after a few more minutes had passed. "The node, I mean. It's like, in Liteworld, people cut themselves up into tiny little parts so they can fit into the way things work. That's what makes them the Dead. . . . And then they come here, and everything they do is suddenly wrapped up in everything else, I mean the things they make are wound up with partying is wound up with eating is wound up with the families in their warehouse and everything, so it's like all of a sudden they are whole people again, for the first time, the way they were as kids. Trouble is, only whole people can feel pain wholly, see what I mean? All the little pains they had when they were cut up they felt in little ways, but here it all comes out at once, whoosh, typically a few weeks after they move here. People call it 'turning blue,' for obvious reasons."

Soledad was not really listening. And she had come from the *cruce*—another node—so she did not count herself among the cut-up people. Molly's voice was gentle and soothing and just the sound of it made her feel protected, sheltered from the fog.

"I bawled for four days straight when I got here," Molly continued, "but I was worse than most. I mean, I thought I was happy—like I had a husband I loved, I went to the opera every two weeks, I had a manicurist who painted little Nativity scenes on my fingernails." Molly stretched her scarred, stubby fingernails and laughed. "And I had this great job: I was assistant director of planning for the whole county of San Francisco, and it wasn't mean-ass work, man, we were looking for ways to debug the future because the percentage of unwired—you know, the offline, the intractably indigent, Darkworld immigrants like you—they were shooting up in numbers, clogging the skyways and vegetarian food-courts, and it was taking up more and more of the emergency budget. Made the taxpayers feel uncomfortable, who wants people pushing their gross unhappiness on the rest of us, right? We had parallel processors up the wazoo, an army of programmers to model what was going on.

"And Eugenio Zatt was the director of research, that's how I knew him. . . . Well, one day Zatt rolls in, I use the term advisedly, I had no idea about him then, thought he was just another chiphead. He says, an' I'll never forget this, 'You look like you still have a couple circuits open, I want you to look at something.' "

One of the Navigators was arguing heatedly with the Puta jefe. "If the chain of command doesn't suit you, I wanna know who's going to deploy them when the time comes." The Puta answered, "I don't give a fock 'bout your chain of command—way things work here, we stay flexible, stick by our own." Molly glanced over, not looking at the Navigators but at Will Grammatico, who sat somewhat apart, twisted in his chair, gazing up at a pushscreen that showed his brother's workshop. The lines of Molly's face straightened, and grew tense. Then she turned back toward Soledad.

"Ah, shit," she sighed. Her arms had not shifted. "Anyway, where was I? Oh yeah, Zatt. He calls up this regression analysis he'd worked on, a real beaut. It correlated, in person-hours and credits and other shit, the effort our agency was making in the field. You know: trainee recidivism and medium-term job placements and ESL graduations and soup-kitchen attendance rates and TeeDee hospice occupancy—matched that with the effort being put into org interests.

"Org interests," she repeated patiently, glancing at Soledad again. "Internal administration, interdivisional legal expenses, protective coinsurance, intramural conflict resolution, departmental mergers, that kinda thing. Guess what?"

Soledad shrugged. She knew Molly did not care if she guessed, or even understood—that Molly was talking the way monks chanted, to ease distress, to put off inevitable mourning.

"The field effort," Molly said, her voice regaining some of the heat it had lost when she looked at Will, "was weak, to say the least. Sometimes nonexistent." Molly removed her arm from Soledad's neck. The absence of weight there, the cooling of exposed flesh, seemed to enhance the grief still raw in the sump of her. "Org interests, though, were off the chart. In fact, over the previous fiscal quarter, the biggest area of efforts was directed at coordination with security agencies against the so-called irregular elements we were s'posed to work with: the gangs, the jaggers, the spindle smugglers, the weed-pirates—Hawkleyites especially."

Molly twisted around again, staring behind her for a long stretch of seconds. Twisted back, talking faster.

"I resisted it for a long time, what Zatt said. I thought it was your basic Hawkleyite paranoia: Oh sure, like, the orgs were really going to move, unconsciously but brutally, against direct threats to their power. Against groups that could—that wanted to live disconnected. Ones that simply learned to live without the orgs. Zatt said they would crack down first in the margins; on isolated squatters, like it happened to the Sausalito boat people, the slum cooperative groups, the barter 'hoods, the copyright smugglers, the slower Wildnet ISPs. But eventually org security would move against any node that was getting close to the thirty-seven—"

"What's going on, Molly?"

Will moved around their table so fast that Soledad jumped.

Molly did not react. It was as if she had been expecting him, as if she'd been talking specifically to fend off Stix's brother.

Soledad pressed down her squirm of disappointment at the thought. It was perfectly possible that Molly had other reasons for talking to her besides consolation. It also did not mean the consolation was feigned. When Soledad had switched into a younger emotional role, she had allowed her thinking to regress. She would have to be careful, as vulnerable as she was to what was going on around her, not to make a complete ass of herself with people who were simply being nice.

"You won't believe," Molly told Will false-brightly, "what's happened with Soledad—"

"You know what I mean." Will's voice was stretched like a drumskin. "That."

He jerked a thumb at a vidscreen clamped between a plate with Eisenhower's face engraved on it and a Hamilton Beach blender. The screen showed autoRodan, now rolled to a cleared alley beside the torpedo factory. "That—" Another vidscreen displayed a techie gently screwing something into the pterodactyl's fuselage. "That—" At Stix, tapping on three networked jambooks piled before the architect's wall-screen in the factory control room. Will held himself very straight, his arms almost pinned at his sides. He glanced periodically upward, into the silvered wedge of his half-sucker.

"Stix," Molly agreed. Buying time, Soledad thought.

"What's he doing, Molly?" Will interrupted loudly. "He cut off his vox, I can't talk to him."

"He's gonna fly the bird," a Ludd-Kaczynski at the counter answered, waving one arm around so that the sleeve of his long monkish garment dipped in his French toast. "Lotta bullshit infotech."

"I'd like to use that thing for jis'," a smuggler commented.

Molly said, "You heard them."

"That's not what I mean, any fool can tell he's gonna fly that thing. But he's doing something with *that*." Will spun and pointed to the vidscreen showing MSNBC footage of San Francisco airport, where a double-decker Airbus with EU colors was disgorging a pack of blue-suited functionaries. "He's gonna do his guerrilla-art act, you know it." Will swiveled again, jabbing a finger at Molly. "He told you, didn't he!"

Molly smiled sweetly.

"Molly!"

Soledad, who had been staring at Will's face, thought that he looked like a seven-year-old boy who just found out that his brother preferred playing with another friend to hanging out with him. The hurt and grief in him were as total and unitary as a boy's would be. The way his eyes tilted when angry made him look more like Stix than usual.

Impulsively, Soledad touched his sleeve, meaning to comfort him. But the movement had the opposite effect, for Will glanced down, shocked, and the boy look disappeared completely. He jerked away, pressed his throat mike to his windpipe. "Stix! Goddamn you, talk to me!"

"He never hurts anyone," Molly said, and her voice, while still soft, now made no pretense at friendliness. "He'll be cool."

"It doesn't matter if he's 'cool'—he doesn't know what he's tangling with. He'll bring down the hornets' nest."

"Thought choo wanted that," a Putamadre seated nearby remarked. "Thought that was the *point,* man."

"We're not ready," Will said. "When everything is set, then we can provoke 'em, but now—"

"There she goes," the Ludd-Kaczynski shouted. "Fly-by-wire controls: *separation.*"

"Shut up!" someone yelled.

Fat Zeenie, the fry chef, touched the diner jambook, grinning so widely the cigarette in his mouth fell out and he had to catch it in one greasy palm.

All the vidscreens, including the ones showing the end of the warehouse concert or the ninja potato-stander or a child-care center, flipped to one of these images: a view of the empty alley from Stix's warehouse, the shot of Stix's face, a techie pulling chocks from autoRodan's wheels, the MSNBC anchor.

"And now the Dutch prime minister," a vidscreen announced. "Since the Netherlands is currently chairing the EU, he's the de facto president of Europe—Jan Poldroon is stepping onto the podium. He's been one of the loudest voices, Brian, warning about another Infocrash, and he's sure to bring that up in discussions. Now he's followed by the French president, Jacqueline Cohn-Bendit, and General Cheng, of the Chinese People's Liberation Army."

In the frame of camera lenses, autoRodan began to move. It gathered speed at an increasing rate. The view of alley vibrated sickeningly and the walls on each side slid backward so you could tell one camera was hooked to a camera in the bird's vindictive beak.

Then, seen from outside, autoRodan's beak tilted upward. The onboard camera took in nothing but sky. The alley envirocam tracked the bird's gawky outline until its indigo wings faded into gray and it disappeared into the mist over the bay. The activity now was restricted to two screens. One showed Stix, bent intently over the thumbsticks of his jambooks, flicking his eyes between the controls, the fog-rich view from auto-Rodan's camera, and a navigational program; and MSNBC, on which the president of the United States, leaning over the podium, was clearing his throat, ready for speech.

"Oh my fucking God," Will whispered.

The view from autoRodan was split between gray fog overhead and the waves of San Francisco Bay rolling dark and chiseled underneath. Stix had to be piloting it only a few feet over the surface, and it could not be an easy task for the view kept shifting jerkily, right, left, up, down, pitch and yaw and bank. A navigation buoy appeared and vanished a second later. "The fairway," one of the smugglers grunted, "he's headed almost due west." At one point the screen tilted surreally, and the viewers in Molly's diner caught a single glimpse of a maroon and black hull, with a giant green-white bow wave, almost filling the lens before Stix took evasive action and the screen was full of nothing but fog, or the mix of harbor and fog, once more.

Someone whooped. MSNBC continued its running commentary. Otherwise the diner was very quiet. Soledad could not keep her eyes off the screens. This was new, because normally she had no trouble resisting vidpull. Then again, the screens showed someone she knew and he was doing something daft and the alternative was to dwell on her usual losses, or think about her second miraculous victory over stage fright. Too much thinking about that, she felt, might kill the miracle; therefore watching was easier.

So she too remained twisted around to watch as autoRodan continued its strange journey; as the red-lit words ECM*WARNING*J-STAR appeared on the readout from the bird's nosecam.

"Shit," Will whispered, "they picked him up," and stabbed his jambook repeatedly. Briefly the nosecam transmission was replaced by snow, eliciting a general groan from the diner audience. When it blinked and came back on, Will suddenly stood straighter and murmured, "Got him. Stix," he continued in a louder voice, "you read me, over?"

"Don't bother me now, bro," Stix replied, adding sarcastically, "Over."

"Turn it around," Will said urgently. "You have no idea what shit this is gonna cause. Over."

In the workshop envirocam, Stix glanced up briefly from his jambook controls.

"You're not the only one who can take direct action, Will," he said. "Leave me alone."

"You saw where it got me," Will said angrily. "It's dangerous; if you don't time it exactly it will—ah, Jesus!" he spat out, and ripped the 'sucker from his face. "He scrambled the channels on me."

But no one else was listening to Will, either, because the nosecam view, which for three minutes had shown almost exactly the same picture, suddenly changed.

A cluster of pilings bearing blue, then orange lights appeared out of the fog and vanished beneath the nose of the speeding drone. Another cluster appeared, followed by a riprap of black algae-covered rocks and a field of cropped grass dotted by junk gulls. Then an endless parallelogram of concrete, striped with the yellow chevrons of runway, was hinged into the grainy infinity of fog by a row of Christmas-blue lights on either side. AutoRodan hedgehopped a Cathay 787, a red-and-white radar truck, then banked jerkily to follow a runway at right angles to the first, with the number 12 briefly visible on the apron.

On MSNBC, the anchor fell silent. A Chinese security man whispered urgently in the PLA general's ear. Important people looked around, beginning to notice something out of kilter. It was one of those moments that later on might be described by pop chroniclers as "frozen in time."

AutoRodan zoomed steadily down the tunnel of tarmac and fog that was Runway 12.

Then, chaos happened.

Secret Service men and black-clad SAS/Delta teams vaulted aboard the podium from all directions and threw themselves on the various dignitaries in order to protect the VIPs by shielding them with their own bodies. Unfortunately, since there were almost twice as many security goons as

VIPs, the goons found themselves playing a rapidly accelerating game of musical statesman, with the final half dozen bodyguards forced to throw themselves on top of each other in order to prove their commitment to executive protection.

Bright TV spots, flashing police lights, a confusing mix of aircraft and other structures appeared on autoRodan's nosecam. They grew larger by the second, dead ahead.

Three blurs—too dark to distinguish, followed by plumes of bright fire—lit the fog as they flashed past autoRodan from separate directions.

The anchor, meanwhile, had found his voice again.

"Snipers probably, from the control tower!" he shrieked. "Clearly at least seven or ten of the people have been shot! Oh, Hoffa save us!" The camera gyrated wildly, then located the anchor on his hands and knees in the shelter of a luggage cart. "Don't point it at me, you moron, point it at the president!" the anchor shrieked, patting his hair back into place. Then his eyes, already wide as tea saucers, grew wider still. "Hoffa!" he wailed. "Air attack!" And disappeared permanently under the cart.

AutoRodan was almost on top of the lights, cameras, aircraft. It jerked left, right, left, to avoid one of the same domed and snouted armored cars that had chased Soledad down an Oakland alley, as well as two conventional armored cars and a TV van, clumsily maneuvering. Then it resumed course for the podium with the huge banner reading CASPIAN CONFERENCE ON WORLD SECURITY stretched along the railing.

The hockey scrum atop the podium now filled autoRodan's nosecam and the four vidscreens in Molly's diner showing its point of view.

In two other diner screens, Stix, crouched like a jumping spider over his jambook controls, abruptly pulled the joystick, leaning backward in empathy.

"Go," Molly yelled, leaping to her feet in excitement, "bombs away."

"*Bombs,*" Will shrieked, "whaddya mean, he's gonna bomb the leaders of the *whole fuckin' planet*?"

The autoRodan cam jerked upward, briefly revealing the mothership glow of the San Francisco control tower. Then the pearl of fog shrouded everything once more as the remotely piloted bird climbed bravely into airspace over the security area.

The B-Net cameraman had recovered by this time. His lens followed the disappearing wingspan of autoRodan, and what looked like a ticker-tape parade of paper fluttering in its wake. When the gawky bird had been disappeared by the overwhelming power of fog, he pulled the camera downward, tracking the drifting papers as they landed on the men and women still squirming in panic under the relentless bodyguards.

One of the Putamadres started to laugh.

"Napalm!" the B-Net anchor was screaming. "Cold napalm! I've been hit! Jesus, it's gonna burst and kill everyone—"

"Tracts," another voice interrupted. Apparently the producer or the cameraman had commandeered the voice link. "Hundreds, no thousands of tracts, they have just been dropped by what appears to be a small jet painted to look like—"

"And some kind of chemical, Brian," a third voice interrupted excitedly, "it's white, I've been hit, we can't rule out nerve gas here, omigod it's on my elbow and look, look at the president, omigod this assassination attempt, it's still happening, it's *still going forward*!"

The B-Net camera zoomed closer to the pile of suited limbs and leather briefcases and bulletproof vests, out of which a few individuals were now being extracted by the more quick-thinking members of the security squad. Tightening focus framed the features of the American president. The rugged cragginess that had won him the last election was easily recognizable; so was the smatter of white that sat like a giant glob of birdwaste on the left shoulder of his jacket.

"Vanilla," the second voice said in a calmer tone. "I've been hit, too, and it smells like vanilla."

The ECM readout on the nosecam display blinked a little faster now.

"It's—cream," the first voice whispered, and then, louder, shock breaking his voice into schoolboy registers, "I don't believe it, it's *whipped cream*!"

The barrel out back, Soledad thought. Stix had asked her, the first time she came to this diner, if there was too little vanilla. Molly had made whipped cream for him, in industrial quantities that he apparently had just dropped on San Francisco International Airport.

"Merde," she said, almost inaudibly.

The nosecam readout blinked steadily green on the gray worldview of the jet-powered bird. The flashing numbers were ominous in their intensity. Again the fog went white as a missile came from nowhere, went nowhere, then filled the nose camera's lens with pink as it exploded somewhere else over the harbor.

"They're coming from behind, Stix," Will said into his throat mike. "Answer me, goddamn you!"

"Crapola." Stix was trying to sound cool, but his voice broke in excitement like the TV man's had. "Infrared seek-ers."

"Not around an airport," Will replied urgently. "What's your heading, over?"

"Uh—ninety-eight degrees true," Stix said. "Over."

"Listen, Stix," his brother said, pressing the mike hard into his throat as he watched the monitors, "they're not using infrared. They're gonna track down your beam. You've got to bail out, cut the uplink. Do you hear me? Over."

"I hear you, bro." Suddenly Stix's voice was calm again. It was as if all he'd wanted, all along—so Soledad thought—was to get his brother to work on a project of importance with him. "Let me check GPS." A pause. "I'm well over the bay now. I'm locking the controls, now. I'm cutting the uplink—now."

The Putamadre had stopped laughing. The diner was silent again. In the control room video, Stix pushed himself away from the row of jambooks, flipped up the face-sucker, rubbed the heels of his palms against his eyes—then flipped the 'sucker's screen down again so he could see what happened next.

He was only just in time. Without flash or warning the nose camera's point of view went mad, briefly showing the sawtoothed black waves—but on *top* of the screen, upside down. Then came white fire.

And the four screens turned into snow.

"Airburst," Will said.

"Poor autoRodan," Molly whispered.

"You *see* that?" a smuggler asked a Puta, doing the complicated congratulatory sign. "You see *that*!" Like schoolchildren when the teacher has left the room, the diner's clients turned to each other and started to babble. They fell silent as Will roared, "Shut the fuck up!"

Soledad jumped. While autoRodan flew, while Stix's whole weird magico-political trick was literally up in the air, she had hung on to the last traces of comfort from the concert, from Molly's embrace.

But Will's yell startled her, as did the sheer controlled attention in his voice. The way he stood, grim and rigidly still, his eyes fixed on nothing in particular, filled her with a cold feeling she tried not to analyze.

A ship hooted once from the direction of the bridge.

Bacon fried loudly on the grill.

A trembling started beneath their feet; it grew sharply in intensity, rattling tableware and ceremonial plates and sending the more professional Californians running for doorjambs.

The round view of sky behind the diner's portholes flashed twice.

Then a massive sound, somewhere between a crash, a pop, and a roar, covered the driftwood structure, as if a sea monster of noise had rolled over the node, crushing all other sound to bits.

Subsequent explosions were various and confusing but faded quickly. The echoes shuttling back and forth between warehouses, dry docks, and water took somewhat longer to die.

Even Will could find nothing to say in the silence that followed the last echoes.

It was a measure of her familiarity with despair, and the fruits of resistance, that only Soledad found it within her to fill this void, drawing on knowledge she had won at such cost in the *cruce*—croaking "An *air-sol,* d'ye ken what that is, an air-to-ground missile" with such authority that nobody in this headquarters of squabbling in a community of instinctual quibblers bothered to venture a different opinion.

EIGHTEEN

THEY ALL WENT OUTSIDE, like children drawn by the banging of a fiesta band. Crowding through the diner's hatch, splatting in harbor mud. They were so deep in the embrace of tall piers, and the fog was so thick, that they could not see actual flames—all that was visible was a patch of pinkish fog wavering over a decommissioned fuel dock.

But this abstract color had an effect on Soledad well out of proportion to its intensity. She felt her breath come short and her limbs grow numb from panic. Ever since the destruction of the *cruce,* she had never liked open flame. The way she was looking at it now, over a horizon line at dawn, brought home the similarities in both appearance and circumstance to the morning she had woken up and found Ensevli ablaze.

No one else seemed scared. Awed, maybe; uncertain, some of them, about what had happened. Two of the more cautious smugglers dragged dinghies off the mud and rowed to their sharp-prowed craft. A number of Putamadres decided they were mostly angry, which was not an atypical reflex. A couple yelled at or around each other, checked magazines on tape-handled automatics. Leaping into their respective Lincoln Mark Vs and Caprice Classics, they pumped up the hydraulics and fired the engines in a blast of missing mufflers.

At that, the rest of the Putas raced to their rides, followed by everybody else. One by one, the chopped and channeled jalopies skidded around the muddy parking lot, switched on fog lamps, and bumped crazily into the principal access tunnel. Molly, riding in the second to last, spoke into the ear of the driver's helmet. He jammed on the brakes, skidded to a halt ten meters from Soledad, and peered at her irritably.

"You coming?" Molly called.

Soledad was suddenly aware of herself as Molly must see her, standing alone and a little hunched in the mud in her wrinkled travel blouse and borrowed bell-bottoms, both hands folded over her lower abdomen.

"I—" Soledad could not get the word out. For a second she was terrified that with this latest onslaught of flame she might have again lost the ability for speech.

"Get back in the diner," Molly said, nodding in reassurance, "you'll be safe there." The Putamadre jammed his gear-shift into drive.

"No!" The word broke out of her, harsh as a crow's caw. Soledad broke toward the smoker as if trying to catch up with her own motivation, which had to do with staying with Molly and fleeing loneliness. Above all, it consisted of this idea: that she had once sought refuge in a safe place by herself and that had turned out to be the most dangerous place of all, so what price the diner's "safety" now? Molly and a Puta hauled her over the vast sides of the ancient jalopy, and then they were off in a cloud of illegal exhaust and spattered mud and gangbanger *coños* and *maricón de chingadas*.

The tunnel was shorter and simpler than the one Stix used. It ended back in the storm culvert that formed the south wall of the jag market, right under a giant vidwall framed in torn black drapes showing a black room and a black-dressed pianist under a storm sky slowly plinking out Verdi's *Requiem* on a boulder of ebony with a keyboard set in a vein of quartz. This was a TeeDee area; a number of the afflicted emerged from structures built of old Zenith radios, listening to the cellphones strung around their persons, gazing blearily after the cars.

Soledad hung on grimly, one hand wound in the leather jacket of a backseat Puta and the other grasping a tear in the upholstery as the souped-up Brentwood screeched out of the culvert, accelerated down the side of two small warehouses, took a ninety-degree curve so hard she was crushed between Molly and the Puta to her right, and accelerated into the double haze of fog and exhaust from the black sedans ahead.

Down another alley, then left between a rank of cranes and a gray basin of stale water. And suddenly she was breathing sharp smoke, not car exhaust but a smell bitter and specific as a bite of something rotten—could see flames licking the top of a dockside warehouse, French-kissing the fog. The fog was so thick it looked like the flames were burning mist, but the fire was well established in the dock buildings as well, scarlet fire with tongues of daffodil framed by gaping warehouse windows—RDX, ergo ordnance, thus air–ground missiles, with that greasy black smoke occasionally lit by streaks of platinum powdering itself to death into the swirl of humidity that steamed from further conflagration below.

A giant cat's toy of red-leaded steel that had once been a set of antennas balanced precariously between the near side of the warehouse and the smashed cab of a giant crane.

A firetruck with the words U.S. NAVY still visible on the side careened onto the wharf, blocking their path. It was manned by a group of teenage hackers. The Puta driver howled, and flipped the hackers a black-gloved finger.

The wharf was crowded with nodistas. Some had arrived by boat, mooring against the side of a barge that lay abandoned and serene as an old monument in the middle of the basin. It was then she realized this was the dock where Stix had taken her to be tested by Doctor Zatt on the first day. She turned to focus on the gantry crane with the crushed cab—yes, it was the second one on this side, the very crane where the crippled man had set up shop.

Molly leaned over the driver's helmet, pointing. He gunned the car around a knot of onlookers, over the crane rails, following the tracks around the basin, bumping heavily over debris and loose cobbles. They moved slowly because of the crowds and rubble, and Soledad could have gotten off anytime without injury. Instead, she lay back against the Naugahyde, keeping both hands on her stomach. Shutting her eyes against the scene she was about to witness, ignoring as best she could her own need to find out what had happened to the yellow-skinned cripple. She had no great affection for him, but he was one of the few people she knew in this place. She realized, with a kind of tourist surprise, that such connections had become important to her, somewhere along the line.

The problem with closing her eyes was that it seemed to amplify the message of sounds, and those sounds were full of ominous portent: the fear in mothers' voices, the blithe excitement of children, the vapid urgency of men who did not really know what to do about this but insisted on shouting orders nevertheless so as to disguise their milquetoast terror. The words "cannons" and "attack" and "stealth" and "cruise missile." The acronyms "BON" and "MOUT." Utter despair grew inside of her, like a fruit of void sending its roots into the cracks of her character.

Because she had heard those words before, in another language. The situation had been pretty damn similar. And Soledad now knew, absolutely and with no possibility of further doubt, that this Yanqui *cruce* was doomed as surely as her own *cruce* had been.

She had heard someone in the diner say this missile strike was a simple act of retaliation against Stix's act of Rube Goldberg hubris. In a psychological sense, she surmised (with a tiny flowering of "eureka!"), this was the paternal revenge Stix had always sought. But the timing was similar to what had occurred in the *cruce,* in that it was the *second* act, the second explosion deliberately aimed. She understood rhythm, this was why she was a musician and a composer, rhythm was the key to her. And she therefore understood that the reason for this particular missile was irrelevant.

What mattered was, here was the *second* stanza in this moronic backbeat of aggression. And nothing would sway the beast that danced to such vicious rhythms from carrying through its campaign.

She was not going to hang about and wait for the beast to finally finish what it had started here. The conviction was deep and seized up inside, already solid around the little glow of life that she knew, with the same kind of instinctive certainty, lay curled in the hub of her womb.

Alone, she might have considered staying. She would have focused on the dissimilarities and the fact, above all, that this was a Yanqui city and the gringos did not allow themselves the same murderous luxuries they allowed their clients farther south.

But she was not alone anymore. She was keeper of this spark so new it was not even as big as a minnow. Her baby. Jorge's baby.

She opened her eyes. Molly was staring at her hands. Their eyes met, Molly's eyes dark green, a shade or two lighter than Jorge's had been. Soledad opened her mouth; then the car abruptly stopped, throwing them both against the front seat. The Putas beside them vaulted out of the jalopy. Molly and Soledad sat up and looked around. The fire truck had followed them backfiring around the basin. Now a squad of hackers was wrestling the brass nozzle of a hose, arguing about trajectories and flashbacks, aiming the curve of pressured water neatly through one of the windows above, where it turned immediately to steam.

Molly was gone. Her blue apron flashed amid a small group active by the legs of Zatt's crane. A couple of neodoctors ran past, clutching diagnostic jambooks. Zatt's bald head shone in the middle of the crane group, his face turned toward the warehouse. He's alive, she thought; it seemed a good omen, because luck was irrational and in its randomness often dragged more luck in its train. Zatt yelling, "Jeezus, ow!" as the neodoctors checked him over, and then, "Listen, Stix, it came through this morning, the Marsh—*gently,* goddamn it!"

Soledad climbed out of the car. She checked out the crowd, carefully not looking upward, where the fire made happy sounds of chewing and crunching and angry sounds of hissing and tearing. A boy ran by, clutching a twisted chunk of titanium and circuitry, much as a month ago a boy rather like him had run through the debris of the Slave Market. Down the wharf a man sloped stealthily out of a warehouse door, humping a boxful of switching components. He was immediately jumped by Putamadres.

Then she saw Stix, marking him first by the iridescent scarf. He stood beside another knot of half-trained medics.

Soledad moved closer. Two people lay on the moist cobbles. A Zero Cola cap was collapsed incongruously in the middle of a puddle of blood. A fat middle-aged man wearing an old-fashioned printer's apron yelled, "All these games of childhood, and what about the people who only came here to work for themselves, they got nothing to do with your fuckin' toys, and now he doesn't have an *arm*!"

Molly, both hands gripping Stix's healthy left arm, bowed her head to this statement that required no answer. Stix stared down at the neodoctors, who were using oxygen now. His face was so pale the skin looked transparent. His eyes were dark and empty, his hands clenched as if he were about to punch someone. He had big hands, Soledad noted once more; workingman's hands. "Not bandages, a sling—whaddyamean we don't have a sling?" a neodoctor shouted. Slowly, Stix unwound the scarf from his neck and tossed it beside the medic, who picked it up without looking where it came from. The crowd shifted, as crowds will, for no reason, allowing Soledad a glimpse of Will Grammatico talking alternately into his half-sucker and to the three Navigators beside him, gesturing toward the west and shoreward end of the node. He walked slowly up the quay in their direction. "The Farnsworth," Zatt was screeching. "Stix, the Marsh said they were over the limit every time. When she dreamed, she dreamed of *weaponry*!"

But Stix did not hear. Watching Stix, Soledad had the momentary fantasy that his whole being had been squeezed out and was hovering like one of those out-of-body superstitions over the neodoctors and the people they tried to help. Even as she imagined this, Stix caught sight of Will. For a good twenty seconds the brothers stared at each other across the excited crowd. Will's face was as rigid as a fjord wall. Stix's features were soft, weakened and made changeable by whatever emotion had taken him over. Maybe there was an instinctive freemasonry of pain, Soledad thought. Maybe she automatically felt sympathy for someone in such deep distress. Or perhaps the night of bodily contact, chaste though it had been, had opened her to the moods and currents in this man.

At any rate, Soledad felt a corresponding softness and vulnerability inside her, lying almost as deep as the baby's nest. I could love him, she thought, given the right time and coincidences. She started to move toward Stix, wanting at least to give him the comfort of another touch; and got as far as Molly, who noticed her but did not shift to let her in close.

Fine rain from the fire hoses moistened their hair. The Putamadres threw the looter they had caught into the basin.

The neodoctors spread out, stowing gear, getting ready to pick up the armless man. Stix shrugged off Molly's arm, bent to take a corner of an improvised stretcher, and was brushed away in turn by a medic. The neodoctors lifted the stretcher swiftly and effectively, along with a jumble of IVs and oxygen tubing, and trotted up the quay toward a commandeered jalopy. Stix, after a couple seconds of hesitation—during which Soledad got an even stronger sense that he was suspended outside his own body, naked and without protection and confused—limped swiftly after them. Soledad called his name, but the only one who noticed was Molly.

"Look at that," a woman said, "now he's trying to be a paramedic. Hasn't he done enough damage?" Molly whipped around to face her, hissing, "Has it ever crossed your mind that maybe this was not really his fault? Maybe sending a fucking missile because of a *prank* was just a teensy bit *criminal*?"

The wounded were gone now, the fire halfway to being doused. The crowd had no reason to stay in the same place. Molly trudged, head down, back to the jalopy they had come in. A pushpanel on an undamaged warehouse blinked stupidly in purple letters: TOWN MEETING/URGENT/COME NOW NOW NOW/QUORUM CALL 20 MINUTES.

Soledad started to follow Molly. Then she stopped.

She glanced at the twisted antenna, the crushed crane gantry, the blackened and broken warehouse wall. With the heat so much lower now, the slabs of fog moving in from the bay could settle over the damaged structure without being breathed upward by the fire. The roof of the warehouse was blurred again, as was the end of Zatt's crane jib, still lifted stubbornly over the empty black water of the dock.

Half alone, Soledad thought. That was her status now and for the foreseeable future. She had taken her hands from her belly while pushing her way closer to Stix. Now she put the hands back where she thought the baby was. It might have been her imagination, but she was sure there was a slight swell there, from water retention only at this stage, but still a clue that he was in her, healthy and growing. She had no doubt it was a boy, though she also knew such certainty was unfounded.

She turned away from the signs of disaster and—picking her way carefully among the broken bricks, the scraps of rubbish, the torn pages of feathered lovelies from Zatt's magazines—made her way toward the alley that led away from the quay.

SHE WAS NOT THE only rat who figured the ship was going down. When she reached the tunnel under the Wall of Novas—which was the route the Proto-Panther had used back into the node after picking them up in Berkeley the night before (there had been no security checks coming into the node, at least at that point)—she found a line of cars and handcarts and people laden with suitcases waiting to negotiate the narrow tunnel. It was an odd sight, one she had never seen before in this enclave where, crowded though it was, people never seemed to have the patience or temperament for queuing, preferring instead to argue and cluster.

But now they had slotted back into this Liteworld tropism as easily as if they did it every day. And it all added up to a vision that was grayly familiar in a variety of ways: the moss-streaked sides of a warehouse towering up on one side, the surreal stack of crushed jalopies soaring up on the other, losing themselves in fog and perspective; the twisting line of humans, hues leached out of their clothes by the poor light, faces pale and taut with the tension of what they were doing and what they were running from. It reminded her of an image she could not exactly place: Poles leaving Warsaw in the early stages of World War Two perhaps, or refugees on their way out of Amritsar after the tactical nuke, or Spanish Loyalists fleeing the siege of Gijón. Such were the real unifying forces of human history, she thought. Violence and misery and ignorant armies powered by fossil fuels. All constants, as was the urge to flee them, to protect the illusions and the children.

> *They have no country*
> *and thus no name*
> *for the ferns and lupines they knew,*
> *all gone to ash.*
> *Even the plaster birds*
> *whose songs they hum at dawn, fled north—*
> *why stay?*
> *when even the music has gone*

"Jorge," she whispered, then said it louder. "Jorge." It was the first time she had uttered his name aloud since she left Bamaca. The child in line beside her, a three-year-old boy, tugged his mother's hand and said as if in complaint, "She's crying."

His mother had pretty, Italian looks, faded somewhat by time and work. She wore a handmade scarf and the tunic of a Ludd-Kaczynski. She turned, and with her free hand gave Soledad's hair a single stroke.

It was the second time in one hour that Soledad had attracted a gesture of comfort. Instead of going through the
same displacement as earlier, however, Soledad found herself
thinking of Molly, and wishing she had said good-bye.

Too late now. Soledad wiped the blue off her cheeks and
shuffled forward with the line. The woman's husband smiled
at her, tracing the line of her body with his eyes. In the gray
heights of the Wall of Novas, Navigators stood perimeter. A
Navigator carrying a wireless jambook and a GPS receiver
walked up and down the line, looking hard at the faces of tall
men, who made insulting or suggestive comments that the
Navigator ignored. This reminded her of a logistical problem
she had ignored the whole time she'd been inside the node. It
was a problem that, having to do with the time before she arrived here, seemed like local color from another life, another
country.

But this Navigator, with his closed expression and position-
finding gear holstered in his belt and the tight tunic so many
of them wore, reminded her of a flic. And of course the
thought of policemen brought into sharp relief the fact that
some form of flic was on the hunt for her out there, had almost nicked her under the Nirvana Motel.

It didn't matter if, as seemed likely, the soldiers who
gassed her in front of the bird-configured crane had done so
only on general principles and not because they were looking
for Soledad in particular. The dark intent of that ambush in
the Tenderloin had been such that she must assume they
would scan for her among this column of refugees streaming
out of the closest equivalent to the Bamaca *cruce* in the western United States.

Soledad examined the queue before her, trying to find a
line of disguise that might slip her through the cordon outside. A woman with very long red hair, dressed in a cape,
boots, and Russian Army trousers, stood by a silver Airstream. She verbally whipped half a dozen men into reloading
architect's wall-screens and rolls of blueprints into the trailer.

The Ludd-Kaczyinski woman beside her made a comment to her husband, and both giggled. Soledad marshaled the words she needed, and touched the woman's shoulder.

"Please," she croaked, and cleared her throat. "Please, would ye give me a—a *châle*?" For some reason, though she knew the word, it would not come to her. "A cloth thingie." She made the gesture of wrapping something around her throat. "Only until we're out of the node."

"Your scarf," the man said. "You want my scarf?" the woman asked. She took the handloom from her neck and tossed it to Soledad, who looped it over her own head, hiding the mouth.

"Beautiful and mysterious," the woman said.

"I wouldn't worry," her husband told her, "BON's giving everybody amnesty if they leave in the next twenty-four hours. It was on the pushscreens. That's why so many of us are leaving now," he continued, smile fading, "because we don't have the courage of our convictions."

"We also have a child," his wife pointed out.

"Ninety-six percent," the man continued without acknowledging her, "that's what the *Smuggler's Bible* says. Ninety-six percent respond primarily to fear. I thought the node was different."

"We have a *child,* Peter," his wife repeated tiredly, and when she looked at Soledad next the generosity was gone from her eyes, as if Soledad, by bringing up the political realities, was the one who had caused this problem.

The scarf, the rumor of amnesty, combined to reduce the panic that had underlain her every thought since autoRodan was destroyed, and Soledad felt herself starting to daydream. Her mind roamed in short inconsequential flights as her eyes wandered over the seventy-foot cliff of staring headlights, crushed tailpipes, folded hoods and trunks and tires of the Wall of Novas. She noticed a couple, then four or five big-assed ring-tailed creatures waddling like furry Sherpas up the pile of chrome and rusted steel.

The coatis are leaving, too, she thought.

Something was holding up the line.

Half an hour passed, then forty minutes, an hour.

Time seemed to both stretch and compress. Soledad realized she was reentering the mind-set of the professional refugee. The refugee spent most of his or her time waiting for the circumstances of the outside world to shift in such a way as to allow another hot scurrying flight to the next skived mode of transport, the next borrowed shelter. But always the emphasis was more on running from capture than toward safety, because capture was always by far the more powerful and immediate reality in the refugee's life.

She had shed that mind-set so easily, Soledad thought in wonderment, shed it without doubt or caution or even noticing; and that was a tribute to the power and attraction of this node she had landed in a mere five days ago. There were times, in the limestone huts of Antioquia, in the swamps of the Tapon de Panama, in the endless dust-swept vans and trucks of Chihuahua, that she thought the paranoid coloring taken on as she fought her way north would stain her forever. Thus, even if by some miracle she achieved the nirvana of a *cruce* refugee—for example, a Nansen grant for residence in Norway, the only nation in Europe that accepted Hawkleyites without fuss—if she found herself one day in a comfortable suburb of Oslo, married to a blond assistant professor of genetic semiotics, with a wooden country house on a fjord farther south and three café-au-lait children, two of whom were also blond—she could never look out her opened door except through the dust-tinged haze of the refugee's panic.

The idea of the blond assistant professor made her smile a little. The vision was hackneyed, built on ignorance. The thought of marrying a man so foreign was a joke; she would jump in surprise every morning because the face on the pillow beside her did not belong to Jorge. And through the eyes of the brown-skinned Norwegians she might give birth to, Dolores would always be staring out in wonder and confusion and hurt. "You are like her"; she could hear her father's voice ring on the soundstage of her memory. "Leaving is something that comes naturally."

It was true, as her father believed, that she had practiced a scorched-earth policy in her own life, taking over territory, consuming everything she could, leaving it black and sterile in her wake as her mother had done. She knew that this realization should leave her trembling, curled like a fetus on the ground, because it was a flaw and shame as basic and damning as the volcanic fault underlying this area of San Francisco Bay.

Yet for some reason she continued to stand, examining the cascade of carburetors and planet gears of the junked cars. Like an inoculation of memory and emotion, what preempted her circuits were the faces she had conjured up prior to her father's words: Jorge, Dolores. Their faces would always be stronger than words because they slotted exactly into the contours of her own mind—her own story of herself, as Jorge would have put it. It was a fact that her love for these people, in less than a year, had permanently altered the geography of her own character and life. It was the reason Stix and Molly, whom she had first met a few days before but who lived in the same breathless tension, the same commitment to deep living as Jorge and his daughter, would always carry more weight than a man she married in circumstances that cut against the grain of her geography.

In that gallery of faces, she could see Stix as she had seen him last, his features pale, his thick hands clenched in grief. And Molly watching him, bent forward from the waist.

The line started to move again.

Three families in front, the silver trailer carefully negotiated the tunnel of Novas. "There she goes," a man behind them said. "The great white hope of modern architecture, right? But the thing I always liked most about Vanny Kemp was her carrot-top." Soledad whirled, trying to locate the speaker, but the line was shifting forward. The Ludd-Kaczynski family pulled their bicycles ahead, leaving tracks in the carpet of rust. "Hey," a woman behind her called, "could you move? It's like HolocaustWorld here, there's a penalty for waiting."

Soledad turned, but did not move forward. Her heart was slamming as hard as it had been when she saw the first glow of fire from this morning's missiles. Her eyes, she thought, must look as pathetic and terrified as those of a tree sloth caught in the beam of a *selva* poacher's torch. "Sister," a man down the line said, "you got to make up your mind."

"But who am I," she whispered, staring at the road that stretched behind her, "if I am not with them?"

"Come on."

"Speak up!"

"She's jis'ed out."

"Leave her alone."

Even now, in this sad and embarrassing line of surrender, in the chaos of her own contradictory thoughts, she found a second to admire how these people gave her a chance to explain, instead of cursing and shoving her out of the way. She licked her lips and said more strongly, "Without my mates, it doesnae matter anymore. For me. For my baby. Without a *place*," she continued desperately, "where would I go?"

She thought, at the same time, that this was a specious argument from her fetus's point of view. She wrapped her hands more firmly than ever over her stomach. From her baby's viewpoint, the only thing that mattered was a chance at life, at light and touch and milk, and to hell with the hang-ups of the people whose job it was to give him these things.

But still she did not move on after Vanny Kemp's Airstream, or the van that had followed it. The line shifted faster now. A six-meter gap had opened up between herself and the L-K family, which was only a car and eight people from the dimly lit tunnel formed by six crushed Camaros and a half dozen timber supports.

After another ten seconds of waiting the family behind simply walked around her to close the gap. The rest of the line followed, describing a meander around Soledad as she stood gazing up where the top of the Novas disappeared into the fog, like Joan of Arc seeing a vision of Detroit as the sea wind handled the borrowed scarf around her throat.

I'm going to go through it again, she reflected tiredly. I am going to risk my life, and my baby's, because I am *lonely*.

But the outrage in her mind was no match for the warm surge of comfort that wrapped her gut like a blanket of *vira puru* feathers. When she finally did move, turning away from the Wall of Novas and skirting the line of refugees who had come after, she walked progressively quicker and with increasing confidence, until by the time she reached the jag market she was running.

THE MAJORITY OF THE pushscreens on the node's bigger thoroughfares showed images of town meeting, featuring thumbnails of speakers, spotlit by old-fashioned arc lights against a shadowy background, gesturing atop yet another big and unrecognizable hunk of junked machinery. Shift-shin wafted gently from screen to screen, echo bouncing to echo: pastoral laments, friendly techno riffs on voyageur ballads. Many screens displayed shots of a high factory with skylights that Soledad figured must be the town meeting building. Giant arrows flashed in what presumably was the right direction.

But the arrows, though accurate in space, were misleading in time; too late. As she strode down the streets where the arrows pointed, Soledad met a stream of nodistas all coming the other way. Most of them, silent and glum, moved fast. Jalopies and bike-carts sped dangerously through the crowd, their drivers intent, now that public business was finished, on private urgencies. A few of the walkers still argued, as if the high of discussion was something that should be discharged slowly and with care—as if it mattered, when the arguments must have already been played out, a decision, popular or not, defined and entrenched.

Soledad slowed down, paying more attention to pushscreens, which showed replays of the meeting that had just ended. On one, a large bearded man in a full-sucker spoke poorly, self-consciously, arguing a point she could not discern. In another, Molly said heatedly, in close-up, "They *know* how people work. They know how to follow a Flash trough. They know, if something comes in they want to paper over, they just pump up news bulletins on Infocrashes till people could give a fuck if the world is about to blow, they're so drunk on what the Flash is telling them in 3-D and bright colors and star appeal. And they will *use* that trough to finish us."

"Tell us, babe!" hecklers howled in the background. "Resign! Blow me!"

But most of the pushpanel clips featured Will, standing on a catwalk on the building's far end. That sector of the factory had been invaded by black water, and a light mist rising off the tide made halos in the spots around him. With his military bearing and dark uniform, he looked like a prophet from the old days, when prophets fought grimly and hand-to-hand.

What was most impressive about the views of Will, though, was the sound track; the town meeting building must have been lousy with speakers, and they'd all been in use and at fair volume. Every kind of tympanic equipment imaginable seemed to be present: sheet metal, snares, garbage cans, she even caught a *bombo* in there. On a screen behind Will, images of Sarajevo and the Killing Souks of Samarkand were synched with clips from ancient movies: the burning of Atlanta from *Gone with the Wind,* the pilots' pep talk from *Star Wars,* the PT boat-attack from *In Harm's Way,* the prebattle lull from *Exodus*. And all these images, in turn, were syncopated with samples stolen from Beethoven, Fred Frith, Kurt Cobain, Clam Fetish, Rouget de L'Isle, Tan Dun, woven together in the same wild rhythm but with minor and seventh chord patterns nicely meshed by the hand of someone who knew exactly what she or he was doing.

The sound track behind the next clip was softer but the base melody there was something Soledad knew very well. It was her *"Souche"* song, only minus Jorge's lyrics, cut and bent to fit into a driving 2/2 beat.

Soledad felt her earlier comfort wash away like runoff from a cloudburst. She wished only to lie down and rest. She did not have the energy to manage the new and uncouth feelings welling inside of her: of anger because they stole her tune for this; of automatic letdown, because the attack music had waned; of utter resignation, because the node was dying, and she most probably with it, and her baby with her.

"To fight back is not to take a chance, it is our *only* chance." Will's voice came calmly and with utter conviction from an encryption booth to her left. "To make their attempt to destroy us so lurid and fiery and costly that it will explode into the Flash and the B-Net news like a Roman candle. And they will be forced to give it up, and negotiate, and accept that an alternative structure—Hawkleyism, and the nodes that are built on it . . ."

A camera trained on the audience showed nodistas tallying up hands raised like a field of pale sunflowers.

". . . voted for armed defense," a man passing Soledad commented bitterly, "but *only* if Liteworld uses it first."

In the streets, the crowds grew thinner. As she walked against the weakening current of stragglers, Soledad for the first time stopped looking at the pushscreens, avoided listening to the sounds that came out of them. She covered her ears with her hands when walking close.

It did not really work.

When she got to the factory with the skylights she found it almost empty. A clutch of female Proto-Panthers drank steadily in a gray pillar of fog illumination thrusting down from one of the skylights. One of them called, cheerfully, "Yo, it's all over, babe, and you missed the show. Now it's time to kiss your honky ass good-bye." "Have a drink first," another suggested, "anyway," proffering a bottle of Coastal Chardonnay.

There was no sign of Stix, or Molly, or Will, or anyone else for that matter. Soledad trudged slowly into the middle of the factory, staring up at a ruined, three-story-high gas-turbine engine that dominated the great floor. On one side of the engine, bolted and cabled to its rust-eaten injectors and fuel-returns, a pushpanel ten times the size of any she had seen before glowed and shifted with the trades of a functioning node:

400 CRATES OF NONORGANIC APPLES, 86 BARTER-CHIPS— SADDLE MOUNTAIN COOP///FOR///3 J. DEER 220 DIESELS, REFURBISHED, SKETER WORKSHOP, WAREHOUSE 44 [900 CAYMANS]

It was Lo Pano, Soledad realized belatedly, or the Yanqui equivalent. This half-sunken wreck of a building was the Oakland node's barterboard; the soul, brain, and digestion of any real *cruce*.

2 SWITCHING DEVICES, 23, D. DUNCAN, UNION, MAINE/// FOR///16 PLANET PROGRAMS, JEDDA & SLADE, COMPROMISE WORKSHOP, 20 BARTERS PLUS 3 CAYMANS

She sank into a crouch on the algaed concrete, ignoring the echoes and flicker from hundreds of now-dimmed thinscreens on the rusted walls of this condemned building; watching only the board in the middle as it flashed like the EKG readout of a patient in the darkest and most hopeless unit of a hospital ward that everyone had forgotten about long ago.

———

STIX DISCOVERED HER ALMOST two hours later, slumped against a silent speaker in a corner of the building, still staring at the giant barterboard which continued to record transactions, though no one else was in the place. No one had to be there, Soledad realized, because everyone bartering was electronically logged onto the dozens of envirocams permanently focused on the board.

He had found her through the envirocams, Stix said— hadn't even been looking, not specifically, though he was anxious to know where she was—spotted her, a detail in the darkened "town hall," in a pushscreen on random-scan in his workshop.

He pulled her to her feet and looked her up and down to see if parts were missing. Took her hand and led her into the sacred daylight, where his spiderbike cleared its throat on the littered cobbles. Strapped her into the "abdomen" and ran her slowly through the gray alleys, slotting into Nimitz Way, to the sub-base tunnels. She knew where she was going. Through the reeking conduits to Molly's Diner.

But the diner was closed. A sign on the door read "gone to town meeting." Fat Zeenie was loading a boxful of cast-iron frying pans into a rusted Cherokee. "I ain't stayin' around while these idiots play hero with Navy Seals," he grunted. "Just hope that amnesty is no Flash bullshit."

"Where's Molly?" Stix asked him. The fry cook lifted his chin, apparently straight in the air, but Stix must have known what he meant because he glanced across the cove toward the abandoned submarine. And Soledad, who had never looked closely at the wreck before, took notice for the first time of the web of ladders and scaffolding leading over the pressure hull to the conning tower; and a rub of smoke, almost indistinguishable against the fog, rising from the tallest periscope.

The spiderbike made it halfway around the cove before getting stuck in the mud. As they slurped on foot down the cove's shoreline, the sub, which from the diner had seemed as black and lethal and unapproachable as all its kin, was revealed to be the same kind of disused, misused, reused hulk that characterized the rest of the node. Acoustic-cladding tiles hung off the metal like peeling scabs. Russet scars marked where the hull had been cut open to take out the reactor and then crudely arc-welded back together. A midden of thrown-away missile casings, welding rods, computer carapaces and wiring, as well as more recent junk brought in with neap tides, filled the dark spaces between the inward curve of hull and the harbor mud.

The boat had in any case settled, somewhat canted to port, so that half her port bow plane was dug into the viscous silt. Stix clambered up the ladders to the base of the sail, and Soledad followed without hesitation. She had lost touch with the issues that first plagued her when she came to this node, of who followed whom, or how to avoid the easy path; none of it seemed vital anymore.

The sub's interior was cramped and gloomy and filled with pipes and wharf cats and half-cannibalized instruments. All the films she had ever seen about submarines had been, she thought, quite accurate. Down a series of ladders, lit by occasional Coleman lamps, past three tiny but comfortable cabins with stainless-steel sinks and bunks piled with blankets. Somebody was curled up in one of the bunks, and two cats wedged tightly on each side of the sleeper unsheathed long yellow looks as they went by. Across a gangway, to a door marked COMA, with the explanation underneath— COMBAT OPERATIONS MANAGEMENT AREA.

Behind this door lay a big room, by pigboat standards. The curved walls were covered to a depth of meters with computers, or rather, the skeletons and panels of computers. For the guts of each machine had been ripped out of them, none too delicately, and broken boards and multicolored wires sprouted from every surface like postindustrial fur.

In the wounds and cavities so created, people had obsessively inserted household objects: book racks, Hokusai reproductions, Indian prints, wind chimes, plants—dozens if not hundreds of shade-loving plants, and flats full of mushrooms, and a system of copper piping meant to water all of them at once.

An enameled woodstove squatted on two-by-fours over the periscope well in the middle of the room. The stove's flue led through the housing of the attack 'scope into the ceiling. Broken-down armchairs set on threadbare rugs on the deck surrounded the stove, whose mica judas glowed cherry from the fire within.

Molly sat sideways on one of the armchairs, her neck and knees supported by armrests. The boy was behind her, seatbelted into a swivel chair next to a former sonar set, busily playing with the one computer terminal that had been spared, or perhaps repaired. His coati fiddled with different knobs and levers, constantly checking the display above to see if he was having any effect.

In the armchair beside Molly, cradling her head with knees and hands in ways that made it clear their intimacy was not a recent development, sat a tall nervous figure, dressed in updated and expensively modified evening dress of the type Stix wore. The figure looked so out of place in this position, in this node, in this abandoned machine of long-distance death, that it took Soledad a few seconds to accept the label her own mind assigned to elil: Randy, the giggling impresario from the Cloud Forest gallery.

"It happened like I thought, homey," Randy said, letting Molly's head go gently, then leaping to elil's feet as they came in, catapulting the black tom who had been lounging beside elil onto a carpet—fluttering around Stix like a butterfly unsure of its flower. "The Infocrash. Started this morning in the Mumbai exchange. Thirteen-thirty-eight Zulu, Vonguey-Krain announces negative earnings, the AI systems decide they can short their leveraged positions on Flash margins. Wrong! Took the whole thing down. You shoulda seen the Bloomberg vidscreens, like Amritsar, like Hiroshima. My NASDAQ hedges tanked 78.68 percent in less than ninety-two seconds."

"It's like they knew," Molly said softly, giving Soledad a glance quite empty of hostility. "They played us like a cello. The tunnel attack, and autoRodan. They predicted exactly how we would jump, and planned around it."

The black tom stalked away from the stove, thought better of it, and curled up on a rug.

"They have this amazing guy, at BON," Randy said, blowing elil's cheeks out to demonstrate just how amazing. "Psychotherapist. Client of mine, works for RAND, told me. Hector Pereira, his name is—he has predictive models for whole cities, their psychology, like they're patients of his, he can predict how they'll work with other cities. True fact." Randy giggled.

Soledad stared at elil, trying to remember where she had heard that name before, and in what context.

Someone had described what Hector Pereira did, and it was associated with what Randy said.

It had not been in Oakland, however, and it had not been recently.

"I'm wondering," Molly said without opening her eyes. "Did they trigger the Infocrash on purpose? Not that we're so important as all that. But I'll have to ask Zatt to put it in his model—it's interesting, no?"

"In Polis," the boy said softly, "all rollerbladers were supposed to have been taken to the Hythe County laboratories, but there is no trace of them there."

"I was ready, anyway," Randy said. Elil poured coffee into navy mugs and looked at Soledad. "I couldn't stand Cloud Forest anymore, or the gallery on Market Street. I got to the point," elil added cryptically, "where I was sick of *approximating*."

Stix stared at elil as if they had never met before. Soledad who, in her fatigue, in the aftermath of this day, in the great psychic diving of this abandoned sub, had given up trying to make sense of people's thoughts, watched the mushrooms. The raccoon stared at dead dials. Molly kept her eyes closed. After a while she said, in a voice as calm as if she were discussing which of her pies was less runny, "This civilization should have died. Died like the poor old U.S.S. *Dubuque*. Been replaced by a whole system of nodes, little city-states, some of them nasty probably but overall they would take care of people, respond better to climate changes, that kinda thing.

"But the orgs got so big, like maggots breeding and breeding in a dead body till they can make it move—*they're keeping it all alive*.

"There's nothing so dangerous," Molly continued, "as something that knows it should have been dead a long time ago. Because you see, it has nothing left to fear."

Soledad did not turn away from the plants. A coldness grew

in her, a chill created by Molly's words the way fast evaporation cooled reefer circuits, by something being whisked away out of her; what was it—the last dew of illusion, of hope?

She did not let herself think, *Dead like me, like me,* but the space for that thought was present inside her, and she was aware of it.

"Something so dead," Molly continued remorselessly, though no one responded or even made eye contact anymore, "once you give it the pretext to attack, it's not gonna be too fussy, you know? It's gonna kill, and keep on killing. Anyway," her voice dwindled, "node people are better off dead, where BON's concerned—they make such lousy prisoners. Last bunch went to Oakdale Penitentiary, they had a shiv barterboard going in that place before you could say *Smuggler's Bible.*"

No one talked for a while after Molly fell silent. They sipped coffee and watched the boy try, without success, to restore communication with his lost rollerbladers.

Eventually the stove cooled. And at length Soledad glanced at Stix, and kept glancing at him till he noticed she was trying to tell him something. Soledad would have been hard-pressed to describe exactly what the message was, but what it came down to in rough draft was that time seemed to have come to a halt. Or more exactly, the rhythms that had governed their lives so far were about to change violently, jump to a totally different rhythm, and it was important to mark this, to remember.

There were so few ways available to do this for someone like her, she who made memory years after the fact in notes and bars of music; so few ways to inscribe memory at the instant it was happening.

He must have gotten the message, or a précis of it anyway. He stared back at her for a few seconds, then lifted his eyebrows.

Stix leaned forward and kissed Molly on the lips. And Soledad, leaning over, after a second's hesitation did the same.

Molly put her hand flat against Soledad's cheek. Molly's

skin was cool and hard, not hard like old steel but tough like a tree that had weathered and learned in the weathering how to protect itself. Like Jorge's, in a way.

"Take care of him," Molly said softly. "Though I doubt you can."

"I need to know this," Soledad said. Her voice was still rough with lack of habit, and she had to clear her voice pipe again. "I need to ken what happened to your husband."

Molly's eyes widened. Her gaze flicked back and forth between Soledad's. Then she settled back into the ripped cushions. And smiled, a good wide smile that now reminded Soledad of herself when she had been happy, or at least fully engaged in something pleasant, a smile that worked out every millimeter of the corners of Molly's mouth.

"Oh, Geoffrey," she said, and laughed softly. "We had problems, anyway. He wanted a son, I had endometriosis, couldn't have kids. But what finished it was the node—he just couldn't take it. He tried, poor dear, but the node just wasn't his style; too dirty, too dangerous, too many rats.

"And then I fell in love," she added, pointing at Stix. "With his brother."

It took a second for Soledad to register.

"With *Will*?" she croaked; shocked, for a brief instant, out of her calm resignation.

"Will hadn't gone all religious then," Molly said. "And he hadn't gone all military, which is what inevitably happens to the religious types. There didn't use to be so many beliefs, then," she added. "Back when the node was small."

"Only s'posed to be a joke, Hawkley said." Randy picked up a piebald cat, who hissed and tried to scratch elil. "Navigation religion."

"Anyway, Will was cute," Molly continued, "cuter than him—" Again she pointed at Stix. "I picked the wrong brother, so sue me." She looked at Stix with eyes that were very steady and green. Then took the piebald from Randy. The cat hissed, settled into her lap, and began licking its asshole.

"You can't take care of him," she repeated, certainty in her voice. The smile, cooling like the woodstove, lingered in her eyes. "But, honey, at least take care of that li'l critter in your belly, OK?"

———

THE WATER-FILLED MATTRESS WAS cold as the cement sides of the torpedo-testing tank that in turn was cold as the girders of Stix's factory.

They took off everything they wore out of an unspoken agreement that this of all times was no time to allow protection, or holdback, or separation of any kind; not when the aim was contact, alliance, physical warmth, all opposites of the processes so deeply and unstoppably gearing into action outside. He did not reach for latex and she did not ask him to. The need for that type of protection was also gone, on whatever level you cared to examine it.

They hugged each other till they stopped trembling. They explored each other, respectfully at first and then with increasing haste, as if the very fibers of their muscles were aware of how little time was left for this. She wanted to— tried to—touch every square millimeter of his body, from the follicles of his hair to the knotted muscles of his left thigh to the deep ridges at the joints of his toes. He responded in kind, and each touch conferred diplomatic approval on the next caress. Every piece of him was individual, a new man to her. And to begin with, it reinforced her first, deep data on him: smooth back (openness); taut knee (damage); the soft part of his buttocks, where they folded into his thighs—the place where vulnerability twisted into strength.

She spent a long time caressing his ass and then, when the desire got so strong he was shaking again, she rolled on top of him and, opening her legs, slid down the sweat along his body.

And he was inside her, easy as a submarine diving into a tropical sea. She shut her eyes and saw one thing: a corner of seawall in Bamaca Harbor. Heard one thing: a flute, a *pito*, a single note.

Then everything changed. Every difference between the man beneath her and the man she had left behind forever faded like sugar into water. She was reading this act like braille, by touch and feel and smell and sound, the script parsed in the deeper skim of memory. Now all the dots and dashes read "Jorge Jorge Jorge," the name and the *pito* and the lip-smack of fishing-harbor waves rising like the ocean of missing him within her. "Jorge."

He shuddered and thrust deeply into her, *Jorge,* and she bore down on him, the opposite of giving birth, *Jorge.* Feeling the blue tears further reduce the friction between her breasts and his chest, all the way to zero, oh—

the sound of waves

the harbor wall

the *pito* flute

zero:

Like the point she had attained in music, where everything had happened, and nothing had ever happened quite like this before.

NINETEEN

AND SO THE FLAMES come for her, and consume her, or so she assumes.

Then, for some reason, they let her go.

And she finds herself lying in a chiropractic position across what feels like the hardest and sharpest corners in the world have been assembled as a mattress for Soledad alone.

Her head aches badly. That is her first and strongest sensation.

Her back is twice as painful as before. Her forearm, too, complains to the brain. Her lungs are raw and constricted. After a few seconds, when she has been awake long enough to require more air—for she must have passed out, she has no clue how long ago—they jump and burn from irritation.

She coughs, without relief, long and hard, like an inmate in a TB ward. Coughing is agony for her lungs, and racks her throbbing lower back against the corners of whatever she's lying on.

Her eyes opened as soon as she regained consciousness but the darkness is so deep it's as if they were shut. She knows that the air is still full of smoke, because she smells it, bitter and inimical; because of how her lungs are reacting.

There is light, though, in some primal form. After a few seconds or minutes her eyes collect enough of it to distinguish unclear shapes through the grim haze that surrounds her, surrounds everything.

Rocks. Masonry, cracked and piled in a heap beneath her. A chunk of brown limestone thirty centimeters across lies on her left ankle. It doesn't hurt, for some reason. It appears to move, approach, recede. Her eyes stream with tears from the smoke. The smoke pulses, as if she were caught in the guts of some giant dark animal, a black dragon perhaps, watching its lungs expand and contract, watching the vapor of its breath, the orange glitter of distant fire up its long throat.

And well, yes, there *is* fire. She was trying to avoid that fact. Between a giant coil of smoke creeping down from the roof of this long tunnel and the outline of broken masonry below, around a curve of distant passageway, its yellow-red fingers flick and curl.

Her first reaction to that is terror, terror without bounds, scampering madly abandoned like the rats she hears, cheeping and scurrying to get away across the lower slopes of her rubble mound.

Terror, because she was unconscious till now and at the fire's mercy; because she is lying on her back, the classic position for rape, ready to be violated by flame and the hard twisted plans of those who made the fire come.

Because she may well be paralyzed, or pinned by the block of stone across her leg.

She yanks her left leg convulsively. Her ankle scrapes easily free from under the block of limestone, most of whose weight had been resting on another stone by her instep. Groaning with fear and relief, she crawls downward, sliding on a huge block, plowing through crumbled stone till she reaches a surface that feels level. And continues crawling, touching the right wall of the tunnel to keep her bearings, groping in front of her, more and more often, as the light of flames recedes and the air around her turns into a purer mixture of smoke and darkness; her mind still obsessed with the pulse and rhythm of the dragon, the sourness of its breath, the flicker of its nerves and combustion.

Except that the flicker is gone now. Her knees and hands are raw from crawling, and the parts of her brain that have come free of dragon-thoughts register the fact that this passageway is clear enough to warrant getting to her feet.

Which she does, twisting around to look behind her. The

fire is out of sight. Not even a whisper of movement in the
slight reddish tinge that remains to the air, a color that casts
shadow in the fire's direction against the cracks of masonry—
which means it comes from *behind* her, in the opposite direction from the earlier flame.

She spins, wrenching her back again. A light burns far
down the length of this corridor. She walks toward it slowly,
still coughing, trying to rid herself of that overdose of particulates. As the light brightens she recognizes the worn flag-
stones, the rough-hewn walls of the convent tunnels.

Always, in the back of her mind, she knew she was still
here.

The light, when she gets to it, reveals itself to be an oil
lamp with a red glass chimney burning calmly in front of a
gilt icon of Saint Sebastian. Saint Sebastian, or Oxum, god of
hunters; lord of the festival she played at once with Jorge, it
might have been yesterday, it could have been years ago. Her
sense of time, it seems, was destroyed when she was put to
sleep by that heavy beast of fire, smoke, and stone.

But time is relevant only to connections with people, and
here she is alone. She could be dead, Soledad thinks. She is
alive but, trapped in the deep passageways of Santa Karen, it
does not matter. No one will know the difference, no one will
find her, which is both good and bad: good because she will
not be hunted down and killed like Jorge and Dolores and the
others in this *cruce*.

Bad, because no one will find her, ever, not before she
goes mad or dies of thirst in five or ten days or however long
it takes.

Dolores, though. That gets through. That name reminds
her of unfinished business, of the direction she was moving in
before she passed out. Is direction, too, a function of time, the
way speed is? She knows, from the fact that she even asks
herself this question, that she is still light-headed. She wonders if she got a concussion, and feels her head delicately
with her fingers. A definite bump has arisen on the rear right

side. There is a little wetness, a little blood. Maybe her brain is swelling; perhaps she will start to think even stranger thoughts and die here and now, over the course of only a few minutes, as the broken vessels seep blood between her dura and her cerebellum and the pressure shuts off single neurons, then entire sectors of consciousness. She wonders if it will hurt. She thinks it might be painless. Or at least far less painful than the ache in her stomach that comes from the name, "Dolores."

It all comes back then, playing like a rerun film: the flames over Ensevli, the helicopter swooping overhead, the tanks lined up in the distance on the *cruce*'s northern fringes. The people playing dominoes. The wind blowing curtains in Dolores's room, over the girl's empty bed.

Soledad stands straighter, runs her fingers through her hair, brushing out the dust and ashes accumulated there. The lamps in this passageway are red. The ones she saw earlier, she recalls, were blue. This may mean she has wound up in a different part of the convent altogether. She remembers dim light overhead when she woke up; it would make sense, if an explosion had blown up the passage she previously stood in, for her to wind up on debris where it fell in the tunnel below.

Her brain, she thinks gratefully, is working fine, or as well as it can under these conditions. She suffers through another fit of coughing, then picks up the oil lamp. Holding it high, she walks determinedly in the same direction as before, away from the rubble mound.

Only fifty paces on, the floor trembles and jumps in a way that feels familiar. The terror comes back. It seems all the hard work and emotion she put into reducing its ambient levels was as useful as building sand castles to hold back the Atlantic tides, the way she used to as a kid on the beach of Santa Maria del Mar. A fierce wind surges down the corridor from behind, blows out the lamp, submerges her in smoke and darkness. "Dolores!" she screams, stupidly. She knows it's useless, and screams again anyway. "Dolores!" Her cry becomes a cough, for the smoke is once more so thick it scratches her throat as she breathes, so thick she can taste it against her tongue, almost chew it between her molars.

She walks as fast as she dares, scraping her left hand now against the wall, lifting her blouse to wad its hem against her teeth as a filter. It is useless, the particulates are thicker than they have ever been. Her lungs rebel as they breathe. Breath and coughing are one and the same at this point. Her back spasms furiously from the strain of it. Her eyes are streaming so hard she shuts them, but they fly open immediately as her left hand finds emptiness.

Soledad stops. The passageway forks at this point. While the opening to the left is black and uncertain, the right-hand tunnel is visible, an aura of rose shimmering through billows of smoke rolling in from behind her and the fire she just left.

So she goes right. What choice does she have? The tinge of rose comes from another lamp in a tiny cell; nothing but stone walls, a straw mattress, a crucifix, a wooden door with a tiny judas. The chambers of the Inquisition, she thinks. The idea has been in the back of her mind ever since she was blown into this lower passageway, though she has no evidence to support such melodramatic fancy.

She takes the oil lamp from this cell. Another haze of reddish light is already visible farther down. This reveals itself, after a few seconds of walking, to be an identical chamber, with the same lamp and bloodied crucifix, the same door and straw mattress. Only this time the cell is occupied; someone is curled in sleep on the mattress.

Soledad takes a single, slow step into the cell, raising her lamp to add light to the scene.

It is a teenager with long black-purple hair, like an Indio. He has the long eyes and prominent cheekbones of a Manopani, though his nose and lips are European and thin. The familiarity of his features slams into her like a tram accident—which is to say, among the variety of terrors she has undergone so far today, against the renewed and growing fear of what might have happened to Dolores and Jorge, what might be happening to them even now—it slightly increases her difficulty in drawing breath, boosts her heartrate a notch:

Jean-Philippe—

What she remembers mostly, however, is not so much his features as the curve of him asleep, the slope of his neck and long back. She used to leave him in that position, in the hunters' hut they sneaked to a grand total of three times; the hut hidden in branches over the slow-coiling river and the rotten straw mattress on which he taught her how to make love. She so frightened of becoming pregnant, and he terrified of being caught by her father, taking her well outside the perimeter of the *estancia* as no one was ever supposed to do.

It was in part to dispel their fear, of fathers and fetuses and cloud vipers, that he brought out his tiny accordion and sang *Vallenatos* to her, *"Vent de la Selva"* and *"Les Yeux de Stéphanie,"* in that rough twanged accent of a Campo native. She was never in love with Jean-Philippe but *putain* she cared for him so, and her body cared for his. And she loved those *Vallenatos,* she remembers them note for note. She remembers them so hard she finds herself starting to mouth the words through the grit of smoke between her lips and in her throat. Which is impossible, too many particles have clogged her mucous membranes and she doubles up in a fit of coughing and a long rasping wheeze that leaves her exhausted, leaning against the joined stone.

The boy, Jean-Philippe, never stirs. The smoke billows again around her. She hears music now, disconnected instruments down the passageway, the direction she is going in; but no accordions, no *Vallenatos* she can discern. "Jean-Philippe," she whispers, then turns abruptly and leaves, continuing down the hall, remembering that Jean-Philippe, too, is dead. Maria Gisela told her he was one of the thousands in the *selva* villages who, having never even heard of a vaccine, much less having access to one, died when the Kundura swine flu came invisible down the dirt roads in the dust of lumber trucks.

Jean-Philippe was a cousin of Maria Gisela's and she had

grieved for him. Yet there was a note of grim Catholic satisfaction in her tone when she told Soledad, because she had a very good idea of what the two of them had done. The sound of his cheap accordion, long notes over the rush of river . . . Soledad had hated Maria Gisela at that moment, for the first and only time in her life. But she does not want Jean-Philippe to wake up now, not after five years buried in some *selva* graveyard.

The music gets no clearer as she walks on. The flagstones tremble under her feet from yet another blast. The gust of air and smoke from this one is nowhere as powerful as before. Her lamp flickers but stays lit, allowing her to spot the next cell, which does not have a lamp in it at all. Soledad averts her eyes from the doorway—she cannot take the emotional risk of seeing another *lombuage,* recognizing someone she has no wish to see, someone she perhaps had not known was dead—though the ghosts so far have stayed in their territory, not permitting trespassers in either direction, allowing her only a glimpse through the intervening glass, like a prisoner led to the window for his wife to see he has not yet entirely disappeared.

There are ghosts, she knows, who would not respect the conventions and she has no time for these, no time for the exhausting emotions that such shades demand. She is beginning to lose confidence, beginning to doubt that a way out exists. She is beginning to shed, in her fatigue and various pains, the will to fight her way clear of Santa Karen.

The thought terrifies her and she turns her eyes right, away from the cell door on her left—and sees little flashes of light reflected on the yellow limestone of the right-hand wall. They must come from a spectacle more urgent and contemporary, to judge by its complexity and violence. Which means, in turn, they might offer her a clue to getting *out*. So she looks through the door, stepping back against the far wall this time, wadding the blouse against her teeth once more as if this would protect her from anything but smoke.

And looks through a window that is no window

And in that window a city is burning

She looks away, eyes streaming. She knows at gut level that this vision, if that's what it is, crawls with information. The information may cause her utter despair, but it might also show her Dolores.

She mops away the smoke-tears, looks again.

It is Bamaca, it is not Bamaca, the way the window, which begins like a black panel built fifty centimeters inside the cell door, is and is not a window. The rough rectangle frames a sky filled to bursting with smoke; black smoke from flames, a man-made brownish smoke meant only to obscure, and a grayish-yellow smoke that catches up to people and leaves them asleep in its wake. Flame has made free with this city; she sees the Slave Market burning now with white phosphorus, and giant buildings like the factories around the airport only much bigger than anything in Bamaca, shuddering under the magic blows of rockets, blossoming red and yellow and black.

The picture is full of movement. As the vortex of this motion draws Soledad's gaze she understands the first rhythms of the waltz danced here: how the giant choppers swooping in low circles are part of a broader plan, for they hew to the philosophy of the Mobile Operations in Urbanized Terrain squads, which is one of vertical mobility. Black-clad men drop fast as ceiling-spiders down lines from the great choppers, while gunners overhead lay covering fire from the surrounding rooftops, and pre-positioned snipers fire into apartments and other places they already know about.

In the tunnels below, in the sewers and adits surreptitiously bored under walls of garbage and ramparts of cars, paired platoons slosh through the fetid water, aiming for a *treffpunkt* in the air, on the middle story of buildings. Street control: they move block by block, neighborhood by neighborhood, taking a building on one side of the *calle* from above while the next one down, on the other side of the street, is stormed from the basement.

Far overhead, above the stealth bombers guiding their

rockets with wire and light, an intelligence jet glides in circles, mapping the district with infrared. Its vast computers
sort through every radio, cable, and Wildnet message, corre-
lating data so the snipers know where to fire next, the MOUT
squads where to divert a pincer movement or surround a stubborn building.

Back to detail: A huge bulbous vehicle, like a tank only
larger, sighs down a lane blocked by militia. It shrugs off
the blasts of rocketpropelled grenades, the cheerful fire of
Molotov cocktails. It blinds its opponents with lasers and
vomits brown-yellow smoke until the roadblock is at first
silent, and then invisible.

Giant figures wearing masks and hydraulically powered
armor rise like Teutonic myths out of manholes well in front
of the vehicle and sway off in different directions. They are
monstrous dancers in metal and high explosive who always
know the next step.

And they do know; Soledad repeats this to herself; they
know from data hidden in the music they hear, though she
cannot term what accompanies this obscenity of military precision "music"—it is *antimusic,* a collage of melodies she
recognizes just enough to gag at the use being made of them.
This bad music is not the intelligent plan behind the attack,
but it is a key to the whole because it is intricately wired
into a frequency being transmitted to every part of this battered *cruce,* in blared loudspeakers from the hovertanks and
choppers, in pirated transmissions to the Wildnets and to
sound systems in markets and warehouses and jagger bars
and brothels, in powerful downloads to street-corner vidpanels, to the jambooks directing what was once good music,
cruce music, Shift-shin and *Cumbia,* merengue and slapp,
streetfight and *lanto.* All gone now. They have researched to
death every frequency in this place, jammed them all with exact rhythms that first dampen, then invade the transmission
channels, until the only thing she can hear, all they can hear,
is antiharmonic: horror tunes, rodent rhythms—a multimedia
version of total war, a theme park devoted to jamming.

And looking up at the invisible sky, Soledad knows she was wrong in her earlier theory. No spy plane alone could do this. It is a whole web of far greater birds, a system of Teledesic satellites in low orbit zipping data back and forth, and a command center unrivaled in speed and sophistication. Only organochips and parallel processing could coordinate something so lethal and big as an entire combat environment, warfare suffusing most of a city. Only a system that big and fast could design both a frequency its own troops dance to and another one that slows the defenders; one harsh but logical music that directs its tanks and smart rockets, and one so delicately tuned that, well, *listen*—a couple of pieces of the *"Souche"* song. Except here the melody is corrupted into stupid fascist oompah-band rhythms, and the words, the lovely words Jorge made, turned into parody—

> *If my stomach was a dog (oompah,*
> *oompah-pah)*
> *it would* (disco rhythm) *eat itself up*
> *and then crap its own dinner (oompah,*
> *oompah-pah)*
> *in a place you would step in*

And how can you fight men who repeat such sick tunes even as they *break* every beat, sabotage every transition in the sweet medley of music that is the heart, lungs, and blood flow of the *cruce,* her neighborhood, her home.

Soledad retches. She holds her hands, first to her mouth, then to her ears, but it makes no difference. It's as if the bad music is being transmitted in ultralow frequencies straight to her biggest bones; it thrums her like a drum box; she cannot move fast while the corruption of it is going on. No one in the *cruce* can flee or fight with any coordination—she sees them, the *cruce* people, trying to escape her own perverted song and the corruptions of tune; trying to run through the streets to the fish market and its smell of eel, through the dark pre-Columbian alleys of Ensevli. They move as quickly as possible, men, women, and children hauling their gear in jury-rigged carts, gang members and grave robbers and men in half-familiar uniforms falling back, sometimes with a semblance of military order she would never have thought them capable of—but it does not work. They are sapped by wrongness. The armed bands fail to cover each other, they lose lines of communication, are surrounded or exploded or broken up into routed remnants. And the rest move slower than the bone-colored smoke being blown at them by floating tanks. The smoke builds around their ankles and knees, thicker and thicker, and the people move like sloths as the smoke rises. The smoke is so thick now as it hugs the cobbles that it resembles cement. They struggle feebly, and give up, because how far can you run when you are buried in hardening foam up to the thighs of men and the necks of children?

She has no breath left with which to watch this. Her vision is vague with tears and the increasing depth of smoke flowing between her and that nightmare doorway. The corrupt music has sickened her so badly that for all she can't breathe, she shuts off her airway and vomits, gasping out smoke and despair and spit and a couple of stretching strings of bile. She is doubled over against the cold limestone with an entire world of paralysis and devil-music happening in the room before her. Still puking, still trying to breathe, and somehow sobbing at the same time as the places and people that define her are pinned down and raped by a perversion of what she once made.

So helpless that when a squad of men, their bodies clad in tight-fitting black clothes, their heads in face-suckers, close in like giant bugs out of the smoke around her; when, after checking her for weapons, they twist her arms behind and frog-march her, still retching, down the tunnel in the same direction she had been going: she barely resists.

She even welcomes, in some sense, the inevitable brutishness of the male plan that now at last controls her.

How violence is the default option for them, she thinks;

how predictable the way women fail to resist and even become complicitous in the event, when the nicer plans and
prettier ideas they hoped would save them are revealed to be
defective, and worse, irrelevant.

———————

THEY TAKE HER TO a cell somewhat bigger than the others. The end wall is rounded, suggesting the shape of the
outer bastion. A single window, more of an embrasure really,
is set high in the curve.

A corner cell, no doubt, she thinks wryly, *for one of the
executive monks.* It includes a massive table of black oak. A
crucifix, black of course, under the window. Two chairs, two
men, flagstones, a vaulted ceiling, a pinch of music—not
good, not loud—nothing else.

Or so she reckons; she does not notice details at first. The
black-clad escorts thrust her into the room, salute, and leave.
The thick door slams theatrically behind them.

The two men waiting for her are also clad in black com-
mando uniforms. They wear pistol holsters of green webbing,
and lightweight combat boots. One is thin and of medium
height and wears a major's star-and-bar on his shoulder boards.
His face is pleasantly ugly, fleshy, capable of mirth. His
mouth is set in a half smile, his eyes are thoughtful.

The other is the man from the brothel, the one who
watched her window for so many days and nights; or someone who looks like him, she cannot be sure. Maybe F2 re-
cruits only men like him, people in their early thirties of
medium height and broad build and regular, quiet features.
He motions toward one of the chairs, a formal gesture.

She shakes her head, though her back is in agony and her
arm stings and she is breathing phlegm in and out and struggling to control nausea and trembling because the sight of
that burning city has sucked every atom of courage out of her
and every molecule of Soledad cries out to rest.

The watcher shrugs. The major leans over the table. That

is when she starts to register other details: a jambook computer with built-in bubble antenna, probably where that thread
of music comes from; a lightweight envirocam; a rank of
truck batteries under the table.

A tattoo, vaguely familiar, on the major's inner right forearm. It is a tapir, nicely worked in indigo.

Shackles, black from age, bolted at each corner of the table. Crocodile clips, shiny and new, at the brassy-frayed ends
of wires coiled beside the batteries.

So she was right. That is Soledad's first thought. She
ended up, like the conclusion to some boring Freudian
proposition, in exactly the place she fought most fiercely to
avoid—among the chambers of the Inquisition, the lair of
those gentle priests who approved the burning of everyone in
Xelixec on the grounds that because the images of Toltec
gods had been so deeply carved in the cliffs there they could
not be removed, the natives were not baptizable. The same
friars who burned Giordano Bruno because his idea of infinity was not as big as theirs; who made candles of stubborn
Jews all over Spain. What was it Jorge had said? He had said
so much in their short cohabitation. "Oh, they were really not
as bad as their PR," which is like saying vampires had their
good points. But he also claimed—he was talking of living in
Barcelona, under the prison of Montjuich—that they were all
the same: the cells above his house, the cellars of Prinz
Albrecht Strasse, the classrooms of the Naval Engineering
School in Buenos Aires, the barracks of Uranium Plant No. 2
on the Mangyshlak Peninsula. The mechanics of pain pathways, he pointed out, were identical in every case.

And she is certain this blankness in her must be the same
as the blankness in every victim who arrives at a place like
this, for how else do you confront the likelihood of your absolute reduction, through humiliation and agony, to nothing—
even less than nothing, to the very denial of that identity? The
idea being that you assume the identity of your torturer, in
order that he might see clearly, and by introspection, every
secret you possess.

"You have something to tell us," the major says in a voice that is neither harsh nor friendly but abstract and, above all, confident.

She stares at him, trying to keep her gaze level against the constant itch to cough, the neon background of terror.

"You know what you want to tell us," the major continues. "Is that not the truth, Mademoiselle MacRae?"

She can't help it, she has to cough. The effort breaks her stare. She tries to avoid feeling that this is the first in a series of defeats, because that will logically lead to imagining all the melodramatic details they will use despite or even because they are melodrama: the surge of current, the elemental agony when the cells in your own body begin to boil, the smell of your own flesh burning, the dry bruise of rape. Always worse, she thinks desperately. The image is always worse than the reality.

"No," she whispers, "no, I don't know." No, I have nothing to tell you. No, I will not tell you. The last two sentences not said aloud but thought, silently, to herself.

"Where Echeverria is," the major continues in that same casual tone. He taps a few keys on his laptop with one hand. He frowns, then rubs his knuckles. Purses his lips. "Where he goes when he is, shall we say, emotionally threatened, yes? You know this. You are his whore—no, let's be polite—his mistress."

He smiles. His eyes don't show emotion one way or the other. Soledad thinks, He is wrong; I am no longer Jorge's mistress, or whore. She needs to not think about that truth—it comes much, much too close to answering the question the major poses. However the fact that he is wrong in that first, crucial statement fans a minuscule cinder of hope in her.

They are *not* all-powerful. They do *not* know everything.

And like the spark breaking into flame in the bracken of the upper *selva,* as happens every fifteen years or so after one of the rare droughts, the hope spreads and makes flame of vast areas of her motivation. It becomes something different in the burning—not hope, but resolution: the intent to resist answering, for as long as she can, the major's question, and more; the resolve to shove away from her consciousness, no matter what the pain, no matter what they do, the information he seeks.

The major taps one key on his jambook. Rubs his knuckles again. He has arthritis, Soledad thinks, his hand hurts. To her amazement she feels a real, if brief, flash of sympathy for him. The major taps another key. The music, with its uncut rhythms and poor syncopation, increases in volume by a notch. The static lines and diagrams on his thinscreen shiver, and disappear.

The major smiles. He likes it when a tap of his finger has such an immediate effect.

Soledad clears her throat, looks away. The black crucifix catches her eye. To carry through on her resolutions she needs to ignore not only crucial data, but the F2 men themselves, and their undoubted proclivity for this kind of work. She must graft instead onto the anger already existing within her, the despair that was born with the sight of that city burning; the sense, strong black and vibrant, that she knew what that wee Galilean was about when he hung up there between two thieves: not that there was really hope or a cosmic second chance, except in metaphor, but rather that the immensity of pain in human life logically demands a denial different from the one elicited through torture. Because the existence of such misery must cancel, not only your fool's notion that there really is some loving order to this world, but also your pretentious notion of self, *unless* it be via empathy with other victims of torture, through common suffering and pain and death. Because sacrifice through compassion is the only way, in the end, to achieve that unity which human consciousness both rejects and needs. This was the greatest insight of jisi yomo—so Haddad had muttered once. And if it's not strictly true that the word "jisi" is a corruption of "Jesus," rather than the Manopani for "Panthers, crying," it should be. Because jis' brings on that same Jesus reflex, that quest for ultimate empathy, although in painless and more socially acceptable fashion.

That jambook is doing funny things. The upper body of a man is framed in the oval screen. He wears a suit of the type that is popular with American tourists, a shirt half blue, half white, as Yanquis wear them. He has a rim of gray hair, a semblance of ears, a wedge of chin and neck that defines the limits of his head. Where his face should be, however, there is nothing, or rather, there is too much: billions of shifting pearly pieces of data appearing and disappearing too fast for the eye to track: one hundred thousand features melting into a shifting absence of face, an absence so odd it is funny, so funny it is terrifying, so terrible it is numbing, so numbing it hurts.

The faceless gringo.

The music has increased in volume yet again. Now, once more, she recognizes the chaotic grab bag of dyschord and cheap sampling. She knows too well by now the logic that seeks only to kill fine rhythms and distort sweet harmonies like her *"Selva,"* or the theme song of that city being crushed and burned to painful death in the cell down the hall.

And these wrongnesses combined part her brain briefly from her intestines, which try, mercifully without success, to void themselves.

The major says something. Soledad drags her eyes away from the featureless Yanqui in that screen. She shuts her ears to his evil tune, though that is more difficult; it is all strange and horrifying, but irrelevant to the drama just beginning here. Like an actress whose career depends on one first-night performance, she needs to concentrate on the role at hand.

"You will *have* to talk to us," the major repeats. "It is not a matter for discussion."

Soledad stupidly looks at the ancient table, which she now notices has a gutter running down the middle of it, for blood she assumes, for the vomit and shit and piss of bodies pushed beyond the limits of will.

"Oh, no." The major feigns horror. "Not the table. We would never use torture on you. What do you take us for—Argentines?"

The watcher laughs, politely.

"Of course," the officer continues, "we *could* use pain, and it would work. Oh yes, believe me. However—" He leans forward to stare into Soledad's eyes. "I have heard your music. I think I know you—does that seem, I don't know, presumptuous? But I believe you have a capacity for shutting down, for going away in your mind. That is bad for hypnosis, bad for physical—persuasion, also. It might take longer, yes. And the mess—" He looks at the gutter and waves one hand, almost effeminately.

"You may not believe me, but I don't enjoy this kind of situation. It's a job, and I will do it, but it forces me to dehumanize myself, ever so slightly." He rubs the knuckles of his bad hand, not knowing he does it. "I take on, with every scream, a very thin layer of, of a monster.

"When I go home," he adds, not looking at Soledad now, not looking at the screen either, "I feel a little bit more disconnection from my children. And my wife. No, I don't like this at all.

"But why," he continues, straightening, almost smiling, "why rub two sticks together, when you have a Zippo lighter? Why kick down a door, when you possess the key. Do you follow?"

"You have a gift for metaphor, Major Uraba," the watcher says, just south of sarcasm.

"Thank you, Lieutenant." The major stares at him for a beat or two, glances at the screen again. "I have said enough. You have said enough also, Lieutenant, using my name as you did. We'll discuss that later. Bring the other one in now."

The watcher opens the door behind Soledad. Sharp footsteps, a dragging sound. Two of the black-clad soldiers support someone so thin and small in relation to the men that Soledad imagines, for a second, it is a child. When they wheel in front of her she sees it is in fact a small woman, dressed in the smock of a Santa Karen patient. Her hair is gray-black and full; the rest of her appears ancient. Her hands are clasped around a small *bombo* drum, the kind they use for therapy here.

Soledad for no good reason keeps looking back at the woman's face, which is deeply lined but somehow over-loaded with emotion—although all of a sudden Soledad is no longer sure whether that emotional charge comes from the woman or from herself.

The woman's eyes are too big and wide, always too wide, for her face. The shape of her small, determined chin seems ridiculously familiar given she is a convent *loca* and no one Soledad remembers seeing in Bamaca before. Her mouth also is wide, so broad that the ends of it disappear into the heavy sagging folds of her cheeks, *the way my mouth does,* Soledad finds herself thinking, *or the way it will when I get old.*

Just like that, the bottom drops out of Soledad's ability to make things happen differently. The great suppression of hor-ror, of pain, moves aside just as Major Uraba suggested it should. Her blazing determination, quenched, steams fruit-lessly. Her inner structure without warning is filled with gray vapor, just as her lungs still burst with bitter reek from the smoldering convent.

"Maman?" Soledad whispers.

"Very good," the major says, "you recognized her. She doesn't look *anything* like her pictures. But blood will tell, eh, Lieutenant? Blood will tell."

"That's right, Major." The watcher no longer sounds sar-castic. He sounds as though he has slotted into his assigned role of straight man, even fool. He nods twice. "That's right."

The old woman, who was looking downward at the flag-stones as if in reaction to the upward lift from her two escorts, glances at Soledad. Her eyes have trouble focusing. They are pink-rimmed and watery. Their irises are the deep brown Soledad remembers, full of possible love and also potential ruthlessness, and all the egotisms of hurt. It surprises her a little that with the intervening years, the different layers of her mother's eyes should not have altered in any significant way.

The major, the two soldiers, the watcher are bit players now, removed from proscenium to wings by the power of this script. The F2 does not matter in this second. The cell, the Inquisition, the armed destruction of her *cruce,* even that obscenely combusting city down the hall and the corrupted sounds associated with it, no longer signify.

The principal action now is she, and her mother, and Soledad's own tune, a single note of pure sound rising in her ears, raised in self-defense against that noise from the laptop. Or maybe it is not self-defense, maybe it is an act of purest creation, a single note to preserve who she is against losses past, present, and to come. It is the first pure, unwavering note from the *pito* flute, A-minor, that marks the instant before dawn in the opening movement of *Selva.*

"I have to know," Soledad says, and coughs. "I have to ask—"

"Isn't this—" Major Uraba interrupts loudly. "Isn't this where I'm supposed to say, 'I ask the questions here'?"

The lieutenant smiles.

"Why did you leave?" Soledad ignores the major. "Where did you go?"

Irena says nothing. For a few seconds a horrible doubt pervades Soledad, that she is wrong, the victim of a con. They searched and searched for a woman of the right age with some resemblance to Irena MacRae, and how does this compute in terms of what F2 seeks now? What could possibly motivate the expense and logistics of such an operation?

The old woman's eyes widen, as if surprised by her own decision to talk. She licks her lips and says, "Listen to me." Her voice is paper-thin and clear at the same time, like the west wind coming through the screened porch at Glen MacRae, Soledad always thought of it as F-major, a breeze the exact pitch of her mother's voice. Now her doubt vanishes for good.

The major nods. The lieutenant walks around the trio of two men and prisoner. He takes a sponge from his pocket, reaching from behind Irena, and wedges it between her jaws. Then, opening an army bandanna, he expertly knots it behind her head, securing the sponge in place.

The soldiers drag her to the black table. They toss her drum to the floor. Then they lift her, gently, and lay her on her back. She does not resist. They pull her arms and legs straight. Her limbs are pale and thin, with varicose veins and the splotchy marks of dermatitis.

They open the giant manacles, which seem far too large to confine wrists as thin as those, but the mechanism can be tightened with a key and the watcher does so, cuffs and attached chain clinking musically as the wormgears turn.

Irena looks placidly at the vaulted ceiling. In Soledad's ears, the *pito* dies, as it's supposed to. What happens next, though, was not part of her score—for the bad tune never stopped its gradual climb in volume, and now it is very loud. The image in the jambook screen has not changed, but whatever program is in control has injected combustion into the sound track. Snaps of burning wood, cracks as rock and brick break under tremendous heat. Soledad squeezes her eyes shut and grinds her fists into her ears. The firewall will break, it's all she can think about; the horror of that burning and the malevolence of that music and the psychic focus implied in the presence of this old woman on the table; all those elements will crack her protection. And then it will be exposed, tiny and round and shining like a pearl, the information they want, the one detail she must forget she knows; the answer to a question she must not even think of for fear it would open a channel through her resistance.

She hears movement and—it's a reflex of survival—opens her eyes again.

The lieutenant pulls a short blade from his belt. Soledad

gasps, involuntarily. He slices open the front of Irena's smock, revealing breasts that are wrinkled and dusty-looking and sag to either side. He picks up the crocodile clips and attaches one to each nipple, the nipples Soledad sucked on as a baby (for a week only, Maria Gisela said, it was too hard for her, which is why they hired Maria Gisela in the first place, but at least she *tried*)—

Irena cries out, once, as the first clip springs shut.

"Maman," Soledad whispers.

The major looks at her encouragingly.

The lieutenant glances at the major. The major nods.

The woman's body arcs as if a rope had been attached to her navel and winched half a meter in the air. Her eyes pop, her head slams from side to side. The bandanna slips sideways and a continuous hoarse rattle escapes the sponge and the woman's clenched teeth, overcoming the buzz of a capacitor at the table's edge.

It lasts two seconds; then, as if the rope had broken, her thin buttocks slap back on the black oak and her head flops to the right, away from her daughter.

Soledad feels as if the electric current had burned through her body as well. Her feet seem welded to the stone beneath her. Her breasts ache fiercely. A smell of urine rises from the table. Her mother says, clearly if hoarsely, "But this is nothing, Soledad. I am so used to this—this kind of treatment. They said it would make me better."

"She was in the state hospital, in the capital," the major adds conversationally. "Then they sent her here with the other hopeless cases. They are big aficionados of electroshock in the capital. But not the way we use it. Lieutenant—"

The invisible rope jerks tight once more. The woman's nipples are erect as if in passion, and seared red around the clips. The rattle is deeper, more agonized. Her mouth is spread all the way open. The rictus unfolds her cheeks at the corners, where bubbles of saliva appear and pop.

It lasts longer this time. When it's finally over, Soledad's tear ducts are producing water like industrial pumps. Her chest and throat hurt with the pressure of it. Her nose is full of liquid. In the blur of tears she senses the major nodding at his subordinate and cries *"Stop!"* in a voice hoarse with strain and mucus.

"Where is Jorge Echeverria?" the major asks.

"I will tell you. I will—"

"Now."

"No." Soledad mops her nose, her mouth, her eyes with the sleeve of her blouse. She can see better now. The major stands with both hands behind his back, at ease. Her mother lies still on the great black expanse of table. The faceless man, the Yanqui in the laptop screen, shines and shimmers like one of those African "flowers" that turn out to be made of uncountable, tiny, multicolored beetles.

"No," she continues in a voice just strong enough to make itself heard over the jambook. "This is my bargain. I will talk to my mother. And you promise, if you find him, you will not hurt him."

The major shakes his head, doesn't even bother looking at her.

"I cannot promise you that. It is not up to me. You know that, Mademoiselle MacRae."

Soledad nods. She does know that. She is thinking of Pytagoro as she does this, how he places bets in dominoes, how he bluffs when he plays the important games—how he withholds what he knows, until it's time.

"Then you will let his daughter go. Dolores, she is nothing—"

"I have no orders about his daughter. But it's the same thing there. I cannot make promises that are not mine to make. Lieutenant—"

"No!" Soledad throws her hands toward the major histrionically, like an Edwardian actress, but she must not let him run that current again. "No—only just let us go, me and my mother. I will tell you." Panting as if she'd had to sprint to get this far.

Major Uraba chews something small in his mouth. His

eyes shift—he is looking at the computer. The evil music pauses for a fraction of a second.

"You're joking," the major says, and he sounds genuinely surprised. "Your mother can't function out there, Mademoiselle MacRae. You would do better to leave her here."

Soledad remembers what she must face on the Outside, even if these torturers live up to their bargain. Uraba is probably right, her mother would not survive.

What she says is, "That is not the point. Maybe my mother will decide to stay. But it will be her decision." Thinking, as she says it, What a *cruce* thing to say, this irrational obsession with choice in a world that includes the kind of pain Uraba dishes out.

The major makes a quarter turn to the right.

"You have two minutes," he says, and checks his watch. "Time them, Lieutenant."

Soledad goes to the table. She touches her mother's arm. It is astonishingly cold, for one who has so recently been overdosed with electricity.

"Maman."

The woman shudders. The smell of urine is strong. Liquid plinks through the gutter to the floor. Soledad's tear glands continue to produce their own liquid, which she mops once again with her sleeve. She reaches for the right words, can't find them. Ends up where she started, with the only real question she had.

"Maman, where did you go? I looked for you—"

"I know."

"You knew?"

"I—heard." The old woman turns her head so she is looking at the ceiling, closer to looking at her daughter but not all the way. "But I had found—a refuge. In Los Altos.

"It was so hard for me," she continues. "I knew you were there. Such a little girl. But not as hard as the other—the alternative, I mean." She grunts, clearing her throat.

"See, you were hard, deep down; I thank God for it. Like your father."

"I don't understand," Soledad whispers, leaning over the table. "I was fourteen." The face beneath her seems alien now, unrelated not just by blood, but by race and species and history. Her pity, the pickled love and missing of the girl she once was, alters for an instant to raw anger. She wants to grab those scrawny arms in her own strong hands and crush them, break them if necessary, to get at the truth. It has been so long in coming, this truth, and she has only the two minutes Uraba gave her—only one minute and a few seconds, now. "I still don't understand *why*."

"But it *is* why." Irena licks her lips. The bubbles are drying to a cream-colored scum. "You could not know the real torture. Not this—" She moves her arm, and the manacles clank against their chain. "Oh, I never knew if it was really what they said. A disease."

The ghost of a shrug. "Does it matter? Or just the torture of a way of life. I was in jail there, Soledad. In that finca. So much worse than . . . I was going mad, you see. And when I finally burned the new studio; yes, I burned it. I used kerosene and cotton, it burned very well I thought. I knew I had to go away. To protect you. To protect myself."

"And Papa?" she asks quietly. "What about my father?"

"You two were always covering for each other," Irena said. She let her head loll leftward briefly. Soledad had to shut her eyes. The woman's gaze was so full of venom and love that it would change her forever if she accepted that combination. "You *always* were, you two."

"Time," the watcher says.

"No," Soledad calls despairingly, "just one more minute!"

"The electricity," the major calls, "Lieutenant?"

"The City of Boats," Soledad says, very firmly and clearly, and takes a step backward, her hand rising to her throat as if to cut off, too late, the words it just let pass.

The major turns, slowly, until he faces her.

"Go on," he says.

"That is all I know." She whispers it so low he asks her to repeat it. He smiles when he hears what she said.

"We will find him. It will take longer, and I guarantee that your mother will not survive the process. These electroshock treatments—" He clicks his tongue disapprovingly.

"Ha-ha," the watcher says.

Soledad's hand is tighter around her throat. The pain halves the intent in her—to tell him, not to tell him. At last it's a dearth of force in either direction that finally allows the real drive to surface. And that drive is a crude and utter inability to watch her mother arched again like a violin string against the bow of electric current.

"The *Fumiste,*" she whispers. The major leans close, looking at the lieutenant. "It's a smuggling launch. Nestor Prin's. Next to where the *Fumiste* is moored is a sailboat, a sloop—I don't know the name. It belongs to a girl at Lo Pano."

"And?"

Her windpipe is bruised from the grip of her own fingers. She squinches her eyes shut, as if this might insulate her from the hard fact of what she is doing.

Against the dark of her eyelids she watches a small and vicious movie, of Uraba's men moving in on the sailboat, and finding only the Lo Pano girl. They shoot her instead of Jorge, leaving her in a heap on the cabin floor, her blood reddening the bilges. A brief and nasty joy rises within her, and is quickly swamped by disgust.

"And that's where Echeverria is? On the sailboat?"

Something in her—some lost DNA strand from Francis MacRae, quickened perhaps by the mention of Jorge's name— forces her to open her eyes again. She must do this with her eyes open. She will watch herself betray the man she loved, the city she loves, the people who are her friends.

She nods.

The major straightens. He glances at the jambook. He grasps a half-sucker, places it on his head. The image of the faceless Yanqui blinks and vanishes. The music of nightmare fades more slowly.

"I promise you," Uraba says, and Soledad will never be sure afterward if he is talking to her or to someone on the wireless connection, "the city will be the better for this. Now it is split, you see—gone schizophrenic and *mad*.

"But we shall make the city whole again."

He starts to issue a series of orders in neutral, short, jargony phrases most unlike his way of speaking with her.

For a few seconds she feels lonely, cheated of his attention.

The feeling disappears almost as fast as the Yanqui did.

———————

SOLEDAD STANDS BESIDE HER mother in the same position as before. Over the last hour the major so thoroughly sucked all available power in this cell unto himself that they all look to him for guidance now, even in matters already concluded.

"While the torture continues"—Soledad recalls a line from *The Vultures of Estremadura,* Jorge's second book—"the victim holds the power." He was referring to his marriage but it is a good metaphor, it works in all directions, even the obvious.

Irena lies peacefully, eyes closed, on the table.

Soledad lets her hand fall from her throat. Partly because of that grip, her windpipe feels unequal to the task of forming speech.

But the torture here is finished. She should be happy about that.

She feels instead as if her value, by any form of reckoning, has been reduced to zero; not so much because of the shame of what she has done, but because the major so clearly classified her as "unimportant" the instant she told him where Jorge was.

Which is why he might even stick to his bargain. How much of her worth in this *cruce,* she wonders, ever really came from herself, and how much from association with

Jorge? God help her, she can still find it in herself at such a stage to be jealous of the man she is helping to kill. *Was it jealousy,* she wonders, *that allowed me so easily to tell Uraba what he wanted to know?* She remembers her little fantasy of the Lo Pano girl's death.

For an instant, she feels like she's going to throw up again.

She leans over, grips her mother's shoulders. Using all the forces of her own disgust, she pulls Irena to a sitting position.

The major, his eyes hidden by the silver of the half-sucker screen, doesn't react. He continues to issue orders as Irena, fighting a nearly uncontrollable trembling, tries to stand up, and the watcher, moved by some maintenance level of humanity, summons two guards to help.

As they falter out the door, the F2 major is still focused on what he sees on his half-sucker screen, murmuring the sharp intimate phrases of combat like a man seducing a future lover.

———

IT TAKES A LONG TIME, even with the guards' help, to negotiate the stairs and floors of the undamaged portion of Santa Karen. The explosions grow in power and the air takes on further palls of smoke, though never in the proportions Soledad saw when fleeing on her own.

Finally they reach a tiny cut in the massive walls. It ends at a small steel gate. The watcher speaks into his radio. Then he takes out a key, unlocks a giant padlock, swings a bar out of its joists, and pushes the door open.

Bright light washes in.

Soledad, squinting, glimpses the northern part of the Bahia de las Animas. It's like a curse, as if the gods wanted her to see immediately the fruits of her betrayal; for this perspective overlooks the City of Boats. Only she can't see it, even when the snakes of smoke curling around the convent slide aside to reveal that portion of the bay. Almost all of this district of docks and rafted craft is shrouded in brown smoke from burning, and black from RDX and petroleum fires. Maybe they've already sunk that woman's boat, Soledad thinks, quite dispassionately; maybe everything I told them was irrelevant.

But if they found the Lo Pano woman, then surely they would have found Jorge as well?

She turns toward her mother. The two guards have disappeared. Only the watcher remains, presumably to make sure they leave and don't let anyone else in. She clears her throat.

"Come on," she croaks. Her words are rough as the croak of a horror movie ghost. "We'll—we'll find a cellar. Or something." She coughs. The saliva she spits out is gray with the smoke she has breathed. Tugging at her mother's smock. "Come *on*!"

Irena doesn't move. Until this moment she has kept her eyes cast down like a shy novitiate, looking at the floor, looking at her little drum, which she retrieved, unbeknownst to Soledad and at Exu knows what physical cost to her own shaky constitution, from the floor of the major's cell. But now she looks up at Soledad for a few seconds before dropping her gaze again.

"I can't come," she says softly. "You know that. You always knew it."

"Please," Soledad rasps, "there's no time."

"The soldier was right." Irena's voice is even softer now; calm and very clear compared to her daughter's. "I don't belong outside. I belong here." She waves weakly at the thick walls.

"But why did you come this far? You must not be sure—"

"I am sure," Irena interrupts. "But I am weak. Nothing but weak. I wanted to be with you . . . only a few minutes, really."

"*Stay* with me, then." Soledad coughs again. The spasm doubles her up. She leans against the wall until it passes. The turbine-scream of a jet makes speech impossible for a further ten seconds.

"Be with me more," she repeats. "Be with me always."

"Good-bye, Soledad." Irena reaches out to touch Soledad's cheek with shaky fingers. She has to look to see where she puts her hand, yet she does not look up far enough at the last to see her daughter's eyes.

Irena turns, and starts shuffling back down the passage-way. And Soledad does know, after all. She knows her mother is right. The mass of Irena's first decision, the momentum of all the intervening years, are much too great to cut with the single blade of such an encounter.

That is what she knows.

The girl in her, the one who still, in some sense, in some angle of her mind, tramps around the high country dressed as a Gypsy and living off the alms of strangers to continue her search, has no such certainties or belief. *"Maman!"* she screams, *"s'il te plaît!"*

The old smocked woman does not turn around. She shuffles to the central tunnel, brushing the wall for support, then totters left, the way she came.

At which point the lieutenant, anxious about leaving the secured portion of Santa Karen vulnerable in this way, grasps Soledad none too gently by elbow and shoulder, shoves her into the smoke and disaster, and slams the postern shut behind, making the walls of the fortress whole once more.

———

SHE LOSES TRACK OF where she goes. The smoke, though not as thick as it was in the convent, and irregular by virtue of wind and the breath of explosions, is very dense and black when it settles over the alleys she flees through.

Even in the upper part of Bidonville, where the damage is not bad, she has trouble finding her way around the maze of stack-dwellings and workshops and the intervening dirt roads. She had started off running pell-mell down the nearest alley, away from her terror and disgust; but soon she slows to a trot, and finally a furtive lope.

This wedge of Teton Mountain has turned into no-man's-land. A few looters trundle goods out of smashed workshops, looking around fearfully for *guaqueros,* who would shoot them on sight if they caught them. One of the thieves, running hell for leather out of a jag workshop, drops a pack of triage spindles. Soledad picks it up, attracted as a child would be by the scarlet foil wrapping, and stows it without thought in the big pocket of her blouse.

Three times she spots a group of older people playing dominoes as if nothing unusual were going on.

But everyone else has fled. The explosions are so massive that she has to put her hands over her ears, it has become a reflex by now, and stay clear of some of the more precarious tenements, which have a tendency to fall in the backdraft. Yet she can tell the shells are not falling close, but well to the north by the City of Boats and southeast in the Slave Market. Sometimes, incomprehensibly, they fall south, near the volcano.

Before the explosions, the hollow rush of bigger shells from tanks, from the frigate.

Sometimes, the lighter rush of mortars and rifle bullets from *crucista* positions.

Her strength wanes. The constant coughing wears her out. The accumulation of discomfort from her swollen throat and pounding head, her burned arm and twisted back, the small cut in her foot, slow her further. After ten minutes she stops in the lee of one of those thousands of tiny raised gardens that perfume Bidonville. She collapses in the alley dirt, in the shelter of a lovingly espaliered avocado tree, and curls up with her forehead touching the rough wood of the garden's bulkhead.

When she closes her eyes she doesn't see Irena, or Dolores, or the shape of thoughts. All she discerns is the after-image of smoke coiling and drifting, inside as well as out. Through some therapeutic trick of consciousness, what she is most aware of is her catalog of physical irritations, and the way the cool humidity of the alley's dirt soothes them, like a balm.

She lies there for a long time. She has lost all motivation to do anything else. She stays there too long. The explosions grow louder from the south, and this has to be a bad sign.

She opens her eyes once, watching the smoke drift; watching, between a couple of intricately guyed shack towers, in the holes the wind makes, how busily the choppers hover and jink under the volcano's cone as they ferry troops and mountain howitzers to the army's beachhead there.

San Isidor. It is the one place no one ever figured the army could pass.

She closes her eyes again, and resolves to keep them closed. Chooses not to move. An avocado, shaken loose by a mortar round exploding two alleys away, lands on her cheek, and she barely stirs.

Eventually a mixed group of *guaqueros* and emerald poachers, falling back from positions behind a line of metal workshops that have literally been run over by tanks, comes across her sleeping form. Most of them think she is dead and ignore the corpse, but one of the *guaqueros* is a pal of Diego, Dolores's ex-boyfriend. He recognizes her and looks closely enough to notice she is breathing. He grabs her elbow, just as the F2 men did, and pulls—this is no time for the niceties of first aid.

Reluctantly, she looks upward, takes in his face, his *guaquero* attire.

"Soledad," he is saying. "Soledad?"

She opens her mouth to answer. No sound comes out.

"Soledad," he repeats, "come on!"

The urgency in his words leaves her absolutely cold. To move now would force her body to change shape, and then her mind would have to keep track of that, and who knows what might slip through the filters of a mind busy with movement?

Soledad.

The *guaquero* is strong and determined. He is yanking at her now, which she hates. The smoke before her eyes is parting, which is also not what she wants, she has no desire to see clearly again, yet he pulls again and sideways till she is forced to react—

TWENTY

—AND SHIFT IN THE same direction, if only to keep him from pulling her arm off.

She opened her eyes, in pure reflex. The brain didn't like the body to move without checking first for possible dangers.

And absorbed difference. She should have been growing familiar with this process, of course, yet the embarrassing innocence of her waking up seemed to be fashioned anew every time; and now everything was altered from the smoke and shelling and that dusty exhausted platoon of *guaqueros* and poachers.

The here and now was cool and flat with electric light projected against dark interior. A poster of Winston Churchill in the background; in the foreground Stix's face, so close to her own she could smell the savor of QuikViet shrimp rolls on his breath.

"Pereira—" This was what her lips wanted to say. It was something from her dream, one of her dreams, that finally had made the leap to consciousness. At any rate, she remembered where she had heard that name before. Hector Pereira was the real name of Doctor Fernsehen. Jorge had referred to it early on, when she had first come to Bamaca.

Which implied—because, on the submarine, Randy said a psychiatrist of that name was consulting for BON—that Fernsehen was now working for the enemies of the node; for the men who destroyed her *cruce*.

The fact, if fact it was, seemed quite irrelevant right now. Stix touched her left cheek, then her right. Smoothed azure against the sheets. The linen was damp on her bare skin.

"Jorge" was what she actually said, or whispered, rather. "Jorge." The tears welled out of her eyes. She could tell she had been crying for some time, not only by the dampness but by the fact that no obstacles existed in her throat to try to restrain her sobs.

"Ô Jorge, qu'est-ce que je t'ai fait?"

Stix's eyes were wet as if he'd been weeping also. She noted this almost impersonally. Her mind felt dully sectioned off, compartmentalized. Perhaps this was the effect of the strong dreaming she did, it shut off affect in the compartments for the here and now, and let emotion run free in the story she remembered. That was a powerful tropism and, like a big locomotive, could not be stopped on a dime. When Stix leaned over and put his arm around her neck she felt a hint of anger because in her dream he would have been a stranger. She also experienced the physical opposite, a hearty ripple of lust that loosened her from scalp to toenails.

The dream-Soledad, annoyed that she could be distracted by something as casual as sex from the end of everything, ordered her to go rigid.

Her body did what it wanted, though, which was something she'd always liked about it; raised her left hand and stroked Stix on the back of his neck then down his spine, and not whispering "Jorge" anymore.

She shut her eyes and saw the *cruce* again, the ripped tapestry of smoke and occasional sky behind the melodramatic foreground of Bidonville burning. She was grateful for one thing, and this was a pleasure the brain firewalls could do nothing about: Her lungs were clean and free of smoke. She smelled no conflagration in California.

The sound of chaos remained, low but insistent, like an aural hangover from the *cruce*. Which was worrisome. It meant that, even as she stroked Stix's back and grew wet because of his presence, she might at any moment slip back into sleep, and Bamaca; find herself in Santa Karen again, with Major Uraba and her mother, and Dolores still gone—

She looked around her. The triple windows that connected Stix's bedroom with the outside were filled with deep black. She was certain, for some reason, that dawn was not far off.

Another day in Oakland, then. But this one felt different. It was raw and fresh with possibility, with plan.

I have to go back; I have to find out what happened to Dolores.

It was as if the idea, spawned fresh only yesterday, after the warehouse concert, had required time and dreams to become whole. Like the Islay whisky her father loved, which in order to mature needed to sit in Amontillado casks already pickled in wine from a warmer, sweeter climate.

The sounds did not stop. They were radio or pushwall noise. The trio of envirocams was aimed at her from the overhead brackets, as usual, but their red lights were dull and disconnected: not running. Something that had sat heavily on her sense of trust and ease in this node suddenly got up to leave, and left her lighter into the bargain. Only once before had she woken up in this room without seeing herself on camera.

The noise came from a wild-speaker in this room. It reverberated against the glass that separated the sleeping cabin from the control room.

She listened harder. It was tough to get a fix on it but she was starting to make out rhythms that stopped and started in different times, and broke off in the wrong places—unresolved chords, most of them minor but making no sense overall. Like a Virtix soap-opera sound track played backward.

She stopped rubbing Stix. The air remained clear, yet once again it was hard for her to breathe. Though he was leaning against her, her chest felt as cold as indifference. A chilly blue light played against the wall facing one of the ancient naval workstations.

Her stomach filled with a nauseous certainty.

"It is starting," she whispered. "At last."

He nodded, chin nudging her collarbone.

"I'm sorry," he said. "It's why I woke you up." He shrugged, glancing regretfully at her breasts, which no longer were covered by blankets. "There are things I have to do now. You should get ready, too."

He adjusted his bathrobe and left the cabin. Soledad sat up in the water bed, which as usual wallowed and jiggled beneath her. She was growing used to the instability of it. She was growing used to the nausea that greeted her waking. Calmly, she slid off the bed's rim, put on her blouse, and walked down the length of the control area to the washroom, ignoring everything except what her body had to do at this point. There, she vomited in a sink, neat as a cat; urinated, and washed up.

As her nausea subsided the sounds regained their previous importance in her ears. She looked at herself in the washroom mirrors. Her mouth was wound tight by the winch drums of her cheeks, her facial bones stood out with strain like a skull's. It was a familiar expression. It was the expression she wore when she was scared.

Her cheetah tights still hung on a hook beside the shower stalls. They were wrinkled, and torn in three places from traveling. They were not as warm or strong as the navy pants she had borrowed but that didn't matter; it was time to return her borrowed gear, time to put on what was hers.

She blew through the washroom's double doors, noticing more now. Stix held the half-sucker by its throat mike, talking low into the pickup as he stared out the factory window. He grabbed a spring roll from a Styrofoam box and took a bite.

The ancient workstations, their screens visible from this angle, showed nothing but gray-blue blizzard, though the volume of bad music coming from them was already perceptibly stronger than it had been a few minutes ago.

Someone spoke behind her. She turned, startled, because no one had been there before. And no one was there now in the strictest sense. But the architect's wallscreen showed Zatt in his bent wheelchair, parked in a cramped and unfamiliar room, his lap deep with blankets and copies of *Feather,* his fingers on the ever-present jambook.

In a secondary screen wired to the wheelchair's structure, the boy's raccoon worked a Polis thumbstick.

Zatt was looking at the jambook's thinscreen. He hummed thinly, a tune that was more rhythm than melody. The definition on his jambook screen was so good, it appeared to be a perfect image on its own.

In the screen, Soledad lay rigid on Stix's water bed, talking fast and obsessively in the clicking whir of Lanc-Patua, her cheeks blue with tears.

Her hair was spread over the pillow like the map of a flooded delta. Her shoulders were bare. The blankets had slipped down, exposing her left breast, its nipple small with cold and fear.

She had woken up naked here only once, and that was five minutes ago.

The humming stopped. "There it is," Zatt said, "hold it." He hit a key, and the image in his laptop froze. "*That*'s an anageism." Pause. "She said that? Yes, yes, exactly." He listened to the half-sucker again. "Yes, but they didn't *have* screens like that."

The nausea came back, but it was not, it did not feel like, morning sickness. What it felt like was, she had been filmed by these men so many times, over and over, reproduced and freeze-framed and fast-forwarded and reversed in slo-mo, that she was finally getting motion sickness, a kind of jet lag of the psyche, a gut revulsion to the unnaturalness of having her image, her precious, unique and analog self, repeatedly converted to ones and zeros, and back into image again.

She realized now just how comforted she had been, how much reassurance she had found, in the fact that the cameras over that water bed had been dark when she awoke this morning. The disappointment, the sense of betrayal, the sense of weight coming down on her again as she realized they had merely been switched off, perhaps seconds before she regained consciousness, were twice as heavy as a result.

She walked up to Stix, shoulders back. He looked up at her, a half smile on his lips, which melted away as soon as he saw her expression.

"You filmed me again, didn't you?"

He glanced at the pushscreen. Shook his head. "Soledad—"

"*Isalop*. Bastard. *Sassenach!*" It had been her father's worst insult and she used it now, grinding the hard Scots "ch" into the roof of her palate. Her emotions were being twisted deeply enough that it seemed she had to reach way back for curses potent enough to match them.

She stamped her foot. This, too, a throwback, ridiculous in a grown-up. Wiped her cheeks with one clenched fist, looking away from him.

"I *canna* trust you." Her voice was better this morning, she did not have to cough or clear her throat every three words. "I should know by now, yes? I cannot trust *anyone*. Because they are all—" She searched for the right word in English. It was important that they understand what she was saying. "They all betray you in the end."

Except for her mother. Irena MacRae, the first traitor, had not betrayed her at all. Irena had performed the ultimate act of loyalty: she had tried to preserve her daughter from the mother's instability, not only by committing herself to Los Altos Hospital for the Insane, but also and especially by sacrificing her daughter's kind memory of her in the process.

It was the hardest kind of sacrifice, Soledad thought. It was the opposite of what Charlie Rickle had done on the Wildnets, in that tacky ranch house in Berkeley.

For if you deliberately destroyed memory—made abominable the "life-box" others held of you, that story of yourself they treasured in their mind—it had to be a far more lasting and effective destruction than dying or otherwise disappearing from their lives, even if you did that as well.

She wondered, without worrying too much about it, if that was why she had blocked for so long the memory of what happened in Santa Karen: to preserve a convenient hatred of her mother—and also to perpetuate the easy image of herself that went along with it. Soledad the victim. Soledad the loyal friend. She was glad when Stix interrupted that train of thought, blurting, "Soledad, look—"

But she was not ready for him to explain himself. She had too much explaining and reassessment to do on her own.

"Did ye film us fucking?" she asked. Her voice was working perfectly, she could use every modulation and hiss that had ever been available to her. "Were those cameras on—" She thought back, could not remember, what a *fool* she had been not to check. "Did you film us so that auld man"— she stabbed a thumb at the wall-screen—"he could wank off watching the hochmagandy? Play it back, and back, and back *again*—"

Stix closed his eyes. He waited. She waited. Her fists hurt, they were clenched so hard. She felt like hitting him. She had never hit anyone in her life, not even Miguel.

She did not wish to think about Miguel. She did not want to think about Santa Karen. Concentrated on keeping her fists tight at her side. Finally he said, "No."

"Liar."

He opened his eyes.

"What do you want me to say? I can't prove a negative, Soledad. But I wouldn't have done that." He winced, as if it hurt to utter what he was about to say. "I'm in love with you, Soledad. Or starting to be—I guess that's more accurate, really. It's not a—an excuse." He sighed, and looked at the wall-screen once more. "I just wouldn't do that. I did turn the cams on, but much later, when you started talking in your sleep again."

She followed his glance. In the twisted wheelchair, the yellow-skinned cripple watched the square of video clip that showed what went on in Stix's control room. Looking at them. Listening to them. Soledad felt an acute wave of homesickness for the *cruce,* for a culture that did not have to record everything all the time, did not have to monitor and play back and "save" itself in cold electronic memory; that allowed real memory to live, in its own unique process of degradation and accommodation, of remake and forgetting, choosing or changing the apparent facts to suit the climate and temperature of an ongoing human life, the way a well-built house would weather and soften and be repaired to fit the changeable landscape it was built for.

It struck her then that this concept of recording everything and transmitting it back and forth was a dangerous one, a lie, because even an envirocam could not capture the totality or even the greater part of the lives and events it filmed. Only a human mind could come close to doing so. And perhaps the process of memory, for that mind, was one that *deliberately* distorted images and sounds to fit more accurately the gigantic mass of other data it had accumulated about an isolated event or person—to fit, also, the complex and ongoing tale of the human doing the remembering.

Soledad sensed she was on to something important here, something that would change forever the way she thought about herself, about people like Irena, and Jorge; about everything. Perhaps someday she would have time to truly think about this—to parse what pushwalls and dynamic audio added to a town meeting such as the one she had "witnessed" yesterday through the medium of playback as she walked the node's main streets. Perhaps then she could also discover what it took away, in terms of a single human's ability to control a process that moved so fast, and was so amenable to quick cutaways and edits. She got a visual, truly vague, of a Scandinavian library—of herself, much older, with glasses and stretch marks, writing in a red-checked notebook. She had no time to follow that fantasy any further.

"Soledad." The voice from the pushscreen.

"Still listening, Doctor Zatt?" she asked him. "Still spying, no? In this node, ye live on the Flash in your own way, I think. It is a smaller Flash than Liteworld's, but—" She shrugged her shoulders. The sickness in her stomach was pure puce anger and it had not gone away at all.

The man did not stir. His eyes hid behind refracting lenses.

"It has nothing whatever to do with personal feelings," he began. "It has to do with trying to salvage this movement, which is an attempt—"

"You think I saw something," Soledad interrupted. She ran her fingers through her hair, twice. "You think I saw the future. You are such bairns, such children. It was dreams of Bamaca, *dreams*—I saw nothing there I did not already know."

Zatt touched a key, and a graph popped into view on the wall-screen, beside the thumbnail of Stix and Soledad.

"It's not a theory," he said, and a cursor moved up and down on the graph's livid colors. "These are data from Livermore, and there"—the graph altered subtly—"from the Teller Lab in Berkeley. All from the last three days, all complete to exactly, uh, seven minutes ago, because they're updated online and realtime. They are recording the average incidence of the P-272 particle, which Farnsworth postulated was the catalyst to the opening of a Bell-Everett event."

"Zatt," Stix warned. He was looking alternately at the factory floor and at the naval workstations, where the snow was gelling into images now, but so briefly and fitfully that nothing definite could be seen in it; just an apparent attempt, on defined frequencies, to assemble control from madness. Zatt nodded, but did not speed up his discourse.

"You see those spikes?" he said. "Way off the average. Up in the seventy, eighty million range—it's usually forty, fifty mil in the deuterium tanks. Now look at the time, the dates. I correlated them with the tapes we made. And they correspond *exactly*."

"Exactly to what?" Soledad asked in a calmer voice, though she already knew.

"To when you dreamed." Zatt slumped a little, staring at the graph. "Specifically, to about 4.8 seconds before you dreamed the anageisms—the bits that were inconsistent. The weaponry they never used in your country, the stuff they haven't even used here yet. The burning city in that cell you saw.

"It was *our* story you saw, Soledad. Or one of the stories that could happen." His voice now hit different ranges, like the spikes in his graph, making him sound at once satisfied and depressed, tired and energized. "The one, it appears, that's going to happen."

"And that shows you what, exactly? Nightmares, that's what I saw. Things I extrapolated, you know, fantoosh? Things I made up."

"It shows us what they are going to do," Zatt insisted. He hit the keyboard and the graphs vanished. "It shows us how they are going to do it. You never saw what you dreamed before, not in real life."

Soledad thought about what Zatt had said. It was hard to believe that her dreams had room for anything besides the emotions she had felt in Bamaca. Right now, for example, the memory of the last one was too fresh. That burning city had injected tremble and terror so deep in her muscle fibers that she knew from experience it would take a long time to go away entirely. The exhausted, defeated group of *crucistas,* the filthy bandages, the warm-barreled rifles—she could still feel the sting of the avocado on her cheek, the strain in her arm where the *guaquero* had stretched it. Though that might have been Stix, pulling in real life.

Whatever real life meant, at this point.

"Maybe you'd better tell Will," she grunted, still thinking of the *guaqueros*. They and the emerald poachers and some smugglers were the ones who did all the fighting in Bamaca. Just as only Navigators and that street gang—and Stix, oddly enough—had participated in what could be called resistance here, during that first and telling probe. "If what you saw is the truth, then shouldn't he know?"

In the wall-screen, Zatt looked away.

After a pause he said, "Will discounts everything you saw, Ms. MacRae. He still thinks that you're some kind of agent provocateur, sent here by BON.

"I sent him a vidclip, anyway," Zatt said and held up one hand as if to ward off her anger. Which made Soledad reach for that anger, in reflex, only to find it had subsided, mostly, without her knowing. "I'm sorry. He'll see your tits, of course, but it's too important to wait for editing."

Soledad smiled. She didn't mean to. Zatt's words had triggered a train of thought that should have made her frown. But she couldn't shake the incongruous image of her bare nipples moving at the speed of light through the node's Wildnet links, carrying, if Zatt was right, far more important data than erectile tissue normally could bear. She turned to stare at the battleship gray computer terminal to her right; it was a primitive reflex, sprung out of associative magic, as if she might catch a glimpse of those electronic breasts passing through every computer in this enclave, like a face glimpsed on a cybernetic express streaking through a local station. And the smile slowly died on her lips.

"Did you get hold of Molly?" Stix was asking.

"I couldn't raise her," Zatt replied. He was back on his keyboard again. "She's not at the diner, or the *Dubuque*."

"Anyway," Stix continued, "I got drive-train problems on the Creeping Jesus, I'll never get it ready in time. And Mojo needs to get on the tug and she does too, before—" He stopped. "Soledad?"

She said nothing, did nothing. In this culture—it was a continuation of a thought previously interrupted—you did not have to. The eye always took its cue from the nearest pushwall, or jambook, or interactive monitor.

Stix followed her gaze. He looked long and hard at the navy computer, at the silver-blue chaos on its ancient screen, which had slowly morphed into a mass of smoke.

At the bits of flotsam and driftwood in that gray smoke-river which, as the camera panned and pulled focus—there was always a strong directorial hand in these pictures, she realized now—resolved into the tops of black sedans, with chunks of circuitry or steel welded in symbolic shapes on the hoods. Sedans whose drivers lay still, heads slumped against the wheel or on seat rests or door panels.

Where the smoke-river shallowed she discerned knees, or

buttocks, or shoulders, bent the way humans folded when they had lost awareness.

And the river moved less and less, for it was not a river, just a gray expanse that had been pumped through these wrecked canyon walls on which people had once fastened gardens, proscenia, catwalks, and balconies.

And finally the river, too, was immobile, as if its molecules had altered, bonded, set into something as solid and unfeeling as concrete. The camera dwelled on that scene for a moment—gray stone, strapped bodies of darker gray—then tracked up the black walls to lose itself in the fog that confused everything with its similar and limited palette.

"Nimitz Avenue," Stix whispered. "Shit, if that's real, they didn't waste any time."

Soledad's stomach was still upset, and the sight of that waking nightmare did not help. She did not have to look at it, was going to look away, but the trouble with Yanqui videos was that the production values were good—they knew the secret to holding your eyes, and the secret was, Keep things moving.

And the gray was changing, becoming darker, while at the same time streaks of warmer colors came through, until suddenly the camera broke out of a bank of mist and swooped low over a fantastic chaos of palms and thorn trees and alleys and stucco walls painted blue and orange and yellow; Roman-tiled roofs, many of them built into teetering towers and extra floors; the whole climbing like a suicide wave of details up a steep volcanic hill, trying to flee the much greater folly of red-orange fire and its dark smoke billowing and roaring in so many places the helicopter, or whatever the camera was mounted on, had to bank and climb and dive continuously to avoid the walls of conflagration, the curtains of smoke being snapped into greater fury by La Loca.

Because yes, it was La Loca; yes, it was Bamaca. She kept catching glimpses of familiar spots: a far-off snapshot of the Walled City, a corner of the fishing harbor, and—her lungs froze—a lazy shot of a terrace, with Ionian columns supporting a grape arbor, a thin bridge connecting that roof to one of those stacked-dwellings next door, a roof topped by two VW chassis.

The camera lingered fondly on the terrace's tall windows. Their long curtains billowed as fire engulfed the entire structure, Jorge's building, hers. The apertures pumped out sparkling embers, splinters of tiny ships exploded free from their confining bottles, gray ash of guitars like the remains of music; blue ink boiling, penholders aflame like tiny torches. All transubstantiated into a river of reek that flowed through the smudged windows of the study, her piano room, into the tapestry of greater smoke and flame that was the sky over the dying *cruce*.

Macaws, trapped in their cages, screamed as they were consumed.

She turned away and sank into a squat against another workstation, holding both arms against her stomach. Stix dropped his keyboard and crouched beside her. His arms circled her shoulders, protectively. She did not mind, she barely noticed.

"Soledad," he urged, "let's get you outta here."

She shook her head, more in commentary than refusal. She was still wired mentally into what she could not remember; did the *guaqueros* manage to sneak her out one of their safe routes before everything burned? But Stix could not know the answer to that question.

"You *have* to get out," he insisted. "Just like last time. It worked once, we'll get you on the *Razzle-Dazzle,* doesn't matter if it's late, you know I always run late, things work out."

"Are you," she croaked, "are you coming, too?"

"Not now—"

"Then I'm not going."

"I'm gonna come later," he said. "I have a ton of things to do first."

"I am biding," she insisted, and looked up at his face, taking in his pudgy cheeks, the soft umber of his eyes, not in present affection but in storage for when clear emotion would again be possible. "I do not leave anymore. Not people I—I could love.

"I do not love you, Stix," she quickly added. Seeing him wince a little, she thought wryly how vulnerable people were that, in the midst of massive onslaught, she could still hurt this man with a hung sentence. "I *could* love you," she continued.

"I do not want to, though," she added fiercely. "I am *so sick* of leaving places that are good for me—where I fit in. Och, do you understand? This place . . ." She stopped, suddenly confused, remembering another vow made only a short while earlier: to return to Bamaca and find Dolores.

Surely that meant, logically, that she should escape this node, make her way as best she could, back the way she had come? The borders would be a lot easier to negotiate going south.

She closed her eyes and saw at once, in the screening room of her mind, that window of Jorge's piano room vomiting sparks and charred papers. Her head felt crammed with cinders and sparks as well, each a half-consumed emotion, an unfinished thought, like this one: If Fernsehen was advising BON, and he believed the Bamaca *cruce* to be the subconscious twin of the Oakland node, and if she somehow was allowed to come here—an agent provocateur, as Will thought, albeit an unknowing one—*then what in the name of Exu had been her true role in this story?*

If she really was an agent provocateur it might answer an earlier question, about how she had gotten out of Bamaca when almost everyone else had been trapped: because F2 *let* her escape, so she could flee north and carry the virus of Bamaca's way of death to this northern *cruce*. Which meant—here was a side deduction, popping up like an unexpected message from the subconscious—that whoever first directed her to Oakland had also been an F2 agent. She knew someone had directed her, but the person's name was just out of reach, slightly beyond the scan of her memory.

She squinched her eyes tighter against that obscene music. Everything used to be so much simpler and cooler in the old days. When the emotional temperature got too high, when the psychic wind blew too peart, she simply threw her clothes into a bag, hitched up the Fourneaux-Dallapé, and left.

And she never thought about it much afterward, at least on a conscious level.

Her father. Jean-Philippe. Miguel. Jorge. She had deliberately mimicked her mother by leaving, in order to punish others as Irena had hurt her, in order to hurt herself most of all, because children always took the blame and punished themselves, it went with the territory. This was a psychiatric chestnut, one she had long ago accepted and, using her self-awareness as a crutch, blithely ignored from then on.

What was new here—it had started in Bamaca, when she climbed up Lo Pano and made that fatuous and, in the end, dangerous speech—was her refusal to follow that pattern anymore.

She shifted in Stix's arms, wanting him to stop hugging her, dreading the withdrawal of touch. He shifted, too, looked longingly at his jambooks, but did not let go.

Yet was staying not still part of that pattern, in a way? Because even if she was rejecting it instead of automatically going along, she was still following, by antiphony, the melody of initial hurt, and the pattern of flight that devolved from it.

The one thing she knew was, she was tired, so tired, of being in a situation where she had to choose. She had slept well in Stix's arms last night, but now she felt exhausted to the point that even lying against this enemy computer dangerously taxed her reserves of energy.

The machine throbbed against her spine. Its noise sliced through her thoughts. The beat was stronger still than when she had returned from the washroom; more cretinous, more repetitive also. People howled like jungle animals in the background. An explosion, not near but not too far either, shook the workstation and the concrete floor it stood upon.

She struggled to her feet. Stix helped her up. She held on to him, dragged him away from the terminals, back to the bedroom.

Stix gently pulled her fingers off his arm, and let her slide against one of the test-tank stanchions to the ground.

"I got to go now, Soledad," he said. "When things start, they're gonna send squads around, they might even send one here, 'cause of what I did yesterday." He sighed.

"I'm not gonna force you to leave, if you really don't want to. It's not what people do here."

"Stix," she said, looking up at him, and suddenly her eyes were hot with the tears wanting to come, "I don't know what to do. I don't want to leave you. I don't know where to go."

"But you don't," Stix said softly. "You don't leave people you—you care for. Or places, even. If you really love them, in some way I mean, they always stay with you.

"You know the Fernsehen," he added. "People are only the stories you make up about them." He slapped one hand with the other fist. "I really have to get out of here now."

He opened the door, which Soledad had deliberately shut, and went back into the control room. And the music came in stronger. But even the surpassing evil this music sprang out of and embodied did not affect Soledad as it had when she was next to the workstation.

Part of it was the greater distance, but part of it was the sense Soledad now had of going beyond her fatigue, through layers of soul exhaustion she did not even know she was capable of, and breaking through into a sort of colorless empty space where by the grace of utter indolence she was exempt from the laws of gravity, from any strings or attractions no matter what their source—as warm and clueless and floating as the tiny fetus that lay in her uterus, upside down or right-side up meant nothing, all that counted was the steady gush-thud of his mother's heartbeat and the certainty, built into his very structure, that this heartbeat would never go away.

I am a mother now, Soledad thought. I cannot go away

anymore. She saw Irena's face as she'd seen it last, shadowed in the gloom of the postern tunnel. She recognized, in the same part of her that held the baby, that her mother also had felt this way. Perhaps the night after the studio burned she had stood over Soledad's snakewood bed, looked down at her daughter, and thought the exact same thought, the meaning Soledad sought, the understanding that she was trying to avoid, no matter how many liars had used these words before, the truth: *I will never leave her in a real sense.*

And that, Soledad realized, changed everything:

Because when you cast aside the words and recriminations, the who-left-whoms and who-stayed-behinds, what mattered was only that you aided, whether by your presence or your absence, the ones who needed help.

In Soledad's case, the people she had decided to protect—the baby, and Dolores—were those in whose interest she must flee Oakland, in order to best assist them. Out of range of the explosions and whatever nightmare horses of fog and murder were going to gallop through this node in the next few hours.

She would have to take Stix and Molly with her in the way Stix had described, as stories that she could grin over, or cry about, depending. It was the pride and grief of these enclaves that the inhabitants demanded, and were accorded, the absolute right to do the wrong thing at any given time.

Another explosion came, much louder. Gray dust hissed from the ceiling in dry slides. Light glowed a muddy orange, then dimmed against the Churchill poster. WE SHALL NEVER SURRENDER. The glow was so short and so faint, filtered as it was through three soot-encrusted windows, that Soledad could never be sure if it was a resurgence of flame that prompted her to scramble to her feet. She had finally, utterly lost what little ability she'd had to tolerate flame.

She slid open the door and ran back into the control room. Dust shaken loose by the blast haloed every light. The wallscreen in which she had seen Zatt earlier was a wash of colors in the haze. Stix, oblivious to the echoes of that second explosion, stood with a half-sucker lowered over his eyes, tweaking the thumbstick on his jambook, following whatever was happening on the top half of his screen.

She came to a stop behind him, coughing from the effort and dust. He raised the visor, and looked closely at her face. "Good," he said. "You're outta here." She thought she traced a line of disappointment in the set of his eyes.

She looked away. And, as if the shift in vector that came with decision unlocked another dammed channel of her memory, she had a brief but diamond-clear glimpse of Haddad handing her the fire orchid after her Lo Pano speech—Haddad saying, news of what she'd done would someday spread as far as a *cruce* in California.

Haddad, in Pytagoro's on the day everything burned, had told her the lie that led her to the convent, and the reluctant torture of Major Uraba.

The discovery did not seem very important and, finally, she looked back at Stix and nodded.

"Good," Stix said again. The word came high and strained. He shut the jambook and slung it over his shoulder. "Let's boogie."

———

THEY TOOK THE ELEVATOR. She held back, didn't want to—they had cut the electricity first thing, at home—but he looked at her with a kind of gentleness and said, "Don't you get it? With all they've invested in pushscreen propaganda, last thing they'll shut off here is the juice."

The factory floor was thick with new dust. Some bricks had fallen. And the machines were mostly gone. Only the giant hand and the Creeping Jesus remained, looking confused and abandoned in the absence of their mechanical fellows, amid the confusion of workbenches and racks and wayward shadows and the first rays of dawn light touching the inside of the old torpedo workshop.

She said nothing, though she felt a rush of sadness that reminded her, of course and inevitably, of Bamaca, which was the last place she had felt anything like this awareness of loss. Her moron heart had already got used to this place, to these surreal machines. Self-love was at work here, she knew, the missing of herself-in-safety, a refuge that would shortly be gone except for what she managed to preserve in her memory—in her dreams.

This time, instead of going to a side door, Stix limped straight to the factory's huge central gates. She realized she did not know why he limped, had never asked. She had assumed, at some early point, it was something his stepfather did to him, although Will was the one who physically confronted the man.

Perhaps there were some scars that no one should know the origin of.

One of the gates had been slid halfway open. And the rest of the machines were lined up outside in the lightening mist: a green toilet-rocket, the screaming navy man, the horse-carcass flinger; trembling as their various motors turned and the different programs on Stix's jambook goosed the retard on one and tested electrical servomotors on another.

He was already opening the carcass-flinger's engine cover, peering at a gauge, kicking a compressor. Such an American, Soledad thought. When things fall apart, they try to solve everything by tinkering with the machinery.

She watched them for a few seconds: the giant cannoli, the target-dragon, the scale model of autoRodan. The sadness she had felt a minute ago took on colors of real affection now, because she understood these mechanisms. She understood the side-pulled logic of intricate belts and gears all driving and spinning—always late and a bit off-center—to run something that served no useful purpose; the ludicrous movements of his figurines and skeletons; the great violence and noise of them, that they ended up turning in odd directions, flinging squid, crashing into their brethren, squirting cream; above all, the great reference made to themselves, by themselves, through exaggeration, surprise, and pratfalls.

Like any good machine, only facets of their creator.

She stood braced against the ache in her hips. Her eyes were dry but she could not look at him. Maybe he felt the same, because he came up behind her, slid his arms under her breasts, and leaned his chin on her shoulder.

"I'll see you afterward," he began, but she shook her head, thinking of Molly's words, of how dangerous the orgs had gotten. She did not want to follow through on this thought, and what she said was, "No, please, don't give me promises. I don't want promises—I only want you to say what you said before."

"Before when?"

"That we don't really leave each other. When you said we go with each other?"

"I was trying to get you out of here," he said. "It was only half true."

"But it's the half I want."

"All right, Mystery Woman," he said softly. "You never leave the people you love." His arms pulled so tight around her gut she felt afraid, suddenly, for the baby, and turned around, wrenching her back, feeling his body against hers. She kissed him, quickly, on the lips.

"The tug," he prompted gently. "Scram."

"I am not sure," she began, "that I know the way—"

"You know, Soledad," he interrupted. "You always knew."

He let go of her and turned back to his machines, going straight to the carcass-flinger, which clearly had a timing problem because it juddered and shook unevenly so that its noise sometimes coincided with the disjointed beat now wafting from co-opted subwoofers down the alley.

Taking a screwdriver from his pocket, he slid the top half of his body under the juddering chassis, and out of Soledad's sight.

After a couple of seconds of watching his workboots, which were cracked along the instep, she turned and walked quickly down the street that led to the harbor.

———

STIX WAS RIGHT. She did know the way. The main alleys and thoroughfares of the node had, unbeknownst to her, been seared into her neural pathways over the last couple of days.

At first the alleys seemed eerily quiet, as if the fog contained a factor that squeezed people out; trees waving lonely from balconies, abandoned boxes by loading docks. So many had left, she thought, and was glad.

The pushpanels were still active, would remain active, even when their people had gone. Many were still busy with node concepts: doomed bridges, the leaning faces of dead kings, a chorus in the bass warehouse singing Orff. But a number now also played impostor images jammed onto node circuits by overpowered or stolen servers: a crowd of bright-eyed Yanquis simply laughing, at first in normal fashion, then more and more obsessively; a shot of a prison, with a sign reading OAKDALE FEDERAL PENITENTIARY/FEDERAL BUREAU OF NATIONALIZATIONS/VIOLATIONS DEPT; gates slamming shut; an aerial of the node itself, an ultraviolet mosaic of cool blue and green colors with clusters of giant red things grappling onto four hot spots on the perimeter—surely Photoshopped, she thought. And things far worse, shots so fast-wrapped they registered only in broken-off pieces: a woman torn apart, something lovely and violet crushed in shit, something alive and in so much agony that it wished it were dead. The concept of blindness. A raindrop of violet loneliness so pure and distilled it could kill a city. A bar of music sick and cold and loud enough that if it were ever played it would permanently freeze every atom of air on the planet.

The sound on these vidpanels was low in the first two alleys Soledad traveled down. But she was well aware of growing volume as she approached the avenue of blue cadmium that led toward the underground sub base, sound that might have been real or manufactured but that was in any case discordant enough to be more frightening than the much louder explosions coming regularly now from the direction of the Wall of Autos.

With no warning, an altogether different noise grew from overhead, to the left, and she froze because it was the *"Souche"* song, or rather the variation—she recognized it immediately—that they had improvised in the bass warehouse here. But of course it had been stolen, of course the Dead had poisoned it, sampled its pure notes into a crass horror-movie theme, sullied it with plumbing-product jingles, made it stink with noise recorded in a slaughterhouse. She shrank under a balcony thick with St.-John's-wort, catching in the corner of her eye a black-brown thing with twin turbines, bat-like wings, and a poke of envirocam under its fuselage. The noise grew for a second to intolerable pitch, then faded as the drone disappeared over the horizon of buildings, and was gone.

Putain, she hated this. She pulled her hands off her ears. They were trembling like an old woman's. Fifty meters away from the avenue an odd smell touched her nostrils, something metallic and sweet, a flavor pleasant on the outside and filthy within, like the bathroom disinfectant from a freeway rest-stop she thought. It set her coughing so hard she had to stop.

When her coughs subsided, she noticed the color of the fog in the avenue had changed, gone slightly russet among the folds of gray that rose and fell with the sough of wind along the avenue's blue axis. What she saw among those folds—by this point it came as no surprise at all, rather as something almost welcomed, like the left-hand harmony for the melody you played with your right, a Yanqui mirror-image of that flight down Teton Hill—what she saw was people laboring mightily toward the harbor, away from the mass of workshops. Fathers pushing children atop bales of marimba or crates of computer spindles; hipsters struggling in wrong shoes; TeeDees dragging chains of broken communications gear; Kundurans in cloaks and caps that might hide their deformity outside the wall; women with strollers, clutched cats, caged hamsters—while, like a countercurrent, chopped black Impalas and Crown Vics crowded with Putas and a few squads of Navigators and the occasional Proto-Panther

moved toward the growing smoke, toward a sudden reflection
of flame that lit the fog from within, until the explosion fell
in on itself and the only light left was the cyanide glow of
co-opted vidwalls and the indigo of cadmium, and the sparkle
of lamps and vidscreens and candles still lit in the forsaken
warehouses.

That, and impossibly delicate fingers of roseate light that
pointed like the fingers of a god out of an invisible high place
and played among the refugees and Putamadre jalopies.

A roar of small rocketry tore the cacophony from close
by. One of the Puta cars shuddered, smoked more than normally, and rolled to a stop in a cloud of azure dust. People
scattered, not the way people normally would move from fear
but rather as if they had lost the conviction of their actions
and were going through the motions, slowly, as in Tai Chi.
Seeking comprehension in the parsing of time.

A mother pulled her child into the shelter of a doorway,
casually, and sat down. It took her fifteen seconds.

A man ran with such lack of interest that he did not pick
up his feet out of his own path and tumbled comfortably to
the trash and cobbles to lie there in the cadmium, watching
the fog. A Putamadre raised his Glock, then stared in disbelief
at the pushwall beside him, where Will Grammatico's face
appeared in precise digital relief—Will with an SS *TodesKopf*
Division cap on his head and a thousand tarantulas crawling
in and out of his mouth. The sound track played, simultaneously, a football song crammed with meaningless obscenities
and a *Marseillaise* mangled by firehouse bands.

The Puta's gun fired anyway, into the air.

The fog shook as if something big had run through it.
There had to be cause and effect, but it was neither clear
nor demonstrable at the end of it why a Navigator hung still
and upside down from another smoking car. The digitalized
face of Will jumped from pushwall to vidscreen, following
the now-disorganized Putas and Navigators as they took off
down different streets. Someone screamed, not in terror, but
as if it were called for, something the director insisted on.

Even the gang members in their casual discipline moved slower and slower as the russet gas took hold.

Soledad turned, and moved back the way she had come, slower than she wanted to but without much lag between decision and movement. From this she knew that the gas had not dissolved deep into her bloodstream.

Another drone passed overhead. She barely noticed. The air looked cleaner in this direction. For a few paces her sandals seemed very heavy, as though filled with sand. As soon as she reached cleaner air—she could taste it in her mouth, the sweetness gone, the fog tasting only of water and metal and untended plants and garbage and oil, like the rest of the node, and it was colder too—the gap between what she wanted and what her body was capable of started to shrink. She trotted to the next alley, turned right, then left, running now, progressing at right angles toward the bay, toward the smaller entrance Stix had used the last time she had been on *Razzle-Dazzle;* toward the sub tunnels where the sleeping gas would not yet have penetrated.

She held a vague chart in her head, a shifting plan that allowed her to flee knots of explosion and chopper noise and gas smell while circling nearer to the base, but she did not know the node well enough to avoid trouble entirely. Crossing one alley, she glimpsed an entire MOUT platoon in operation, men in gas masks clutching silenced .45s as they rappelled from olive choppers.

Identically clad soldiers bursting out of manholes were pulled like sorcery up thin lines to windows above.

In the middle, a bulbous black vehicle sat on a cushion of air. It was a hovertank covered with snouts and radomes. Its speakers blasted Shift-shin in such a way that the sound was not only discordant and ugly but also timed to stolen images on the flexscreens protecting the hovercraft's skirt: digital composites of Mojo scratching his toes and Zatt drooling over glossies of touch-lovelies—timed also to the back-and-forth rhythm of the two MOUT squads now advancing, one after the other, the first leapfrogging ahead up the warehouses and workshops and hydroponic gardens lining this street, then halting to provide covering fire from rooftops and doorways for the second.

And then, when the street was clear, climbing back aboard the choppers and tank, and ratcheting away into the mist.

No hope, she thought, shrinking back around the corner of the alley. Nothing could resist an attack from people who manipulated rhythm with such ease. Not the crowd grouped around a Hoffaist pastor wildly waving cashchips to pay off Jesus and avert this doom; not Stix's squid-flinger, lying still amid a circle of stink bombs it had been throwing, black marks of fire smudged across its machinery; not the knot of weed-pirates and smugglers standing in clean fog only a few meters from the secondary entrance ramp to the submarine base.

They closed ranks protectively when she approached. Faces both hard and hopeless, angry and cowed. One of them stepped aside so she could see what they protected: a body curled on the crumbled asphalt; a rucked-up apron, a jagger's tunic.

Dungarees, half-laced workboots.

A long blond forelock.

Soledad walked into the circle.

Molly's face was pale and peaceful and still. Her eyes looked at the fog the way people did when they looked inward—as if she had been calmly trying to trace what the projectile did between when it made a neat purple hole in the left-center of her forehead, and when it exited in a mess of mauve shredding on the other side of her brain.

"She said she would see me later," Soledad said, turning to the man who had let her through.

The man did not reply, only stared at her, free of empathy.

"Molly. That's what she *said*."

Soledad had no idea why she was saying this. She did not reject the fact of Molly's death. She did not discount the danger of a sniper's lurking even now among the rooftops from where he had drawn a bead on Molly. She could not overcome her astonishment that Molly's words, her voice and intonation and tone, could be so big and real in Soledad's brain, while the woman who had felt and spoken them lay with her own brain turned to pudding, leaking out of holes in her head to the asphalt at their feet.

"You never should have come here," one of the weedpirates, a female, muttered.

"It was thanks to you," a young man said.

"Stix was just trying to impress her," the woman added, "with that fancy bird."

A third man completed the thought. "It gave Will what he needed. A reason to start shooting. And now look what happened."

Soledad stared from one to the other of them. Their words had not gotten through to her. It was as if she had lost her ability to understand English in any meaningful way. She gasped for air—once more, she had forgotten to breathe. She knelt beside the diner chef and touched the rivulet of purple liquid that ran from the hole in Molly's forehead, thinking, It makes sense that our blood should be purple, if our tears are blue. But what she really felt was a deep loneliness, because Molly had given her pie, and now Molly would never make dessert for anyone again.

Then she got to her feet and wiped the purple onto her tights. The convenient monomania of escape was back upon her, like an obsessive friend; someone who replaced uncertainty with doubt, hope with action, a drug. She had truly lost the habit of it while she felt safe in this node.

She wondered—it was a stray thought only—if that small lowering of her refugee's guard was what had allowed her to dream about Bamaca in the node.

But she had not been in the node so long that she had forgotten how to flee when necessary.

In any event, she recognized the habits of escape, she even welcomed them. There were no difficult choices involved in being a refugee, and thus no moral dimension. The single decision left to you was simple: run, or be caught.

She walked fast down the ramp, through the hatch, and into the seaweed-flavored world of the underground base.

———————

AFTER THAT, IT WAS almost easy. The occasional vidscreens in the sprawled tunnels furnished just enough light for her to make her way.

What was more, someone was paying attention to the bad rhythms those MOUT soldiers used as the guiding logic and EKG of their attack. Because node techies had defended this part of their Wildnet with cybernetic antigens, or perhaps they had reconquered this sector, to show a whole series of Polis environments where naked children used wands to create patterns of light in tower rooms. The structures were reflected in weather that kept an invasion fleet (long metal boats like red birds) beating futilely outside the harbor wall.

Also, clips of node spindle workshops, and a Thanksgiving feast in the engine factory, and a Hawkleyite school, and an Afro-Peruvian combo doing the third movement of "*Souche*." There was even a clip of herself in the bass warehouse, crying so hard as she played that the ivory on her Hohner was lightly blued. To see herself thus did not surprise her. She knew very well how addictive "*Souche*" was, even to others, and she found herself humming the third stanza, against the tearing in her lungs that was the effect of the russet-gray sleeping gas.

> *ah but we have our ships*
> *our midnight trains, our jets*
> *to show us what we've lost*

She passed the sub pen she had first seen when Stix hauled her in the spiderbike along this route, and was afflicted by a massive and totally unexpected wave of nostalgia for that time, only four days previously, when Molly had been mixing whipped cream and the node was new to her and full of possibility.

> how dark the volcano's cone
> from such a distance
> how perfect the circle of this harbor
> how much you loved me

The music gave her courage and also a rhythm by which to twist her footsteps around heaps of junk. A blue light appeared down-tunnel—she walked faster, thinking it was the tug, then slowed. The light was plainly in motion.

> a thousand leagues away

(the song would not die quietly)

> warmed by a foreign wine
> finally
> I remember

As the light passed before a vidscreen she discerned the bizarre profile of Zatt's twisted wheelchair, with its jury-rigged keyboards and monitors, and the fat cripple himself, hunched as he drove his rig in fast-forward. She hung back for a second—that hovertank had impressed her, the way they caught Will and cartooned him on the protective screens for all to see. With the intelligence and resources they seemed to possess, might not the node's enemies have made a facsimile of Zatt himself, and sent it out to add god-knew-what infernal dimension to that twisted plan of theirs?

But she heard a snatch of muttering, and humming that was not her own. It was the sound the yellow-skinned cripple gave voice to when he was performing a mundane task and thinking about something else.

So she sprinted as fast as she dared over the algaed surface of the ramps. Caught up with him at a crossroads, on the

other side of a bulkhead she was sure was close to the pen
where the tug was moored. He started violently when he saw
her, and slewed his machine into a ridge of rubble that had
washed from a tunnel opening to the left.

A deep rumble of diesel was audible from here. The tug
was indeed not far. They said nothing to each other. She was
out of breath anyway. He threw the electric motor in reverse,
and when the chair jammed on debris, she hauled it clear.
Both of them focused totally on the diesel, the short-term
goal down the tunnel before them, so they did not hear the
scrape of equipment, nor notice the figures that slid, spinning
slowly, from an opened hatch at the tunnel's top and dropped
noiselessly to the concrete behind them.

The first was slim, the second anything but. It braked its
fall with a mechanism that whined briefly, hit the ground with
hard boots whose crunching sound caught both Soledad's and
Zatt's attention at the same time—he flicking to a backward
video shot, she whirling—catching a brief view of a gleaming metallic giant and a tall, thin soldier on the ground.

A couple more giants rappelling down from the hatch to
block their escape.

Two of the giants simultaneously popped flash-'n stun
sticks that filled their ears with noise and their eyes with
acetylene.

Soledad fell back instinctively. Zatt caught her round the
waist and hauled her with surprising force across the painful
bars and softscreens of his wheelchair, into the padding of
magazines in his lap. He jammed his engine throttle against
the stops. Soledad could hear nothing over the ringing from
the stun stick. All she could see was what the magnesium had
burned into her retinas: armored men, the same ones as she
had seen in that cell in Santa Karen. Even in that split second
she recognized them with certainty—the jackal eyes of infrared night goggles, the snouts of chemical warfare masks,
the laser half-suckers. And there was more, these American
monsters were all equipment: chest packs of grenade launchers and flamethrowers, belts full of shaped charges and

grappling apparel and door-slammers, plus Kevlar padding and minicams so they could see 360 degrees and still absorb the unexpected fire.

In a way, it was nothing new. What was surprising—what shocked her more than the stun stick—was the tall black-clad MOUT captain standing hipshot beside them. Because, though she looked very different in an SAS jumpsuit and combat boots; though she carried a silenced .45 instead of an outmoded handbag, and her face, instead of being heavily made up on one side and not at all on the other, now was uniformly gray with camo paint; yet the captain was a mestiza, and her features were those of the electronic hooker who had offered Soledad a short-lived job in the haptic arcade in San Francisco.

Which penciled in a couple more factors into the equation, but there was no time for that now. Zatt's wheelchair might outrun armor-restricted nightcrawlers: it could never evade a fit MOUT officer.

In any event, Sha'Oprah was not going to bother racing.

"Yo, *sugar.*" The voice carrying well in the tight concrete tube. "Give ya till five, and I blast the crip. One, two." Zatt's wheelchair hit a chunk of rubble and lurched sideways. It scraped into the wall and stopped.

Soledad, with a heave that made her back burn, staggered off the chair to her feet.

"Four, *what*? Spread out, flank positions—"

Motor sounds came from the side tunnel.

The nightcrawlers swiveled, and kneeled in firing position, bringing headlights and laser sights to bear on what looked like a giant section of sewer, a huge tube of yellow-white over half-hidden caterpillar treads roaring over the ridge of rubble into the main adit. A deep voice suddenly blared, in decibels well over the safe limit for such a small place, maxed-out speakers shrieking:

"Do not grudge our loyal, brave people, who never flinched under the strain of last week—I do not grudge them the natural, spontaneous outburst of joy and relief when they

learned that the hard ordeal would not be required of them at the moment."

It was the voice, more than anything. The orotund Twito-cratic vowels clicked her out of the magnesium shock and into a sort of perception. Four-meter-high fiberglass casing, a mound of Styrofoam "whipped cream" with the barrel-sized "cherry" stuck in the middle; the bulging sheet of plastic filling at the business end of the vast cannoli.

The sheet split under the pressure of a meter-wide jet of cream-colored foam. The foam expanded instantaneously as it was released from its tank, flooding the section of tunnel around the access adit within five seconds.

The nightcrawlers tried to straighten up from firing position and move out of range, but their size slowed them down. Already the foam was up to their knees, hardening quickly as its level rose, from froth to cream to slurry to the consistency of wet concrete.

They moved more slowly as it hardened, as it reached their thighs and shoulders and CBW masks. Their training had been thorough, and they opened the internal oxygen tanks before the foam engulfed them totally.

"But they should know the truth." The cannoli had fallen victim to its own filling, which had entered the air intakes and stalled the engine, but its speakers were still above the cream and operative. *"They should know there has been gross neglect and deficiency in our defenses; they should know that we have sustained a defeat without a war!"*

Sha'Oprah, unimpeded by armor, had leaped out of the foam's reach. But the cannoli had cut her off at the landward end of the adit, and now the foam created a solid cofferdam that prevented her from pursuing Zatt's wheelchair. In frustration, she emptied the .45 blind. A couple of slugs, braked somewhat by the foam, rattled randomly around the tunnel. The rest were absorbed by Stix's giant pastry.

The foam was at speaker level, but the volume was such that Zatt and Soledad could still hear, at ever-lower power, the Churchillian monologue as they resumed their way down the tunnel toward the tug.

"They should know that we have passed an awful milestone in our history, when the whole equilibrium of Europe has been decayed, and that the terrible words have for the time being been pronounced against the Western democracies: Thou art weighed in the balance, and found wanting. . . ."

Three minutes and two sub pens later, they rounded a bulkhead and spotted the *Razzle-Dazzle,* her navigation lights white and green in the darkness. The boy and the weed-pirate stood by the singled up gangway, almost jumping up and down with impatience as they waved at Zatt and Soledad to hurry.

EPILOGUE

SHE DIDN'T WAKE UP, because she wasn't asleep, not really. Dozing while your brain let out the clutch, releasing overheated images so they could bounce somewhat around your synapses, did not count as sleep.

More to the point, she had not relinquished control, not enough to let dreams happen, or other images that might be too painful to bear with any grace. Dozing only let go a backlog of neurotransmitters, bleeding them away so as to goose her small chemistry a few microns toward release, setting off the dominant images: the sharp silhouette of a destroyer, radar churning and missile ports open, chopper fueled and ready on its stern deck as it glided through the fog like a floating castle, only eighty meters away; or the North American coati, turning a crank in the glare of the tug's searchlight, doing it on his own while the boy laughed in wonder and the ancient, three-hundred-ton, nuke-proof casement scraped slowly open onto the pearl mist; or the wheelhouse of this tugboat, soaked in green light from the radar and computer displays, much too cramped for the silence and tension building within as the old weed-pirate conned her gently past the sunk pilings and shoals leading out of the disused base; as the boy and Zatt together sweated over codes that were supposed to signal ships and patrol craft in deeper water that this was only another Navy unit on standby to pull damaged craft out of range of criminal waterborne elements of the former Oakland node and free market.

Soledad could not allow herself to believe they'd made it out.

She lay, wrapped in a filthy sleeping bag, under the jumbled radios of the wheelhouse chart table.

It was too cold and damp, and she was far too much in need of warmth, to lie outside.

The tug's saloon was full of nodistas, crying babies, laboratory raccoons, and cats. Its atmosphere was rank with the smell of diapers and old socks and fear.

They *should* not have made it. The cordon around Bamaca was no tighter than this. Of course, the frigate of the Flota Nacional that lay in Bahia de las Animas was not hooked into fancy computerized battle-management systems, either. It just shot the hell out of everything that moved.

She lay with her hands folded over her stomach.

Molly's face, with the single purple dot in her forehead.

Stix's brave squid-flinger, burnt out and silent in a circle of its own destruction.

She kept her eyes open mostly, to cut the power of such images. Did not allow herself to think beyond the visual. She would have gotten up, concentrated on easy things, like keeping her balance in a seaway, going to the bathroom, finding something to drink, but she was too ill with aches and fatigue.

Finally her bladder got too full to ignore. She went below to the toilet. It reeked so badly of throw-up and shit that she barely managed to keep from vomiting.

In the galley, someone handed her a cup of coffee, which settled her stomach a little. She made her way to the one unoccupied portion of the settee and knelt there, looking out the porthole; it was a trick the smugglers had taught her, on the voyage around the Tapon de Darien. Watching the horizon, they said, quieted the little piezoelectric crystal that controlled the balance center in your inner ear. She leaned her forehead against the cool salt-and-tallow smell of the porthole. Drank the liquid slowly, letting the coffee smell take up places other smells could use. She looked across a wilderness of scattered mist to a ragged-looking sailboat, a schooner with a green hull and tan paint peeling off its upperworks. The sailboat appeared and disappeared behind the green-blue shoulders of Pacific swells, heading the same way as the tug, perhaps two hundred meters off.

For no reason she could fathom, Miguel's face popped into her head, very vague but it was him all right, with that one refractory cowlick and the slight stoop.

It was more than just his boy, she found herself thinking; I should never have done that to Dona Serena. For the second time in only two days a slow flush of shame spread across her cheeks.

I should never have done that to another woman.

The flush made her sweat and unsettled her stomach again. The smell of socks was stronger than ever. She spotted a pair of large and knobby feet, sheathed in crusted gym socks, poking out from under the settee. She turned from the porthole and the sailboat and headed fast up the companionway to the wheelhouse.

A thinscreen hooked over the radios on the chart table showed a low-altitude aerial of fire; fire scarlet, with a flash of daffodil, framed by oily black, platinum-streaked smoke of RDX explosive from high-precision mortars. Silver from phosphorus shells. No orange, no napalm, but maybe they didn't need it, the warehouses this camera focused on were burning fiercely already. A B-Net logo flashed in the corner.

A different angle, made grainy by the ubiquitous haze of smoke and fog, showed a line of people in the messy motley of civilians being herded by dogfaced MOUT nightcrawlers into buses.

Another shot showed only smoke. Now the announcer's voice cracked high with excitement. The smoke cleared, and the camera swung to cover the MOQ where, so the voice-over claimed, a bunch of jaggers and Putas had feigned a fallback, then circled around to capture a squad of urban soldiers.

A hovertank floated cautiously up the next road. At that point, a man rolled out of a smashed lab, swinging his fists aggressively. He was larger than life, and dressed in the uniform of a naval petty officer. Soledad imagined him shouting

"Front and center, 'ten *hut,* ten days in the brig!" as he advanced on the hovertank, and as a dark group of resisters took advantage of the tankmen's distraction to fade out of one ruined building into another.

The tank's turret swung briefly. The mechanical man flew apart. There was not enough time for flame even, his torso vanished, nothing left but scraps of machinery and one foot in regulation navy brogans rolling very slowly down a gentle incline toward the harbor.

She put one hand over her mouth. She knew, for the first time she really knew there was no hope for him. The tears nibbled hotly around the edges of her eyelids. "Hawkleyites make lousy martyrs," Molly said once, "they are dangerous alive only." Or something like that. She tried to think of Stix's face, his body, the man she made love to only a few hours ago, the man whose microscopic seed still fruitlessly swam toward the spot inside her preempted by another.

All she saw was that stupid pastiche of a naval petty officer swinging its fists at an approaching tank; and the cannoli, the pastry he had placed to protect her, holding off a MOUT squad with foam and Churchillian bluster.

She wondered—no, she hoped that Stix and Will were together at this juncture. In a way, it was what Stix had always wanted: to fight something head-to-head, as Will would do.

She kept her chest moving, breathing in and out, pumping oxygen one way, CO_2 the other. Life, she thought desperately— we are only useful *alive.* She felt right now that she could sob forever; for Stix, for Bamaca, for Jorge and the node and Molly, tears copious and blue enough to rival the Pacific; but she would be out of commission while she cried. And incapacitation was not a luxury she could afford. Not on the run, not with a baby in her belly.

There would be time to cry later, if they made it to safety.

So she turned very deliberately away from the screen, to check out instead the wheelhouse, the boy at his usual post, Zatt with his nose buried as always in the data of a terminal.

No surprises here, she thought, it was yet another *putain* of an eavesdropping video, a tight shot of her, Soledad, rocking her head back and forth on the soaked blue mesa of Stix's pillow; muttering a song, warbling in such a queer and sleep-drugged fashion as to generate another wave of hot embarrassment under her reflexive anger.

At least her tits did not show in this one, she reflected, and knuckled away the moisture that had gathered on her cheeks.

> *Of what use is a root*
> *That does not touch the volcano's sex*
> *Of what use is a love*
> *bound by the shadow's track?*

the woman in the video sang.

> *Desdichado*
> *Desdichado*
> *this land is sad*
> *as a wound*

The diesel rumbled. The thud the tug made as it ate into swells triggered creaks and complaints from other parts of its structure. Computers feeped. Everybody kept doing the same things as the boat plowed into the waves and its small circular horizon of mist. She felt herself wanting to turn back to the news, just in case she was wrong, just in case Stix might have—

It was to prevent herself from doing this that she said at last, "Why don't ye wank off to yer own fuckin' magazines for a change?"

Zatt ignored her. He always ignored her. From close up she saw that his screen was split between her image slotted on the left-hand side, while on the right a midi-program parsed her tune into digital frequencies, and a graph tallied numbers under the original Lanc-Patua version of Jorge's text.

"Where's Mojo?" Zatt called, not looking around.

"Saloon," the boy said.

Eventually the weed-pirate went below, complaining, and came back followed by the connection of electrocuted hair and stinking footgear that was Mojo.

Soledad stared at his socks again, wondering why on earth the American Megorg considered him a target. Yet a bump of respect was raised on her idea of him when she remembered Mojo as he was in the bass warehouse, pulling all the different musicians and ateliers into Soledad's improv. She had not noticed his socks then. There might be a lesson in that memory.

"The reason is here," Zatt commented suddenly, scrolling down the right side of the split-screen. He twisted to look at Mojo. She tried to beat away the front of revulsion blowing over her at the sight of two men bent so lasciviously over a glowing screen. They seemed to bear no scars from, pay no respect to the destruction going on behind them; the wiping out of their home, the death of Molly. "It was in this song— the 'Souche,' you call it? I did slow regression analyses on all her songs, melody, meter, lyrics; this clearly was the important one, in terms of stochastics. And finally"—he tapped out a command on the keyboard—"it's the only one that got results."

Soledad did not want to ask these men anything.

Then again, they were talking about the *Concerto de la Selva* here, talking about something as personal as that glimpse of breast in another part of the video.

"What results?" she asked finally.

"Really puerile code," Zatt said. "The numerical value of the first letters, ancient stuff; people say their version of Voodoo has a lot of Qabbala in it."

"Voodoo?" Mojo, touching his crotch, started to jerk his thin frame to the tune the screen-Soledad still warbled, through quite good speakers really.

"There is a clear pattern of similar numbers," Zatt continued. "Look, *A quoi sert une souche:* the *a*, of course, has a value of one. The *q* in *quoi*, seventeen. *S* for *sert*, nineteen, he never counted prepositions, which is convenient. 117.9. The next stanza, *qui ne toucherait le sexe du volcan,* is 191.8. I got to admit, I couldn't figure out what linked those numbers for a while. Then I ran them through a stochastics program, working off the marsh, the AI link, remember? And it mentioned, like an afterthought, they were all numerals between 10^4, and 8×10^7, divided into bands by ratios of ten. That mean anything to you?"

"Palm trees, voodoo," Mojo moaned.

"Radio frequencies," Zatt explained, after a few seconds in which he really seemed to think they might guess. "Which means Wildnet bands, in my book. I figure," he went on, "Echeverria was in touch with Hawkley, or some pal of Hawkley's. But what we have here is Wildnet frequencies, plus a random iteration based on the beat of the music it's hidden in—6/8 in this case, is what he says." Jerking a thumb at Mojo.

"Making it one whole network of Wildnets, changing randomly, untraceable, unless you have this key, in which case you hook into the network on a permanent basis, easy as pie. Keep in touch with a whole grid."

"How dark the volcano's cone," Mojo commented, not listening to him at all. "I wanna riff on that line."

"An 'internode,' " Soledad said. "That's what Charlie Rickle's group called it. That's what they think the next type of node will be."

Zatt's eyes shone the way they always did—bright and somewhat cold. So different, she thought sadly, from Molly's.

"Stix really showed you around," he commented.

"Texas shortwave!" Mojo wailed. "Internode!"

"It does not sound like a good place for dinner," Soledad said softly.

Zatt kept staring at her for a beat or two. Then he turned back to his jambook.

"Well," he said, "it's real on some level." Jerking a thumb to the right, where the schooner chopped into the Pacific swells, canted starboard by the wind. "That boat's on the same Wildnet."

"Oh, magic," Soledad replied. "An electronic yacht club."

Zatt ignored her sarcasm.

"It's going to be diffuse," he said. "Networks of really small groups, big families really, connected by Wildnets. Barter and trade long-distance, working back up to the thirty-seven percent—"

"A system of shared music." Mojo was looking steadily at Soledad now. The crazy jerking was gone, as suddenly as it had come. He smiled in a way that, while it was somewhat dreamy, was also close to sane. His wrinkles were harsh in the silver light.

"I don't understand," Soledad said. "How could he know you would look in *'Souche'*? How could he know I would sing it?"

"Oh, he knew you'd sing it all right," Mojo said. His grin went weird once more. "Volcanoes burning, coming like fire-sperm? Maybe he didn't know it would be in your *dreams,* but he knew his words would come out, somehow."

Soledad watched him for a second.

"But I don't want to chase after this network," she said at length, in a voice that was very close to a whine.

The tug hit a wave higher than most; she was caught off-balance, and had to hang on to a chain overhead. A deafening mechanical hoot erupted from outside. Her heart seemed to somersault in her chest. The raccoon chirred, and chucked a pair of dividers in her direction. The boy and the weed-pirate glared at her, then went back to their respective jobs. Soledad let go of the whistle chain, found another handhold, and said firmly, "I have to go back to Bamaca. Or nearby. There is something I have to find out."

"You're not safe there now," Zatt muttered, moving wedges of frequency around like solitaire cards on his screen. "We used this frequency system already and we found an in-ternode site in Astoria, Oregon. Little bit west of Portland.

Tug's got just enough fuel, Ahab says. We can get some rest, score some chow, set up fake UCC accounts. Wait till the heat is off."

"So easy," Soledad whispered. "Just flit on to the next thing, like a fucking butterfly."

Zatt was silent.

"And how do you know for sure?" Soledad insisted. She found she had no great drive to make these objections—she had returned fully to escape mode now and was looking for cracks in the plan as a matter of discipline, the tradecraft of the refugee. Though the emotions trembled deep in a cave inside her, like a jisi hangover, still wounded and demanding of care.

In the few hours since she'd been aboard this tug she had already gotten better at isolating her emotions, and ignoring their soft and treacherous comfort.

She thought: If she was a child before meeting Jorge, and the *cruce* was her rite of passage, then this style of living had become her maturity. It was a maturity that meant routine acceptance of the world's random hardness—of the fact that, even if love, and the story of her loving, were the antidote to this hardness and the reason for going on, she could only deal with one impossible love at a time. "All stories are equal." The words echoed around her head for a second or two before she remembered where she had first heard them.

She continued, more quietly, "How do you know this place near Portland—this internode—how d'ye know it's safe? If the government can destroy a node, these wee things are nothing. It could even be a trap."

By her question's end she was speaking so softly that Zatt cupped his hand behind one ear to make out her words. She leaned back against the radios, wishing only to curl up underneath as before, to fold her hands over her slight stomach and doze—only doze.

"But it's not a trap," Zatt answered. "You told us that, too." He pointed at the vidscreen, his stubby fingers caressing the neck of the miniature Soledad as she writhed and muttered in LCD. "*You* knew this place, Miss MacRae. Do you remember the words, the words that kept coming up in your dreams like a refrain—*except there was not a trace of them in Echeverria's lyrics*?"

Tired as she was, it took no effort to recall the words.

"*Ciment d'os,*" she whispered. "Bone cement."

Zatt's fingers rattled on the keyboard. The image of Soledad was replaced by the Wildnet site for a barter zone in Astoria harbor. A pocket video showed a gaggle of battered craft sheltered among the docks of a former dockside factory. The craft were moored in the kind of pattern that suggested a connection greater than the requirements of tide, access, and shore power. The number of solar panels and charging windmills was great.

In the pocket vidclip, mist weaved in and out of the masts, rigging, smokestacks, laundry lines. It formed vortices among the dock pilings; it climbed and parted to reveal a World War Two–era harborside factory. On the cracked and shored-up wall of the plant, in huge fading greenish capitals, were painted the words: A. J. BONE CEMENT CO INC

"Oh," Soledad said.

Then she bent low, and crawled under the chart table. Into the pocket of smells, of salt and warm diesel, of hot circuitry and rust. Curled with her buttocks to the throbbing steel bulkhead, folded her arms gently over her belly, and lay there for a long time with her eyes open.

She was pretty sure that, since she was back in the routine of flight, when she went to sleep this time she would dream of nothing—not the *cruce* or Jorge, not Stix or Dolores. But she was not so certain of it that she could allow herself to crash without great caution.

The old tug rumbled and creaked, punching its way northward toward Oregon.

ABOUT THE AUTHOR

GEORGE FOY is the author of eight novels, including *Contraband* and *The Shift*. He lives with his family on Cape Cod, Massachusetts, and in New York City.

HORSE, FLOWER, BIRD

Horse, Flower, Bird

STORIES

Kate Bernheimer

COFFEE HOUSE PRESS

MINNEAPOLIS 2010

Coffee House Press books are available to the trade through our primary distributor, Consortium Book Sales & Distribution, www.cbsd.com or (800) 283-3572. For personal orders, catalogs, or other information, write to: info@coffeehousepress.org.

Coffee House Press is a nonprofit literary publishing house. Support from private foundations, corporate giving programs, government programs, and generous individuals helps make the publication of our books possible. We gratefully acknowledge their support in detail in the back of this book.

To you and our many readers around the world, we send our thanks for your continuing support.

LIBRARY OF CONGRESS CIP INFORMATION

Bernheimer, Kate.
Horse, flower, bird : stories / by Kate Bernheimer.
p. cm.
ISBN 978-1-56689-247-6 (alk. paper)
1. Fairy tales—Adaptations. I. Title.
PS3602.E76H67 2010
813'.6—dc22
2010016257

PRINTED IN CANADA

1 3 5 7 9 8 6 4 2

FIRST EDITION | FIRST PRINTING

ACKNOWLEDGMENTS

Stories from this collection have appeared, or are forthcoming, in the following publications. The author expresses her gratitude to the supportive editors of: *3rd Bed, 5_Trope, Born Magazine, A Galaxy Not So Far Away, Filter, The Portland Mercury, The Press Gang, Radical Society, Sou'Wester, Western Humanities Review,* and *Tin House.*

"Shall we let them have a little music?" asked Emily, and she wound up the musical box. It went "tinkle, tinkle" and Darner stirred in his dreams.

Mr. Plantaganet could not tell one of its tunes from the other. "I have to have words," said Mr. Plantaganet. "Words help me to know what it is. Like those carols, Tottie. Do you remember them?" And he began to hum "God Bless the Master of This House." "Do you remember them, Tottie?"

"I remember everything," said Tottie, listening to the music.

"Yes, I suppose you must, and for so long," said Mr. Plantaganet. "Such a long time, Tottie."

"Yes," said Tottie.

"Things come and things pass," said little Mr. Plantaganet.

"Everything, from trees to dolls," said Tottie.

"Even for small things like us, even for dolls. Good things and bad things, but the good things have come back, haven't they, Tottie?" asked Mr. Plantaganet anxiously.

"Of course they have," said Tottie in her kind wooden voice.

"Good things and bad. They were very bad," said Mr. Plantaganet.

"But they come and pass, so let us be happy now," said Tottie.

"Without Birdie?" asked Mr. Plantaganet, his voice trembling.

"Birdie would be happy. She couldn't help it," said Tottie.

And Birdie's bright tinkling music went on in the doll's house, and on her hat that still hung in the hall, and on her feather broom, and on her bird, and on her parasol, the colors and the patterns were still bright.

—RUMER GODDEN
The Doll's House

A
Cuckoo
Tale

A **Cuckoo** Tale

Once upon a time, there was a little girl who liked to atone. She especially liked The Day of Atonement. Atoning, she felt at one.

On that glorious day every year, with the leaves in colors like fire, she got to feel bad while wearing her nicest outfit—a calico dress with lace collar, puffed sleeves, and nude nylons—and she also got to not eat. And not only did she get to not eat, but she got to do it in an auditorium downtown. There she would sit and stand and sit and stand and, not eating, become dizzy from the perfumed women around.

They were all not-eating downtown because on Yom Kippur many wanted to fast and pray together. The temple elders rented a hall in a fancy hotel. The actual temple, old and small, used to be a church. It had uncomfortable pews, making praying quite pleasing.

Discomfort is often a virtue. Nevertheless, the perfumed ladies atoned downtown happily, as did the girl.

Neither she nor the perfumed ladies were much interested in God. They were interested in forgiveness and, the girl vaguely understood, people who had been cooked inside ovens.

The girl was also extremely interested in her Catholic friend, Lizzie Murphy, who had perfectly freckled skin. She and Lizzie had identical rag dolls and a favorite game called Confession. They would take the dolls by their limp little hands and go into the bathroom. One girl would step behind the shower curtain and the other one would stand outside it, reach in, and take the doll's hands and the girl's hands. The girl inside the curtain was a priest. There was much talk of sin in general, but never in particular. All was forgiven in an elaborate ritual involving water and chants.

There was no talk of heaven or hell in the girl's household. It was all about pogroms and rape. But on Yom Kippur she got to lean over and kiss her older sister's dry cheek in the auditorium-temple, upon command of the Rabbi, and say intensely, "I'm sorry I said I hate you this year." Dizzy, she'd stare into the sister's cold eyes.

The sisters shared a bedroom and often the younger sister dreamed that a life-sized doll sat on the edge of her bed and scared her. She would whisper, "Help me!" to the cold sister. The cold sister offered no help, just as no one had helped the family up in the attic after they had been discovered, the family with the girl who kept the diary, the girl the younger sister admired and loved, and wrongly envied.

On Yom Kippur the father watched football while the mother prepared breakfast for dinner. Pancakes and bacon, matzoh ball soup, angel food cake. A mysterious name for a cake. She heated the food in the oven until it was night, and when it was over-cooked, then they would eat.

The young girl was scared of the oven, and there was a reason for that, which was that her grand-mother had told her stories of children who got shoved into ovens and of families that were so over-crowded, the babies had to sleep in pots and pans on the stove. In some of the tales there was a witch who cooked little girls in order to eat them. "Mmm, I smell a Russian bone!" she'd say, and grab at their legs. One of these story-girls wanted to marry her brother. "Think of the sin," her sister warns her. But they do marry, and then four little dolls are placed in the four corners of a room and they cry like cuck-oos. *Cuckoo, he takes his sister, Cuckoo, for a wife, Cuckoo, earth open wide, Cuckoo, sister, fall inside!* After a while a witch shows up and says, "I smell a Russian bone!" She tries to cook the girl who has married her brother. (This sort of witch has quite a longing to eat sinners, you see.) Yes, then the woods become so dark that not even a fly can find its way home. The dolls' heads are chopped off. Then the girl's sister chases the witch into the sky, where she burns. The married brother and sister now are set free. The sister marries a different man, and the brother, his sister's best friend.

As a child the girl would often not eat to get free of sin. Free of someone? That witch, she was always trying to get the dolls and roast the girls. Girls became doves to get away from her, even. And the dolls in the corners cried like cuckoos.

Cuckoo.

A
Tulip's
Tale

A Tulip's Tale

I was but a smallish bulb—a bulbette, really—sleeping cozily beside my mother, when quite to my horror I was wrestled from that safe, underground home and yanked into the face of an unblinking sun.

The shock of blue sky wide above frightened me, and I never grew to my fullest size. Too young for such solitude, I became forever sad.

No longer could I root happily into my mother's company and find comfort in her rounded shape. There was no one to tell me the facts. How much nutrition to pull from the dirt? Would the beetles bring harm? And what of the worms? Friends, foe, or nevermind?

Is it any wonder I was always so silent? Always so small?

No, I was *not* ready to leave her at all. I was but a tiny bulb—a bulbette, really—quite at home beside my mother, when those wretched hands dug me out of my peaceful slumber and moved me into that cold plot of land. There I had no playmates to speak of, no playmates for miles. It was a bewildering journey from the very beginning.

I cannot say that I have appreciated it at all. No, not at all.

Then one day, nearly a hundred years after the trauma, I became blessed with a friend. She happened upon me and pulled me out of the ground. To me she whispered thoughts of great feeling: "Poor little thing, poor ugly thing," she said. How those words brought me comfort!

She said she could see I had a difficult life, never allowed to see the sun. With my best effort, I communicated agreement. This was not easy because my skin was tough and quite immobile.

She continued, "And we will *not* pretend to ignore that you are misshapen. Just as my mother taught me when I was young to accept my homeliness, so must you accept yours. My mother and father love me despite the plain features on my face. But none has a plainer face than you! Oh my dearest and ugliest friend!"

When my friend found me, she covered her heart with one hand and rested the other tenderly against my hard little body. She told me that her childhood memories were like those little boxes containing dried nuts, or fruit, that her mother sometimes received from guests she did not seem particularly eager to greet. The guests were men in black garments, clutching tiny books. This was an elaborate narration that she ended simply by trailing off her words, and stroking my spindly roots.

And then my pretty friend put me in such a box, for her to keep. At times she opened the box and licked me. Why, she loved the taste of my dirty skin! And I liked my little box, that wooden box lined with pink paper. It fit in her apron pocket. Unlike heated potatoes—surly relatives of mine—I did not keep her warm.

She kept me from missing my mother too much.

This was all in the town of Sneek, near the Wadden Zee, just north of the Zuder Zee.

Her father was a fishmonger, her mother a fishwife. Though her father's family trade had been in diamonds, the family was of the Jewish kind. The Fishmongers Guild did not restrict, so he made the switch. From glinting stone to lively flounder!

There is more life in fish than in jewels, though diamonds do glint.

little reflective bits take reader
of of context + provide a more
complex backstory of narrator
→ like narrator isn't so much a
fairytale character → too complex

And indeed, her father loved everything alive. It was this love that eventually brought him to ruin, but through no fault of his own. And she, the girl who suffered most badly for his tender spirit, never blamed him. Yes, he and her mother had provided well for the girl from north of the Zuder Zee, a pleasant life that they designed in the meticulous manner of the era.

The mother kept the home as clean as perfection itself. The mother also labored long and hard as a bleaching maid.

(The smell of bleach and fish made the girl swoon
for all her days, and still would if she were living.)

When first she found me, my friend and I and her sisters slept in a drawer. The drawer pulled out from underneath the parents' small bed. Together the sisters huddled through hard winter nights, and the sister clutched me in her hand. And the mother, so rosy-cheeked and kind! She kept the drawer warm by piling hot potatoes inside. The potatoes she would remove just before bed. Then the girls would clamber into the drawer and whisper stories and poems.

When you hear the Cuckoo shout, 'tis time to plant your tatties out.

While they slumbered, their parents sat by the fire and ate.

As her sisters and mother and father slept, she would open the lid of the wooden box just a crack and whisper to me. Her hot breath against the pink tissue paper moved it a bit, making a nice, wrinkling sound that made me swoon.

We shall discuss your amusement in time. It interests me because otherwise you appear so small-headed, as I appeared as a child.

My friend had several friends who had to sleep in the oven. Yes, the oven! Poor little Anneke K——, whose mother forgot she was in there when she fired it up in the morning! But they all rather *liked* her singed hair. It had the most unusual crimps and curls!

And just because poor little Anneke K—— slept in the oven does not mean her life was bad. Oh no, her life was good, my friend related. Her family lived well, and kept their wooden floors clean and their tiny home scrubbed and finely sparkling. At night there was much drinking of wine, much cheer all around in poor little Anneke K——'s fine house.

Just like my friend, Anneke K—— eventually was auctioned. This took place at midnight, in the town square. My friend came home for the very last time and she told me.

"There was little interest in me," she said sadly, "I am dried up like a prune at thirteen: they said my face was sour, though inside I feel fine."

"In the end, I was taken for a moderate fee," she told me. "Now I'll be taken to my new home, and to this man who I fear will beat me."

And then she left me.

So now I feel death coming closer each day—*'tis time,* I almost can hear him say. But I am here for your comfort. I am here to make sure that you grow. I was surprised to see you sprout from my withered body, but sprout from me you did.

Lying beneath a man—I don't mean to shock with that phrase, it was common in the time to lie with men, you are so sensitive for such a rough one!—I believe she must have often thought of her parents' house. And of me?

The home in which you reside is not forever.

That swept front stoop. That waxed oak door. Even the mother's feet had brushes upon them, on their soles! This pursuit of cleanliness was performed by all of the husbands and all of the wives in all of the homes on that small and oak-lined street.

From the time my friend was five, she created a ruckus. Her poor mother, trying to clean off the door! Always, my friend insisted upon rushing out-side, shoving aside her poor mother. And upon her return she always forgot to remove the straw covers that covered her shoes. The filth. What reprimands she received. And deserved.

She cared not so much about cleanliness. I believe this was part of her attraction to me—indeed part of her country's fascination with my type.

It was a pity they auctioned her off so young. But it was a pity for her parents most of all. The Jewish fishmongers. They were not allowed in many trades. They could have made a bundle in tulips, but how could they know?

But they had no idea of our worth, nor of hers.

I was inside the trundle, inside my box, wrapped in pink tissue paper just as she'd left me. They received news of her death. This arrived in a letter she had sent before tossing herself into the icy cold sea. The letter gave strict instructions to plant me in earth.

It has been a long, cold winter. Will the spring never arrive? My dear Jewess, my beautiful friend!

Come back.

Come back.

Come back to me.

A
Doll's
Tale

A Doll's Tale

Once there was a musician who played ukulele, fiddle, accordion, and banjo with a group specializing in country tunes for weddings. At one such wedding, Jewish in style, he met his future bride. Sitting between a spread of lox and onions and another of herring and cream, she watched him play. He had longish blond hair, a pale blue suit, and an ironic gaze. He looked like a cowboy-cum-criminal-cum-angelic deceiver. How they actually got introduced is unknown; and in fact, this is not their story. It is the story of the future bride's sister, who was neither at this wedding nor at their own. This Astrid herself never married.

As a very young child, Astrid had enjoyed many activities along with her sister. They shared a bedroom and had twin beds, and with a sheet draped over the space between the two they played Runaways in Tents. In summer they gathered frogs in a pail, left them in the sun, and shellacked their dried bodies in the basement. They used a tiny oven to make tiny cakes on numerous occasions. They also had great fun playing Little Matchbox Girl, fake-starving.

Yet this all came to a halt on Astrid's ninth birthday, when she received a life-sized doll from which she quickly became inseparable. Astrid named the doll "Astrid," too, though Astrid the doll was far less plain than Astrid the girl. The doll had blond hair made from a horse's mane, pink undies made of silk, and lengthy limbs of Plasticine. Astrid found the Astrid-doll rather haughty and mean. Confused by this feeling—for Astrid was a kind and gentle being— her ambivalence became a kind of devotion. "Oh, my doll! My precious friend!" she'd say, and press her lips on Astrid's own.

However, after not very long, Astrid the doll was lost in a hotel on a family trip. This loss was perhaps Astrid's own fault: a laundry chute was involved. As her mother phoned Miami Beach from home, Astrid held onto the telephone cord, sticking her finger into its coils and drawing it out, keening after the doll. She listened suspiciously as her mother described the scene of the crime as Astrid had described it to her. "She was in the bed," Astrid's mother said. "She is a big doll, the size of my girl." But although Astrid's mother attempted quite valiantly to retrieve the lost doll from Housekeeping's hands, it did not work. Poor Astrid, left alone to swelter in Florida. Poor melting Astrid, Astrid desperately thought, smiling.

⤷ like anti-fairytale

Then, out of guilt, or perhaps mere childish loneliness, Astrid soon invented an imaginary friend in exactly the same form as the beautiful doll. This new Astrid accompanied Astrid everywhere she went. Hand in invisible hand, they trundled along in the snow. Eye to unblinking eye, they told tales in bed, tales of madmen and beasts. How Astrid adored this new, imaginary friend! Silently she fell in love. "Oh, Astrid," she would mouth, nearly writhing with joy. Pressing a little ear to an absent voice, she listened as her very own Astrid mutely crooned of love.

Quite disappointingly, Astrid's new and fragile happiness only served to bring about the most unfortunate of consequences. For Astrid's sister now had her own room with a green shag rug and intercom. After listening through the white box affixed to the wall one afternoon, she'd broadcast, "Now entering the Astrid Freak Zone" through the house over and over again. It was no surprise that soon, a tragedy inexplicably occurred: Astrid ran away quite without warning. Not the girl, but the friend. Invisible to begin with, she vanished again. Frantically, Astrid told her parents about the disappearance. "We were lying in bed, and you tucked us in, and when I fell asleep she leapt out the window, I think." She paused, gasping for breath. "She's afraid of the dark," she said. "Of the men that come in," she added, elliptically.

Astrid's parents responded to the disappearance with reason. Her father masterfully guided their luxury sedan throughout their small town, down each and every narrow alley and unpaved road in search of this invisible friend who had been—indeed!—the very best friend for his delicate, odd little girl. Astrid watched her father's hands on the shift, so strong, so masculine. For a long time he steered them around and around. But at dusk he brought Astrid home, completely forlorn.

→ She's not even trying

This second loss proved too much for her, really.

Doll-less, invisible-friend-less, finally more comfortable in fear than in gladness, Astrid began to live in her head. Or rather inside a small tunnel—a hole—in her head, through which she watched everything gaily depart. She nodded this head and pretended to listen. "Bye-bye," she would hear from within, even when grown up and schooled. To outsiders, this inside-conversation lent her a remarkably pleasing air, since she never had reason to interrupt anyone's talking. "Bye-bye" she heard over and over. "Bye-bye, little doll, little friend."

And as you perhaps have gleaned from this story, our Astrid didn't much thrive.

A
Petting Zoo
Tale

A Petting Zoo Tale

This story takes place in a small house, not too different from any other. From outside, the house looks sweet and simple. Made of wood, poppies growing all around. Painted white. Dog on rope. Though plain, this house, like its couple inside, has a charismatic feel. Often people stop to gaze. Day and night they pause and stare and don't know why. Do you want to know? No one else does.

The girl of the house has built a petting zoo inside. Though the zoo is a secret, not being legal, it lends the house a certain air.

So far the girl has two laying hens, a miniature pony, a goat, and three rabbits. Partitions made of chicken wire separate the animals, yet allow ample socializing. To offset the look of the wire, the girl has painted the walls various shades of pink. She has draped sparkly gauze over the windows. From the ceiling hang strand upon strand of Christmas lights. These electric bulbs have many settings: blinking, fluttering, glowing, traveling, and the chickens' favorite, a syncopated combination of all four.

Each morning, before the husband comes to break-fast, the girl goes down the basement stairs to feed the pets. At sunrise animals must be fed. She remembers this from school. Patting the goat's head, she admires its melon eyes. Finding the rabbits in hiding, she scolds. "Bad rabbits!" she says brightly, putting them back in their pen. They do have fun. Yet the miniature horse seems unhappy. This worries the girl to no end, because the entire zoo has been planned around his small majesty.

Each dawn since his arrival she has braided his mane carefully and tenderly brushed his legs. In a closet sits a tiny saddle, which occasionally she places upon him. She perches a stuffed monkey there for rides; she leads him around the room. This takes place in the afternoon when the husband is gone. The girl had—and continues to have—plans to construct an exit from the basement to the yard so the pony can get appropriate exercise and exposure to fresh air. But how might she do so without arousing the suspicions of that kind husband?

Each day, the husband is away at work, "litigating" and "trying," and probably wouldn't notice. Of course he pays his girl much good attention. He tells her in an absorbed and charming tone each evening about his cases, which have a language of their own she finds amusing. *Slip-and-falls. Emotional claims. Pierces in the corporate veil.* Because his work is so involving, the husband never ventures into the basement, the domain of "ironing" and "washing." In fact, the girl has had the washer and dryer removed to make room for a water trough. She goes to the Laundree-Mat on Division Street for all such needs. The Laundree-Mat is a wonderful place, but not a place he'd want her to frequent. There you exchange your money for tokens. They have pinball machines with women that moan!

The husband is really a delicate man. But she could get away with a lot more than a petting zoo, it seems. So very mindful inside, he doesn't notice a thing. How chicken feed is delivered each week. How catalogs to order live monkeys pile up by the bed. How the girl daily carries two perfect eggs from the basement in her hands, and takes them to the fridge and pretends to remove them from a tray. Bent over the newspaper, his shoulders droop.

→ There's this weird fear of men/male presence throughout whole book "always some guy crawling through the window"

No, the girl thinks. A revolving door to the yard, gar-lands of red roses on tiny wooden jumps, stacks of eating hay? It could take a while, but eventually the husband would look outside, see the frolicking pony, and become quite alarmed. The girl would never for-give herself for upsetting the husband's sweet balance. He must try to keep calm, for how else could he daily don a button-down shirt, a checkered tie? Dress in a suit, as if to accompany an organ grinder through town? All he lacks is the little cap! "Look at me! A working man! Yeep! Yeep!" That sound you hear in the primate room at the actual zoo.

It's just too sad. The girl must help him keep calm as best she can so they can pay for their excellent home, for her wonderful petting zoo, for her petting. The animals sleep well there at night, the animals in hiding.

All good animals have secret lives.

A
Cageling
Tale

A Cageling Tale

Once upon a time a girl of seventeen, or maybe eighteen, got a parakeet and kept it in her room.

The girl's mother, with whom the girl lived alone, didn't like this at all. The mother thought birds, whether herons or doves, peacocks or wrens, defined filth. Bird-hating was a strong, female tradition in this family, with a not very interesting history. For example, one old aunt had lost her mind and imagined birds everywhere. She'd yell "Birds! Birds!" and wave her arms around whenever anything—a branch, someone's hand, even the wind—got too near her body.

And the girl's grandmother had a vengeance for birds. (She had very bad vision and once, mistakenly, got a chair upholstered in a fabric that depicted garish birds. Strangely, the girl's mother, whose mother this was, seemed to take some kind of wicked glee in the error, and never revealed it to her.)

The girl was against phobias both in general and in the bird particular. That's why she got a parakeet and caged it.

However, she pitied the sky blue bird for being confined. It looked happy enough in its cage, staring with unblinking eyes, licking its wings, but could it really be happy in there? Soon she took to letting the parakeet out of its cage when the mother was out of the house. The bird knew not to soil the room, and only to soil the square of sandpaper that perfectly lined its cage, so the girl's mother never knew the bird often flew willy-nilly. Furnished in pink, yellow, and green, the bedroom complimented the bird's powdery blue.

Lying in bed, watching the pale bird toss itself through the pastel scene, the girl felt in the best way—pastoral, nearly.

The girl grew to love the parakeet so much it was painful. Sometimes she imagined roasting its sweet body, putting the poor thing onto a stick over a fire—it was so small and delicate, it was hard not to think this.

Previously, the girl hardly liked anything at all that could breathe, let alone talk. But thankfully, unlike human animals, the parakeet could only say what she let it. So far it could speak her name (Edith), its name (Pretty Eyes), and one saying: "You're sexy." Pretty Eyes was close to saying "hot lady" and "nice rack." This was to scandalize the mother, who had phobias about words like *sexy, lady,* and *rack.* The bird was a loyal friend.

Sometimes, though, Edith became quite tired of her (though the gender of the bird was unknown, Edith thought of it as "her"). Edith was very moody, and many of her moods were not good. And when in a bad mood, Edith could stand nothing to see her. This presented a bit of a problem with Pretty Eyes, whose smooth bald head—despite those feathers, it was smooth as a tiny, little ball—was all eyes. "You're sexy," she said, making eye contact. When Edith was sad, this comment crushed her.

But Edith quickly discovered a solution to the trouble of juggling moods and the bird. All she had to do was cover the birdcage with a dark plastic shroud, shaped perfectly to the cage, and make the bird think it was night. Once covered, it shut up and slept. So, as the moods came often, Edith often covered the cage. She felt no guilt about it at all, however. Just as with her resistance to phobias, Edith had something against guilt, another devious maternal vice.

Yet Edith felt she owed Pretty Eyes something for having to so passively bend to her will. Thus, she began to allow Pretty Eyes free range of her room at all times, even when the mother was home. This meant the lithe blue creature got to flap through the room at very late hours, when it was dark outside and the lights were on. Then, the windows reflected the room back into the room, so the parakeet could not see the window pane that separated the room from the world. The pink-flowered walls and yellow rug and green curtains seemed to spread beyond where they did, into a whole other room identical to this one.

(There was thick glass and then dark woods, full of
crows and mice and men who chased you home.)

But Pretty Eyes was just a bird with a small parakeet brain! She didn't know. So, after not very much time had passed since Edith began letting her out of the cage when the outdoors had blackened, Pretty Eyes flew into the window and died. With horror, Edith quietly placed her back in the cage.

The next morning, she began to fake-weep when her mother entered the room ("Wake up, Piglet! Another day in which to excel!"). To Edith's dismay, she soon found herself in actual mourning, pointing wordlessly, sobbing, at the dead bird. Her mother just stared, and then said with a frown, as if she'd rehearsed, "You may eat like a bird because you like the disgusting look, but you never fed this bird what birds ought to eat. No wonder it's dead. You'll probably be dead soon too. I don't miss the bird and I refuse to miss you."

Edith either misinterpreted this last phrase or not, and assumed her mother meant she wished Edith had never been born.

It took little hesitation for Edith to leave. She packed a bag, buried the bird, got on a bus, and moved on. Flew the coop, as it were.

So it was in diffident anonymity that Edith began to work as a topless dancer in a city far away where, suspended from a red room's ceiling in a cage, she swung on a bench and tilted so that her long hair spilled down her back and flew out of the cage in wisps. All the girls had roles they played, and Edith's was advertised as "The Cageling." In her role she didn't do much except stand around in the cage, or swing, or sometimes crouch in a bird-like manner at the edge of the cage and kind of lean against the metal rods of the cage, looking sad.

Between acts, she'd sip a beverage at the bar. In her pale blue bathrobe with its wide gauzy sleeves and with her small eyes, she looked rather like her poor dead bird.

This job suited Edith well. It was easy, the men were nice, and she didn't have to talk to anyone while she performed. "I can be any kind of bird I want in the cage, right?" she had asked the manager upon being hired. "I don't have to be a *talking* bird?" to which he agreed with a scornful laugh. "My girls don't talk," he said in exactly the nasal drawl one expects such a man to use. So it didn't matter if she was in one of her moods at this job. Bitterness, sadness, unpleasantness, horror—they were all the same to a girl in a cage, standing around with a bird's blank stare in her eyes, feeling nothing but air on her bones.

Eventually, of course, Edith got too old for the job; the place preferred its girls young in addition to quiet, and when she turned thirty, they let her go. But like other girls who worked there, Edith had made the acquaintance of some men at the club and together, they pooled some dough and kept her up rather well. This was common. Some girls wanted swimming pools, some wanted diamonds and leather and pearls. Not Edith. She wanted a modest allowance—enough for food, which she barely required, electricity, and movies. She didn't care for a phone, not wanting her mother ever to find her.

Grateful, Edith was kind to her men. Not prone to speaking, how could she fail to please them? Eventually she was able to afford a two-bedroom apartment. One bedroom was for sleeping and the friendships that paid. The other she kept closed to the men. Inside the room she began to build a cage for herself, the cage of her dreams. It was made of metal she found and lugged home, scraps of automobiles, machinery, saws. She'd stand in the room for hours at a time, welding that cage into perfect submission, with tools she'd received as gifts from her men.

She asked for tools such as blowtorches, vices, and saws. (Curiously, her gentle friends never asked why she'd want them.)

Finally, after many months of work, Edith has finished. The cage has round steel edges that nearly touch the sides of the room in which it's contained. And when you open the door and look in, you can see through the bars and windows to outside, where spreads a thick, brick wall.

This cage is very helpful to Edith.

Though her life is nice enough, what with her income and her lack of phobias and guilt, those moods still come and go, despite her sweet men, despite how well things have worked out, when you really look at them. But if she didn't know better, Edith would start talking aloud, staring too much toward the brick wall outside. For now, Edith simply enters the cage, closes the door, and sits down. Not moving, she feels calm. And when you really think about it, what makes that so wrong?

A
Garibaldi
Tale

A Garibaldi Tale

Garibaldi, Garibaldi.

When I was a child in Garibaldi I had few concerns.

Nothing could trouble me, morning or night. Mornings I spent with my aunt. Like me, my aunt was not sent to work. My mother worked. My father worked. My sister worked. My uncle worked. They worked on the docks. The men hauled and the women boned. Hauling boning, hauling boning, off they go to holy bones. I didn't know why I didn't go, I didn't know why my aunt didn't go, but I did know that my aunt and I deeply resembled each other.

In Garibaldi my aunt had few concerns and watching her through the days I learned to be the same. Like me she had a round face, partial deafness, and webbed toes. Like me my aunt liked laundry and dirt and bread smeared with butter eaten at the top of a hill on a cloudy day when the birds cawed often. Like me my aunt did not speak much and when spoken to like me my aunt only on occasion would respond. But my aunt went away early on in my story. Though I missed her, this did not overconcern me much. I knew of the resemblance but I was not certain I preferred the resemblance so when the resemblance was gone so was my uncertainty about it. While she lived everyone was kind to us. However I felt that they thought of me as a version of her rather than simply as me, the child with few concerns.

When I was a child in Garibaldi we were always referred to this duplicate way, as Auntie and Auntie. "Is dinner ready? Ask Auntie and Auntie." "Are my long johns laundered? Ask Auntie and Auntie." "Are we ready for church? Call Auntie and Auntie." I was Auntie and Auntie and if I had any concerns at all, it was this repetition of names. *Auntie and Auntie go to the moon, Auntie and Auntie died too soon, Auntie and Auntie see the birds, Auntie and Auntie know what we've heard.* I made that up in my secret shack. It was there I wrote my best poetry. Auntie and Auntie times two.

Garibaldi, Garibaldi.

When I was a child in Garibaldi on weekends we went to the city nearby. Our schedules were otherwise smooth. Daily my mother and father and sister and uncle went to the docks. There the fishing and boning took place in a rough fashion full of odors. While this occurred Auntie and Auntie stayed home. The end of the days followed a straight line from the kitchen also with smells to the bed where I slept dreamlessly alone. But on Saturdays we drove to Tillamee to shop. On Sundays we drove to Tillamee for church. The city was where cheese was made and what my mother called "sundries" procured. Sundries, cheese, Sundays, church. I could not fashion a rhyme but believe me, the coincidence of the shared first letters did not escape me. Because I had no worries I could notice such things.

Scrutiny!

Tillamee, so blessedly near Garibaldi, was lovely lovely lovely to me. As an example: all the stores featured free cheese. My sister and I both admired the samples on toothpicks. While my father and uncle went to the barber and my mother and aunt went to the market, my sister and I admired the cheese, the opposite of fish. Yellow cheese and white cheese, cheese in strips, in cubes. Cheese with holes! Cheese with sausage in the holes! My sister and I would reach a frenzy of cheese and then we would take a long walk, a rather long walk down a lane, and admire the boys in the town. Apparently all of them worked in cheese. Oh, my sister and I shared many admirations. This was different from the sharing and liking I did with my Aunt.

Garibaldi, Garibaldi. In Garibaldi there were two shores and one had a smokestack and one had the docks. The smokestack did not go on working once I was born, but there is no relation between these events. The docks were our livelihood, they were our blood. This was obvious to all who happened to visit our good town for all of Garibaldi smelled like the docks—like brand-new fish just caught or killed or rotting fish left behind in chunks—or, if you went to the docks at four a.m., as I often did, to stare in the water and think, the smell was of swimming fish left living for the time being. Fish figured largely in our days and our nights and this made everything friendly. We ate fish for breakfast in the form of pick-led herring. We ate fish for lunch in the form of a fry or a sandwich. We ate fish for supper in stew. We ate fish for snacks as dried jerky. When I was a child I liked all sorts of fish.

Because of this affinity, I didn't like to stray far from the sea. Not seeing the sea did concern me. But there was one place to be. Behind our house and beyond the hill where Auntie and I watched the birds before Auntie died was my shack. This shack was far from the fish. From there one could not view the sea but one could hear the waves on a windy day and from time to time in a strong hale breeze, smell the boning going on. Inside the shack I would put on my sack. My sister had pilfered the sack from behind the cheese factory in Tillamee. I had asked her to take it for me. Because I did not speak much, when I made a request it was always heeded. I would share this secret to persuasion with a select few if it would not take speaking to do it. Besides, I save my talking for things that will benefit me. Come now, don't think that's selfish. I never do anything unkind unlike others I see. Being a simple child of few concerns from Garibaldi, I was often confused in Tillamee when I saw people exchanging hard words with one another, shaking their heads and contorting their faces as if they were having fits. Right on the street corners.

Ever since being a child, I have preferred to sweetly gaze, to finger, to smell.

In Garibaldi I had few concerns, but people leave children alone, particularly simple children with round faces, partial deafness, and glorious webbed, beautiful webbed, those special webbed toes. I make no mistake this unconcerned disposition was an achievement of mine.

Before Auntie died as she sat nearby on watch I would dress in the sack that my sister had taken upon my request and kneel on the floor and spread out my poems in order to speak. I liked a poem especially I had done called "The Sea." The poem went something like this: *See what will be spent in the sea, See what will become of thee, See how my coins will weigh you right down, See how I've saved them see how you drown.* This poem was based on a coffee can full of pennies, nickels, dimes, and quarters that I had been saving for several years. At first I had planned to spend the money on a pink dress I had seen in the Sears catalog, but then the catalog was discontinued. This made me so angry that I decided to write a poem about how, if I found the person who had discontinued the Sears catalog, I would offer him my coffee can full of coins while he stood by the sea. I would cry deeply but quietly as I told him the pink dress tale and it would sadden him so deeply that he would throw himself into the sea.

Weighed down by my can he would drown.

I remember that poem because of what happened with the sack, which had to do with the pink dress I had wanted.

When I discovered I could not have the pink dress because of the discontinuation, I was for the first time in my life distraught. I was in a bind, for once I had sidled up to a boy at the cheese factory while sampling a particularly gooey variety, which I'd taken with my finger. Under the pretext of wiping my hand on my pocket, I had taken the photograph of the pink dress out of my pocket, and held it toward him and raised my brow. He understood the question and smiled. He had nodded his head, with vigor, I might add. For several Saturdays that followed, I noticed him looking at me.

Garibaldi, forgive me! For in fact he had been mis-led. One should not flaunt a pink dress, the promise of a pink dress that is not owned. As penance for my deceit I wanted a burlap sack. If I presented myself in a burlap sack he would see the real me and he would not expect any other. With his eyes he would arrange to meet me at the edge of the docks and toss me around like a buoy and I would laugh loudly as the gulls got confused about the girl in the brown burlap sack who resembled their particularly ugly gull brother or aunt. All Garibaldi would hear my song. The song of a girl whose family smells like fish; a girl so simple she isn't allowed to herself.

I never made it to Tillamee in the sack. My parents would never allow me. The first time I tried, I simply wore it and they sent me to change. The second time I tried to sneak it under my clothes but I was so slim, the bulges gave it away. The third time I put it in my purse but the clasp would not close. Finally I just gave in to pining away. I took to putting on the sack and going to the shack and lying on the dirt floor crying *I love you, cheese boy, I love you, cheese boy, I love you I love you I love you so bad.* This was not one of my better poems. It had no rhymes.

Of course, I didn't love him. I was a girl of few concerns, and love was not one of them. I knew that I
liked the sound of the word. Words. I liked them all!
But "love" I did not the boy.

To my great misfortune, my sister heard what I said. Auntie had gotten sick and could not keep watch while I spoke in the shed. My sister told the boy and he laughed hard. "She is tortured by the loss," my sister said. My sister, a young woman of few concerns but not in the positive way, told me of what she had done. My sister liked to use the voice. This is how we differed. Of course soon I noticed a terrible thing. The boy stopped looking at me.

But because I was a child of few concerns I had no inclination to explain. "No, I am not tortured," I would have to say. "I know that I don't love you. I know that you don't love me. Do let's eat some cheese and go back to how it used to be." But everyone knows that an insisted thing loses all meaning. The more I would say I did not, the more he would think that I loved him. And there was the lament to defy me, which had been overheard and translated. I got into fits in the shack in that burlap, but my sister, being the unfit kind, did not understand the difference. Perhaps she liked him better than me.

Is it any surprise that I decided to cease writing poems? This was not difficult at all. However I had trouble giving up the burlap sack because I had become quite accustomed to the rough feel it gave the skin. My aunt, who had not yet died but would soon thereafter from some kind of brain fever, who liked similar things, made me some nice brown clothes. She knit me a cap, and a poncho, and altered a flannel shirt of my uncle's into a dress. In knee socks and the rest I looked serious and quiet and warm. I was dressed in this outfit when a nicer boy happened upon me in the shed. I laid down the burlap sack and kissed him. Then some other things happened. Though the things were unfamiliar they caused no alarm.

After that I didn't stay in Garibaldi long.

When I was a child, I had few concerns. From most places I could see the water where most of my family worked. The fish that they caught and then boned flew through the air in a smell that entered my clothes. Because I smelled fish, I thought fish, and fish have no use for voices. I occasionally used my own, and occasionally I still do. But because I did not work in the rough trade of boning and calling out to the men, my voice was a seldom thing.

This is no one's concern. They will learn, or drown.

A
Star Wars
Tale

A Star Wars Tale

Once there was a little girl and an older sister, and they had this game they played, and in the game they played Princess Leia and Darth Vader and Luke Skywalker. The younger sister played Princess Leia and the older sister played Darth Vader and Luke Skywalker. This all took place in the kitchen, papered metallic silver with yellow flowers.

First the sister who played Princess Leia rolled her hair into balls on the sides of her head and was locked in the pantry, but as the pantry didn't lock, it was pretend-locked by the other sister who, at the time in the game when the locking took place, played Darth Vader.

The Darth Vader sister had a black plastic garbage bag over her shoulders like a cape and spoke with a raspy voice. This Darth Vader sister would say, "You must be locked inside this soundproof room because you were very, very bad and you will never, ever get to see the handsome Luke Skywalker again." And always the Darth Vader sister would threaten the Princess Leia sister with "beating, rape, and other forms of torture."

→ men are presented as predators, enemies

While threatening Princess Leia, the Darth Vader sister would sometimes close herself into the pantry along with her sister. She would stretch her arms imposingly across the door. This was a cue for the Princess Leia sister to throw her arms around the Darth Vader sister and cling to her in thrilled terror. Then the Darth Vader sister would tilt back her head and cackle in the raspy voice. She'd leave the pantry, fake-locking the door. Back in the kitchen she would pretend to pluck a yellow flower from the papered walls and stomp on its bloom. Rasping, she'd cackle again.

Now the sister playing Princess Leia became terrified, and screamed. "Help! Help me Luke!" and the sister who was playing Luke Skywalker, who had just been playing Darth Vader, would quickly, quickly remove the garbage-bag cape from her shoulders and put on a white shirt of the father's (which the mother used for baking) and say, in a voice full of passion, "Princess Leia!" But because the pantry was sealed off from sound, being soundproof, Princess Leia couldn't hear Luke Skywalker, even though Luke Skywalker out in the kitchen could hear Princess Leia calling for him. "Help! Help me Luke," Princess Leia sobbed again and again. Yet Luke Skywalker, abjectly, only could listen.

Pacing the kitchen, Luke would wave his arms in their long white sleeves to the rhythm of Leia's cries. That he could hear her at all was an auditory curiosity, a miracle of sorts, a fatal glitch Darth Vader had not predicted when he locked the princess in the room. At this very moment in the crisis, each and every time the game was played, Luke could hear Leia crying for help from inside the soundproof room. In fact, the game hinged on his hearing her. How else would he know to save her from rape, beating, and other forms of torture?

Yet as Princess Leia could not hear Luke from inside the pantry, telling her how he would save her (which would prove that he loved her), Luke Skywalker would make tapes for her to listen to on a cassette recorder. He would speak into the microphone as he paced around the silver kitchen professing his "deep and unfathomable love for you, Princess Leia, my only sister—I mean lover—who is locked away forever and can never hear my voice again and might be beaten, raped, or tortured!" He would then rewind to the beginning of his message and open the door to the soundproof room, hand Princess Leia the cassette recorder, and slam the door shut again, hard. The Luke Skywalker sister often forgot whether to be tender or mean, having to juggle so many roles.

Princess Leia, clutching the machine to her chest, would hit PLAY, listen to his message, and then record one of her own. She whispered close to the machine: "Luke Skywalker, I love you with all my heart, you are my one and only lover and I will love you for all time even from inside this soundproof room in which the wicked Darth Vader has locked me for all time, and where I will be punished again and again in so many unspeakable ways." She would attach a yellow flower from the wallpaper to her message, placing the flower on the recorder with care. After rewinding meticulously to the beginning of her message, Princess Leia would open the door and hand the recorder to Luke. Sniffing the flower with great fervor, the young Luke would cry.

So it continued along. Back and forth Luke and Leia would pass the recorder and profess their love with only the occasional interruption by a garbage-bagged Darth and his threats of beating and rape. And though it made the sisters glow, no one ever got saved.

Whitework

Whitework

The cottage into which my companion had broken, rather than allow me, in my desperately wounded condition, to pass a night in the thick-wooded forest, was one of those miniaturized and hand-carved curiosities from the old German folktales that make people roll their eyes in scorn. This, despite the great popularity of a collection of German stories published the very same year of my birth! As to the justifiability of this scornful reaction: I cannot abide it, nor can I avoid it by altering the facts. This is where I found myself: in a fairy-tale cottage deep in the woods. And I had no use of my legs.

When we came upon the cottage we were certain, by its forlorn appearance, that it had long ago been abandoned to the wind and the night, and that we would be perfectly safe. Or rather, my dear companion was certain of this. As for me, I was certain of nothing—not even of my own name, which still eludes me.

There were but few details for my enfeebled mind to record, as if the cottage had been merely scribbled into existence by a dreamer's hand. Tiny potholders hung from the wall in the kitchen, beside tiny dish towels embroidered with the days of the week. In each corner of each room was tucked an empty mousetrap—open and ready but lacking of bait. At the entryway, on a rusted nail, hung a miniscule locket, along with a golden key. As to whether the locket ever was opened, and what it contained, I have conveniently misplaced any knowledge. About the key I will not presently speak.

My companion placed me onto a bed, though I would not know it was a trundle bed until morning. I had only vague notions as to how we had arrived at the cunningly thatched cottage, but I believe we had walked through the forest in search of safety. Perhaps we sought some gentle corner where we would not perish at the hands of those who pursued us. Or had we been banished, from a kingdom I no longer recall?

The room in which my companion put me to bed was the smallest and least furnished of all. It lay, strangely enough, down a long hallway and up a stairway—I say "strangely" because the house was so diminutive from outside. I realized, upon waking in morning, that I lay in a turret. Yet from outside, no curved wall was visible. With its thatched roof the house had resembled a square Christmas package, a gift for a favorite stuffed rabbit—a perfect dollhouse of a cottage, the sort I had painstakingly, as a child, decorated with wallpaper, curtains, and beds.

Though there was scarcely any furniture in this turret room, the sparse pieces were exactly correct—nothing more, nothing less: the trundle bed, empty and open, and the walls bedecked with no other ornamentation or decoration save whitework, the same sampler embroidered with the same message over and over. It was embroidered in French, which I do not speak: *Hommage à Ma Marraine*. In the center of each piece of linen was sewn an image of a priest holding two blackbirds, one on each hand. The edges of all the whitework were tattered, and some even had holes. On these white-on-white sewings my foggy mind immediately fastened, with an idiot's interest—so intently that when my dear companion came up to the turret with a hard roll and coffee for breakfast, I became very angry with him for interrupting my studies.

What I was able to discern, looking about me while nibbling the roll after my companion had left, was that some of the whitework contained a single gold thread as the accent over the *a*. Why the gold thread was used, I had no idea; and in considering this detail, along with the remarkable fact that blackbirds had been so expertly depicted in white, I finally asked my companion to return to the room. I called him and called him before he returned—disconcertingly, for it seemed he had only returned by accident, to fetch my empty teacup—and when he took it from my hand he gazed into it for a very long time without speaking a word.

At last, he closed the shutters of the windows tight, which was my wish, as it allowed me to see the whitework more clearly: I find I see better in the dark. A candle in the shape of a bluebird sat on the floor beside the bed, and I lit it and turned it just-so toward the wall. Luminous! I felt I had not, in many years, experienced such nocturnal bliss—even though the broad daylight shone outside the curtained windows, at least a day as broad as may shine in a deep and thickly wooded forest where real and grave danger does lurk.

This activity transfixed me for hours upon hours and days upon days.

In time, my companion and I so well established ourselves in the cottage that we felt we had lived there our entire lives. I presume we had *not* lived there our entire lives; yet of the event that drove us into the forest I cannot speak, and not only because I cannot recall it. But I can tell you that we had so well established ourselves in this cottage that I was shocked one morning to discover, under my feather pillow, a miniature book that had not been there before. It purported to criticize and describe the whitework on the walls.

Bound in black velvet, with a pink ribbon as a place-holder, the volume fit precisely in the palm of my hand, just as if it had been bound for me to hold there. Long—long I read, and devoutly, devotedly I gazed. Rapidly and gloriously the hours flew by and then the deep midnight came. (Not that I knew the day from night with the curtains so tightly drawn.) The bluebird was guttering—just a puddle of blue now, with yellow claw-feet fashioned from pipe cleaners protruding from the edges of the blue pud-dle. I reached my hand out to try to build the wax once more into the form of a bird, but I achieved merely a shapeless mass of color. Regardless, the can-dlelight flamed up and shone more brightly than ever upon the black velvet book with onionskin pages.

In my zeal to illumine the onionskin, the better to learn about *Ma Marraine* and so on, the candle's light had illumined the corners of the room too, where sat the mousetraps. Yes, this turret had corners—quite a remarkable thing, as the room was a circle. If I failed to perceive the corners before, I cannot explain . . . truly this architectural marvel of corners was a mar-vel-inside-a-marvel, since even the turret itself was not visible from outside.

With the corners of the room thus illumined, I now saw very clearly in one corner, behind a mousetrap, a very small portrait of a young girl just ripening into womanhood. I don't know how that phrase comes to me—"ripening into womanhood," for I would prefer simply to describe the portrait as a very small portrait of a young lady. But, to continue, I could not look at the painting for long. I found I had to close my eyes as soon as I saw the portrait—why, I have no idea, but it seems that my injury was not limited to my crippled legs but had also crept inward to my mind, which had become more . . . impulsive or secretive, perhaps. I forced my eyes back on the portrait again.

It was nothing remarkable, more a vignette than an exposition. The girl was depicted from top to bottom, smudged here and there, fading into the background, reminiscent somehow of the *Kinder- und Hausmärchen*—yes, you could describe her portrait as an illustration. She was a plain girl, not unlike me. Her eyes were sullen, her hair lank and unwashed, and even in the face and shoulders you could see she was undernourished—also not unlike me. (It is not. my intention to plead my case to you or to anyone else, now or in the future; I merely *note* the resemblance.)

Something about the girl's portrait startled me back to life. I had not even realized what a stupor I'd lain in, there in the turret, but looking into her sullen eyes, I awoke. My awakening had nothing to do with the girl herself, I believe, but rather with the bizarre execution of this portrait, this tiny portrait—no bigger than that of a mouse, yet life-sized. And it was painted entirely white upon white, just like the embroidery on the walls.

Though I felt more awake and alive than ever before, I found that I was also suddenly overcome with sadness. I don't know why, but I do know that when my companion brought me my nightly black coffee, I sent him away for a pitcher of blueberry wine. I asked for him also to bring me a pink-flowered teacup. My needs felt at once more urgent and delicate, and thankfully he was able to find articles in the cupboards that satisfied them.

For quite some time, drinking the wine, I gazed at the portrait of the sullen girl staring out of miniature eyes. At length, wholly unsatisfied with my inability to decipher the true secret of the portrait's effect (and apparently unaware that I very nearly was standing), I fell into the trundle. I turned my frustrated attentions back to the small book I had found under the pillow. Greedily, I turned its onionskin pages to the girl's portrait. "Flat, unadorned," the page read. The rest of the description was missing—everything except a peculiar exclamation for an encyclopedia to contain:

SHE WAS DEAD!

"And I died." Those are the words that came to my head—but I did not die then, nor did I many days and nights later, there in the forest, where I lived with my companion quite happily—not as husband and wife, yet neither as siblings . . . I cannot quite place the relation.

Soon, of course, I thought of nothing else but the girl in the painting. Nightly my companion brought me a teacup of blueberry wine, and nightly I drank it, asked for another, and wondered. *Who was she? Who am I?* I expected no answer—nay, nay, I did not wish for one either. For in my wonder I possessed complete satisfaction.

It was of no surprise to me, so accustomed to confusions, that one morning I awoke to find the painting vanished—and not only the painting but all the little priests with the little birds from the walls. No whitework, no turret, no companion. No blueberry wine. I found myself in a different small and dark room, again on a bed (not a trundle). An old woman and a doctor sat by my side.

"Poor dear," the old woman murmured. She added that I would do well to take courage. As you may imagine, the old woman and doctor were at once subjected to the greatest of my suspicions; and as I subjected them privately, I also protested publicly, for I knew I had done nothing to lose all I had learned to love there in that mysterious prison or home. No: I should have been very happy to be lame and blurred, to have my companion bring me teacups of wine at night, and in the morning my coffee and rolls. I never minded that the rolls were so tough to the bite that my teeth had become quite loose in their sockets, as loose as my brain or the bluebirds in the forest when their nests are looted by ravens.

Cheerfully, the doctor spoke over my protests. He said that my prognosis relied on one thing, and one thing alone: to eliminate every gloomy idea. He pointed toward a room I had not noticed before. "You have the key to the Library," he said. "Only be careful what you read."

Acknowledgments

As a writer, I owe a great deal of gratitude to so many family members, colleagues, and friends, but in the case of this book especially Brent Hendricks, Willy Vlautin, Joyelle McSweeney, Donna Tartt, and Peter Buck, along with Chris Fischbach and everyone at Coffee House Press. I need to thank Anne Marie DiStefano for a late-night conversation about childhood games that we had at La Cruda in Portland, Oregon, and for giving me permission to animate one of her memories in a short story. Inspiration for the book's title comes from a childhood naming game played—still to this day—with Diana Selig, Rachel Heckscher, and Sarah Madsen Hardy, friends I am so lucky to have had for so many years. The story "Whitework" is an homage to Edgar Allen Poe's "The Oval Portrait" (1848 version) and to an article about Karoline von Wolgozen's *Agnes von Lilien* (1798) by Jeannine Blackwell called "German Fairy Tales: A User's Manual. Translation of Six Frames and Fragments by Romantic Women" *(Fairy Tales and Feminism: New Approaches,* ed. Donald Haase, Wayne State University Press, Detroit MI, 2004). Finally, I hereby officially name Rikki Ducornet, Maria Massie, and Lydia Millet the three graces of *Horse, Flower, Bird,* and thank them for their incredible kindness.

KATE BERNHEIMER is the author of two novels and the children's book *The Girl in the Castle Inside the Museum*, a *Publishers Weekly* Best Book of the Year. She is also the editor of *Fairy Tale Review*, and three anthologies, including *My Mother She Killed Me, My Father He Ate Me: Forty New Fairy Tales* (Penguin, 2010). She lives in Lafayette, Louisiana, and Tucson, Arizona.

THE COFFEE HOUSES of seventeenth-century England were places of fellowship where ideas could be freely exchanged. In the cafés of Paris in the early years of the twentieth century, the surrealist, cubist, and dada art movements began. The coffee houses of 1950s America provided refuge and tremendous literary energy. Today, coffee house culture abounds at corner shops and online.

Coffee House Press continues these rich traditions. We envision all our authors and all our readers—be they in their living room chairs, at the beach, or in their beds—joining us around an ever-expandable table, drinking coffee and telling tales. And in the process of this exchange of stories by writers who speak from many communities and cultures, the American mosaic becomes reinvented, and reinvigorated.

We invite you to join us in our effort to welcome new readers to our table, and to the tales told in the pages of Coffee House Press books.

Please visit www.coffeehousepress.org
for more information.

Colophon

Horse, Flower, Bird was designed at Coffee House Press, in the historic Grain Belt Brewery's Bottling House near downtown Minneapolis. The text is set in Goudy Village.

Funder Acknowledgments

Coffee House Press is an independent nonprofit literary publisher. Our books are made possible through the generous support of grants and gifts from many foundations, corporate giving programs, state and federal support, and through donations from individuals who believe in the transformational power of literature. Coffee House Press receives major operating support from the Bush Foundation, the McKnight Foundation, from Target, and from the Minnesota State Arts Board, through an appropriation from the Minnesota State Legislature and from the National Endowment for the Arts. Coffee House also receives support from: three anonymous donors; Abraham Associates; Allan Appel; Around Town Literary Media Guides; Bill Berkson; the James L. and Nancy J. Bildner Foundation; the Patrick and Aimee Butler Family Foundation; the Buuck Family Foundation; Dorsey & Whitney, LLP; Fredrikson & Byron, P.A.; Sally French; Jennifer Haugh; Anselm Hollo and Jane Dalrymple-Hollo; Jeffrey Hom; Stephen and Isabel Keating; Robert and Margaret Kinney; the Kenneth Koch Literary Estate; the Lenfestey Family Foundation; Ethan J. Litman; Mary McDermid; Sjur Midness and Briar Andresen; the Rehael Fund of the Minneapolis Foundation; Deborah Reynolds; Schwegman, Lundberg & Woessner, P.A.; John Sjoberg; David Smith; Mary Strand and Tom Fraser; Jeffrey Sugerman; the Archie D. & Bertha H. Walker Foundation; Stu Wilson and Mel Barker; the Woessner Freeman Family Foundation in memory of David Hilton; and many other generous individual donors.

This activity is made possible in part by a grant from the Minnesota State Arts Board, through an appropriation by the Minnesota State Legislature and a grant from the National Endowment for the Arts.

NATIONAL ENDOWMENT FOR THE ARTS

MINNESOTA STATE ARTS BOARD

TARGET.

To you and our many readers across the country, we send our thanks for your continuing support.

Good books are brewing at www.coffeehousepress.org

HORSE, FLOWER, BIRD